CUT IN HALF

IN ALL JEST WORLD BOOK A

D.E. KING

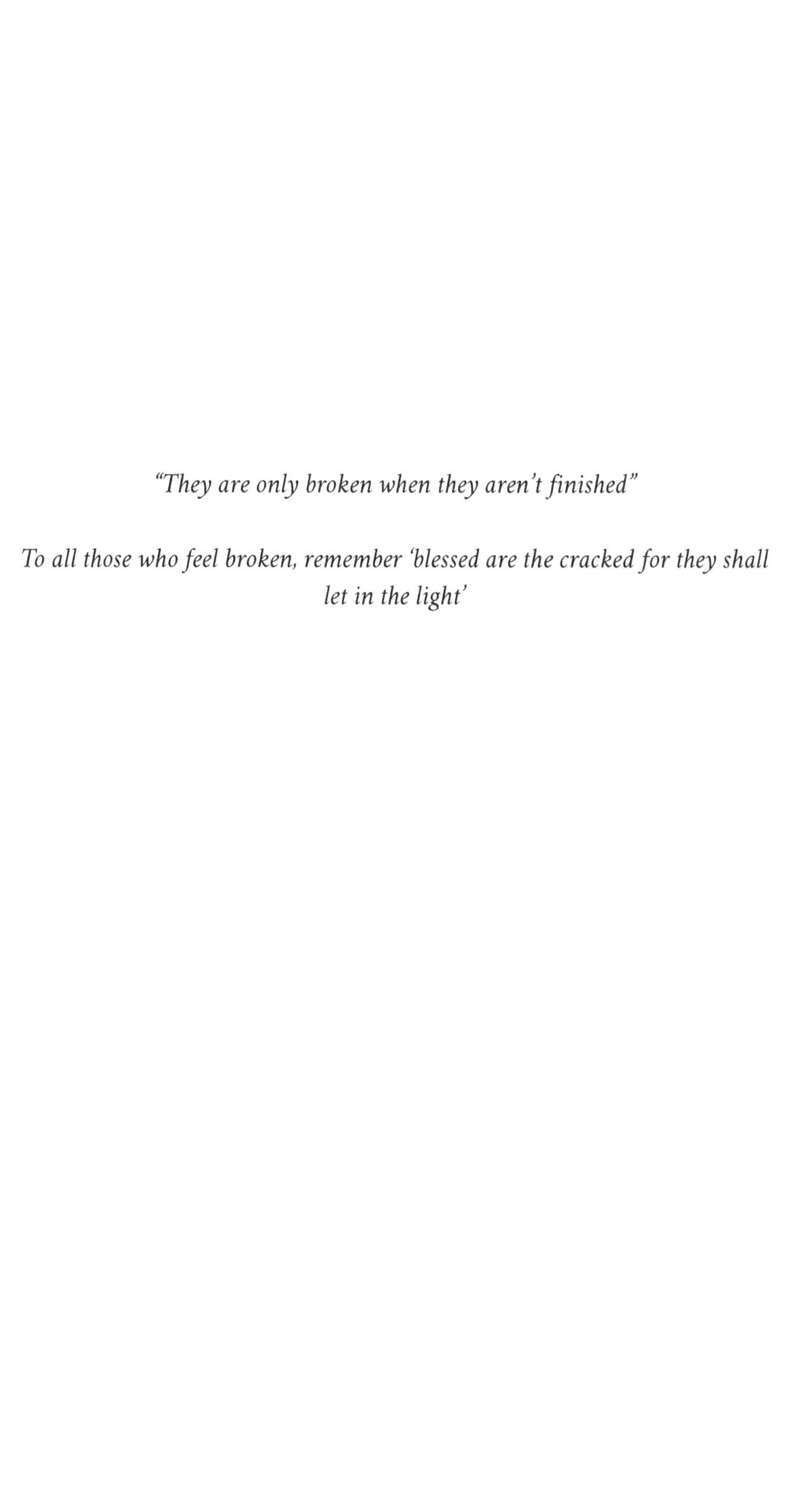

"They are only broken when they aren't finished"

To all those who feel broken, remember 'blessed are the cracked for they shall let in the light'

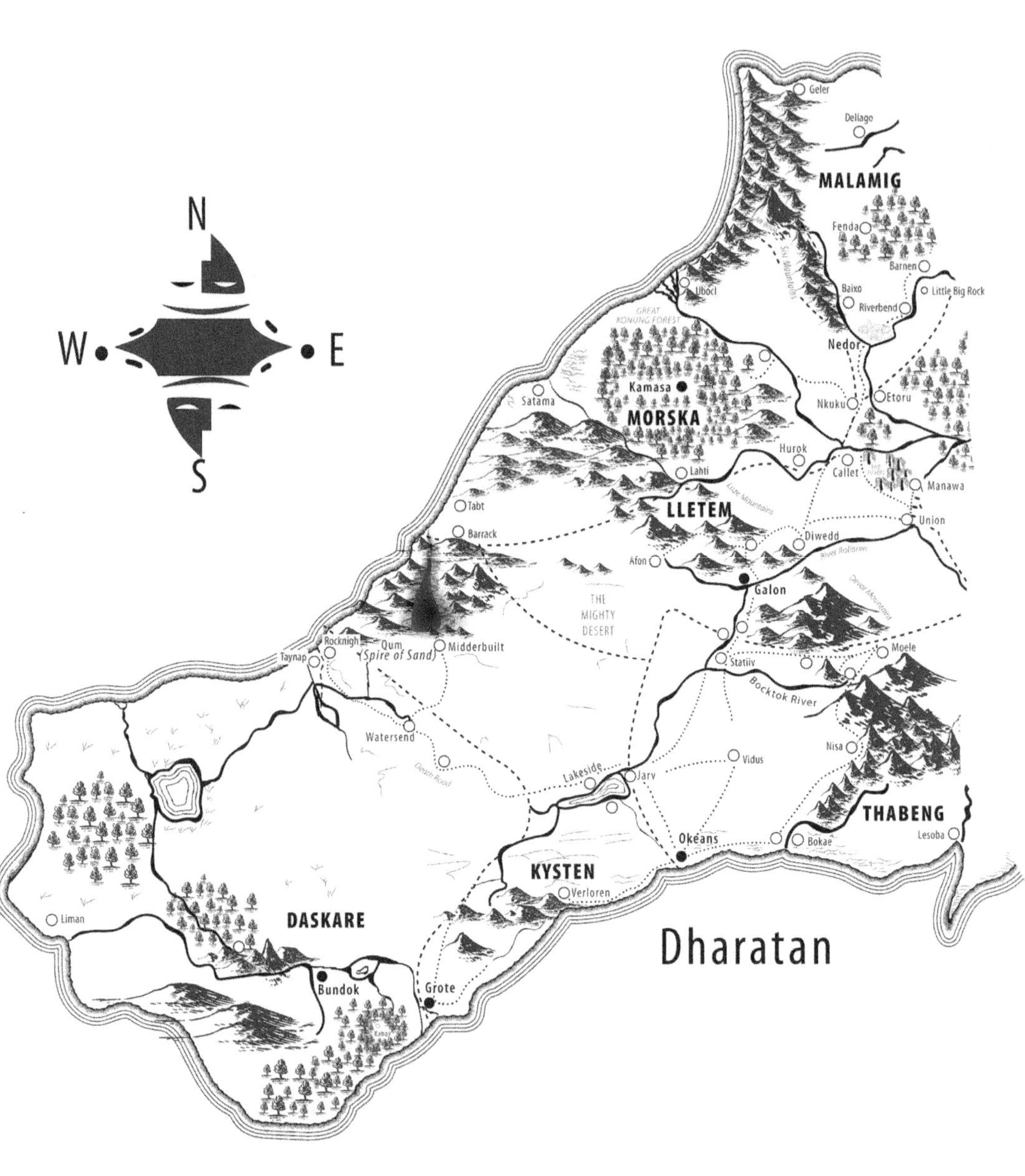

N
W
E
S
Geler
Dellago
MALAMIG
Fenda
Barnen
Ubocl
Baixo
Little Big Rock
Riverbend
Ski Mountains
GREAT KONUNG FOREST
Nedor
Satama
Kamasa
MORSKA
Nkuku
Etoru
Hurok
Callet
Manawa
Lahti
Tabt
LLETEM
Union
Barrack
Diwedd
Luze Mountains
Afon
River Rolloren
Galon
Denor Mountains
THE MIGHTY DESERT
Moele
Rocknigh
Qum
(Spire of Sand)
Midderbuilt
Statiiv
Taynap
Bocktok River
Nisa
Watersend
Denn Rock
Lakeside
Jarv
Vidus
THABENG
Lesoba
Okeans
Bokae
Liman
KYSTEN
Verloren
DASKARE
Dharatan
Bundok
Grote
Kanar

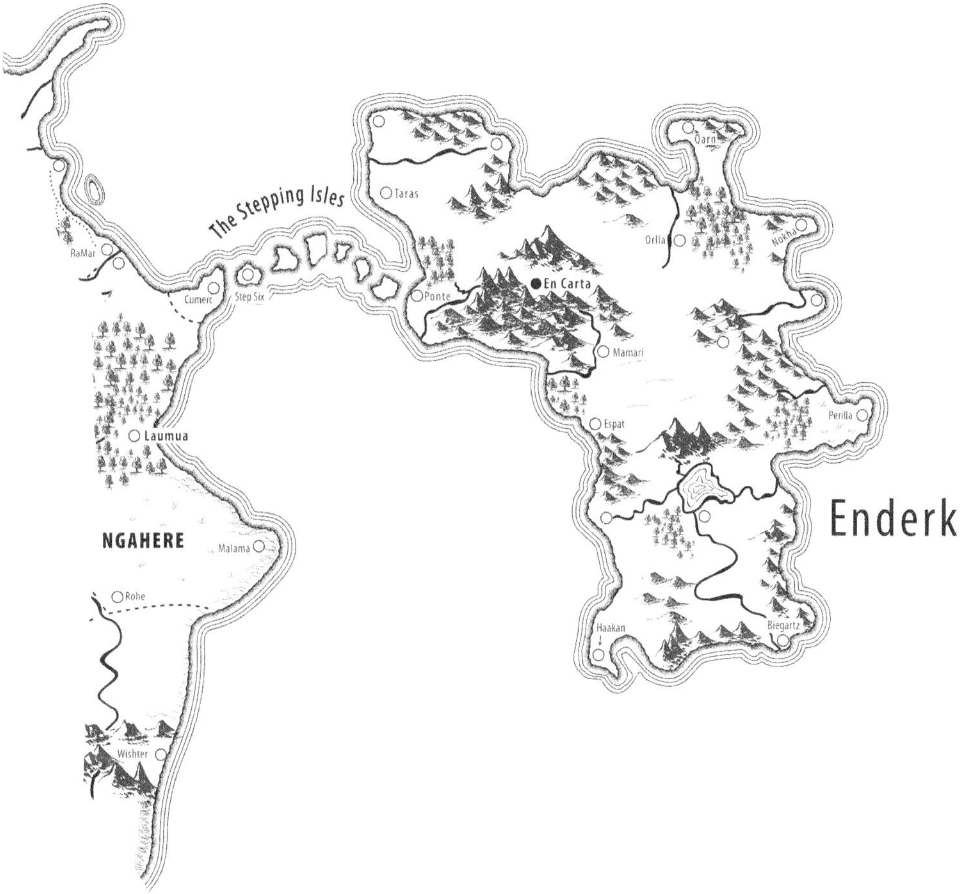

Map of
Mid Scurra

INTERACTIVE MAP

This book is accompanied by an **online interactive map**, which you can find on my website: kingdarryl.com/maps

Enter chapter numbers and **see pins** showing where characters are within the world. You can also see a large version of the map to zoom in on.

PROLOGUE

Out to the east of the land known as Dharatan there lay an island. While the people of Scurra knew of the seers that came from here, none knew of this island.

Few normal people had the ability to build boats that could travel such a journey, but even if they could, they would never find it. The island was protected by a magic that came from the deepest sources within this world.

The gods could skip around it but they couldn't change it. And on this day Okicheck arrived, stepping out on the lone jetty. He arrived at the harbour, out of the air, and caught the sole worker by surprise.

This woman couldn't see him, despite his physical presence, because she was without eyes. That didn't stop her from knowing he was there, nor from detecting he wasn't one of the ordinary people of the world.

"Shall I lead you?"

"There is no need, Miressa, I know the way."

The woman was a little surprised to hear her name from someone she did not believe she had met before, but not enough to be startled. She returned to sweeping the jetty.

Okicheck walked the path that led to the inner part of the island; into the massive temple carved out of the mountain that was home to The Eyes. He smiled at the irony of their name but not irreverently.

Those he had come to see were not gods, but neither were they like people of the other lands. And there were many lands in this world, many more than most were aware of.

Quite a few were empty or hardly inhabited, and not for reasons he knew. Why so many congregated in certain places only to leave others alone was an oddity of the people of Scurra.

The Eyes lived in the space between the source magic of the world and regular people. Okicheck had often pondered why it was that he and his siblings weren't able to access what The Eyes saw but he had never found an answer.

Their role was important, fulfilling a role that was both a help and a hindrance. They learned of things that even he could not see, and yet they always delivered it within a riddle. He'd never met an Eye that could tell you straight what it was they knew.

Having reached the steps to the main ceremony area he paused. It truly was a beautiful place; that those who lived here, protecting the temple, could not see it saddened him.

"We have all seen it in our lifetime, Okicheck."

It wasn't often that Oki was startled, but Valina, the head of The Eyes, had crept up on him without him sensing anything.

"You reading my mind now, Valina?"

"That would be a most terrifying experience, Oki. I can sense your feelings as you stand in awe."

"I am not sure awe is the right word."

She didn't reply.

"So you know what it looks like?"

"I saw it as a child before my eyes were removed. It is not something you forget."

"No, it is not."

"I stand here each day and look up at it, seeing it towering over me, from my young perspective. I feel the awe I felt then, and it reminds me why I am here."

"And why am I here?"

"Because you came."

Okicheck laughed, his hearty laugh, one that many people back on the mainlands enjoyed.

"And why did I come?"

"A better question."

"I heard your voice on the wind."

"Let's go inside."

Despite his instinct to do so there was no need to lead her. They walked side by side until they reached the sitting space. Valina stood for a while saying nothing then lowered herself into a seat.

Okicheck had hoped to be done quickly, there seemed to be so many things to do, but Valina would not be hurried. He sat and let his eyes feast on the beauty of the temple.

"There was a foretelling."

Okicheck turned back at her words. "Do I want to know?"

"You don't wish to hear it?"

"I am here am I not?"

This time it was Valina that smiled. "The time of growth is over."

"What does that mean?"

"The lands that you watch over, are no longer infants. There are many people and many interests, peace will not remain."

"They haven't been particularly peaceful in some time. It seems the way of people."

She shrugged.

"Tell me."

"The words are a little oblique."

"When are your messages not?"

"I can only tell you what was received."

Okicheck waited.

"*In one of eight, so lives the night. A single tear, to grow the seed. Fed by lust, dark shines bright. Its prize divine, not easily freed.*"

She paused and Oki wondered if she was done. The message meant little to him at this point, but he would have plenty of time to ponder it with his siblings.

"*One seeks two, two are one. Innocence doth mark its plan. Siblings missing, some are none. The darkest light will swallow man.*"

Another pause.

"*Should what remains perish too, Then no answer for the daughter. Guard, nay shelter, with no clue. Hide it with the depths of water.*"

Then she stood up abruptly. "That is all."

"I don't suppose you can provide me any insight to it?"

"You know there is nothing but delivery, Okicheck. Although, I can tell you that the message was received on the land of Enderk."

"You have people there?"

"Our people go where they are drawn. At times we are everywhere and nowhere."

"Significance in the location?"

"Only that it came there, which would indicate some relevance. Were it to come across the White Sea one would assume it was relevant there, but it did not."

"Thank you. Is there anything I can do for you?"

Expecting her usual reply, Okicheck was surprised she said nothing. If anything, he sensed hesitancy and spotted a small smirk on her face.

"What is it?"

"It is the strangest thing."

Oki chuckled and looked around, sweeping his hands. "And this isn't?"

Valina smiled back at him. "Come with me."

She stood up and led him along a narrow corridor to a room that he had never seen before. Within it were shelves full of objects of many shapes and sizes.

"The room of the world."

"Sorry?"

A small smile formed on her face. "Whenever our people return, they bring with them distinct objects from where they have served or been."

"Ah." Okicheck let his eyes run over some of the items. "So how can I help?"

Valina pointed to a spot on the floor. "It was the oddest thing. I came in here after the latest foretelling to place what was returned from there." She walked over and picked up a tin cup. "This was brought from Enderk."

He nodded.

"I noticed an old item, something personal to me, was missing. I found it on the floor, smashed to pieces."

"What was it?"

She let out a small nervous laugh. "A tooth from an ice bear. Your brother gave it to me many, many moons ago when I was small."

Okicheck wasn't sure where she was heading with this.

"It has been there for a very long time, and yet it was as though a wind swept through here and blew it down, breaking it."

"A wind? But the weather cannot touch this island."

She shrugged.

"Couldn't it have been one of your people?"

"My first thought, but that I checked. As you know The Eyes cannot lie."

"Doesn't mean they always tell you everything."

"But when asked a direct question they cannot lie, it is the way. And no one on this island broke this thing."

He knew that was the truth and it would be pointless for them to hide it, it would serve no purpose. "A visitor?"

Valina shook her head. "None can come here without my knowing. Not even you."

"What would you ask of me?"

"It might seem silly, but would your brother be able to replace it?"

Okicheck laughed.

"What?"

"Of all the things I might get asked to help with, you want me to ask him to find you another tooth?"

"I know it seems silly, but it matters… to me… to this collection. I'm sorry if it's too silly for you."

Okicheck was amused but also humbled that such a thing was so important to her. "I will ask him, but you know there's no making him do anything."

"I would be most grateful."

He looked across the many objects in the room, noticing how many of them were very simple items. None were what people would call valuable like jewels, and yet they were displayed here as though they were.

With nothing more to say Okicheck left, walking slowly and soaking up the beauty of the temple. On the occasions that he visited he'd often wondered who had made it, but still had no answer.

It hadn't been he or any of his siblings, so either the first of their kind had made it or... he didn't know, and while it was a curiosity, it didn't really matter. Some things just were.

That someone or something might be able to reach here bothered him. It was a sanctuary meant to be kept far from the people of these lands. But as he knew, nothing ever stayed the same. Like the prophecy, it needed serious consideration.

Before he reached the outside of the building he was gone from the island and back in the place people called the Void.

His brother was waiting for him. "And?"

The abruptness of Hembleth contrasted with the serenity of the island.

Hembleth stared at him relentlessly, expecting him to speak for what felt like an age. Okicheck spoke.

"A riddle."

"When is it not? Spill it then, I have little to do at the moment, it will be good to ponder something new."

"There's also something else."

"What can be more important than a prophecy?"

Okicheck told Hembleth about Valina's request. Then he told him of the prophecy and the two of them wandered endlessly through the space that was their home considering the options.

As they threw ideas back and forth Oki watched Hembleth roll the teardrop-shaped gem between his hands.

Okicheck couldn't remember when his brother had first received the tiny replica of the Citadel stone, but he always rolled it like this when he was thinking deeply.

Over the next few days that passed neither mentioned the prophecy to their other siblings, not for any deliberate reason, but more because they quickly became absorbed in trying to figure it out.

1

NIGRIV

igriv held his breath as he eyed the fox down the length of his blunt arrow. The sound of the bowstring releasing reached the animal only moments before the arrow and it had no time to flee.

The weapon was only just sharp enough to maim or kill but not cause significant damage to the creature's coat.

With little concern for noise now, Nigriv hurried across the snow, his snowshoes keeping him from sinking. The fox was still breathing so he twisted its neck, putting it out of any further misery.

"Tie it up, we should find your brother."

He turned to see his father coming from the east and nodded. He used some twine to tie the feet together and slung it over his shoulder. Nigriv felt for his brother and sensed his presence. "He's that way." He pointed to his left then set off in that direction with the older man now alongside.

Father had long since given up asking how the boys knew things about each other; the connection between them was natural to the twins but unusual to others.

Ligriv was knelt beside a creek bed, tying up his small shoulder bag and slinging it. He didn't have any catch, nor did he comment on what Nigriv carried, and without the need for words all three set off toward home.

At the base of the ridge closest to their cave, Father slowed, looked back over his shoulder. "Catch up, El." He didn't wait for him to do so before beginning the steep climb up what they called the staircase.

Rough rock steps worn and cut into the cliff allowed for a much quicker climb than other routes, but it was narrow and fell away on the right side. Nigriv lost sight of his father until he too reached the top and turned onto the ledge that led from the stairs over to solid ground.

Father nodded slightly at him before he continued. A bit further along the ledge he turned again, looking back past Nigriv, and as he did, he misstepped.

Nothing out of the ordinary, he just placed his foot a little off the line he should have. They walked this way often so all of them knew it well, but that step was enough. As he lost his footing, he turned, staring at his son with his nearest arm reaching out.

It was entirely instinctive -- a primal urge to save himself. Father was such a pragmatist he would have already accepted his fate and wouldn't pull his son over with him.

Years later, Nigriv would wonder how that must have felt in the moment knowing what was about to happen. But as a ten-year-old he had no concept of that at all.

There was concern, not fear, in the older man's eyes which Nigriv didn't comprehend. Father should have known that Nigriv and his brother would be fine.

They were trappers, hunting and trading pelts for what they needed. He'd taught them how to survive out here in the harsh wilderness of Northern Malamig.

From an early age he'd shown them how to kill, skin and prepare their work, as well as how to feed and look out for themselves. It had always been just the three of them.

Mother had been killed by a bear when Nigriv was too young to remember. The rug on the floor of their cave was the only revenge Father could exact.

Once in a while, Nigriv wondered about her, what life with her would have been like had she been around. Not in a way that made him discontent, it was simply from curiosity.

Some people from Geler, the nearest trading town, had told Father he needed help with the boys, but he ignored such words. He made it clear to them he neither wanted or needed their advice.

They only ever went there to trade, which appeared to suit his father's desire for isolation. Nigriv didn't know why he'd chosen this of all places to live and now he could never ask.

Perhaps it was simply that which resembled concern on the older man's face, that he was leaving them alone, before he was gone over the edge and out of sight.

Neither called out, there was nothing words could do to change what would happen, and shouting would alert predators to their location.

Nigriv stared at the spot where Father had just been, as though he might reappear, hearing the loose stones, from the crumbled edge, clatter down the rock face.

His father thudded to a stop at the bottom. Nigriv carefully sidled to a secure spot at the edge, holding on with one hand, and looked down. The body lay broken at the bottom of the small ravine.

That didn't upset him, he didn't feel things the way others did, like his brother, whose mood changed at every emotion he experienced. Nigriv knew father's death wasn't a good thing, but in his head, it was just another event to process. It happened, that was all.

When his brother felt things Nigriv was able to sense it through the unique connection between the twin boys, but he struggled to relate to them.

Living out here that connection had served them well, each signalling danger to the other without words on many occasions. The sound of Ligriv's footsteps crunching up the steps to his right caught his attention.

"Brother, what is it?"

Nigriv pointed down between the rock faces. "He slipped."

His twin joined him and looked down.

"No!" Ligriv gasped and Nigriv saw his brother's eyes water.

"It will be alright."

"How?"

Nigriv didn't know what he needed to say so he just stood there alongside Ligriv, staring down into the ravine. What he could sense now, his brother had previously explained as sadness.

Why don't I feel such things?

After a couple of minutes he asked, "Are you alright, El?"

His brother shrugged, wiping his eyes with his fur glove. "What's done is done, that's what he'd say isn't it?"

Nigriv nodded. In that way he and his father were very similar, yet he could feel Ligriv didn't really mean it.

"What should we do?" His twin's eyes were still glistening.

"Take his things and leave him to the animals, El. There's little we can do for him now. But we should do it quickly, before they come for the body."

His brother's face scrunched as Nigriv said it but, like always, Ligriv wouldn't argue. It was just the way things had become between them.

There was nothing to be gained from trying to lift the heavy body of their father out of there. This would be his grave now. It had been snowing a lot these last few weeks, maybe it would cover him before creatures got to him.

Their father's clothing, weapons and tools were not to be wasted. Each had been traded for or made by his hand. The boys could use it all now or in the future.

As a family they lived a simple and frugal life. They had never been greedy, trying to gather more furs than they needed to survive; Father had always been respectful of the land. *Only what we need and a little more.*

After securing a rope to a nearby pine they carefully walked backwards down the rock wall. Nigriv tied what was worth keeping into a bundle and waited while Ligriv climbed back up and hoisted it out.

Then his brother helped to pull him up. At ten years of age both boys were much stronger than similarly aged children, but then they didn't live like others. Out here they had to be fit, strong and smart to survive.

Once out of the ravine Nigriv didn't look back, remembering one of his father's regular statements: *What's behind you is gone, boys, you can do nothing about it but learn from it.*

What lesson they'd take from father's death, apart from staying away from edges, Nigriv didn't know. He would ponder it another time. Neither boy spoke as they trudged back to their cave.

His brother immediately set to rebuilding the fire that was always left smouldering throughout winter. Once the space had warmed enough Nigriv removed his fur coat.

He looked at his brother, still sensing the sadness within him. It would take Ligriv some time to put it behind him. Nigriv had no idea how long it would take but knew he would just need to let him work through it.

"I'll prepare us food."

Ligriv said nothing, his eyes fixed on the flames.

"Come eat," Nigriv told him once he'd made up a board of food.

Ligriv joined him and picked at the dried meat and cheese.

"Do we have much left?"

"There's some supplies we'll need from Geler before long, but we still have plenty of meat."

"What will we tell them when we go to town?"

Nigriv thought about that for a few minutes before answering. "Nothing, El."

"What do you mean?"

"You know what they'll say, what they'll want."

Ligriv looked at him, his face scrunched in a question.

"Do you want them to take us there, to live with someone in a house?"

"No."

"Then they don't need to know."

"I'm worried."

"Don't be, El, he taught us what we need to know. We just have to be smart."

"But won't they ask where he is?"

"We'll tell them Father set it as a task for us. That he wanted us to be able to do this on our own."

Ligriv stared into the fire and nodded.

After a minute Nigriv put an end to it. "We tell no one, El. It's just us now, we'll be fine."

Ligriv nodded.

Nigriv had no reason to doubt that they would be fine, but he got a sense, almost words, that he heard in his mind different to his normal thoughts.

For a time at least.

Nigriv didn't understand where it came from, and a chill ran down his back which he had to shrug off.

Ligriv looked at him quizzically. "What is it, brother?"

"Nothing." Nigriv shook his head. "Just a chill."

His brother could probably sense the fib... it didn't matter. Nigriv pushed the thought away and got about the business of tidying up. He'd only remember it many years later but by then it wouldn't matter.

NIGRIV

Nigriv woke to the little daylight that found its way through the wooden wall and door which blocked their cave entrance. First light would normally be when Father returned from his morning walk, but not anymore.

With a stretch, Nigriv rose from his bunk and looked across to where his brother was still asleep, strangely hugging his small bag.

Nigriv pulled on his boots and wrapped a rug around his shoulders to keep the cold at bay. His breath turned to a frosty cloud as he let it out.

Up until four days ago Father would have added wood to the fire when he rose, warming the cave before the boys woke. Nigriv reached the fireplace and used kindling to poke at the few embers left while he waited for it to ignite.

For no specific reason he felt it was his responsibility to oversee their lives now. Yes he was the oldest by a few minutes, not that it meant much. But he still felt as though it was his burden.

He looked over at his brother again. While physically they were mostly identical Nigriv knew they were not the same. He was very pragmatic, more like Father, whereas Ligriv was much more emotive.

His twin felt things deeply that Nigriv did not. He would hold a grudge, fester over an injustice or problem, while Nigriv could brush it off.

In many ways it made their relationship stronger. If their personalities were identical life would be very dull, or so he reckoned.

From time to time, they would sit and talk about their differences. For Nigriv it opened his eyes to things he could have passed by, and in return he helped his brother get things off his chest.

While Nigriv had no need to talk about what had happened he knew that Ligriv would and that they'd need to discuss it. It's how he was.

Father always struggled with that side of Ligriv. He was a quiet man, in many ways similar to Nigriv. He used as little speech as he could, it was him that had shortened their names. *El and En.*

The less he had to say, the more it suited him. He'd said the shorter names didn't end the same and helped remind him they were different. Nigriv often wondered why they hadn't been named differently but perhaps that was their mother's decision. Father wouldn't have changed them if that was the case.

By the time the fire was burning strongly he sensed his brother beside him.

"I will never understand how you do that."

"What?" Ligriv sounded groggy.

"Sneak up on me. I didn't hear you; it was only my sense that you were there that let me know."

"You were making so much noise with the wood, I can understand why."

Nigriv grinned; he doubted his brother knew how he did it. He was simply able to move without making a noise.

Together they squatted staring at the flames for a time before Ligriv broke the silence.

"What's our plan?"

"We hunt, same as always."

Ligriv said nothing and Nigriv could sense he was still pained.

"How about fish?" Nigriv asked.

Ligriv shrugged, which was as good as anything.

Without any hurry they prepared themselves; there was never any rush in this house. Father had always said that only a fool wanted to be first, a wise man preferred to be prepared and arrive last.

With the rivers and lakes all frozen over it was ice bear season. They needed to be vigilant, or it wouldn't just be Father that would be lost.

Another chill ran down Nigriv's back. The thought of losing his brother touched him in a way he wasn't used to and he choked on his own breath.

"What is it, En?"

Nigriv shook his head. "Nothing, I just need a drink, my throat is dry."

The thought of not having Ligriv around caused his whole body to feel odd. Before he realised it, Nigriv was scratching at the scar on his forearm, a carryover from the first time he'd learned to prepare fish.

His knife had slipped out of the fish he was gutting and sliced the underside of his left forearm. Father had wrapped it and scolded him for his lack of attention, but it healed.

Often, he'd find himself doing what he'd started now, scratching at the scar unconsciously, until it almost bled again. He grabbed his things to stop himself doing it. "The cave will be warm by the time we get back."

His brother nodded, slinging his small bag over a shoulder, not giving any indication if he sensed the lie his twin had told. They left the safety of the cave, closing the wooden door behind them. The contrast of the outside temperature quickly changed Nigriv's focus.

Both carried their axes in one hand while lightly gripping the bows across their shoulders with the other. They headed northeast toward a spot where they usually had success, at the point where the river met the lake. At this time of year the water beneath the ice moved much slower, and there the fish gathered.

As they approached the lake both boys slowed before crawling up the last ridge. At the crest they lay down in the snow and stared out across the expanse of the frozen water.

Patience mattered most at this point. Once down on the flat they would be visible to any animals in the area.

After a good while Ligriv slowly turned his head. "I think it's fine."

"Me too, let's go."

They walked down the slope, Nigriv's eyes darting around the wide expanse of the lake, looking for any sign of danger. At the river's edge, Ligriv did what he always did, using the back of his axe to break the ice around the spot they fished.

It was thinner from regular use which made it easier and quieter work. Nigriv kept his eye on the main expanse of the lake, his bow in his hands, an arrow nocked.

Usually, Father would act as guard while both boys fished. *Not anymore.*

Something flickered on the distant shoreline which grabbed all Nigriv's attention. He stared in that direction but saw nothing of concern. Out of the corner of his eye he could see Ligriv drag a fish from the icy water.

Maybe it's just wind in the trees.

Nigriv's eyes stayed focused on that distant spot for a good time. *Nothing.* He went back to scanning the whole area, periodically returning to that spot, but nothing stood out.

"Will we be alright?"

There was still a strong sense of unease coming from Ligriv. As much as he didn't want to talk about it, Nigriv knew this was his brother's way.

"Why wouldn't we be, Ligriv?"

His brother shrugged. "It's just…"

"He taught us how to survive, we know how to hunt, how to skin animals and set them for the traders. As long as we look out for each other, we'll be fine."

Nigriv continued observing the open space around them while his brother processed what he'd said. There was still nothing out there, or at least nothing he could see, which was good enough for him.

"It was my fault."

That got Nigriv's attention, and he turned to look at his brother. "What do you mean?"

"If I wasn't lagging behind, he wouldn't have looked back."

Nigriv wanted to say he was wrong, but he knew as well as Ligriv that in a way what he said was true.

"I couldn't help it."

"What do you mean?"

"I..." Ligriv struggled to speak. His eyes were glistening as he looked at his brother. "I found something... It grabbed my attention, and I forgot what I was doing."

"What did you find?"

His brother lay the wooden stick he fished with across his lap and reached into his bag. When he brought his hand out, he held something shiny in it. "This!"

Nigriv moved a step closer, looking at an orange stone which filled his brother's palm, reflecting the sunlight. "Where did you find that?"

"In the creek bed where you caught up to me... it was like it was calling me."

"Calling?"

"Not like words... it was like things are between us. I just knew something was there and when I looked, I could see it wedged under some sticks and other rocks."

Nigriv reached out to it, but his brother quickly pulled his hand back, confusion crossing his face.

"I don't know why I did that. You can look if you want."

His brother's reaction concerned Nigriv but he was just as happy to leave the stone alone, he'd only reached for it out of curiosity which had disappeared. "You didn't cause his death, brother. He slipped and fell, that's all there is to it."

Ligriv looked at him grimly before nodding. He put the stone back in his bag and picked up the wooden rod. "I guess."

"It's true, brother. Yes, he looked back, but Father knows... knew, what he was doing. He shouldn't have been so close to the edge."

Again, his brother shrugged.

"Do you know any magic?"

Ligriv turned back to him and his face was scrunched up in confusion. "What?"

"Do you know any magic?"

"No, of course I don't -- magic is nonsense."

"Well then, you can't take us back to that day, can you?"

Nigriv watched his brother shake his head.

"Then you can't change what is. It's done and that's the way of things. All we can do now is look out for each other and move forward."

Ligriv didn't respond and Nigriv went back to scanning the lake and surrounding land, leaving his brother to reflect on what he'd said. Ligriv pulled out another large fish.

"Two's enough, El."

His twin nodded and began to roll up his line. "Who's that?"

Nigriv had only looked down for a moment at his brother's catch, and was surprised as he looked back across the frozen lake to see a person was walking toward them. *How did I not spot them?*

"What do we do?"

"Pack everything up, I'll keep an eye on them."

He slowly lifted his bow, so he was better prepared to use it, if necessary, although he didn't feel any concern. His logical mind knew they should be cautious but whenever he focused on the stranger any concern flittered away.

The man, no taller than the boys, but broad of girth, stood out for his bright red hair that hung down well past his shoulders. He was ambling across the ice of the lake with what seemed not a care in the world

Ligriv stood, ready to go, holding the two fish in one hand. Nigriv placed his hand on his brother's shoulder.

"Let's see who he is, brother. What he wants."

His twin looked at him confused but like always accepted his decision.

LIGRIV

The man's voice was friendly. "That's a good catch, boys."

"Who are you?" Ligriv sounded flustered which matched how he felt.

The man looked casually his way as though nothing unusual was happening here. "I'm a friend."

"We don't know you; how can you be a friend?"

"Friends come in many types, Ligriv…"

"How do you know my name?"

A grin broke out on the man's face and Ligriv felt himself relax just a little.

"I'm the type of friend that knows many things but also someone who keeps them to himself."

Ligriv didn't understand what the man meant but his presence had stopped bothering him. He could sense that Nigriv wasn't concerned either and out of the corner of his eye saw him lower his bow toward the ground.

Something strange was occurring. Ligriv had an awareness of that even though he couldn't explain it. He muttered to his brother, "What do we do?"

Nigriv ignored him and spoke to the stranger. "What are you doing out here?"

"I needed to speak to you both, it's important."

Neither answered.

"Boys, I know your father is dead…"

"No he isn't." Ligriv spat it out quicker than he wanted.

The man's smile disappeared, if anything he looked sad. "And yet Nigriv watched him fall. I could take you to the site if you want."

Ligriv felt uneasy about what was happening. Somehow this man knew things about them that he shouldn't. His brother's words about the townsfolk wanting to interfere came back to him.

"I don't want to take you away; I just need to tell you some things. Like I said, it's important."

"What things?" Nigriv asked.

The old man looked at them both, then looked across the open lake surface. "Perhaps it might be safer to go elsewhere, the ice bear on the far side is a little unhappy with me."

Ligriv turned and stared across the lake. "What bear?"

"Can you see the twin green rocks, almost straight ahead from where you're looking?"

It took Ligriv a moment, but he locked in on the spot and nodded.

"Right side, half a dozen paces or so back there's a small copse of trees. There's one lying forward on his paws right there if you're patient enough to watch."

Ligriv was and he stared that way. The bear twisted its head a little, moving its muzzle enough that Ligriv could see it wasn't just bush.

"I see it."

So did his brother. "Me too. Why is it unhappy with you?"

The man pulled a large tooth from a bag Ligriv hadn't noticed before; it was still bloody. "This."

"What did you do?"

"I didn't have time to fossick for buried ones, so I relieved it of this. As much as I am fond of them, I'm a bit time poor and I needed to find you boys."

Ligriv was stunned, he couldn't imagine this funny little man besting an ice bear, let alone removing a tooth while it was still alive. He wanted to laugh at the thought of it.

Any apprehension he'd held about this strange little man was now gone, as though they'd known him for a long time. Ligriv sensed the same calmness in his brother.

"Follow us." Nigriv turned and started back up the hill.

On the trek back they followed different paths from earlier. Their father had always taught them to not use the same way in and out of anywhere, whenever possible. He'd warned them that predators, man or beast, liked their prey to follow patterns, that it made it easier for them to hunt.

"Use a different path and you'll always have an advantage."

As they walked Ligriv began thinking about how silly it was to be taking a back way to their cave. But as soon as the idea formed it immediately slipped from his mind.

Once inside their cave Nigriv tended to the fire and all three of them began to take off their outer robes and gloves.

"This is a nice spot, much warmer than out there. Can I trouble you for a root tea?"

In all his years Ligriv couldn't remember a time when any adult, other than his father, had been in their cave and it made him uncomfortable. Usually, he had no issue talking but now he struggled for what to say.

"How can you tell us apart, when we've never met you?" It was all he could think of.

"A good question, Ligriv. I have a few tricks up my sleeve."

"We don't need any tricks. What do you want from us?"

"I need to ask you some things, that's all."

"What?"

The older man sat at their table and didn't answer until Nigriv had brought him his tea. He held the mug and blew on it before he took his first sip.

"That's better." He looked at them both. "Do you know what a foretelling is?"

Nigriv answered. "Father says they aren't real."

"Did he?"

"He said that they are tricks told by townsfolk at fairs to part people from their coin and worry them needlessly."

"Wise words, especially if you are at a fair and being seduced by someone in a stall. Those witches are tricksters for sure, but I'm not one of them."

"How do we know?" Ligriv asked.

"That I will have to prove."

He said nothing else, and the cave fell silent apart from the crackling in the fireplace. Ligriv never liked silence amongst people even when it was around his father and brother, despite that being their preference. He knew he'd feel better if the conversation got going again.

"Did you find something out in the woods, Ligriv?"

The man's eyes bored into Ligriv's, not painfully, they just stared at him so intently that he couldn't concentrate. In the end all he could do was nod.

"I see, and was it a gem?"

He nodded and the stranger looked over at the fire. Ligriv's mind regained its focus and he shook his head.

"Sorry, son, I just needed to make sure you were the one."

"What did you do?" Nigriv sounded concerned.

"Just a trick I know, to help make someone tell me the truth."

"I thought you said you weren't a trickster."

The man laughed. "You're a sharp one aren't you? I said I wasn't a trickster, not that I didn't know any tricks."

"But..."

"Enough!" The tone in his voice was enough to silence Nigriv. The stranger turned back to Ligriv. "Can you show me? I won't try to take it from you, I promise."

Cautiously Ligriv reached into his bag and eased the stone out. Holding it close to his body he turned his hand over and opened his fingers. The stone sat in his palm.

All the firelight in the cave appeared to get drawn into the stone and it glowed as brightly as it had out in the sun.

The older man squinted a little as he studied the stone. "So, it's true."

"What is?"

After a few moments he looked at Nigriv and answered, "The foretelling."

"It told you about this stone?"

"In a way, Nigriv, yes it did."

"Why does it matter?"

"That isn't just any stone."

"What does that mean?" Nigriv still sounded annoyed.

The stranger lifted his mug and blew on it again before slurping some more of the tea.

"It has a unique value."

Ligriv couldn't help but grin that he'd found something worth a lot. It felt good.

"Not a value you can measure in gold, understand, the value of this is quite different."

"In what way?" Ligriv was a little disappointed.

"It comes from somewhere a long way away… and it is unusual… very unusual."

"What's so unusual about it, apart from how it looks?"

"Have you ever seen another stone like it before?"

Ligriv shook his head.

"Nor have others. To be honest I am not sure why it is here, or how it got here, but I learned that it was found and as luck would have it, I was in the area."

"How?"

"How what?"

"How did you know it was found?"

"Well, that is quite the question is it not? As is why would two young boys be the ones to find it?"

Neither boy answered and Ligriv watched the older man until he spoke again.

"Can you touch it, Nigriv?"

Ligriv instinctively wrapped his fingers around the stone and tucked his hand against his body.

The man raised a hand. "I'm just curious, Ligriv. Why would it hurt for your brother to hold it?"

Ligriv felt silly about why he'd reacted this way for the second time and opened his hand again.

"What does it matter?" Nigriv asked the older man.

"I'm curious, it would be useful to know."

Nigriv didn't seem happy about it but came to Ligriv and took it from him, his face scowling as he did.

"What?" Ligriv asked.

"It hurts."

"How?"

Nigriv kept moving the stone in his hand as though it was hot, and he couldn't let it settle lest it burn him. Then he dropped it back in Ligriv's hand, shaking his hand afterward. "It felt sharp like it was pricking me constantly."

"Interesting," the stranger said. He stood and fumbled around inside his tunic, pulling out something in his closed hand.

When he opened his fingers Ligriv saw a blue-white stone, polished and shining just as brightly as his own stone. His orange gem was heating up, uncomfortably.

"What is that?" Nigriv asked.

"Why don't you hold it?"

"I don't want to; the other one wasn't pleasant." Nigriv replied.

"I am guessing you'll find this quite different."

Ligriv was surprised he couldn't read his brother's thoughts at all. His brother walked to the old man and took the stone. This time there wasn't any juggling and the scowl on his face slipped away.

If anything, he looked happy to Ligriv. *Why can't I feel him?*

"Doesn't hurt."

"I didn't think it would. How does it feel?"

Nigriv didn't answer straight away, his mind seemingly elsewhere. "It's comforting..."

"Give it to Ligriv."

Ligriv pulled back from the words. "I don't want it!" The words came out before he'd even had time to think about them. He didn't understand his reaction or why he didn't want to touch the stone, but he was adamant he didn't want to.

"Very well, I won't force you. You can put that away now." He pointed at Ligriv's stone.

"What is this?" Nigriv asked.

"That is something I've carried with me for a very long time. It's… it's like a child to a much larger version of itself."

Nigriv held it out to the man who shook his head.

"No, I think you should keep it."

"Why?"

"Balance. I think there needs to be balance."

"But it's yours."

"I have become very fond of it, and have carried it for an extremely long time, but it has never been mine. I've just been carrying it."

Nigriv hovered there, unsure what to do. Ligriv could see he was thinking on what was happening. Ligriv wasn't jealous of his brother, his own stone was bigger, but the white stone bothered him for some reason.

Slowly Nigriv stepped away and pocketed the white stone. No one said a thing and Ligriv just sat watching this strange man as he slurped his tea staring into the fire.

4

———

NIGRIV

The stranger sat with his eyes closed and Nigriv wondered if he was asleep. It wouldn't surprise him given how odd this whole experience had been.

Whoever he was he didn't seem to have a care in the world, which was at odds with how Nigriv felt. Internally he was feeling a conflict -- one part knew that this wasn't normal while the other was able to shrug it off.

They knew nothing about this man and yet here he was in their cave seemingly taking a nap.

"What's your name?"

The man didn't reply straight away, when he did, he spoke softly. "Hembleth."

"Where are you from?"

"Around." The man used his hands to signify a big circle as he sat up.

"That's not an answer."

"I don't really have a place, Nigriv."

"What does that mean?" Nigriv found his non-answers irritating.

"Exactly as it sounds, lad. But don't let that bother you."

"Where does the gem come from then?" Nigriv patted the pocket where he'd put the stone.

"A place a long way from here to the south, somewhere that it never snows."

"No snow, how do they survive?" Ligriv asked.

"Quite easily. In fact, it's so hot there that instead of snow all they have is sand. Oceans of sand."

"Oceans of sand? You're making that up."

Hembleth chuckled. "No, but then I doubt you boys have ever been very far from here."

"We've been to Geler," Ligriv replied. "And to Cragen up in the mountains as well."

"As you would, but there's plenty more than those few places in this world, boys. Just because you've never seen them doesn't mean they don't exist."

"And this stone comes from the ocean of sand?"

"No, but a town that lies in the mountains by the desert."

"Desert?"

"That's the name men give to the ocean of sand."

"What is the town called?"

"Midderbuilt."

"That's a strange name."

"Well, Nigriv, anything that you don't know can appear strange, until it's not."

"Why do you always talk in riddles?"

"That's no riddle, son. Think about it, before you'd ever been to Geler it was strange to you, right?"

Nigriv nodded.

"But now, it isn't because you know it."

"I guess."

Hembleth had a little grin on his face. "And so it is out there. Once you've been somewhere and learned of it, it's no longer strange."

Nigriv both liked and disliked the way this man was making him think. "Why did you foretell us?"

The older man let out a short and forceful laugh. "I did no such thing, lad, but I get what you mean. Those that did the foretelling don't understand the why of it, or why a thing is foretold. It just happens, but usually it's about something important."

"And what was told?"

"Show me your hands, Nigriv."

He had no reason to obey the older man but he did anyway. Nigriv turned both his hands so the palms faced toward Hembleth.

"You're right-handed?"

Nigriv nodded.

Hembleth pointed at the marking on Nigriv's right palm. "See that mark?"

Nigriv nodded, he knew what his hands looked like.

"Have you ever wondered why you only have it on one hand?"

Nigriv shook his head, he'd not actually thought much about the mark at all.

"And Ligriv is left-handed?"

Nigriv knew the answer but turned to look at his brother as he replied, "Yes."

"And he has the same mark on his left hand." It was said as a statement not a question.

"How did you know?"

"It was most likely, all things being as they are."

"What is it?"

"Think about the shape of the gem I gave you."

As soon as Hembleth said it Nigriv knew what he meant, the stone and the mark on his hand were the same shape. The mark had been there his entire life, and he had never given it a second thought.

A line ran down from between his second and third fingers then split into two before rejoining at the bottom of his palm. The shape it made was narrow at the top then spread out near the bottom before joining up again.

"It's a teardrop."

"What's so important about that?"

"That's the interesting part, Nigriv. Those marks mean you can hold the stones."

"How is that interesting?"

"Like I said, these particular stones are different and other people cannot touch them like you do."

"Why not?"

"They wouldn't like it if they did."

"You can!" Ligriv exclaimed.

"That is true, Ligriv."

"Do you have the mark too?"

"No," Hembleth chuckled. "But that's an astute question. I'm a little different as well."

"How so?"

"That's not important at this time. What matters is that you both have the mark and thus you fit into this foretelling."

"Why us?"

"That's a conversation for another time."

Nigriv didn't like that he was only telling them parts of the things he knew. He was about to push it, but his brother spoke first.

"It's not a very interesting foretelling if all it says is that we can hold these stones."

"There's a little more to it than that."

"Such as?"

"You can do much more than just hold them."

"What else is there to do?"

"What's the difference between the white stone and the one you found, Ligriv?"

"The colour!" he answered quickly.

"Apart from that."

Ligriv appeared stumped and it took Nigriv a while to think it through before he had an answer. "Their shape."

Hembleth nodded. "In a way. Ligriv's stone is unrefined, unpolished, almost raw, whereas your stone has been cut and polished into that specific shape."

"And?"

"Do you know what a lapidarist is?"

Both boys shook their heads.

"When you're an expert gem cutter, someone that can select the best stones and work them into true gems, those are what we called lapidarists. For some that is all they do, while others create beautiful jewellery from the stones."

"What's that got to do with us?" Nigriv asked.

Hembleth's eyes locked on Nigriv's. "It would appear that you are meant to work with gems… normal ones as well as these stones… that you're both going to be rather talented."

"At making stones shiny?"

Hembleth chuckled again. "Something like that, son."

"But we don't know anything about gems and stones."

"No, but you can learn."

"So you'll be teaching us?"

A warm smile formed across Hembleth's face. "No, Nigriv, that's the job of a skilled craftsman, not a grumpy old man like me."

"Who then?"

"I don't know yet, but it won't be around here."

"Where?"

"Some of these lapidarists live in the city I told you of, in the desert."

"This is our home; we don't need to be going anywhere."

The older man stared at Nigriv for a short while, making him uneasy.

"It has been, son, but I think Midderbuilt would be a good place for you both. Safer."

"It sounds interesting, brother."

Nigriv looked at his twin and could sense his excitement, which he didn't like or agree with. He turned back to face Hembleth. "Safe from what? We can look after ourselves, we know how to trap and hunt, how to feed ourselves. It's more than safe enough here."

"So it might seem, Nigriv, but there's more to be concerned about than just the odd ice bear."

Silence hung across the cave for minutes. Nigriv felt uncomfortable looking at Hembleth who seemed unconcerned about the tension in the cave.

Finally, the old man's spoke. "I need to go. I won't make you leave, at least not now, but your time will come. You won't be able to stay here forever, it's too exposed, and others will seek you out. More than that, you'll feel the pull."

"What pull?"

"You'll know, in good time. Be warned though, if I can find you so can others, and they aren't going to be anywhere as kindly as I am."

"Who?"

"Others who might want your skills for their own purposes. They might come directly, or they'll use people you know."

"What's different about what you want us to do?"

"I won't force you to do anything nor to leave here, but there'll come a time when the choice to leave might be taken from you."

Nigriv didn't like the way the conversation had turned. The cave felt tiny and tense, and it sounded very much like he'd threatened them.

They'd let this stranger into their home and trusted him without reason. Much of what he'd said made sense, but Nigriv knew Father would have rejected a lot of what he had said as nonsense.

Hembleth stood abruptly, startling Nigriv. "I think I've filled your heads with more than enough new information and I need to be going. I'll let you be… for now. But know that you'd be well looked after in Midderbuilt, I promise."

"It's dark out there."

"Such things don't bother me, Nigriv. Look after each other now, don't go doing anything stupid, and keep those stones to yourself."

Then he gathered his coat and was gone, the door clunking closed behind him, leaving the cave feeling empty.

They both stared at the closed door as if expecting the man to come back in.

"I wouldn't have minded going."

"We're not going anywhere, El. This is our home, it's just nonsense. If it wasn't that you saw him too, I'd think I just had the daftest dream."

He already knew his brother wouldn't argue with him and the cave again fell into silence for a time before Ligriv spoke again. "I think I'm going to sleep."

"You're not hungry?"

"Not anymore."

Ligriv shuffled off to bed, leaving his stone on the table. Nigriv eventually went to bed himself, but he took his stone out from his pocket and firmly grasped it within his hands as he drifted off.

5

———

NIGRIV

Nigriv woke in the dark of night, his face damp with sweat, clutching the white stone. His fingers were wrapped so tightly around it that his hand ached.

Is that what woke me?

He listened for any strange sounds, anything that might alert him to danger, but heard nothing except the occasional snore from Ligriv, which was nothing new to him.

Nigriv sat up and rubbed his temples, noticing that his head ached. *I was dreaming...* He tried to recall what that had been about. *I was underground... looking up at something big.*

He relaxed his fingers and was surprised to see a glow coming from the gem he held. There was a tiny blue light inside it, flickering like a flame.

What on Dharatan?

The image in the dream was completely lost now and the light he thought he'd just seen in his stone had disappeared.

Now I'm just imagining things.

Annoyed that a dream had woken him, Nigriv lay back down wanting to get back to sleep. He put the stone on the floor despite an odd thought in his mind that he should hold on to it.

35

It's not like someone's going to take it.

As he tossed and turned the temptation to pick the stone up kept bugging Nigriv. He fought against it until he eventually fell back to sleep.

When the morning light and the coldness of the cave woke him, Nigriv felt groggy and unrested. He knew there'd be no more sleep and rolled himself upright, finding his hand clenched around the white gem again.

He placed it on the table and busied himself, restarting the fire and rubbing his hands as the flames grew. But it still didn't distract him from thinking about the stone.

He'd never been particularly attached to anything in the past and didn't understand why he was so drawn to this gem. *So much so I even imagined it had a light inside. Just a silly dream.*

Nigriv tried to focus on the fire, adding more wood without quelling its small flames. Still, it kept nudging him, a subtle sensation in the back of his mind, that he'd left something behind.

It's a stone, that's all, and I need to just forget about it.

Nigriv turned his thoughts to the man that had gifted the stone to him. Everything about Hembleth, including his arrival, was odd. He wasn't sure why he hadn't questioned the man more... they'd just accepted what he told them and happily allowed him to enter their cave.

At the time it had seemed perfectly normal, but it wasn't, he could see that now. Even his brother had been equally as welcoming. Nigriv knew that Father would have rebuked them.

He had always been cautious around others; Father would never have let the stranger into their cave. Yet the boys had done that without a care in the world. From the moment they'd first met the strange man Nigriv hadn't been concerned by him at all.

It was one of his tricks... that's what it's been the whole time. I bet he used one of his tricks on that stone as well.

Nigriv looked at his right hand and the mark that he paid so little attention to. They were meant to believe that it made them special, was part of a foretelling and that they should leave here.

We're not going anywhere.

This whole idea of leaving the cave wasn't a thing Nigriv would entertain, this was where they lived, and they were already adjusting to life without Father. There were things to do and they were doing them.

While his resolve was strong Nigriv decided he would put the little gem away out of reach. He stretched up to grab a tin on the shelf high above the fire.

Then he put the small stone in it and returned the tin up high out of the way. *Out of sight, out of mind. You're just a stone and a silly idea a strange man put in here.* He tapped his head.

Ligriv began to stir and Nigriv thought about what chores they needed to do today. He could see that they were running low on wood, considering winter would be with them for at least another six weeks. It would be a good task to remind them both of what needed doing.

In the past it would be Father who did the bulk of the cutting, Nigriv and his twin usually lugged and stacked the wood. Today would be the first time they had to do it all.

His brother had little to say, unusually when he woke, and after they both picked at some bread and nuts Nigriv led them out to get started. Even taking turns at it, the work was hard, and by the time they'd done enough for the day both were puffing.

Ligriv leaned on the axe shaft. "This axe is heavier than it felt at the start."

Nigriv smiled at his brother. "We'll get used to it in time."

Just another thing that had changed. Where there'd always been three now there were two. In Nigriv's mind it was like everything was out of place.

The order he was familiar with had been disrupted and the previous patterns no longer worked. He hoped with time that this sensation would pass and that the new routines would become normal to him.

Routines had always been a big part of the way they had been raised. Completing some of them was much harder without father but he'd taught them well.

While Ligriv would have easily become more fluid in his approach, Nigriv liked the simplicity of those routines and took the lead following how Father would have done it.

Weeks went by and the memory of Hembleth and the stones faded into the background. Even the sensations emanating from his brother went back to a familiar cadence.

As winter ended, the turn in the temperature meant they needed less of the fire and began to spend more time outside. Previously their father dictated what they could do in their downtime, now they got to choose for themselves.

The sun was out. Only a few puffy clouds littered the clear sky and the boys sat overlooking the thawing lake. Nigriv was feeling good about how things were working out.

"No one appearing out of nowhere today, brother."

Nigriv looked over at his twin, surprised that he'd brought up that topic. He didn't want to discuss it so he just smiled. His brother wasn't done talking though.

"The ice will be broken through within days."

"You're right, El. I can't tell if it's earlier than last year or not. That was the sort of stuff Father would know."

"Doesn't matter. I'm keen to get back to swimming in the lake, I prefer spring the most, I like it hotter."

Nigriv didn't favour any particular season, he liked them all when they arrived and was glad for their end when they left.

"Do you think he told us the truth?"

"Who, El?"

"Hembleth… about the ocean of sand."

Nigriv hadn't given that much thought, he'd been glad when he'd pushed those memories out of his mind. "I don't know if anything he told us was the truth."

Ligriv sat quietly for several minutes. "It would be much hotter than spring then, maybe even hotter than summer, don't you think?"

"I don't know."

As much as Nigriv didn't want to revisit the topic, his brother was right. It was an intriguing idea, and he pondered what an ocean of sand would look like.

He'd never seen a real ocean; Father had explained it was like the lake in summer but that it moved and had waves. "Do you think the sand moves, like the ocean?"

Ligriv looked happy that he was engaging with him. "That's an odd question."

"I remember Father said the ocean was like the lake…" Ligriv saddened at the mention of their father and Nigriv paused.

"Maybe it does, maybe the wind moves it like it does the sea." His twin's voice stuck in his throat a little.

Nigriv nodded back at his brother, sensing the pain he was feeling.

Ligriv sat quietly for a time before he spoke again. "I'd like to see a desert, maybe even that desert."

"We're not leaving here, this is home."

"I mean sometime… in the future. Don't you want to travel and see past Geler?"

"Like I said to Hembleth, this is home, I don't see why I'd want to leave here."

"He said he wanted us to go to that city. The one in the desert."

"And we said no. We don't need to listen to what he says." It came out sharper than Nigriv had intended.

"Sorry, I was just asking. Forget it."

But Nigriv couldn't forget it, and while he knew his brother wouldn't say any more right now, it wasn't his brother that was bothering him. He stared out across the thin layer of ice on the lake and tried to understand what was.

What he'd said to his brother was the truth, he didn't want to leave here. Nor was he interested in believing the words of a strange old man and his foretelling. Life was good here, it was home, their home, and they had no reason to leave, so they wouldn't.

A chill ran across the back of his neck and then down his spine. Once again, a thought floated across his mind as if from someone else. *You might not have a say in it.*

6

LIGRIV

The weather had never been a thing Ligriv had ever found himself wondering about before. So, the thought that summer was coming earlier this year stood out as strange.

It had always been his father who would make off-the-cuff remarks like that from time to time, before continuing with what he might have been doing.

Maybe it was, maybe it wasn't true, but the days were definitely warmer, that much he did know. He liked the heat, even though it did take a few weeks to get used to it when it did come.

The idea of never having to wear all the extra clothing to keep out the cold seemed appealing. Ligriv wiped his brow with a cloth he carried tucked into his belt.

Funny how I thought I'd be happy in the desert, surely it would be much hotter than this.

At least once a week he found himself thinking about what that would be like. The last time he'd mentioned it to Nigriv had been more than a month ago and his twin had made it clear he had no desire to discuss it, let alone go.

When it came to making decisions Ligriv let his brother take the lead. He had no desire to argue with Nigriv; it was something he'd never done ever since he could recall.

Ligriv wanted the pair of them to be close and arguing just created division. And that mattered even more to him now than ever before, now that it was just the two of them.

His brother was right, life here was good. They had all they needed; they were safe and things were as they should be. Why would they want to leave here?

"Watch where you're going, El."

Ligriv looked up to see his brother stopped on a rock ledge ahead, staring at him.

"Your head's off again, isn't it?"

"Just daydreaming, nothing to it."

"Pay attention!" His words were sharp, but Ligriv understood why.

While it was different to the spot where father had fallen, this path also had a steep drop-off, this time to the left. Nigriv turned and began to step his way down the steep trail cut into the cliff.

Ligriv looked ahead to the river below. He was keen to get to it. At the bottom they buried their heads in the narrow river to drink and wash off recent grime.

"A swim would be good."

"Not today, El. I want to reach the falls."

"Why you so set on the falls?"

"I don't know, to be honest, I just want to see them again."

Ligriv also enjoyed the falls, but there was no swimming to be had there, and he was hot. But when Nigriv started off again he followed without complaint.

It was a lengthy hike walking and clambering along the river's edge before they reached the spot where the rapids began, and the river widened.

A short while later they edged around the bushland on the southern side to the brink of the falls. The brothers had found this spot two years before, a few feet above and to the side of the falls.

You could sit with your legs hanging off into the air and see the river cascading down below, the only noise the crashing of water.

They sat looking down, at the never-ending flow, totally absorbed by it all.

An hour or more passed before, without warning, Nigriv pushed backward, stood and set off. There was no point in him speaking, the noise of the water was too loud.

Once they were far enough away to be heard, Ligriv spoke. "You seem bothered by something, brother?" While his twin didn't show many emotions Ligriv could sense something off about him.

"Nah." There was a short pause before he continued. "I just wanted to see them."

"There had to be a reason?"

Nigriv didn't answer and they walked for another ten minutes when he suddenly spoke. "I had a feeling."

"What sort of feeling?"

"Like I wouldn't be seeing them in a while."

"Why not?"

"I don't know, El. I just… it doesn't matter, I can't explain. We saw them, didn't we? You liked it didn't you?"

"Yeah." Ligriv grinned and they walked on without any further discussion. It always amused him that Nigriv never liked to be pushed to talk, he had to come to it on his own.

Less than a half-mile from the cliff that they had to climb, Nigriv jumped sideways into the bush. Ligriv didn't ask why, he just followed suit, mimicking his brother as he burrowed into the scrub before stopping still as a rock.

Nigriv held a finger up to his lips and pointed upriver to where they were heading.

Ligriv could see what had spooked him, although he wasn't sure why he'd run away. It was just five men, two at least Ligriv recognised: Falder, a herdsman that lived close to Geler, and Ruskej, a trapper like themselves, whose home was about five miles from theirs.

Two others Ligriv didn't recognise, but they looked like Geler folk by the clothing they wore. Much too flimsy for living out here all the time, more suited to living indoors. The fifth was dressed very differently, his full-length clothing entirely black, and his face and hands very pale, like snow.

They took an age to climb down the trail then walk along the riverbank. The path was only a few feet from where the boys were propped, close enough to hear any sound they might make.

Ligriv held his breath, grateful that the men were talking and not expecting anyone to be so close.

"I can see someone's been down here, it has to be them."

"How can you be so sure, Captain?" one of the townsfolk asked.

"The path's been disturbed recently and there's no one else out here."

"Any other way they'd take to come back?"

"Not an easy way. Can't see why they wouldn't just come back the way they went. They won't be expecting us, or anyone else."

"They're kids, it's not right for them to be living out here on their own."

"We could have just waited back at their cave, Falder."

"If it's as important to you as you say, then it's best to find them."

"As long as we get them." The one called Captain paused and look at the man in black who didn't respond. "They're worth a right good amount of coin to your mistress."

The man in black said nothing.

"You sure you're comfortable with that, Captain? They're still from here," Falder asked.

"Their pa's gone and apart from her, there's no other family. She looks like she's going to give them a far better life than out here or in Geler."

"You really think she's family?"

"Don't know, but why else would she want them? That said, I don't know who pays for their own kin. In the end, if we get them and take them back then we get our reward. And that is fine by me."

As the men kept walking their voices faded from earshot until Ligriv couldn't hear them at all. "What do we do now?" he whispered.

Nigriv's eyes were locked on the path the men had gone down. "Wait a bit longer then up the cliff and home, fast."

After a few more minutes he led the way out of the scrub. Ligriv followed close behind him as they hurried to the path and climbed. At the top they paused to catch their breath, looking down the river for any sight of the men.

"We have family? It doesn't make sense?"

"It's not true, Ligriv, what he said was right, why would you pay for your own? Father told us there was no other family. Whatever this is, it's not real or right."

"I don't want to go with them, Nigriv."

"Me either, El. Let's get back to the cave."

Ligriv liked that his brother had expressed his thoughts, it was often hard to read him through their connection.

They took off at pace, both wanting to put as much distance between them and the hunters as they could.

Ligriv followed his brother, who wasn't bothered about choosing an alternative path back, just getting there quickly.

"Now what?"

Nigriv looked around the cave. He was thinking about something.

"They'll come back when they don't find us down there. Maybe they're already on their way here."

"We can't stay here then."

"Let's get up in the mountain and head to Cragen, we can shelter there until they leave us be."

"Won't we have to go back the way they went to hit the trail?"

His brother stopped his pacing and looked at him, not saying anything for a minute.

"No, we have to go up the rock. They won't be able to see our tracks and we can watch them and see what they do."

It made sense to Ligriv. "How long for?"

Nigriv shook his head. "I don't know. Take anything you need to keep, in case it's more than a day or two."

Ligriv grabbed his hunting tools first: hand axe, knife, bow, then some clothes and a blanket he tied to the outside of his bag.

They owned little else, so it wasn't a big task. He was ready and looked to his brother. Nigriv grabbed a tin box from the ledge above the fire.

"I best take this."

"What is it?"

Nigriv opened it and took out the white stone.

"Why was it in there?" Ligriv wondered; he still carried his with him.

"Something about it was bothering me, so I put it away, but he told us not to let anyone else see them." Nigriv packed it in his own bag and grabbed Father's hunting knife as well, attaching it to his belt.

"We better get going."

Outside the cave they headed toward a spot they'd often climbed before, and Nigriv looked back at him. Ligriv knew why, he was the better of the two when it came to what they were about to do.

"So I'm leading then."

Nigriv smiled. "Yes, brother. You are."

7

LIGRIV

All afternoon Ligriv picked his way up the mountain choosing the best route he could find. It was hard, exhausting work and at times dangerous, but he never stopped.

Nigriv followed behind never saying a word. As he pulled himself over a makeshift wall onto a small ledge, Ligriv stopped, recognising how much cooler it was getting with the sun disappearing over the peak above.

"We don't have much more daylight, brother, perhaps this is as good a place as any to stop."

Nigriv was hunched over panting to get his breath back and simply nodded.

"This ledge will protect us from the weather as much as anywhere."

"It's fine." Nigriv's breath was settling quickly. "It'll be cold, El, but we should be alright without a fire."

Ligriv sat down. "Did you see anyone following?"

Nigriv shook his head.

Ligriv was hungry, they'd not packed anything in their rush to get away, but he knew they'd survive without food for a night or so. It wasn't the first time. All going well they'd be able to go back down in the morning.

As night set in both boys wrapped themselves with the blankets they'd brought, to keep the chill at bay. It would get colder later in the night, but they would manage well enough, there wasn't any wind and their clothing was warm.

Ligriv found it hard to settle. The sounds up here were so different to what he was used to in their cave, his mind constantly fearing about their pursuers, worrying that someone would appear over the rocks out of nowhere.

He dozed on and off, huddled against the rocks beside him. Sunlight woke him from such a nap as it edged up over the far horizon. He stretched as best he could and crawled to where Nigriv knelt looking downward.

"What do you see?"

"They spent the night by the cave. It looks like there's more of them down there now."

"Why more? There's only two of us."

Nigriv shook his head and backed away from where he'd been perched.

"I don't know, brother."

The boys waited, taking turns to watch what was happening below as the sun continued to rise and the day began to warm up.

"Several of them have begun to climb. We should go!"

Immediately Ligriv grabbed his pack and started climbing, his brother close behind. There was nothing to discuss, they just continued up the rock face.

Several hours later Ligriv stopped. "This will make it easier."

They'd reached the main pathway cut into the heights of the mountainside that led to Cragen. This was the trail they'd have been on if they'd taken the normal route there.

Using that path would have been much easier but to reach it would have taken them back near their hunters. This climb had been much harder but at least they were safe. At least for now.

Nigriv stopped beside him. "Let's take a quick break."

They drained the remaining water in their skins. Ligriv knew there was water up here, but he couldn't remember exactly where. He'd just have to hope it was ahead and not behind them.

"Do you think they can see us?"

His brother shrugged. "Doesn't matter. We've just got to keep going now."

Ligriv nodded, before setting off again. Walking the path was much easier than climbing but it wasn't without its own perils. It was very narrow and uneven, and he had to juggle between keeping up a good pace and not twisting an ankle.

An hour or so later he started to feel like things were familiar and shortly after, a smile formed on his face.

"What is it, El?"

"Water, the pond we've used before. I know where we are now, it's just ahead."

They had to climb down from the path over more rocks to reach the pond. The pool sat inside a bowl made by the rocks, a small stream filling it from above.

When they reached the water both boys stripped off and climbed in. It was only waist deep and much colder than expected but they needed it.

Ligriv cupped his hands and drank, soaking up as much as he could. "I'll get our skins." He filled them both before he got out and dried in the morning air.

"What will we do once we get to Cragen?"

Nigriv shrugged. "Rest up, hide, and hope these men give up."

"Why are they after us? I don't understand."

"I don't understand it either, El. All we can do is head to Cragen... we can try and figure it out once we're there."

It wasn't much of a plan, but it was enough for Ligriv. He could just focus on that and avoid spending too much time worrying. A grumble in his stomach reminded him of something more pressing, even more motivation to get to the village.

Bathing in the pool and the cold water he'd drunk perked him up but it only lasted until middle day. The rest of the afternoon was a struggle, his body tired and hungry.

Just before dusk they left the path and walked down the steep walkway that led into Cragen. It sat in a natural basin surrounded by rocky cliffs with huts and tents surrounding an open circle where people were gathered around a fire.

"Ho," Ligriv called out.

A man many years their senior shuffled toward them using a dark wooden staff for support. He said nothing until he was stood before them. "Welcome, boys. Where's your father?"

"Just us, is all." Ligriv replied.

The man squinted a little and eyed them curiously.

"Unusual for you to be traveling this trail alone."

Nigriv shrugged and answered, "Circumstances."

The old man nodded. "You know the rules, no weapons inside the village, you can place them in the hut over there. Then come join us for food."

They quickly did as they were told, placing their bags and hunting weapons inside the visitors' hut, Ligriv's mind now focused on getting something to eat.

In the circle, rocks had been made into benches alongside other sitting stones all facing toward the firepit. A deer was being cooked on a spit above a small blaze and Ligriv's stomach grumbled at the smell.

An elderly woman invited them to a bench to sit. "Hungry?"

"We are, thank you," Ligriv answered.

She returned with some dried beef and crumbly bread. It was tasteless but Ligriv didn't mind, his stomach was grateful that it had food.

"Where you boys headed?" a man across the circle, about the age of their father, asked.

Nigriv finished chewing and looked toward the man. Ligriv watched his brother. "Here is all."

The man laughed. "We're not exactly a major destination unless you have furs to trade, but I saw none."

"We had little choice."

"Why's that?"

Ligriv replied, knowing how little his brother liked to speak to others.

"Some men came looking for us."

"Where is your father?"

Ligriv felt the sadness creeping back in and stumbled a little over his reply. "He died."

"By these men?"

"No... an accident, many weeks back."

Everyone in the group all held their hands to their chests and dipped their heads. "Sorry for your loss."

Ligriv just nodded.

"These men, do you know them?"

"A couple of them, but it wasn't them... they brought others who wanted to catch us to take to someone else. Someone who was paying them to do it."

The older woman almost spat out, "Slavers."

The younger villager looked her way. "You don't know that, Irha."

She shrugged. "Who else pays for youngsters?"

"What does she mean?" Ligriv asked.

"There are those who take youngsters as captives and make them work, on ships, farms, whatever they need. It's a cruel and nasty practice."

Ligriv didn't like the sound of that.

"Did they follow you?" This time it was the original host who had greeted them.

"They were this morning, about a half-day behind," Nigriv answered.

The group sat quiet for a moment before the elder spoke again. "Then most likely they won't be here until daylight at the earliest."

"This was the only place we could think of... to come." All the concerns Ligriv had, came back to him. This little village had no walls and these people weren't warriors; he wasn't sure how much safer they'd be here.

"Few travel the paths up here in the dark, it should be safe enough for tonight. There's little moonlight which will delay them also. The only spare space we have is Yefel's lodge. If you stay out of sight you'll be fine there."

A murmur of agreement spread around the circle, but Ligriv could sense the change in everyone. There was tension now where before there'd just been curiosity.

"Tomorrow we'll learn what these people want."

"We don't mean to bring trouble here, we just didn't know what else to do."

"Rest easy, boys. Maybe they are trouble, maybe they aren't. That isn't something we need to be concerned with tonight. You'll be safe here."

Despite how calm the man's voice sounded to Ligriv it had little effect on his own feelings. He'd thought getting here would solve everything, but it hadn't.

"Come, boys, let me show you to your cabin."

Both of them followed the older lady, Irha, to their cabin. When she was gone Ligriv looked at his twin. "What now?"

"We need rest, brother. I think we try and get as much as we can. Who knows what tomorrow will bring, but if we have to leave in a hurry, we should be ready."

Ligriv nodded, thinking about the best path to his bag and hunting weapons. He fell asleep still worried about what was going to happen.

8

———

NIGRIV

*N*igriv always had a keen ear, at least that's how he explained how the slightest noise could wake him. It was true that he heard things his twin didn't, but maybe that was because Ligriv was often daydreaming.

The cabin didn't feel like much protection. It wouldn't take much for their followers to break in, and being near the entrance kept Nigriv awake for much of the night.

He didn't like this complete lack of order to their life, it made him feel at odds with everything. He was unable to settle down and sleep, envious that his brother had fallen asleep so easily in the other cot.

After the snatches of sleep he did get, Nigriv rose feeling groggy and still concerned about what today would bring. He wanted to be back in their home where everything had a way to it... where he had control.

Getting out of the cabin without waking Ligriv wasn't a challenge as he hadn't stirred at all to any of the slight noises. Outside Nigriv wandered into the circle and stretched his cold muscles.

The advantage of the position of this village was more obvious in full light. The rock walls, for lack of a better term, rose steeply above the basin, leaving only one path of access.

Maybe they won't find us here.

Footsteps hurrying nearby turned him and moments later a single runner appeared at the top of the path and hurried toward Nigriv.

"News of your followers."

Nigriv spun to see the village elder approaching the circle.

The runner met them in the circle.

"What news?"

The man paused just long enough to gather his breath. "They were camped a distance away, but they have started marching with first light."

"How long?"

"An hour, at most."

The elder nodded.

"What should we do?" Nigriv could feel his fear rising.

"That is not something I can tell you, lad."

"We're not going with them!"

"Not what I meant, son. It's not my job to tell you want you should or shouldn't do."

Others were out now and a larger group was heading toward them. The elder waited until enough of them were near them.

"They come."

"He should hide," Irha said.

"Only if he wishes to." The elder turned back to Nigriv. "We're happy to try and send these people away on your behalf, but whether you hide or try to evade them is entirely up to you."

Nigriv's concern was high, but he felt trapped now. There really wasn't anywhere else for them to go. If they tried to get ahead of the men there'd only be a short distance between them. He nodded.

"Then go back to your brother and stay out of sight."

Ligriv was still sleeping when he got back. Nigriv rocked him. "Wake up!"

Ligriv grunted and turned over. "What?"

"Get up and get ready, the men are close by."

That made Ligriv sit up quickly. "Can we escape?"

Nigriv shook his head. "There's not enough distance between us; we'd have to run through the night. They said they'll deal with them."

"How?"

Nigriv shrugged. He knew no more and was too worried to think of any clever options. Neither of the twins could sit still while they waited and paced around the small cabin or took turns peering out the only window behind the cover of a curtain.

When the group that had been following them arrived at the top of the path into Cragen Nigriv whispered to his brother, "They're here."

Only one of them walked down the path into the circle, the man the others called Captain. Nigriv held his finger to his mouth silencing his brother.

"Ho, strangers, welcome to Cragen."

"That's its name, is it?" The captain sounded terse and unfriendly.

"What brings you this way?"

"Looking for some runaways."

"Up here? You're a long way from nowhere, stranger."

The captain continued, "Two lads, young'uns, must have come this way."

"They must have passed us by."

"They're not here?"

The elder was slow to respond. "Have I not just answered that, stranger?"

"Not really."

"I'll be clearer then. There's no runaways here so they must have passed us by."

"Can we look around?"

This time the elder's response was immediate. "You may not." Any pretence of friendliness was all gone now.

"What would it harm if there's no one here?"

"I bet it's the same where you're from, strangers don't go poking their nose into others' business. I think it's best you moved on now." It was said with a lot more strength and resolve than the elder's physical appearance projected.

The captain stood still for what seemed an age to Nigriv, placing his hand on his sword hilt, before he nodded and turned, walking back to his group.

Any conversation held at the top of the pass was out of everyone's earshot, but Nigriv could see it was serious just by their manner. Whatever was decided, they all turned and left the entrance path, turning right on the main trail, disappearing from sight.

Nigriv turned back to his brother. "They've gone"

"Where did they go?"

"The opposite way from home."

"What are we going to do then?"

"Nothing for now. I don't think they'll go far, we need to hide here for a bit."

Nigriv had no idea what they should be doing, he felt completely out of control and at the whim of these villagers. They'd been generous to them so far but who knew how long that might last?

As if triggered by his thoughts the door to their cabin opened slowly and the older woman, Irha, slipped in, carrying a small bag.

"It's something to eat. Sorry for the delay but we aren't sure if they're watching from above."

"What is going to happen?"

The old lady gazed at Nigriv for a moment before she answered. "I do not have answers for you."

Nigriv waited to see if she had more to say.

"We'll hide you here for as long as we can and wait to see what they do. Hopefully they'll move on, and you can get on your way." She turned and slipped out the door.

"Are we safe here, brother?"

"I hope so, El."

Hours passed very slowly and they felt trapped in the small cabin, both hardly saying a word. Irha had come back with more food a second time around middle day. Nigriv was at the window in the early afternoon when two new people arrived in the town.

"They're lugging a cart," he told Ligriv.

"Who are they?"

Nigriv shook his head. "Don't know."

He watched as one of the villagers greeted them much more amicably than the elder had been earlier. They spoke amongst themselves quietly and stood near a hut on the other side of the circle, Nigriv unable to make out what they were saying.

More villagers came to meet them, and many hugs were shared or hands shaken. "They definitely know them; they're all being friendly."

Then several villagers went into the hut where everyone was gathered and brought out furs. The two men who had brought the cart inspected the furs, holding them up and pulling at them.

"I think they're trading pelts, El."

After a while an agreement seemed to be made, hands were shaken and the new men pulled out a pouch and counted out coins which they handed over in exchange. They loaded their cart before setting off back up the path, several villagers helping them get it up the steep slope.

Several hours later, once the sun had gone down, the door opened and the elder came in with another villager carrying some small sacks. They closed the door, and the second man lit a lamp.

"Sorry we kept you in the dark here, boys, but we wanted to wait until the daylight was gone."

"What's happening?"

"Did you see the traders that came through today?" The elder asked.

Nigriv nodded.

"They met the men hunting you just up on the trail. The armed men quizzed them a lot about you two before they let them through. Your followers now know you didn't go that way."

"What does that mean?"

"If I was to take a guess then I think they'll be back. They will know you're here."

"You won't hand us over, will you?" Ligriv asked.

The elder smiled at him. "Not by choice, boy, but I got the sense they will do what they need to capture you..."

"I'm sorry for the trouble we've brought you," Nigriv said miserably.

"We can defend ourselves, but..."

"What?"

"There's another option for you... if you want it?"

"Tell us."

"We agreed to bring you your things in case you want to escape."

"Escape where? They know our cave; there's probably men still there." Ligriv was quite agitated now.

"We have a tunnel. None other know of it. It would get you safely west of here, far enough to give you a big head-start on them."

"And then what?"

"There's paths to the coast or deeper into the mountains."

"Are there any other villages?"

"Toward the coast there's one more, then Ranniko on the water."

Nigriv looked at his brother in the low light. His twin was clearly worried.

"We've packed you some food and skins to make the trip if you wanted to go, and there's this." The elder held up a pouch.

"What's that?"

"Those pelts we sold today, some were from your father, plus others we sold for him over the last weeks. This is all the coin we owe him... now that he has gone it's yours. It will see you on your way down the coast and beyond, if that's what you choose."

Nigriv looked over at his brother who was staring back at him, expecting he would make the decision. He didn't know what they should do, this option seemed too easy.

Nigriv couldn't help but think about the words of the man Hembleth... *you might have the choice made for you.* But he'd been talking about them going to the south, to the place in the desert.

This wasn't that... *or was it?* The strange man had warned them something like this might happen.

What would father say? He was always so practical. Father wouldn't cling to their cave for no reason, certainly not with such a risk. The odds were against them if all of those men came for them.

Two boys against all those armed men... There was only one option if they didn't want to get caught.

A strange calmness came over him. "We'll do it."

Ligriv looked at him and nodded.

"Then you should be going soon. We can lead you into the tunnel and give you light, then you will need to push on through the night. You want to get as far along as you can before daylight."

Nigriv shrugged. To him the decision was made so he was keen to get moving.

The elder turned to his companion. "Keep them company, Broew, and go as far as you feel safe."

Nigriv looked at the older man. "Thank you."

He brushed him away and pointed to his companion.

The younger man nodded. "Come, boys." He handed them their things and blew out the lamp before opening the door and slipping out.

Both boys followed him around the back then over to the rock face. They sidled along that in the low light until they reached a spot where another villager waited.

He lifted a series of mid-sized rocks away exposing a small opening. Their guide slid through, reaching back for their bags, then beckoning the twins to follow.

Once in the tunnel all three linked hands and walked for a bit before the guide found a torch on the wall and struck his flint to light it. He lit a second and handed it to Nigriv. "Let's go."

They walked in silence, not that Nigriv could think of anything to say. Only a day and a bit ago they'd been bothering no one and living exactly where Father had left them... safe. Now all of that was behind them and where they would end up he had no idea.

When their guide stopped, Nigriv knew it was the end of his help, which only made the weight of the moment seem much heavier.

"Just keep going, there's only one way out. You will have to push out the rocks at the end. Please make sure to stack them back so others do not find the way."

Both boys nodded, before Ligriv spoke up for the first time the whole walk. "Thank you."

The guide smiled and patted both of them on a shoulder before turning and hurrying away.

"Here, brother." Nigriv handed his twin the torch.

"I guess I'm leading then?"

Nigriv forced a smile. "I guess you are, brother."

9

LIGRIV

$\mathcal{U}$boci had been hidden by the mountain range until it wasn't. The sharp cliffs and rock walls suddenly became a large hill that sloped down toward a plateau on which the city had been built.

Atop the edge of the mountains a fortified building, many times bigger than any other, loomed over the city below. Smaller and less ornate buildings crept down the hillside into the city proper below.

It was late afternoon as the boat the boys were on pulled into the small port of Uboci and Ligriv was grateful that he'd soon be off the water. While his twin hadn't been bothered at all, he'd spent the entire time seasick.

After three days hiking away from Cragen at first Ligriv had been keen to be on a boat, away from their pursuers, but once out of sight of Ranniko he'd discovered he had no liking for sailing at all.

The seven days they'd spent to get here felt like the longest of his life. He spent most of his time stood at the prow being sick or letting the spray and wind numb him of how bad he felt.

His first step onto land caused him to let out a sigh despite his head still feeling like it was rocking side to side.

Nigriv turned to him and smiled. "Happier?"

He nodded. "Which direction?"

"Away from the port, the captain said we'd be best closer to the inner city." They set off.

It took Ligriv a while to shake off the wobbly feeling that the sea travel had given him, but he was glad to be walking. His mind was ablaze with everything happening around them.

Neither had ever been to a city before and everything seemed new. The volume of workers in the port alone was massive, tenfold the number at Ranniko where they'd boarded their boat.

Wagons rolled past constantly, forcing them to jump out of the way. Wheels splashed water over their boots and people were rushing at pace to and from the port.

The further they got from the docks and into the city proper there were no fewer people. They passed some bars with men spilling out carrying jugs of ale, he presumed, but trying to push their way back in.

Music could be heard over the cheering and jeers of whoever was inside. There were bakeries that filled the street with divine aromas, making Ligriv's mouth water.

No one seemed to care about the boys and would just as easily knock them over as politely push past. A shove here a cuss there, they seemed to be always in someone's way.

Nigriv grabbed him by the sleeve. "This way." He led them off the major roadway they'd been on and toward a square filled with stalls and people.

Nigriv turned to him. "Maybe we can get something to eat here?"

They bought some meat sticks which lasted seconds, reminding Ligriv how little he'd eaten in the week they'd been gone. He'd have bought another, but his brother had already begun to move off.

All around them stall holders were seeking attention, their voices all trying to outdo their neighbour, hollering about what wonders they had on offer.

It felt like a game to Ligriv, not hostile, and he soaked up the fun of it, everything about the place exciting him. A stall to his left caught his attention and he wriggled between some adults to catch a glimpse of it.

An older man, not much taller than himself, stood behind a countertop filled with all sorts of boxes of bright coloured powder.

Despite never having seen him before Ligriv felt a strange sense of familiarity. He had a long beard, which should have been white, but instead was a rainbow of colours.

"Get your chalks, come right up and choose your colour!" the strange little man was yelling out, occasionally clapping his hands causing puffs of colour to burst into the air.

At one-point Ligriv thought the man looked his way and winked at him which seemed strange. He looked about and realised he'd lost his brother, and his chest immediately tightened.

"There you are!" He felt the hand grab his shoulder and spun to see Nigriv. "You can't do that, brother; we'll lose each other in this."

Ligriv nodded and followed closely as they moved on.

They squeezed their way out of the crowd. "I think that's enough of that for now. This bag and stuff just make it harder. We should go find somewhere to sleep."

Not far from the markets they entered a road with multiple inns lined up next to each other. Ligriv chose the first one and went in.

A woman was leaning on a counter in an entry room. "Suppose you need a room, do you?"

Ligriv didn't feel very welcome. "Yes."

"Where's your folks?"

He stuttered a bit. "We're… on our own. From the north coast."

She frowned, showing creases of concern on her brow.

"I've only the one left, but I'm guessing that's all you need anyway."

"Yes."

"I'll want payment up front then, don't want you lads slipping off without paying."

Ligriv didn't realise there was any other option and watched his brother pull out their pouch and hold up a coin.

"You keep that well hidden, there's plenty about who'll see you boys as easy marks."

"What for?"

"To take your money and they won't be bothered about how they get it either. This ain't some country village, it's a city and there's as many who'd harm you as there are those who wouldn't even notice you."

She came out from behind the counter.

"Come on then, I'll take you to your room. It will get rowdy down below once more people arrive and get on the ale, but it won't last all night."

The landlady hadn't exaggerated about how rowdy it would get. Within a couple of hours Ligriv felt like he might as well have been down there, it was so noisy in their room.

Nigriv was lying on his bed, his arms behind his head, staring at the ceiling.

Ligriv couldn't stand still and was pacing about the room. He went to the window and started trying to open the latch.

"What are you doing?"

"Just want to get some fresh air."

After he gave it a serious nudge the window pushed outward with a loud squeak. The noise didn't matter, no one would hear it above the racket downstairs.

While it let in air it also let in more of the noise from outside. Ligriv clambered up onto the sill and then out onto the roof. He could see light from the city across many streets and the noise wasn't just coming from the inn below, the city seemed alive with people laughing and cheering.

He was intrigued by it all; he'd never been anywhere like this.

"We should go take a look around."

Nigriv got up slowly from his bed and wandered to the window. "I could do with something else to eat. But we need to stick together, not like before, you can't go wandering off."

Ligriv could feel the smile on his face. "Sure."

Nigriv grabbed his coat and then paused, turning back to his brother. "We best heed her words about the money." He put several coins into his pocket and left the small pouch in his main bag. Then he picked up his hand axe and tucked it into his belt under his coat before handing Ligriv his.

The main room downstairs was full of people. No one paid the boys a moment's notice as they walked past and headed outside. Ligriv couldn't believe how busy it still was given it was night-time.

"Shall we go back to the market?"

Ligriv nodded. It was as good a place as any, and he'd enjoyed the meat sticks they'd had earlier. He stayed close to his brother's side but that didn't prevent his eyes feasting on everything they saw.

Men lay asleep against walls, others stood relieving themselves in full view of others, and some women stood in doorways calling at men to join them.

The market was still just as busy, and they ate their fill of the same skewered meats as earlier. Ligriv noticed the colourful man was no longer there, nor his chalks.

"Where to now?"

Nigriv shrugged this time.

"I guess I'm leading then?"

His brother smiled. "I guess you are."

With no idea where to go he just went in the opposite direction to their inn. The further they walked, the quieter the streets became as more of the buildings around appeared to be homes.

There were still people passing intermittently but nowhere the same number as there was back behind them. Ligriv was less concerned about losing his brother and let his mind wander over the different houses, admiring many of them.

Some were very ornately decorated on the outside but also had big gates and guards, others still looked massive to him but weren't quite as showy. Such a place was so foreign to him, he couldn't help wondering what they were like inside.

"I wonder who lives here?"

Nigriv didn't answer, he didn't seem to be anywhere near as interested in the buildings.

Something else was pulling at Ligriv. He couldn't have explained it but without all the noise and people he could sense something. Almost as though he was being drawn in a specific direction.

For a brief moment he considered discussing it with his brother, but he wasn't so sure he wasn't just imagining it anyway.

It can't have happened quickly, but he realised that the roads they were in were much darker and dingier than where they'd come from. There was no one around that he could see and while he was still conscious of that sensation, he was also a little anxious.

Nigriv broke the silence. "I feel eyes on us, brother."

Ligriv turned to look at him. "Where?"

"I can't say for sure, but I can feel it, I'm sure of it. Maybe we should go back where there's more people."

They both stopped and Ligriv looked at him, wondering if he was saying they should go back or just suggesting it. Ligriv could still feel that gentle tug, and now it was pointing to his left, at an archway leading into a square.

"Maybe just a little longer, I feel like there's something to see in here."

He stepped through, Nigriv following, and saw an orange glow emanating from a building at the far end. There was little other lighting in the square and Ligriv could make out the shapes of a few people in the shadows.

None of that bothered him and he headed toward what looked like a small temple, the desire to know what was making that light pulling him toward it.

His mind jumped to the stone in his bag back in the inn and he wished he had it with him now.

A small set of steps led up to the entranceway, but the door was locked. It didn't stop him, he just climbed up on the right side of it until he reached the sill of a window.

Ligriv pulled himself up until he could rest on his elbows and see inside. The only light came from an egg-shaped stone, on a pedestal, at the far end. It glowed orange much like the one he'd found back in their cave, and he couldn't take his eyes off of it.

"What can you see, El?"

"Hey, what are you two up to?"

The voice startled them both and Ligriv let go, dropping down beside his brother. A man stood at the bottom of the temple stairs.

"Nothing, just looking," Nigriv called out, somewhat feebly Ligriv thought.

"Don't want to be messing with the temple. Get down here where I can see you better."

Both boys did as he told them, climbing down and making their way down the steps.

"I don't know your faces, who are you?"

"Just passing through," Nigriv answered.

Ligriv saw the man's face was covered with pock marks and his eyes were dark and sunken. He had a skinny build, and his hands looked thin and bony, the right one gripping a walking cane tightly.

Both boys kept moving, intending to get past him.

"Hold up, boys, I want to talk to you." He pushed his cane in front of Nigriv who stopped before tripping over it. "I said I want to talk to you."

"Nothing to say, we're on our way."

"Only if I say so." There was a menace in his voice and Ligriv didn't like the look he gave his brother.

Nigriv went to take a step, and the man tried to block his way. Nigriv pushed his palm out at the man simply to block him, but the spindly man fell backward.

"Oi!" he yelled out as he sat on his arse unexpectedly.

"Let's go." Nigriv took off and Ligriv followed.

"Did you see that? Stop them!"

Ligriv could see who the man was speaking to now, the shapes in the shadows had all moved into the middle of the square, blocking the direct path to the arch.

He didn't have a good feeling about what was happening and knew it was all his fault that he'd brought them in here. He'd caused this trouble just as he'd caused their father's fall... His chest tightened, and he struggled to breathe.

Ahead of him, Nigriv stopped and turned his head to Ligriv. "Let me sort this."

His brother had opened his coat up and had gripped the handle of his axe and pulled it free. Ligriv did the same, his senses coming back to him.

"Why'd you push Trigger? He didn't do nuttin to yu'se. You knocked him over, hurt ole Trigger."

"Didn't mean anything, just wanted to get past, same as now."

The group of boys laughed, but not as though it was funny. Ligriv didn't like the sound of it at all.

"Well, we'll seez what Trig wants to do with ya, now won't we?" There were five of them and they all held knives or blades of some type.

"Like I said, we'll be on our way."

The broadest of the group stepped forward toward them, holding out his blade. "You're going nowhere unless Trigger says so."

"What now, Nigriv?"

It took his brother a few moments to respond. "Father would say it's like wolves on the hunt."

Ligriv understood what he meant. Father had told them many times, *"Take out the main one and the others will scatter."*

"We don't want any trouble." Nigriv took a step to their left as though they'd just go around the group.

The bigger one stepped that way as well. "Too late for that." He laughed and his companions laughed as well.

Before Ligriv realised what his brother was about to do, Nigriv raised his right arm and whipped his hand forward releasing his hand axe. It flew through the air, end-over-end, lodging in the bigger boy's forehead, and he fell backwards startling his friends.

The brothers reacted first, running hard toward the group. When they reached the body Ligriv eyed the other boys who were much less confident and backing away quickly.

Nigriv bent over the dead boy and yanked his axe free before muttering, "Let's go." Ligriv took off with him and they ran out the arch and back in the direction they'd come.

They were long out of sight of the arch and back in more lit roads when Ligriv stopped and stepped into a side alley, his lungs burning. His brother was there beside him but said nothing.

Something wasn't right with him, Ligriv could sense it, but now wasn't the time to ask. He looked over at him. Nigriv was stood, breathing just as heavily, but his eyes were locked on the bloody axe in his hand.

"Put that away!"

Ligriv watched him do it before checking if they were being observed or followed. The way seemed clear, and he turned back to his brother who seemed frozen in place. He grabbed him by the sleeve and led him out of the alley and back along the cobbled road.

Ligriv led him until they found a busy road and mingled in with the crowds. It took a while before Ligriv recognised several buildings. With a little effort he found the way they'd come and led his brother back to their inn and up into their room.

As shocked as he was at what had just happened, he was much more concerned about his brother who still hadn't said a word. Nigriv didn't even take his coat off, he just lay down on his bed and closed his eyes.

NIGRIV

If it was a muscle pain Nigriv would know how to relieve it, but this was nothing of the sort. He was experiencing the same discomfort inside as if he'd overworked a muscle or damaged it but he had no idea where it was coming from.

He rolled to his other side, as if it would relieve it, but changing position did nothing. Even his ears wouldn't let him be, the sound of his heart pounding within them was only broken by the occasional snore from his brother.

What is this?

The inn had closed hours go and all the patrons were gone, leaving few sounds to distract him. Those that he did hear did nothing to ease what was happening inside.

Nigriv was angry at himself and at the lad he'd killed. *Why did he make me do it? Why did I do it?*

He hadn't planned to kill the boy; in the moment he hadn't even been thinking much at all. Everything was simple to process: there was a threat, he'd rationalised it to be like a pack of wolves attacking, and knew he had to fix it.

So, he had.

In the moment it was clear, and they'd escaped, which should have been the end of it. Except it wasn't, and he was more confused than ever. Nigriv had never experienced anything like what was happening to him before.

What didn't help at all was the fear of what might happen next. The only way he could escape the discomfort inside was to worry about someone coming to get them.

Every creak in the inn's wooden floors or walls sent his heart racing, as did distant doors banging or the odd voice drifting into their room. Would it be the guards? Or more of those boys and that man who'd tried to corner them?

He didn't know what their assailants had wanted, nor what they'd do, in the moment he'd relied on what their father had taught them. Except that was in the bush, not here in a city.

Nigriv could remember the first time they'd been surrounded by wolves and the way his body had shaken at the time. He'd begun to panic and wasn't sure what to do, but father had been calm and taken out the dominant animal.

Unlike last night, Father had needed to injure a second member of the pack before the rest backed off and allowed them to escape. Father hadn't expressed anything about the event, he'd been calm the whole time, explaining to them what he was doing.

Last night Nigriv had just acted as he'd seen Father do, the difference being that it wasn't wolves but a person. He'd never been squeamish about killing animals, if anyone was it was Ligriv.

Nor could he say that this was a squeamishness either. Perhaps that was the biggest issue -- he couldn't define what was happening at all. He felt very wrong inside but had no way to resolve it or relieve it.

He sat on the side of the bed to see if it helped, but his hands still shook, and his head was woozy. Grabbing the edge of the bed with both hands, he tried to squeeze his body free of whatever this was.

We should have stayed in; I should have told Ligriv no... he would have done what I said.

"Stayed in… should've stayed in." He repeated the words over and over under his breath.

Now all he could imagine was them being locked up somewhere

or worse. They would have to get out of here, and quickly, before anyone found them. Nigriv didn't know where, but at least his head could reason this out.

Timing would be the key; this place was way bigger than the town of Geler. Back there everyone knew everyone, word of something like this would be throughout the whole town in no time.

It was time to wake his brother and get them out of here, even though he wanted to lie back down and do nothing until everything went away. He went to Ligriv's bed and shook him.

"What?"

"Get up, we have to go."

"Where?" Ligriv was half sitting up and rubbing at his eyes.

Nigriv shrugged. "I don't know, El, but away from here."

"Do you think someone will come looking for us?"

"I guess… I don't know… but we can't get caught here."

Nigriv spun around at the sound of light tapping on their door, putting a finger over his lips and making sure his brother understood.

"Who?" Ligriv mouthed.

Nigriv shook his head at his brother and without thinking crept to where his axe was. Picking it up brought back memories of the night before and he shuddered; dried blood marked the blade; he'd not cleaned it last night.

More tapping. "I know you're in there, boys, now let me in."

It was a man's voice and sounded familiar. *It couldn't be?*

Ligriv got up and raised his hands to Nigriv, looking confused at Nigriv's reluctance to open the door. The tapping began again. Ligriv went to the door and opened it slowly.

Before it was fully open, Hembleth swept in and pushed the door closed behind him. "Bar that again!"

"What are you doing here?"

"Saving you two. What a mess you boys have got yourself into." There was none of the humour in his voice like his last visit, he sounded angry.

"How do you mean?" Ligriv asked.

Hembleth turned and looked squarely at Nigriv. "Killing someone, that was your plan to go unnoticed?"

Nigriv tried to see if he was angry, but he'd never been able to understand others like his brother could. It was only his voice that gave it away. He shrugged, not knowing what to say.

"You're not out in the wilds, lad, you're in a city. Killing someone doesn't go unnoticed. Not only are half the city's thugs and criminals out looking for you, word got to the city guard. It won't be long before someone will pass on your whereabouts."

"No one knows us," Ligriv replied

"Cities have eyes, boys. Not always ones that you can see, it's not as obvious as out in the wild."

Hembleth shook his head and paced about the room muttering something Nigriv couldn't hear.

"Put that thing away." He pointed at the axe Nigriv was still grasping. "The best thing we can do is get you out of the city."

"How?"

"Leave that to me, I have some help." He rubbed his temples. "When I'm gone, bar the door and don't come out until I come back for you. Understood?"

They both nodded and Ligriv barred the door as soon as he was gone.

"I'm worried, brother, what's going to happen to us?"

Nigriv was more confused than ever now. Nothing was going well for them. He wanted to be back home, following the routines Father had laid out for them, but he couldn't.

And now, again, they were being directed by this strange man, and everything was out of their control. The only good thing he could see was that they had help to do what he'd wanted anyway.

"We have to get out of here, El, there's no choice. Maybe it'll be alright."

His brother went and stood by the window, and they waited for the older man to come. Nigriv stood exactly where he'd been when Hembleth had left the room and realised he still held the axe in his hand.

He packed it away and slung his bag on his shoulder. If nothing else, he was glad that someone else was making the decisions. The emptiness inside was making it hard to do anything.

That all changed when a knock came at the door. Something about it bothered Nigriv. He wasn't sure why, but he held his hand up to halt Ligriv who'd begun to head back toward it.

"Boys, boys, you in there?"

It was the landlady. She sounded concerned. Nigriv shook his head at his brother.

"Boys, there's guards here for you. Are you in there? They want to ask you about something. I said I'd get you, are you there?" She banged several more times.

Nigriv didn't know why but his head felt clearer than it had since last night. He knew they needed to move. He whispered to his brother, "She'll be back. We have to go."

"What about Hembleth?"

"He's not here. We'll have to go through the window." He looked down into the back yard and couldn't see anybody. "Grab your things, we need to hurry."

Ligriv led the way and climbed out onto the roof, sliding across toward the stables and roughly down part of the roofing onto the ground. Nigriv followed close behind and they sheltered behind some barrels.

"We can't stay here, we need to find a way out the back and away from the main roads."

Ligriv nodded but before either of them could move the courtyard gate began opening. A horse and wagon rolled through, in no hurry. The man who drove it slowly turned the wagon around, taking several turns, before backing it up right to where the boys were hiding.

He was out of sight for a moment before appearing around the side of the wagon. He was short of height and relatively broad and looked a lot like Hembleth.

Yet his hair was brown and grey, and although tied up behind his head it was definitely shorter than Hembleth's flowing red hair. Apart from what looked to be a permanent smile on his face, the driver's most distinguishing feature was his colourful beard, which should have been grey, but instead was streaked pink, blue, yellow and more.

Ligriv whispered, "He's from the market, I saw him."

"That you did, Ligriv."

Hembleth appeared alongside the man.

"This is them then, brother?" the driver asked.

"Yes, an odd pair they are too," Hembleth replied.

"Are… are you twins?" Ligriv asked.

The other one burst into laughter. "Lord, no. We're nothing alike."

Hembleth's voice returned to its earlier serious tone. "We don't have much time. We need to get you as far away from here as possible."

"Thankfully I was in town."

"Yes, as chance would have it, Oki… Rainbow." He looked back at Nigriv. "My brother will get you out."

Hembleth stared at Nigriv which only brought his discomfort back.

"I see you're not handling this very well."

Nigriv said nothing.

He turned back to the man he called Rainbow. "He's going to need some care."

"I'll see to it." Then Rainbow spoke to the boys. "Let's get you and your things up here in the back behind all this chalk."

"Chalk?" Ligriv asked.

"Just get up, we can talk another time, for now we need you out of sight."

Nigriv did as they were told. Now that someone else was directing things he'd felt the discomfort creep back in and just wanted to hide away.

He and Ligriv lay flat under the bench seat at the front of the wagon between sacks of chalk completely hidden from view.

"No noises from either of you, and you'll not come out until I say so. Got it?"

"Yes," Ligriv replied.

"I thought I said no noise." The man laughed at his joke.

"Enough, brother," Hembleth grumbled. "Get going and I'll close the gate."

"I'll be seeing you."

"I'm sure you will. Just make sure they get on their way to where they need to be and that he's fixed up."

The wagon began to roll forward and Nigriv let the emptiness wash over him. He closed his eyes and tried to avoid thinking about what was happening to them.

As quickly as they'd started to move suddenly the wagon pulled to halt. Nigriv could hear stern voices.

"What are you doing?"

"Captain, is it? Just a trader making my way out of the city."

"What's in the wagon?"

"Chalk, my good man."

Then he heard Hembleth's voice. "What's all this about, Captain?"

"Sergeant actually, but that's of no matter. We're hunting some lads, country boys by the sounds of them."

"Been stealing, have they?"

"A bit more than that. Have you seen them? They were meant to be here in this inn."

"Sorry, can't say we have. We've just packed up our things and are on our way. Good luck with your hunt."

"Right then." The guard's voice sounded uncertain and the wagon began to move. Nigriv remembered how Hembleth had used tricks on them back in their cave and wondered if he'd done the same on the soldier.

Not that he cared how they got away, just that they had and were on the move. There were more than just those soldiers looking for them and nowhere in this city would be safe.

Nigriv knew he wouldn't be able to relax until they were well outside of it, but he had no idea how long that was going to take.

11

LIGRIV

Ligriv was sad to be leaving Uboci despite there being no choice. He'd been fascinated by what little he'd seen of such a city and wished they could stay longer.

They weren't leaving quickly; the wagon meandered along the busy roads, their driver, Rainbow, occasionally stopping to talk to people as they went.

Where Ligriv and his brother were wedged, under the front bench seat, it was stuffy and extremely uncomfortable. They were lying on bare wood and could feel every rock or rut the wheels travelled over.

With a little effort he'd been able to manoeuvre himself so that he could peer out through the sideboards. It was enough that he could take in as much of the sights while he had the chance.

He knew that it was his fault that they were leaving. While it had been Nigriv that had killed that boy, they wouldn't have been in that position if he'd not led them to the temple.

Strangely, their roles were reversed this time around; Nigriv was still disturbed by what he'd done, whereas Ligriv was able to shrug it off. They had needed to get free and what his twin had done made that possible.

Why was I attracted to that temple? It was the first chance he'd got since then to ponder the events leading up to it and what he'd seen.

The stone within he was certain had been what attracted him, but how on Dharatan had he even known about it? *Was that like the pull Hembleth had told us about?*

Except Ligriv knew the old man had been talking about Midderbuilt and not some strange temple in this city. Then there was also the colour and glow, it had been just like his own stone.

Ligriv suddenly fretted about where that stone was. In all the drama that had happened he'd not had time to think about it. To get to his stone he had to twist about and reach over behind him, his shoulder burning at the odd position he put it in.

It had been safely in his bag, but it felt much better to hold it. His thoughts eased about everything, and he felt a smile form on his face. The stone wasn't glowing, and it was very rough in comparison to the orb he'd been able to view in the temple.

Hembleth knew all about the stones, maybe his brother will too. I can ask him when we're safe.

He went back to peering out at the view with his fingers firmly wrapped around his gem. Ligriv could see from side roads that they had circled around the main square.

Some of it seemed a little familiar from last night but it was hard to tell from where he lay. They entered a section of Ubico which looked to be much wealthier than other parts of the city.

He admired the extravagance on display even in simple things like the way the walls and gates were adorned by intricate carved statuettes, some even inlaid with what appeared to be gold.

Ligriv liked what he saw, aides opening doors or maintaining the properties they passed. The further out from the city centre they rolled, the larger the houses they passed.

Then they began to see properties where the land was even larger than the buildings, with spacious courtyards and gardens and others hidden from view by large walls.

Rainbow stopped their wagon and once again was chatting to someone he knew or at least knew him. While they waited Ligriv watch a carriage arrive at the property nearest to them, the main gates still open.

The carriage alone was worthy of awe, red and gold panels shining in the sunlight. When one of the aides walked around the side of the carriage Ligriv felt his chest tighten.

The man's clothing resembled that which Ligriv had seen on their hunters back in Malamig. His head was covered by a black hood that matched the rest of his tight-fighting outfit.

Something about him made it hard to focus on his shape, almost as if the light couldn't settle on him. The best way Ligriv could describe it was that he appeared blurry.

A second man, dressed exactly the same, walked to the opposite side of the carriage and held out his hand for the occupant to grasp. Ligriv's eyes were drawn to the woman as she stepped down to the ground. She was tall and lithe, her dress as glamorous as the carriage.

Her hair appeared golden in the light. She paused for a moment, looking toward Ligriv's wagon, her eyes shifting side to side as though hunting for something she couldn't see.

Despite being hidden behind the wooden planks and the narrow gap between them, Ligriv felt exposed. She shook her head before turning and walking toward the house.

The two men in black followed her a short distance behind. Ligriv hadn't seen the face of the man hunting them back at their cave and toward Cragen but he did recognise the clothing.

It was unusual enough that he was sure these men were the same. Falder and the captain had mentioned a woman who claimed she was kin.

Is that her? They couldn't have got here so quickly... why would they be here at the same time...? It doesn't make any sense.

Had she noticed them, was that why she looked this way? But that made no sense at all, he was just imagining things, maybe because he was attracted to her glamour.

It seemed important, that he'd seen her and her guards, but he didn't know how. *She doesn't look threatening. She has lots of riches, at least that's what it looks like. But who are the men in black?*

Maybe his twin could explain it, but he didn't want to bother his brother, he was still out of sorts.

Their wagon jerked forward and the moment passed. He twisted his head to look back for as long as he could until he couldn't see them anymore. The urge to speak about it began to diminish and before long he forgot about the whole idea.

The view changed, slowly turning from the nicer houses back into merchant buildings, then the main gates and finally they were outside in the country.

Rainbow didn't stop again for several hours, nor did he talk to the boys either. The wheels maintained their slow and uneven roll along the trail, creaking in a regular pattern.

When the driver finally pulled the horse to a stop, Ligriv couldn't feel his shoulder, he'd been lying on it so long. The older man climbed off the wagon, rocking it, and then pulled away several of the sacks that had hidden the twins.

Air rushed into the hot cramped space and Ligriv quickly clambered out, shaking his arm once he'd jumped to the ground.

"Where are we?"

"Just outside a sister city, Beiramar."

"Sister city?"

"They are very close. The river's the main thing that separates them, but the people are connected."

Ligriv nodded. "Are we safe?"

"You're safe with me, don't worry about it, but there's a possibility word will spread within Beiramar as well, which is why we'll stay the night out here."

Nigriv hadn't said a word and Rainbow watched him. Ligriv noticed a small shake of the man's head, but didn't want to comment.

"How far is it?" he asked.

"To where?"

"Midderbuilt."

"A long way, but I don't think you'll be going all the way there."

"I thought Hembleth said we had to."

"That may be true in the future for one or both of you, if the fore-telling is correct."

"What does that mean?"

"Foretellings aren't stories with all the facts. They give parts of the story, pointers to what is coming, but not everything. We have to work out what else there is."

"So where are we going then?"

"You'll be heading in that general direction, but many things can happen before you get to Midderbuilt. Let's get a camp set up. There's more than enough time to talk."

Happy enough just to be out of the wagon Ligriv helped the older man with the task. There were more than just sacks of chalk in the back of the wagon and before long they had a canvas strung between two trees and a fire burning while he cooked them a meal.

Once they were eating, Rainbow started up where they had left off. "My brother told you about your mark, did he not?"

"Why do we have it?"

"That's the interesting part, Ligriv. I can tell you what it allows you to do, but not why."

"He said we can cut stones with it."

Rainbow smiled. "Not just any stones, boys. You both have copies of some very unique stones. No one else can touch those stones without being harmed."

"Really? They're just rocks."

"They're not just any old rocks, Ligriv. I bet you've sensed some-thing about them?"

Ligriv nodded, casually placing his left hand on the stone in his pocket.

"So, while what my brother said about being lapidarists is true, you're not like any others."

"No one else has the mark?"

Rainbow shook his head. "But first you need to learn the basics, which is where I come in."

"How?"

"You need a teacher."

"And that's why we're going to Midderbuilt?"

"Yes and no."

Ligriv shook his head and looked at Rainbow. *He's just like his brother, unable to give a straight answer.*

"I have an idea or two. I get to meet many people in my travels, I'm sure I can find you the right one."

"We'll be travelling with you?"

"So it appears, son. Now, I'm tired and we need to be on the road in the morning, I think we should get some sleep."

With that Rainbow went and lay down and within a minute he was snoring loudly. Ligriv wasn't ready to sleep and watched his brother who'd mostly kept to himself since they'd arrived.

Nigriv had lain down to sleep as well and yet something about the way he looked made Ligriv think he wasn't really asleep. As he played his fingers over the stone in his pocket, he wondered why he couldn't sense his brother.

It had been coming and going all day and he didn't like it. That connection between them, not needing words to understand the other, had been with him as long as he'd been old enough to think.

When they got time and when Nigriv was back to his usual self, he'd discuss it with him. For now, he lay there watching his brother and wondering about this strange man they were with, who that beautiful woman was and why the mark on his hand seemed to matter so much.

Eventually he dozed off. He was woken by a shove from the older man. "Up, lad, time to get moving."

Ligriv felt damp. A heavy dew coated everything, making him feel cold. Sluggishly he helped gather up the camp things and was glad to be sitting on the back of the wagon and not in it when they began to head south.

Once or twice he looked over at his brother, but neither said a thing. Ligriv wanted to ask his brother what was bugging him but he also knew when his twin really didn't want to speak.

He left Nigriv staring down the trail behind them as they rolled slowly along and went back to fondling the stone in his pocket. It felt good to be touching it.

82

BERRELL

The stew's best quality was the saltiness which was good enough for Berrell. He didn't come to the Black Kettle in Tabt for extravagance.

For almost a decade he'd been coming to this town and inn, not to stay -- a room was more than his budget allowed -- but to live a life different to his own for a night.

In his home village of Barrack life was very plain and most just had the essentials. Even something as simple as salt was a luxury. Everyone looked out for each other, they had a roof over their heads and weren't starving.

That was as good as it got. And these regular trips overnight to Tabt, looking for work, were the closest he got to an escape, closer to how it was a very long time ago.

Berrell's wife, Esphe, never came on the trips and he felt guilty that she didn't get to enjoy these little treats. A meal, a few drinks and some entertainment.

But then there were many things she missed out on, by choice. Since day one he knew that she'd never leave Barrack. It was a village created by her family several generations back, and she was the last of them.

Esphe was as close to being a mayor of the village as anyone, simply from that lineage, not anything else, but she took it personally. That there was no one to pass that claim on to was just another thing Berrell felt bad about.

She never mentioned it, nor did she complain in all the time they'd been husband and wife, not when he used to be away for long bursts chasing his gold, or even after their loss.

But then she didn't have to. Berrell couldn't forget, he couldn't put away the blame and the sense of hopelessness, it ate away at him as much as the sickness that had taken old Frank last month.

The difference was that no one could see his illness, at least not on his skin. That was how he explained it to himself. As though he'd caught it and couldn't heal it.

Esphe knew, but it was never spoken about, he wouldn't have it. From time to time, she'd lay her hand on his shoulder or rub his back and he knew that she could sense what was playing on his mind in that moment.

Every day it was a battle. Each task required will, he couldn't just do anything without first having to push himself to it. He wondered what would happen when he got to a point when he couldn't, but that hadn't happened... yet.

He did what he could to be a husband, to be neighbourly and to get through what little work he scrounged up. As much as he could, he tried to avoid the past and yet it was wrapped around him like a dirty old coat that he couldn't remove.

The Black Kettle was his attempt to put on different clothes for one night. The people and their noise, the singer and lute player who were average at best, smoke and energy.

It was the energy he came for, as though it might seep into him and transform him, his life, into something else. Not the past, not who he had been, but into something new, better ... alive.

Tonight, it wasn't working, not even a little, and his mind just wouldn't shut down. Thankfully no one else from Barrack was in here -- he couldn't stand to have to talk to anyone.

All the merchants and farmers in Barrack had to come to Tabt, it was the only place to trade their goods. Some came to this inn; others had their own favourites.

Berrell was here, empty-handed as he generally was. He'd do the rounds in the morning, looking for a commission, or some left-over item from another jeweller that could use a hand, and earn enough.

It was always just enough. That didn't bother him, he could accept enough, although it would be much easier if he hadn't tasted the other side, what having riches was like.

Now he fretted every time their coin dwindled to nothing, wondering how or where he'd find something to do that would earn them a little more. He wasn't at that point yet, but next month he would be if he didn't find something tomorrow.

Esphe had never wanted any more. She'd been born in Barrack and had always told him she'd not leave, which hadn't bothered him when he was courting her.

Shortly after he'd finished his apprenticeship in Tabt, they had married and he moved to Barrack, travelling back to the town every other week to work with his master.

As a junior lapidarist, back then, there'd always been plenty of work. Tabt was the first decent-sized town north of Midderbuilt where many of the best gems came from. That meant some of them were traded here and he got to work on them.

His work equalled his master's within no time and yet he kept improving, despite no one else to teach him. Berrell had always been inquisitive, at least back then.

That too was gone. Now he cared for nothing new, as long as he had enough. He should have been like that when he was young, then maybe…

What's wrong with me tonight, why can't I have one night's break from my own mind?

He put his mug down. It was empty, and while he knew he could afford another, he wasn't sure if he should or not.

"Here you go, perfect timing."

Berrell looked up in surprise as a full mug of ale was plopped down in front of him. Without asking, the man who'd brought it placed another on the opposite side of the table and sat.

"What do you want?"

"That's not very friendly for someone that just bought you an ale."

"Thank you. What's the price?"

"That's a very cynical perspective, Berrell. Just enjoy it while I'm here."

Berrell raised his mug, clinking it against the older man's, and nodded before taking a swig.

"Thank you."

"It's nothing. What sort of friend would I be if I didn't buy you a drink when I'm in town?"

"I wish I could repay the favour, but..."

Rainbow raised his hand, stopping Berrell. "It's nothing. Just enjoy it."

They sat there sipping ale, listening to the music for a while, which intrigued Berrell even more. Rainbow wasn't one to be quiet for long and he'd be out in the middle of a party as much as anyone most days.

Every once in a while, his acquaintance would turn his head and look across the room at a table where two young lads were eating. They were identical, or at least seemed so from this distance.

Without warning he choked up a little, his ale struggling to go down, and had to take a deep breath. The lads would have been about the same age as his... would have been.

Berrell forced himself to look back and saw that Rainbow had been watching him closely.

"Funny thing, them lads."

"Why's that?"

"Well, how should I put it..."

For the first time since he'd met the man, Berrell could see he was avoiding saying what was on his mind.

"Out with it."

"They're in need of a master."

"What?"

"Someone like you."

"I'm no master… not anymore."

The older man clapped his hands on his beard, coloured chalk puffed up in front of him and Rainbow blew it in Berrell's face. It made him choke a little before he coughed it out.

"What did you do that for?"

"Because you're being an arse. You've been an arse for the longest time and you need to get over it."

"And blowing chalk in my face is going to help?" Berrell was annoyed at the big grin on Rainbow's face.

"Well, it's making me happy if no one else."

Berrell shook his head and took another sip from his mug, annoyed at his companion.

"You can't not be a master, once you've become one, even if you stop doing the work."

"I'm done with that; we've spoken of this before."

"Perhaps. But you are not just an ordinary jeweller, Berrell, you've a token and all."

"Don't mention that." Berrell looked around as though the mention of the word would attract trouble.

"Why not, fool? No one here would even understand it. And it's true. There's few that have the skill you have and you're just wasting it."

Berrell's hand had gone to his chest where he could feel the token he still wore under his tunic, hung by a leather thong around his neck.

"I'm no lapidarist, not anymore. Those days are over."

"Moping about, feeling all sorry for yourself and letting your wife suffer more, that's your answer."

"Leave it alone, old man." Berrell couldn't hide the anger he was feeling. "Find someone else."

"That's the thing, there's no one else, at least nowhere close enough for these boys."

"Take them to Midderbuilt, there's plenty of masters there."

"You know as well as I do they can't do an apprenticeship there, and those that stay in that city aren't prone to leave, certainly not to train two at once."

"Not my problem. Send them back home."

"They don't have a home, not anymore. Their father died recently and they attract trouble like flies to dung."

"Great, you want to bring me more trouble."

"Your trouble is all in your head, Berrell. Do you think you're the only one to have lost a child?"

"It's more than that."

"What, that you weren't there? More people are missing in life's worst moments than those who are there. What could you have done?"

"Who knows? I wasn't there, I was so busy in bloody Midderbuilt, addicted to the gems, to being the best, to making more... I left my wife alone. I didn't even know for weeks."

"That was a decade ago, when are you going to let it go?"

"I can't."

"You won't, that's what you mean."

"I can't."

"It's a choice... after all this time you want to be this way, to have nothing, to make yourself pay for the past. It's how you punish yourself."

"I'm not going back to Midderbuilt."

"No one is asking you to."

"There's no work for anyone in Barrack, not enough for me, let alone two apprentices."

"Train them, that's all you have to do."

"I can't."

"What about Esphe?"

"What about her?"

"Would she agree? Would she not want the chance to have some children around?"

Berrell felt stung by Rainbow's words. For all the pity he felt for himself for what he'd done, for their loss, he knew he wasn't thinking about his wife.

He knew that he was causing her as much pain as he felt, just by being the way he was. *What would she want?*

"We can hardly afford to feed ourselves; we can't bring up two boys, sweet Thenis. You're crazy."

"Work will come, Berrell, mark my words. If people in Tabt found out you were working, they will demand your work. The coin will come, you just have to trust me."

"Trust you? It was you that convinced me to go to Midderbuilt and look what happened."

Rainbow ignored his comment. "I'll make it easier for you." He pushed a small pouch across the table. "There's enough in there to feed you all for three months, and a bit more. By then you'd be back in business."

Berrell picked up the pouch and opened it. He'd not looked on so many coins in one place in an age. Immediately he felt the rush, that thing which had drawn him in all those years ago.

He wanted to put it down, to slide it back across the table, except he could imagine Esphe's face when he got home with it. He could take her some spices from the market and maybe a new dress.

But boys... we can't bring up boys.

"Why don't you just meet them and see?"

Berrell put the pouch back down in the middle of the table and nodded, his heart tightening in his chest. *What am I doing?*

13

NIGRIV

The stew they were eating was way too salty for Nigriv's liking and the meat was tough and fatty. Nothing like what they'd grown up on back home. If that wasn't bad enough, he was hot.

Not just from the warm meal but all over. And not just from being inside. The air outside was hot, nothing like where they'd lived up until now. Nigriv wiped his brow with his sleeve before more sweat ran into his eyes.

Ligriv looked up. "This is salty."

Nigriv nodded. "It's food."

His twin put his spoon in the bowl and looked over at him, staring into his eyes. Those were the first words he'd said to Ligriv since they'd left Uboci. It wasn't deliberate, he wanted to speak, to feel normal, but he couldn't.

He had been lost in what felt like mental mud. His whole head felt buried in it and it sucked all his energy and will away. Ligriv and Rainbow had made sure he ate and drank but he'd not participated in anything else.

"Are you alright?"

For the first time there was space for Nigriv to think. "I don't know."

"Can I help?"

Nigriv shook his head and took a spoonful of his own food. "I think it will pass."

His brother slurped sauce from the stew, peering up at him, comically, from the edge of his bowl. It almost made Nigriv laugh but not quite, but he knew that was a change at least.

"What are we going to do?"

This was the problem with his brother, once he started, he wouldn't stop. That Nigriv had now spoken was like opening a door and letting the outside in.

It didn't help that Nigriv hadn't been thinking about any of this either. He'd been so lost in his own head he'd not considered what was happening to them.

He wished Father was with them, that he was in charge of making the decisions. Except if Father was still alive, they'd still be back at the cave, in their home, and none of this would be happening.

Would they have come for us if Father was still alive?

Nigriv had no way of knowing what might have happened. He didn't know who the woman was that sent the men after them, nor any idea how Father would have reacted to it.

At least his mind was freeing up, he was much more aware of his surroundings than he had been.

"What's this place called?"

"Tabt," Ligriv answered.

"What's he doing?"

"I don't know, he just said he knew the man and wanted to speak with him." Ligriv bent down to his bowl and scooped up more of the stew.

Nigriv was still sweating profusely and his back felt damp. There were not enough windows in this inn and too many people, which just added to how bad it already was.

He wanted to get up and go outside for air but didn't want to leave his brother. Going out had been the problem in Uboci that had led to… he closed his eyes and tried to think of something else.

When he looked back at his brother he'd started to scratch at his arm through his tunic unconsciously.

"I want to go home."

Ligriv stopped and looked up. "It wouldn't be safe."

"I want to go home."

His brother looked confused but didn't reply. He wouldn't argue, Nigriv knew that, but it felt good to get it out.

"I know it isn't safe but… you asked what we're going to do. That's what I want to do, where I want to be. If I could I'd be back there right now. Wouldn't you?"

His brother shrugged. "I don't mind it so much, now that we're not in any danger."

"Aren't we?"

"What danger?"

"We don't know him. What if he's trying to sell us to that man?"

They both looked over at the table where the two men seemed to be in a disagreement.

"Then he's not doing so well."

Ligriv's face grinned at his silly comment and he started laughing. Nigriv couldn't help himself, he could sense the joy in his brother and got caught up in it and broke out in laughter as well.

It felt good to him to be laughing; if nothing else, it stopped him scratching. He looked closely at his brother, thankful they were so close.

While many saw them as identical they weren't completely. Ligriv was hairier than him, everywhere, even his face was covered in faint fuzz that Nigriv didn't have.

"Are we really going to be… what did Hembleth call it?"

"Lapidarists."

"Yeah, that."

"I don't know, El."

"What else is there?"

"We can already trap, we can just keep doing that."

"Where?"

"We'll find somewhere."

"Hembleth said we needed to learn to cut stones."

"He's not our master." Nigriv shook his head. "I don't understand why that's so important."

"Because of the foretelling."

"You believe all that?"

Ligriv shrugged. "Why not? I know there's something about the stones. That's what I saw in that temple."

"What?" Nigriv was confused by what his brother was saying.

"In Uboci, before… that glow in the temple, it was orange, like my stone. There was something about it, it was calling me, I could sense it."

"You're imagining things. They're just stones."

"I'm not. Anyway, why not learn something new? Imagine being able to make jewellery and things. It might be fun."

"Maybe." In truth Nigriv didn't hate the idea, he just wasn't ready to write off their old life so quickly. He wanted to change the topic; he didn't like that he had no control over things.

On top of that, the heat and noise in the inn was bugging him and he wanted to go back to their room. Almost on cue, Rainbow appeared at their table.

"You finished?"

Nigriv nodded. Ligriv finished scraping out the last of his bowl and looked up.

"There's someone I'd like you to meet."

"Who?" Ligriv asked.

"Come with me."

Ligriv looked to his brother for a response. Nigriv nodded, stood up and followed Rainbow back to the table he'd been sitting at. The older man dragged up a couple of short stools and plonked them alongside the table.

When he sat back in his chair a small puff of colour leapt from his beard and it made Nigriv smile. He was definitely feeling better.

"This is Master Berrell."

Nigriv could see the stranger's face scrunch up at the mention of his name and he was about to say something when Rainbow carried on.

"This is Ligriv and Nigriv, the two boys I was telling you about."

The man was much taller than them and broad, especially across his shoulders. His hands looked strong like Father's but were dirty. There was a griminess to them that looked as though it had been there all his life.

"Hello," Ligriv said meekly.

"Which one is which?" His voice was deep, as deep as Nigriv had ever heard a voice.

"I'm Ligriv."

Nigriv was happy to let his brother do the talking and just observe the man.

"Why does he call you Master?"

"It's a term of respect."

"Are you important?"

"No, son, it's to do with… work I did."

"What's that?"

"I'm qualified in a trade and that makes me a master of my craft."

"And the word Master means that?"

"It can, yes. Or it can mean that you're a noble's lad."

"Are you a noble?" Nigriv asked.

The man turned to look directly at him and half laughed. "Do I look like a noble?"

Nigriv shrugged. "I guess not. What craft do you do then?"

The man turned back to Rainbow and stared at him for a while.

"He's a lapidarist."

"Was," Master Berrell snapped.

"Are. It's not something anyone can lose. He's just been taking a break from it for a while."

"So, you're going to teach us?" Ligriv jumped into the conversation.

"That's what I'm asking him," Rainbow answered before Master Berrell could reply.

The table fell silent and the two older men sat there drinking their ales, looking at each other. Nigriv felt the tension between them and saw his brother readying to say something.

He used his eyes to indicate 'don't' and waited, hoping it would end soon. The woman who'd been singing earlier started up again and he let the noise of the room capture his attention.

"I won't take them to Midderbuilt." Master Berrell was the first to speak.

"No one is asking you to," Rainbow replied.

"Barrack's no place for an apprentice, let alone two of them."

"They just need to learn, can they do that there?"

Master Berrell nodded.

"They'll be a long way from any trouble there too."

"What sort of trouble?"

"The sort young boys can get into in a big city. Your village will be much closer to what they're used to."

Master Berrell shook his head and looked back at the boys. "Do you understand what he wants you to do?"

"Be apprentices," Ligriv blurted out.

"And do you know what that is?"

Ligriv shook his head.

"You spend years working for your master and only when he signs off to the guild that you're ready, only then do you become a master in your own right. It means hard work and doing what you're told."

He went to take a sip of his drink and shook his mug at Rainbow.

"Very well, I'll get you another."

"It's hard work, boys. You'd have to live with me and my wife. We don't have much, you'd have a tiny room and have to help out with chores and the like. Got it?"

Nigriv nodded.

"We don't have much, but a roof over our heads and good neighbours. You don't do what I say and I let you go, that's it."

Ligriv looked at Nigriv, waiting for what he was going to say. Rainbow arrived back with two mugs of ale and Master Berrell picked his up.

Going with this scruffy man was the choice that his brother

wanted Nigriv to make. The work didn't bother him, if anything it sounded more like their old life than he expected. In a way, they'd been apprentices to Father their whole lives.

"We'd just have to go with you? What about your wife, what will she say?"

The man seemed to tense up at Nigriv's words. "I've no idea what she'll say, but if she doesn't like the idea, then it's over before it starts. I'll not have her upset."

"She'll be fine, Berrell, I told you that. You're the problem."

The master scowled back at their travelling companion. Then he turned back to the boys. "What of it?"

Ligriv was still looking at Nigriv. The connection told Nigriv little he couldn't see on his brother's face, but the choice he was leaving to Nigriv. Either way he wouldn't argue with him.

Rainbow looked his way now. "What do you think, son?"

It all felt too much to Nigriv, he'd only just got his head clear and now he was meant to make a choice for their future based on a conversation. He was tired and his head hurt from all the noise.

Everyone wanted him to decide, but he wasn't sure he could. He still wished none of this was happening, that he was with Father. *What would Father say?*

They'd never had to decide anything like this. The only thing he could think of was what his father had said when he'd asked him about why they stayed out in the cave.

"It's what your mother would have wanted."

Nigriv didn't remember his mother, he had no idea what she'd have wanted. *What would Father have wanted?* Then the idea came to him.

"If she says yes, we will."

"What is that?"

"If your wife says yes, then we'll do it, but if not, then like you said, we'll be on our way."

Rainbow clapped in joy and puffs of coloured chalk flew from his fingerless gloves, raining down over the table. "That's fantastic news."

"We'll see." Master Berrell didn't seem overly pleased at the idea.

"Then tomorrow we'll head there and find out. I'll be leaving at first light."

With a large grin on his face, Rainbow stood. "Come on then, boys. We need to get you to sleep. You have a big day ahead of you."

Nigriv followed him and Ligriv out of the room, taking a quick look back at Master Berrell who was holding his head in both hands and talking to himself.

I hope that was a good decision.

14

NIGRIV

The banging startled Nigriv and as he sat up in alarm, he could see it was still dark.

"Let me in, boys. It's time to go."

He shuffled over to the door, lifting the bar and swinging it open. Rainbow pushed his way in hurriedly. "Best you wake him, Berrell will start off without you. I don't want to give him an easy way out."

"If he doesn't want us, why are we going?"

"It's not that he doesn't want you, lad, he's just a bit stuck in his ways at the moment."

"Feels like he doesn't want us."

"He'll come round, you'll see." Even in the dark the way Rainbow stared into Nigriv's eyes made him uncomfortable. "More to the point, will *you* be alright?"

"What do you mean?"

"Sit down."

Nigriv did as Rainbow asked, propping back on the edge of his bed.

"You know what I mean, you've not been well..." he tapped his head "... up here, since... well, you know since when."

It wasn't something Nigriv wanted to talk about so he looked over at his brother to avoid the man's piercing gaze. His right hand began to rub under his left forearm at his scar.

"That's a good indicator that you're not being honest."

"What?"

"Scratching your arm. There's nothing wrong with being upset about what happened."

"Not upset."

Rainbow didn't reply for a minute. "If you weren't uncomfortable about killing someone, especially a lad like yourself, when you're this age, then I'd have more concerns. Thing is, whether you can understand it or not, your head is upset about it. On top of all this change, son, things aren't going the way you planned."

Nigriv shrugged and kept staring over at Ligriv who hadn't stirred at all.

"You'll be fine, Nigriv, you'll see. But you need to get him up, or Berrell will be long gone."

Happy that the conversation had stopped being about him, Nigriv got up and started rocking his brother to wake him.

"What?" Ligriv grumbled as he stirred.

"Got to get up, we're going."

"It's still night."

"The sun will be up in no time and you need to be on Berrell's wagon before he leaves," Rainbow said.

"With no breakfast?"

Rainbow laughed and spoke to Nigriv. "Is his stomach always the most important thing in his head?"

Nigriv nodded. He didn't want to discuss much with the older man.

Rainbow led them out of the inn and down a roadway toward a large space between several buildings. A lone wagon was parked there and they could see Master Berrell stood beside it.

"I was just thinking about setting off."

Rainbow walked up to Berrell and exchanged words with him that Nigriv couldn't hear.

The comment Nigriv had made in jest last night to his brother came back to him. *Is he really selling us?* As if he could read his mind, Rainbow turned and spoke.

"Just a few coins to help with the amount of food you lads are likely to need."

Nigriv wondered what they were getting into, this scruffy and simple-appearing market trader was handing them off to another stranger.

"You'll be fine, son. I think you'll find Barrack not so different to where you've come from."

But he knew there was no way it would ever be like home. Down here was hot and dusty, people smelled and the towns were noisy and people were very different to him and his brother.

He climbed up on the back of the wagon and as it began to head off, he watched Rainbow who was staring after them. Rather than heading out of Tabt, Berrell turned them toward the town centre. He pulled up a short distance from the market which was only just beginning to open now that the sun had begun to show.

"Stay here and wait for me, I just need to get a few things."

When he returned, he carried two small cloth bags. One was fuller than the other. "There's some food in that, don't eat it all or you'll have nothing when we get home."

The other bag he placed below his seat at the front of the wagon. Then he turned them around and headed out of the town. Away from people and their busyness everything quietened down, which Nigriv liked.

They'd always lived with the sounds of nature not people and he was happier to be away from it. What was newer to him was the constant noise the ocean made as they rode down the road that followed the coast.

Waves crashing on the shore and rocky outcrops helped ease his mind and he found himself not worrying about much at all. Also, the breeze from it had cooled him off and made him feel better.

They saw no one else on the road and their driver said nothing. The two boys sat in the back facing each other with their backs against the wagon sides.

Off to the south Nigriv could see a massive mountain range, the most noticeable feature of which was the lack of snow. He'd always imagined all tall mountains had snow on them, but not this one. It was a mixture of dark greys and brown.

A little after middle day they came to a junction and Berrell veered left away from the ocean. As they meandered their way inland the temperature changed the further from the ocean they got.

He was back to wiping his brow with his sleeve and the back of his tunic was damp. They cut through unruly plains, tall grasses standing at attention, and the occasional bird diving in amongst them hunting prey.

"What are you thinking?" Ligriv asked.

"Little, except how stinking hot I am."

"Me too."

"I prefer the cold."

Ligriv didn't say anything. Nigriv knew he wouldn't argue about it, and he wasn't sure why he kept bringing it up, he'd already accepted they were coming this way for now.

"If you don't want to do this, we don't have to."

Nigriv stared at his brother for a bit. "I agreed we'd leave it up to her. If she says yes then we stay."

"What if she doesn't?"

"Then we'll get somewhere to stay and plan out what to do."

"Like what?"

"I don't know, El. Maybe we go home, they'll have left by now."

Nigriv saw his brother's face had changed but he never understood what things like that meant. He felt for him using their connection but all he could tell was he was hot and uncertain, but nothing more.

They said nothing else for hours until Nigriv spotted a handful of buildings off in the distance. He tapped his brother's leg and pointed in that direction.

"Is that it?" Ligriv asked.

Nigriv shrugged.

Master Berrell turned in his seat and nodded. "Aye, lad, that's Barrack."

They rolled into the village centre and Nigriv could see there was only a half dozen roads and plenty of space between everyone's buildings. A few people were out and about. They all waved at Berrell and he waved back.

Several of them, Nigriv noticed, looked at him with furrowed brows, not that he understood why. One woman shook her head as she walked by but said nothing.

On the outskirts of the eastern side of town lay a compound with a collapsed wall at the front with no sides to it. The gates were open but drooped on their hinges and Nigriv doubted they still swung.

A small house was to their right with a shed on their left. The shed doors were closed and by the tufts of weeds and grass in front didn't look like it was used much.

The wagon stopped and Berrell clambered down. He reached for the small bag under his seat. "Wait here, I need to talk to my wife." Then he marched off to the front door, pausing hesitantly before opening it and stepping in.

"Oh my!"

Nigriv turned to see Master Berrell and his wife coming out of the house. She was almost as tall as her husband but lean.

"Down you get." Berrell didn't sound any happier than earlier. "This is them, Esphe."

The woman looked them up and down, her eyes darting between the pair of them. Tears began to run down her face and Nigriv was unsure what that meant.

"What's wrong, dear?"

She wiped her eyes with a small piece of cloth that had appeared from somewhere on her dress. "Nothing's wrong, fool. I'm just... it's nothing. Let's get them inside, they must be hot and hungry."

The boys followed them in with Esphe turning constantly to eye him and Ligriv. The front door didn't hang straight and Nigriv imagined it didn't close properly.

I thought he was a master, but he doesn't seem to be very good at this stuff.

"This is our home, boys, it's nothing much." She seemed a little flustered and led them into the kitchen. Opposite to outside, this small space was immaculate and well maintained, and he couldn't help but notice the smell of food cooking.

"Come with me first," Master Berrell said and pointed up a small rickety-looking set of stairs.

Each of the treads groaned at their weight and Nigriv wondered how safe it was. There was a small room at the top, the door open. It had a peculiar smell to it and was coated in dust but there were two old beds in it.

"It needs a tidy up, you can do that later. Drop your stuff here and come back down."

When Ligriv placed his bag and bow on the floor, a cloud of dust flew up causing him to cough. He scrunched up his face. Nigriv placed his nearby and got a similar result.

Back in the kitchen, Esphe had set some warm bread in the middle of the table with butter and cheese. She'd also placed tumblers of ale out for them all. "Sit down, boys. I bet you could do with something to eat."

Master Berrell was already sitting, sipping his ale. His face looked friendlier than it had when they'd met in the inn, but Nigriv was still concerned about what they'd walked into.

The loaf wasn't big and Nigriv was mindful to just take a small portion, giving his brother a similar piece. He hadn't forgotten Berrell complaining to Rainbow about how they could ill afford to feed the boys.

It was clear that the couple were living a simple existence; there wasn't much more here than they'd had in their cave.

"Apprentices then, hey?" Esphe said, a smile on her face.

"Yes, dear, that's what he asked from me."

"You know him?"

"For many years… he's always been good to me."

"Did you find any new work?"

Berrell shook his head.

"Thank Thenis for what he gave you then. It'll do."

"You sure you want to do this?"

Her face beamed as she answered him. "Yes, Berrell, I do. Since..." She didn't finish what she was going to say.

He reached over and put a hand on her shoulder. "I know."

"It might not be what we had in mind, but it's the right thing to do, man. My answer is yes. And you?"

The older man looked at the two boys, then back at her. "I said it was your call. If you said yes, then I'd do it. At least until they learn how hard it is… they might not be so keen then."

"Listen to you, that's no way to treat these guests of ours. More than that if they're going to be staying with us. You're such an oaf."

"What if we don't want to?" Nigriv was a little tired of being spoken about.

"What, stay here?" Berrell turned to him, his face darkening a little.

"That, or the apprentice thing."

"I'm not going to force you, lad. If you're not grateful for the chance, you know where the door is."

"Stop it, Berrell!" Esphe snapped at him. "They're just boys, come from Seth knows where, to a strange place, and told this is their new home. Of course they want to know their choices."

The older man slumped back in his chair, rebuked. "You're right, sorry." Then he looked at Nigriv. "Don't feel like you have to, we'll put you up until you decide. It's a good enough trade to have if you're willing to learn."

"Why don't you do it anymore?"

"That's not something I'll discuss with you at this point, son." His response was terse and it was Ligriv that broke the tension after a minute or two.

"How long does it take?"

"As long as it needs."

"How long did it take you?" Ligriv asked.

"Half a dozen years all up, but only three until I had my papers."

"What are papers?"

"It's a term. When you get recognised by a guild then they write you a paper that lets others know you're qualified to be called a master in that trade."

"Oh."

"Enough about this work stuff, I don't even know your names," Esphe said.

"I'm Ligriv, and he's Nigriv."

"You look the same and even your names are similar."

"Our father called me El and him En."

"I can see why. Where is your father?"

Both boys sat silent for a moment. "He died," Nigriv finally answered.

"I'm sorry."

"I think we've asked you more than enough questions for now. Why don't you sort out the room and I'll get some fresh water so you can wash, then we can talk more in the morning."

The boys both got up and went to their room. Nigriv tried his best to clean up the bed and lie down. He was glad his brother wasn't talking, Nigriv just wanted space to himself.

He wasn't tired and it wasn't dark outside but he lay down anyway. It was going to take time to clean this room out properly and he didn't care to do it right now. All he wanted to do was sleep so he closed his eyes and lay there, hoping it would come.

15

―――――

LIGRIV

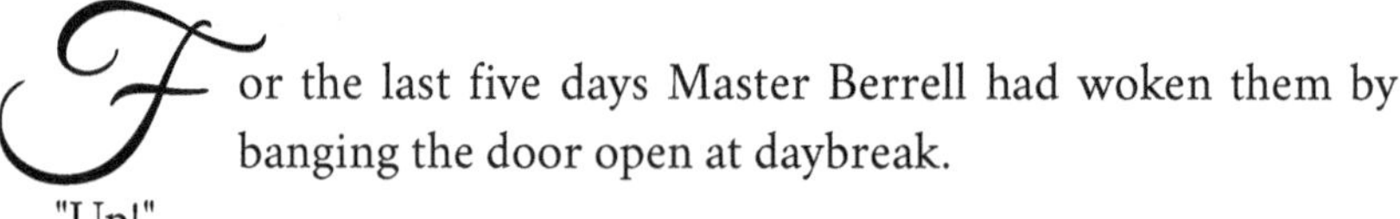

or the last five days Master Berrell had woken them by banging the door open at daybreak.

"Up!"

Ligriv had never been an early riser and struggled with it. His brother was already half out the door, he never seemed to have an issue waking. Ligriv needed every bit of his resolve to pull off his blanket and slide his legs over the edge.

At least it's not cold.

"It's on the table, Ligriv," Esphe said as he walked into the kitchen. She'd worked out the pair of them within a couple of days.

"You might have others confused, but not Esphe."

Ligriv smiled and got stuck into his food.

Master Berrell dropped into his usual seat on the far side of the table. He said nothing while he ate, but once done he looked up at the boys. "I'm splitting you two today. Ligriv, you're off to work with the smithy. You will do a week with him, then you'll swap."

"What about me?" Nigriv asked.

"You're coming with me. We'll be looking for gems."

Ligriv didn't mind the change, anything had to be better than cleaning Berrell's workshop which is all they had done so far.

106

"At your middle day break, come back here and I'll feed you." Esphe patted his shoulder.

Ligriv nodded. He liked being around her as she softened the edges of everything, made him feel more at ease with this new life, even being up this early.

"This is for you two." She handed her husband a bulging satchel.

"Yes, dear," Master Berrell replied, pecking her on the cheek as he took it and led Nigriv away. "Off with you, Ligriv, don't keep Yommo waiting."

Ligriv knew where to go, he'd been there once with Master Berrell, but showing up on his own made him feel a little nervous. The smithy was two roads over and he could hear the clanging of metal on metal the whole way there.

"There you are!" Yommo barked from across the large space.

Ligriv walked toward him sheepishly.

The burly man put down his hammer and, using the tongs in his other hand, moved the long steel object he'd been working on, dropping it into a tub of water. Steam rose as it sizzled.

"Best we get some rules straight from the start."

Ligriv nodded.

"Did someone cut your tongue out, boy?"

"No, sir," Ligriv stammered out. Any warm feelings left over from thinking about Esphe were replaced with apprehension.

"Better. And don't be calling me sir. I'm not your master neither so you call me Yommo or Smithy. Got it?"

"Yes…" Ligriv caught himself, "Yommo."

A laugh burst out of his stubbled face. "You're a quick learner, good. Now, I start when the sun rises, that means you do too."

Ligriv nearly choked on the words he was hearing. *Sunrise, what torture is this?*

"You're young, so I know that will be hard, but you need to figure it out. Before you run home to Esphe for a cuddle you finish early too, so while others are still working, we'll be enjoying an ale or three."

Ligriv had felt his face flush a little at the mention of Esphe.

"Don't worry, lad, that woman even mothers me, so Thenis knows what she'll be doing to you boys. That's all good and well when you're with her, but it's of no use to me here."

Ligriv nodded, still feeling embarrassed.

"When you're here my job is to teach you some of my craft. That means you'll need to toughen up and work hard."

"Why?"

Yommo's face scrunched up at the question. "Why what?"

"Why do we need to learn smithy work if we're going to be working stones?"

The older man laughed again and pulled the rod out of the water before placing it on a bench to the side. "Good ruddy question, lad. Come with me and let me fix my thirst, and I'll try to answer that."

Yommo led him over to a table. "First up, we'll want to dress you properly. Take that off," he nodded at Ligriv's tunic, "and put this light one on. It will breathe better under your apron."

The tunic he threw to Ligriv looked huge.

"It'll be too big but Esphe can help with that. Main thing is your arms will be free and it will keep your back cooler. In case you hadn't noticed, it gets hot in here."

Ligriv felt silly, it hung down past his knees and was very baggy across the shoulders and chest.

The smithy laughed again. "I think you'll definitely need her to work on that. I forget the size difference. It's been a long time since I've had an apprentice."

"Is that what I am?"

"You're not going to be a smithy, but you'll be doing things as if you were." He went to a cupboard and rustled around in some baskets. "There it is."

When he returned, he had a big piece of leather. Yommo brushed all the dust off it and shook it out. "Been a long time since anyone wore this, might need some care. You wear this whenever you work in here, understood?"

Ligriv nodded and took the musty apron, putting his head through the loop and trying to straighten the stiff leather out.

"At least it's the right size, but you'll need to oil it to get it more pliable. You can do that later, tie it as best you can for now."

At least it was the right size for him and as much as he could, Ligriv tied the strap at his back into a bow.

"Here, sit on this stool."

Yommo filled a cup of a light ale for Ligriv and a big mug for himself. The smithy drunk it in two big gulps before burping and sighing.

"Better. Rule number two, don't get too thirsty."

"What do you mean?"

"It's hot work in here, never gets cold, even in the heart of winter, so mark my words, you'll sweat as though you were in the middle of the desert."

That caught Ligriv's attention. He often wondered about the desert, ever since Hembleth had mentioned it.

"Whenever your tongue feels dry underneath, you come and drink. Only time you can't is if you're in the middle of working something in the fire. Otherwise stop what you're doing and get a drink. Understand?"

"Yes."

"I don't want you passing out on me. I have enough to do, don't need to be nursemaiding you. Next, you will hurt. And I mean a lot. You'll be lifting heavy things, working and doing stuff constantly that you've not done before. It'll wear you out and your muscles will hurt. They'll recover. Just do the work and don't be whining at me."

Ligriv nodded. He was used to what his father had made them do.

"You'll get burnt. Ain't no way I can avoid it, everything we work with is hot. When it happens you go and dunk whatever hurts in that vat of water." Yommo pointed at a wooden vat over by the back door.

"In winter that gets as cold as icesheets it does, now not much at all. It doesn't matter how cold or not it is, you put the burned skin in there until it no longer burns. If you take it out and it starts up again, put it back. If you need to get in, get in."

"Right."

"I mean it. Burns hurt and scar." Yommo showed Ligriv his arms and lifted his apron and tunic to show his front, mottled with burn scars.

"Only other rule is... do what I say." Yommo laughed at his own joke. "Do that and we'll get on fine. As for what you're learning here, it's about understanding metals and how to work them. What you boys have to learn isn't just about the stones, you'll be setting them to make jewellery. And while smithy work won't help you with all the fine metalwork Berrell will teach you later, there's plenty about it that will help."

Ligriv nodded and took another sip of his ale. He was already sweating just from sitting here.

"Working metal isn't just banging it with a hammer, you have to be able to work it into the shape you want, balancing how much heating and cooling, when you can shape it and when you can't."

Yommo took another big swig, gulping it down.

"That's part of what my job is, to help you learn about big metal-work, so that when it comes time to learn about the small stuff, you'll have an understanding of the process. Got it?"

Ligriv nodded again.

* * *

HE DIDN'T KNOW how he did it, but all week Ligriv was up before his brother and at the smithy before Yommo arrived. Like magic his body woke him when he needed it to and he quietly dressed and left the house without eating.

The first day, he'd been so hungry when he got back to Master Berrell's place for lunch that his stomach was grumbling fiercely. After that, Esphe left food out for him in a covered basket and he ate it while he walked to the smithy.

Working like this didn't bother him, they'd had a tough father and grew up doing manual labour. Yommo had been surprised at how strong Ligriv was, compared to what he expected.

Even with that his arms did ache constantly and he was exhausted at the end of every day, heading to bed straight after his evening meal.

He and Nigriv only spoke in passing the whole week, but tomorrow was their one day off, and he was keen to spend time with his twin.

"Focus on what you're doing, I need that fire hot," Yommo called from where he was working.

Ligriv stopped his daydreaming and kept his attention on the bellows he was operating.

"Steady, steady, lad. I don't want too much."

Once Yommo had removed the iron he was working on, Ligriv would need to check the coal around the outsides of the fire. He was beginning to understand more about it, putting damp coal on the outside and moving it toward the fire as it dried out.

While he understood why, it was a tiresome activity.

"Don't overfill it now, boy. This is almost done now, we can let it burn itself down."

Yommo had been making new blades for a farmer's plough, one of the many different things the smithy did. Despite the early starts Ligriv had enjoyed being busy, it felt good to be needed.

The next few hours passed slowly as he swept up and set all the tools back where they were housed.

"You've been a great help, lad. Shame I have to teach your brother next. Don't you go and forget what you've learned, you'll be back in another week."

"Thanks, Yommo. We done then?"

"That we are. Go on and get yourself home. I'll be seeing you."

"I'll be seeing you, too." Ligriv thought he caught a small grin on Yommo's face, but it disappeared quick if he had.

It had only been a couple of weeks but Barrack was becoming familiar to him even though other people still kept their distance from him; most of the adults would turn their head away as though he wasn't there.

Esphe was there when he got back.

"Why you looking so sad, Ligriv?"

"Dunno, maybe just a little tired."

"I'm not surprised, Yommo likes to get all he can from his helpers. But there's something more, I can see it on your face."

Ligriv didn't want to say anything but she stood there staring at him.

"It's just… people look at me funny and turn away."

She nodded her head several times before saying something.

"Barrack's a small village, Ligriv, and with that comes some odd thinking."

"What do you mean?"

"They don't necessarily like outsiders."

"We live here though."

She sat beside him and he could sense she was thinking about what she was going to say.

"See how I have lighter skin than you?"

"Yes."

"As do the other villagers, and we're not quite as tall generally."

"Uh huh."

"That's because you're from Malamig and we're from down here. And for some folk that means you're not the same. They like to keep things just amongst themselves… their type."

Ligriv hadn't really thought much about the difference before, he'd just thought of them as grown-ups and he was a kid.

"I've seen other people come through town, travellers."

"Yes, but they don't stay, and don't think for a moment those same people you're asking me about wouldn't be thinking the same thing toward them as well."

"Oh." Ligriv didn't feel better because of what she was saying.

"I wouldn't let it bother you; they'll get used to you in time."

"What about you?"

"What about me?"

"What do you think?"

"About where you're from?"

Ligriv nodded.

"Son, it doesn't matter to me at all where you're from. It's nice to have you boys around, it's filling a hole for us too."

"He doesn't seem very happy about it."

"Who, Berrell? Don't worry about him. I think he's made a habit of being a grump, he'll be fine."

She placed a cup of ale in front of Ligriv. "Now you're in luck. I've been baking some things this morning, and I'd bet you could eat something else."

"Always."

Esphe placed some warm scones on the table, dripping in butter and jam. As he ate Ligriv thought how living here long-term wouldn't be a bad thing at all. He'd get used to the work, and having two adults caring for them was something he could get used to.

Apart from those odd looks, he'd begun to feel safe living here. Living in the cave and always hunting for survival had a degree of risk with it. There was none of that here. And he liked it.

1 6

NIGRIV

As he ate his second scone Nigriv had to admit that he could get used to this. Being out on the mountain with Berrell had been dull but coming back to this kitchen, the smell of food and Esphe, wasn't bad.

"Any luck today?" she asked.

Master Berrell finished chewing before he answered. "Somewhat."

"What?"

Berrell reached into his pocket and emptied his hand onto the table. A half dozen stones of different colours and shapes clattered onto it.

"All of them, just today?"

Berrell nodded. "It was like they were just sitting there waiting for him, we didn't have to do much even to find them."

The older woman looked at Nigriv with a big grin on her face and he felt a touch of pride when she did so.

"That's amazing, Nigriv. He can go weeks up there without finding workable gems."

"So I learned."

"He was right." Esphe looked at her husband.

"Who?"

"Your friend, he said it will all work out."

"It's just a few gems, wife, not bags of coin."

"Don't ruin it, Berrell. This is more than you've had in ages, you can make good with them."

"We'll see."

"How much are they worth?" Ligriv asked.

Master Berrell turned to face him. "Like this, they have little value, but when they are refined and set, that's when they are worth the most."

"Why don't others hunt for them then?"

"You can spend a lot of time out there for no return, most give up. Once in a while you'll find the odd gem hunter that will go looking. But they don't get much for them, it's only when they're worked that they become valuable. That's why."

"Seems like a lot of time and effort for not much reward."

"There's easier ways…" Esphe began but Berrell cut her off.

"This is the only way that matters."

The pair of adults looked at each other and Nigriv saw Master Berrell shake his head. Esphe looked down and said nothing else.

"Will you sell them or work them?"

"They aren't mine to sell."

"I don't understand." Nigriv was glad the tension from a moment ago had eased.

The man shook his head as he wiped his fingers on his tunic. "Son, I can teach you the skills, but what you find is yours. That's the way of the trade."

"I don't understand."

"You find a gem, then it belongs to you. As long as you don't take it from another. The land gives them up for whoever is willing to seek them."

"I don't know what to do with it."

"We'll get to that in time, don't worry too much about it now."

"But you feed us and put us up, we have to pay you then."

"Let's not worry about that. We'll figure everything out in time; besides, I found one of my own."

Master Berrell didn't show it and Nigriv wondered if he was telling the truth, there'd been no mention of this before.

"I'm jealous, brother."

Nigriv turned and looked at his twin. "Why?"

"You found all those valuable gems."

"You'll find yours next week, I'm sure."

Nigriv didn't like that they were apart all week, and it would continue, this time he'd be the one going to Yommo's. He wasn't comfortable not being around his twin, it wasn't normal.

And he'd begun to notice there were times he couldn't sense Ligriv at all. Nigriv wasn't sure why, unless it was the distance, but that didn't make sense either. It was only periodically and he would have to discuss it with him to see if he had noticed it too.

"No work tomorrow for you boys, it's your day off. Maybe you should explore the town." It was Esphe that spoke.

* * *

THAT WAS EXACTLY what they decided to do. Without any reason to be up, Ligriv had slept in like he usually did. Once he was up, they ate and set off to explore the town more.

"Do you like it here, Nigriv?"

"It's alright."

"Do you not like having a place to stay and being looked after?"

"Yes, it's good but it's different."

Ligriv nodded and they walked in silence for a little bit.

"I'm not sure I liked us being apart."

They stopped and Ligriv looked at him. "I know, but being busy at the smithy made it easier for the time to pass."

"It's the opposite looking for gems, you're pretty much on your own. All I had was my own thoughts. Master Berrell doesn't say much."

"I didn't have time to think and my body just ached all the time. I got so tired, even after everything we were used to."

Nigriv was able to feel the connection to his brother again. It was strong, and being close like this made things feel more normal.

"I guess I'll find out next week."

"What was it like with Berrell?"

"Don't let him hear you say his name like that."

Ligriv laughed. "Why, will he belt me?"

Nigriv laughed too. "No, but it wouldn't be right."

"You can be funny sometimes, brother."

"What do you mean?"

"You care about the strangest things. What would it matter what we call him?"

"I just don't think it would be right." Nigriv shrugged. "He didn't say much all week. A lot of it was me panning in a stream by myself while he did the same."

"Sounds boring."

Nigriv shook his head. "Kind of is. He got excited when we found those gems though. Suddenly he became chatty and even smiled."

"I bet."

Whenever they spoke about the gems Ligriv seemed much more interested than usual. They definitely appealed to him, more than they did to Nigriv.

They started walking again, just wandering through the different streets. On one of the roads, they saw a group of boys kicking a ball of reeds amongst themselves. The brothers stopped and watched, intrigued.

"Is this what other kids do?" Ligriv asked.

"I guess."

"You the two twins from the gem man's place?" a stocky, short boy with a skinny head and long nose called out.

"Yeah," Ligriv yelled back.

"Want to join in?"

Ligriv looked at Nigriv who just shrugged. There seemed no reason not to. Nigriv thought this other boy looked a little odd; he had beady little eyes and his arms seemed much longer than the rest of him.

As they approached, the boy swung his arm and threw a handful of dirt which flew into Ligriv's face. The boy laughed, as did the others who'd gathered behind him.

"Freaks!" he yelled.

Ligriv spat out the dirt and tried to wipe it from his eyes.

"You lot aren't welcome here. We don't need strange-looking freaks messing up our town," another boy called out.

"Why did you do that, rat?" Nigriv growled at the boy who'd slung the dirt. It was true, the boy did look like a rodent.

"What did you call me? I'll show you who's a rat." The boy came at Nigriv, his fists bunched and his friends sweeping out around in him a semicircle.

Nigriv was surprised by this sudden aggression. They'd done nothing to these boys yet they were very angry at them. It confused him, but he could still recognise the threat. Just like in Uboci, all of a sudden, his heart rate had increased and he didn't think, just acted.

He sprang forward covering the three paces in no time, and before the boy could take a shot, punched him underneath his chin.

Rat boy's eyes rolled up and he fell backward, thudding into the ground.

"Ren?" one of the others called out. "Ren, you alright?" His voice sounded scared, not threatening.

Nigriv could sense his brother behind him now, protecting his back, but the other kids only hurried over to check on their friend.

"Anyone else want to have a go?" Nigriv's voice sounded as angry as he felt.

"What's going on here?" a man's voice called out and then several other adults arrived with him. "What's up with Ren?"

"He hit him." One of the group of boys pointed at Nigriv.

The tall boy on the ground woke up and coughed. The man leaned over him and dragged him up by his arm. "What happened, Ren?"

The dazed lad just stared up at the man, then slowly as his wits came back to him looked about and saw Nigriv. If anything, he looked confused not angry.

"You two, get back to Berrell's where you belong, I'll speak to him later. As for the rest of you, get to your homes. I'll take this one back to his."

Nigriv didn't say a word but turned and headed back the way they'd come, his brother close behind.

"Sweet Thenis, Nigriv, you clobbered him."

"I was angry… why did they do that?"

"Haven't you noticed it?"

"What?"

"People see us differently."

Nigriv wasn't really sure what Ligriv was going on about. He'd done nothing wrong; the other boys had started it and he'd finished it, that was the way of things. But as they got closer to Master Berrell's he felt the discomfort returning and rubbed at his left arm.

He had begun to like being in Barrack and didn't want them to get kicked out because of something he'd done.

17

LIGRIV

Thankfully neither Esphe nor Master Berrell were in the kitchen when they got home and both boys went and lay down in their room.

"What will they do?"

"We did nothing wrong."

Ligriv understood what his brother meant but he was still concerned about how Master Berrell would handle things.

"If the rat didn't want to get smacked, he shouldn't have done that to you."

Ligriv chuckled nervously. "Rat! He did look like one didn't he?"

Nigriv turned to face him. He wasn't smiling but the mood in the room had lightened. That was until he heard footsteps on the stairs.

Master Berrell's head poked through the door. "Come on downstairs."

Ligriv wasn't sure what he'd expected but the very calm voice of their host wasn't it. Their own father rarely ever raised his voice at them, or certainly not that Ligriv remembered, but he did get angry at things. At those times you were best to stay well away.

"He seems calm enough."

Nigriv grunted in response and stood. Ligriv followed him down to the kitchen where Master Berrell was sat.

"Have a seat, boys."

Esphe opened the back door and came in carrying a basket of clothing. "What's the sombre occasion going on here?"

"There's been some fighting," Master Berrell replied not taking his eyes off the pair of lads.

"Has there now? And these two were involved, were they?"

"So it seems."

"They attacked us." Ligriv couldn't help himself and blurted it out. He could feel Nigriv turn his head and stare at him.

"Did they now?"

"We weren't doing anything, just walking and a group of them called us over. When we got there one of them threw dirt in my face."

"That would be Devlin's son, Ren, I assume?"

Ligriv nodded.

"Sharp-tongued little brat that one. What happened next?"

"Nigriv asked him why he'd done that… and called him a name."

"Rat." Nigriv spoke for the first time.

Esphe chuckled over by the door where she still stood. Master Berrell turned to look at her and frowned briefly.

"What name was that?"

"I bet he didn't like that; people have been calling him that behind his back ever since he was a little'n. Unfortunate how he looks."

"He said they were going to teach us a lesson for it and they came at us." Ligriv stopped then and looked at his brother.

"Then I belted him and he went down. That was it."

"So I hear." Master Berrell sat still for a moment; his two strong hands sat on top of the table while his eyes flicked side to side between the boys.

"Fighting is going to happen amongst boys. It's been a thing since I was a lad and it will be a thing well after I'm gone."

Ligriv began to relax. This wasn't going that badly.

"You didn't start it, I know that, but nonetheless you got into it. What other options were there?"

Both boys sat quietly and Ligriv didn't know what else to say. They hadn't done anything wrong and they wouldn't have fought if the boys hadn't started it.

"Walked away," Nigriv said.

Master Berrell shrugged. "An option."

"Not called him a name."

"Another option."

"What else?" Nigriv sounded broody to his brother.

"Those are choices. It doesn't matter what the choices are, it matters that you had choices."

"I don't understand."

"Are you feeling angry, Nigriv?"

"No." He shook his head.

"What is it then?"

Nigriv shrugged his shoulders.

"You might not be angry but you're not your usual self, why's that?"

"It bothers me."

"Why? It's over, you won. Those boys won't challenge you again, least not like that."

Nigriv sat there thinking for a minute. "Because I hit him."

"So you're upset at your actions?"

"Yes."

"Good, that's the point I'm trying to make. You had many choices. There will be many situations you face in your lives where there's choices. And the only person who gets to choose is you."

He'd been looking at Nigriv as he spoke but now shifted his gaze to Ligriv, making him feel uncomfortable, before turning back to his brother.

"Often the choice is between two things neither of which are pleasant, or ideal, but still, you have to choose. When you make a choice, make sure you do it deliberately."

"How?"

"Choose the option that you can live with afterwards. Do you understand what I'm saying?"

Nigriv nodded.

Ligriv thought he understood. While they were justified in defending themselves, it didn't mean that was the right option.

"You get to choose what you do, and for each choice there are consequences. The main consequence is how you live with yourself afterwards. And are you happy about what happened, Nigriv?"

Nigriv shook his head.

"Then it wasn't the best choice for you. And then there's other consequences as well. This was minor, but I can't let it go unpunished. Next day off you'll stay here and help Esphe. There'll be no exploring."

"But..." Ligriv began.

Master Berrell's eyes turned fully on Ligriv now. "No buts, lad. Both of you had choices, both of you wear the cost. You had a choice to walk away, to laugh or many other things. Next time think about your choice before you make it, not after. Otherwise, you might do something you regret."

The words triggered memories of what had happened in Uboci and how Nigriv had responded then. There was a similarity, even if not as severe, and Ligriv had to wonder if that was always going to be how his brother handled such threats. Their hosts didn't need to know about that but he knew Nigriv would be thinking about it as well.

"Best you go clean up. Come down when it's time to eat, but your day off is over now. You'll need to be in bed early, both of you will be working hard for the next six days."

The boys left the room and went upstairs. Ligriv could hear some murmuring from down below between Esphe and Master Berrell. He thought she was arguing with him but couldn't be sure.

Back in their room Nigriv spoke. "Sorry, El."

"What for?"

"Getting you in trouble."

"I don't care. I'd have hit him too if it needed more."

"He didn't need any more after I hit him." Nigriv laughed.

Ligriv couldn't help himself and burst out laughing too. "Flat rat!"

Both of them had tears running down their cheeks by the time they'd laughed themselves out.

"Those boys won't try that again."

"Good, he got what he deserved, we'd done nothing wrong."

"Yeah, but Master Berrell was right, El, I need to think first."

"Doesn't matter, brother, you know I'll always be there to back you up."

Nigriv nodded. "I know. Same."

As Ligriv lay there a chill ran down his spine and he didn't know why. He knew his brother would always be there for him as he would in return. He shrugged it off, contemplating the day and listening to his stomach grumbling while they waited to eat.

18

LIGRIV

The memory of those first weeks in Barrack made Ligriv smile. Despite it being eight years ago he still reflected on it regularly and how much had changed.

Barrack was their home now, and to all intents and purposes Esphe and Berrell were their parents. The words were never said but that's how it was.

All of the boys they'd fought with back then had become friends and their life here had been good. It had taken a little time for everyone to accept them, but now they were considered locals.

Bit by bit Berrell had become a happier man, and with the boys' help he'd built up enough trade that they got by well enough.

All four of them had restored the house and its surrounds, and Ligriv felt a sense of pride about how it looked now. There was hardly a part of it that hadn't been fixed, even the creaky stairs to their room were strong and silent.

Much like Nigriv.

Ligriv chuckled to himself; as much as the boys were very similar to look at, that was one of the differences between them. Nigriv could go days without saying a word, whereas Ligriv needed to speak.

If he didn't, everything began to feel all twisted and tight inside and he became anxious. There were other things too but none that split the bond between them.

Ligriv was grateful that he had a twin. Others couldn't understand how connected they were, his brother was as much a part of him as his nose or ears.

Now that both had been papered as lapidarists and jewellers, they worked alongside Berrell on any work that came their way. Like old Rainbow had suggested, once word got out that their master was working again jobs turned up from locals, but mostly Tabt.

Ligriv occasionally wondered what would have happened without Rainbow and his brother showing up when they had. Neither of them had been seen again -- not that it really mattered, things had worked out alright.

A year back Yommo had been badly hurt while working on a wagon axle. The prop had slipped, and his legs had become crushed under it. Unable to walk meant his days as a smithy were over.

He'd turned his workshop over to the boys, as their own. That meant they needed to handle the smithy work for the town as well, which Nigriv tended to do more of.

It had always been that way. Nigriv was just as happy with the mundane parts of their training, with the repetitive and heavier work. Ligriv could do it just as well as his brother but he preferred the more skilled tasks.

Master Berrell still found fault in parts of his work and pushed him but Ligriv could also sense the respect when he did so. Pleasing the old man mattered to Ligriv. He couldn't help it; he wanted his approval, but even more than that he needed to be better. To be the best.

Without understanding its origin, inside there was always a drive to be recognised for his work. He wanted people to know he was better than anyone else, even his brother.

When he saw a client's eyes light up it sparked fires of pride inside and drove him to seek more of it. He could never get enough of that and often wondered if maybe he should do more work in Tabt where there were greater opportunities. He didn't mind the coin either.

How would I stack up against the jewellers in Midderbuilt?

Once or twice, he'd tried to ask Berrell about that town, but their master would cut him off and refused to discuss it. As far as the older man was concerned the topic was closed.

"What you daydreaming about now, El?"

He turned and smiled at his brother. "Not you, that's for sure."

"I bet it's Lacey from across town; you've not been able to hide your grin since she let you dance with her last week."

"Leave off, you oaf. I was just thinking about our time here."

"What's that?"

"Just how quickly these years have passed. Do you ever think of…" he didn't want to call it home anymore "… the cave?"

Nigriv shook his head. "Here's home, El. That time has gone, can't live back there."

Ligriv smiled. Nigriv was very pragmatic about everything, he never appeared to think too deeply about anything.

"Are you done? I'm starving."

Nigriv smiled. "You're always starving."

"These muscles won't feed 'emselves."

Both of them had filled out much like their father. They were tall and thickset, which is probably why no one ever picked a fight with them again. That took a lot of food to maintain, much to Esphe's dismay.

Ligriv packed away his tools and cleaned up his workbench, something he repeated every day. He wouldn't leave until it was spotless, unlike Nigriv, who was a lot less organised or tidy, another of their differences.

When he was done, he brushed his hands on his apron, untied it and walked over to hang it on its hook. "I guess I'll lead then?"

"Shut up, fool." They both laughed and Ligriv led them out of the workspace and off toward their home.

Instead of the normal warm greeting when they arrived home Ligriv heard the sound of a stern conversation being had in the kitchen, and a voice he didn't recognise.

"It's been too long, Berrell. Are you so ready to give it up?"

"If I have to, yes."

Both boys entered the kitchen together. Master Berrell was in a serious discussion with a stranger that Ligriv hadn't seen before. The older men stopped as the two boys entered and looked at them both.

"You're back. Boys, this is a -- colleague of mine, Orthtan."

The man stood and held out his hand to Ligriv. He shook it and felt the strength of the man, who was about the same height as Berrell, shorter than the brothers, but wider than any of them and with skin darker than any Ligriv had seen before.

"Nice to meet you." He shook Nigriv's hand as well.

"Where are you from?"

The man paused for a second, glanced at Berrell, then said, "Midderbuilt is where I live."

If he wasn't already intrigued by this stranger the man now had Ligriv's full attention. *Maybe I can finally learn about it.*

"Why are you here?"

As the man went to speak Berrell cut him off. "He's just passing through and wanted to see me."

"Now, Berrell, that's not the truth. Don't you be lying to the boys!" Esphe who'd been busy preparing food off to the side turned around, her hands set firmly on her hips and was glaring at her husband.

Master Berrell turned to look at her and shook his head to which she glared even more. Finally, he looked back at the boys.

"Orthtan is the second in charge to the mayor of Midderbuilt. We've known each other since... since I won my token."

"Token?"

Master Berrell's demeanour had completely changed from how he'd been this morning. Ligriv noted how his posture and expression were much more like when they'd first met him.

He put his hand down the front of his tunic and pulled at the cord that was always around his neck, bringing up the stone disc that it held. "This."

Ligriv had seen it on him many times but never asked what it was. The token was made from a plain piece of stone. The only distinctive thing about it was the small hammer shape engraved into it.

"What is it for?"

"It allows me to enter Midderbuilt. There's only five of them like this. The hammer means I'm a lapidarist."

Orthtan pulled out a similar token from under his tunic and held it out. The engraving on this was a sword. "Mine is the protector's token. Worn by guards, the mayor and myself, those of us trusted to run and protect the town."

"There's two others. A basket which is for wives and others who are needed to keep the town running. There's only as many of them as there are hammers and swords."

"What's the fourth?"

"A wagon, it's for the four traders who're allowed to enter Midderbuilt. Without them the work would be for nothing."

"I don't understand."

"To keep the town running it needs an income source. Think about it, it's in the middle of nowhere, in the desert with no source of food and limited water. The traders swap the finished goods or raw stones for all of the materials, coin and things the town needs."

"But you can find gems elsewhere, can't you?"

Master Berrell answered this one. "As you know, it's slow and tedious and there's no guarantees. What makes Midderbuilt so unique is that there's a constant supply of them and no one has to pan or mine for them."

"How come?"

Berrell looked at Orthtan who nodded. "There's magic there, boys."

"Magic?" Ligriv wanted to laugh.

"It's about the only way to explain it. When you're there you understand. A mountain is not just a slab of rock, at least those mountains are not. Midderbuilt lives under the spire that reaches up to the clouds. At its base there's a small pond. There's always gems in that pond. No mountain on its own just spits out gems like that, there's something else at play."

Ligriv shook his head. The whole thing seemed incredible, and yet ever since Hembleth had told him they needed to go to the city, he'd wanted to be there. He hadn't felt a calling as that man had said but he was very curious about it.

"To protect the town and the source of the gems, access is very limited to only the token holders and those tokens are strictly controlled. Which is why I am here." Orthtan's tone was serious.

Master Berrell's face was dark.

"Your… Master Berrell has been away from Midderbuilt for a very long time, which is extremely unusual. The point of granting access to the city is that the holders use it. They're equally important to the survival and strength of Midderbuilt as the tokens are to their holders." Orthtan paused. "Master Berrell has been gone so long that the mayor has tasked me to bring him back or claim back his token."

Esphe gasped and turned her glare to their guest. "You wouldn't!"

"Hush now, woman." It was the first time Ligriv had ever heard Berrell speak harshly to his wife.

She glared at him and turned back to her work. The kitchen no longer felt warm and friendly.

"It's come to this?"

"This is on you, Berrell. The fix is easy, you come to the city and do some work. You have a duty to fulfil or hand it off to someone who will."

"You know why I don't."

Orthtan shrugged. "Has it not been long enough?"

"Easy for you to say."

"I can't force you to do it, but if you don't then I'll be back for the token and there'll be no choice about it. And with your skill that would be a great shame." His deep voice filled the room.

No one said anything in reply. Berrell seemed to Ligriv to be staring at the far wall and his wife continued working on her bench.

Finally Master Berrell looked at the visitor. "Why now?"

"What do you mean?"

"After all this time, why are you coming for it now?"

"You've not heard?"

"Heard what?"

"Ullia passed several months back. He took a cough on hard and it wouldn't leave. Slowly it ate away at him and sapped what life he had left from him. Which means..."

"A competition."

"Yes. And the mayor decided that if he's to have one, why not make it for two?"

"What competition?" Ligriv's curiosity was piqued now.

Orthtan looked over at him. "It's how a token holder is chosen. The other holders get to present their students as contestants. Whoever is chosen as the winner becomes the holder of that token."

"Can't they be passed on?"

The visitor shook his head. "Only the mayor can select the holder. If someone wishes to leave their token it can only be to the mayor. Are these boys papered?"

Berrell nodded.

"Don't they deserve the chance to compete then?"

"I'll decide what they deserve or not, Orthtan."

The visitor stood. "I wish we'd met on better terms, Berrell, Esphe, but it's not in my hands. You've got until the competition is over to decide. If you've not returned by then, you'll see me again."

"I'll see you out." Ligriv headed toward the front.

Once outside the house he couldn't help but ask about Midder-built. "When's the competition?"

"Four weeks, lad."

"Can't I just come on my own?"

The man shook his head. "That's not how it works. Your master has to present you for consideration, to prove that you've been trained by a token holder."

Ligriv frowned.

"Sorry, son, but you need him. And even though he trained you, if he's not a holder you can't enter in the future. If you're keen on it, you need to convince him to take you."

No one was speaking in the kitchen when Ligriv returned. It was the coldest he'd ever felt the room to be.

He couldn't help himself and he stood in front of Berrell. "I want to go."

Berrell looked up at him and Ligriv could see an anger in his eyes.

Before he spoke, Esphe crossed the room and stood beside Ligriv.

"I let you snap before, husband, but don't be mistaken into doing it again. You'll not be giving up your token over the past."

"You know..."

"Yes, I know! Who do you think carried him? Who was here when you weren't?" Her voice was sharper than Ligriv had ever heard it before and she turned on him, scaring him. "Boys, go to your room please, the two of us need to speak alone."

Ligriv had never seen them argue like this before and didn't know what to expect, but he turned and headed for the stairs right behind his brother.

19

BERRELL

Esphe was glaring at him and Berrell had no response. He wanted to scream, not at her, just out loud, to let it all out, but he couldn't even do that.

He'd sworn to himself he'd never go back to Midderbuilt, to the place where his greatest shame came from. He'd sworn it to her and to himself and yet now here she was angry with him about that very thing.

"You'll not be giving up your token!"

"We agreed... I was never going back there." His voice was little more than a whisper.

"That was a long time ago, Berrell, a long time ago."

"I can't forget."

"Forget what? He's been dead all this time and I've never forgotten either but you don't see me hating on everything about it, do you?"

Berrell shook his head. He didn't know how she managed to be as lively as she was.

"It hurt for a very long time, man, but that's long past. What do you think these boys are here for?"

"What do you mean?"

"They're him, but they aren't. We were given them to help heal our pain, and theirs too."

She came and sat at the table opposite him.

"Can't you see that? It's time to let the past go, and take note of what you have, here... now."

He knew she was right about that. Things had been good since the boys had come into their life and up until today, he'd not thought about the past more than a few times.

"Look at the work that's been flowing your way. If you'd actually put the history of it all behind you, there's more work than the three of you can manage. But you keep holding back."

"I'm worried, love."

"About what?"

"What I might become. That it might pull me back in again and I'll make the same mistakes..."

She shook her head. "You're not the same man as you were back then, Berrell. That's a good thing and a bad thing."

He had no idea what she was saying and his face scrunched up as he listened to her.

"You've not been yourself and I'm as much to blame for that. I let you lock away the very part of you that's yours. You're not meant to live the life of someone else. You're a lapidarist and a fine one at that, else you'd never have a token. But we've let you push that under. You haven't been living this last decade; at best you've been surviving."

"You sound like everyone else."

"Because they're right, and I'm fixed on it not continuing. For you, for me, and for our boys."

Those last few words tugged at his heart and broke through the anger inside. It was an anger at himself and at the gods, at everyone and everything.

He'd been carrying it around about how they'd lost their only child and blaming himself as well as the world for it. Because he'd never had control over it and because he'd let his need for success direct his behaviour.

When he'd turned up back here and learned about their son's death it had broken him. But she was right, these boys were the fix. These last few years had been magical and he knew it.

"So, I take the boys there and let them try to earn their own?"

"What's wrong with that?"

Deep down he knew there wasn't a thing wrong with it. He'd been using Midderbuilt as an excuse, a crutch for his wallowing for too long, but the place wasn't the problem.

His thinking was. Slowly he nodded.

"Then what? I start working there again too?"

"That's up to you, but you have plenty of work here now too, don't you?"

Again, he nodded. "We do. I guess there's no need to stay in Midderbuilt. I can just bring the stones back here with the boys and we can work them as good here as anywhere."

The heaviness that he'd been carrying for all this time, that he'd just accepted as normal, lifted. Like a flash of light bursting into the room his mind cleared and he could see chances for them all that he'd been blocking.

"Then it's settled."

Esphe smiled at him and got up, walked around the table and hugged him from behind, her lips pressing against the top of his head.

"Thank Thenis… things can only get better from here."

"Get the boys, I should tell them."

He watched the two young men as they sheepishly walked into the kitchen and beckoned for them to sit.

"There's some news."

Neither of them spoke, which said a lot, especially that Ligriv wasn't speaking.

"Sorry about all the yelling, you're not used to that I know. Esphe and I are agreed, I'm taking you boys to Midderbuilt for the competition."

"Really?"

Of course it was Ligriv, he'd always been the one to ask about Midderbuilt. Berrell nodded.

"Why don't you live there if you have a token?"

"It was our choice. Esphe's place is here, her family built Barrack and she won't leave it, so there was no choice to be made. When I used to go there, I'd go and come back, that's what the three of us will do."

"When is this competition?" Nigriv asked.

"He said four weeks' time," Ligriv answered

"Did he now?"

"I just asked."

"You've been hot for that place for as long as I've known you. That Rainbow put that idea in your head, I knew he'd get his way."

"How long will it take?"

"Almost every day of that."

"When will we leave?"

"Tomorrow, or at worst the day after. And it's no easy walk either. There's someone I need to see first."

"Can't we ride?"

"What horse would that be on, lad? We've one and one alone, she's old and at best only good for the wagon. No, we walk, that's the end of it. And you carry what you need, food and tools alike."

His words didn't seem to bother the boys, which was a start. Berrell wasn't sure they'd be as easy-going a few days in; he'd never enjoyed the travel but when he'd had the coin, he'd ridden. This was going to be a lot harder.

"What's the competition like?" Ligriv couldn't help himself it seemed.

"Hard, and there'll be fierce competition. A token is worth a lot to its owner. But we'll have plenty of time to discuss that on our walk."

Berrell stood and looked at his wife.

"I'll go and sort that out. We'll need enough food to get us to Darkside, we can restock there."

It was the strangest feeling as he walked toward the inn on the far side of town. He felt twenty years younger, with a spring in his step, and the ever-present sense of dread he'd carried was simply gone.

There was a hint of it on the edges of his mind, like it was there waiting to be called back, ready to sink its teeth in. But he felt good, too good for it to bother him.

At the inn he found the man he was looking for, Aarin, a trader from Tabt who'd approached him the day before.

"Master Berrell, what brings you here?"

"Our discussion from yesterday, do you have time?"

"Of course, sit with me, what will you have?"

"An ale will do me fine."

The man signalled for another drink and then turned back to Berrell.

"How keen are you really on those bracelets you wanted us to make?"

Aarin's eyes had lifted and he smiled. "Very. The few I've sold in Tabt have been very popular, like I said, but two here and there aren't enough. If I can get more and a regular supply, I can push further north… I think they'd be a popular piece for many of them."

"Others will copy them soon enough."

"Maybe, but you and your lads seem to have a keen touch, I've not seen anyone our side of the range that can make something so delicate and consistent."

Berrell nodded. He knew it wasn't him; the twins were good, better than he could ever be, especially Ligriv. There was something they brought to the work that he struggled to match.

And of course, the silver they used was unique as well. The vein he had discovered many years ago high up in the nearby mountain, seemed to react to the boys differently.

That's what set these bracelets apart as much as anything. Something about it changed whenever the twins worked it, something he only wished he could replicate.

Berrell could only hope this trader felt the same way and would wait for them to get back.

"There's a catch."

"What?"

"I have to take them to Midderbuilt, there's a competition they need to enter. They're good enough to win it, and I can't deny them the chance, few get that opportunity."

"When?"

"We'd have to leave tomorrow, and we'd be gone a couple of months."

The man's face dropped. He was a trader after all, and Berrell knew he was hoping to make plenty from the work. "What are you saying?"

"Can you wait until we're back? If you can then we'll put your work first and make you as many as you need."

"Two months?"

Berrell nodded.

"And then how long to make twenty of the things?"

"Twenty?"

"At least."

Each one was a couple of days' work, Berrell knew, and then there'd always be a couple that weren't up to scratch if you were making a batch. But with the three of them... "About a month."

The man rubbed the small beard on his chin, then pulled it downward several times as he considered it.

"There's something else."

"What's that?"

"I'll be able to get a stock of gems from Midderbuilt, we could make a few with stones set in them."

Aarin's eyes lit up and he smiled.

"Done. I can busy myself with some other things... but I need your word that you'll be back in two months." He pulled out a small pouch. "I'm prepared to give you the deposit we spoke about if I have your word."

Berrell hadn't thought that would still stand with the delay, but he was pleased, it would carry Esphe through while they were away. "Agreed. I'll not stay a day longer than I have to."

Aarin held out his hand and the pair shook. Berrell downed the last of his ale and stood. "I'll see you in a couple of months."

"I look forward to it. I think we'll be able to do great things with this jewellery of yours. I'm sure there'll be plenty of work to come from it."

Berrell felt good as he walked home, the pouch in his hand.

In the blink of an eye everything had changed and for the good. It had been an age since he'd felt this good and -- he had to admit -- excited. He had plenty of apprehension about going back to Midderbuilt, to facing his past, but he'd missed how good it felt to be there, around that mountain.

I can't wait. The boys are going to love it.

2 0

───────

NIGRIV

The silence was the thing Nigriv appreciated the most. He'd become so used to living in Barrack that he'd forgotten how quiet being alone in nature was.

Out here on the edge of the desert there was little sound, but for the wind that gusted from time to time and an occasional bird call. At times, Nigriv thought he could hear a voice calling to him.

Just my imagination.

A change had come over Master Berrell the further they got from town. There was a bounce in his step and a level of enthusiasm that he'd never shown in all the years they'd lived with him.

Heading to Midderbuilt mattered to him and he had been speaking much more than ever. Unlike Ligriv, who'd said little over the last couple of days, Nigriv wondered if maybe he'd just talked himself out.

Yet in their whole life that had never happened. Nigriv wondered if he should ask what the matter was, but then there was the other issue. The disconnect between them had returned.

Their sense of connection disappeared for large parts of the day and he knew that it wasn't about distance. They were as close as they could be and yet, just like had happened on their original trip to Barrack, he couldn't sense his brother.

Without even realising it he'd begun scratching the scar on the underside of his forearm. Nigriv pushed his hands into his pockets to stop himself.

Last night Master Berrell had led them into a small mountain village called Darkside. It was tucked away in a narrow ravine cut into the mountain offering a cool rest stop from the desert.

Their path south was more dirt and stone than sand but enough of it blew their way, working its way under their clothing to rankle the travellers.

Nigriv shuffled the heavy skins to ease the straps cutting into his shoulders. There were no more towns before Midderbuilt, which meant carrying enough to reach there.

Each day was the same as the one before, up with the sunrise and moving until it set. Conversation was as sparse as foliage, leaving Nigriv to stare at the endless horizon of beige, and the red mounds of sands, as they walked.

It was hot and hard but there was nothing else to be done. When Master Berrell finally pointed to a spot ahead where a small outcrop stuck out from the rock face, Nigriv felt relieved.

"That looks like as good a place as any."

It wasn't much cover-wise but they'd be able to attach their canvas to it and create a buffer to the evening cold. Nigriv didn't think he'd ever get used to how cold the nights became out here.

As the three sat around the non-existent fire chewing on dried foods Ligriv finally had something to say.

"How does the competition work?"

"You need to understand how Midderbuilt is before I can answer that. It's not like other towns."

He paused and rubbed his hands together.

"All decisions are made by the mayor. No one gets in without his permission and every rule is made by him."

"Isn't that like Barrack?"

"Not really. In Barrack the mayor is picked by the community or it's passed along through a family, but the rules are as much chosen by the town as by the mayor. In Midderbuilt there's no dissent, no argument, you either abide by his rules or you're out."

"Who chooses the mayor?"

"You know what, Ligriv, I have no idea about that."

Master Berrell took another bite and they sat quietly until he was done.

"That's beside the point anyway, when a lapidarist's token needs an owner, it's chosen by a competition. Only someone trained by an existing token holder is able to enter. That's the rule."

"How many others like you are there?"

"There's five others."

"You know them?"

Master Berrell nodded. "Of course. We all lived there… or did."

"I thought they couldn't have an apprentice there?"

"You can't, which makes it much harder than you boys had it."

Nigriv didn't understand what he meant and was about to ask but Berrell continued.

"They take turns going to Watersend, that's where all the training happens. There's a shop there that works the apprentices while their masters are away."

"Sounds daft."

"It's just the way it is. No one wants to leave Midderbuilt for good, but they don't stay there endlessly. It's too much to do that, only a madman could never leave."

"What about the mayor?"

"He leaves too from time to time."

Nigriv wondered what was so wrong with the town if everyone needed to leave. "So why do they care that you're not there?" he asked.

"They didn't, or at least never used to. I guess they kept waiting for me to come back… Like Orthtan said, the point of the token is to use it."

Ligriv wasn't done. "What will we have to do?"

"You recall I mentioned the pond where the gems come to us?"

Nigriv's twin nodded.

"One at a time the entrants get to choose one stone from there."

"To do what?"

"Work it and make a piece."

"Jewellery?" Nigriv asked.

Master Berrell nodded. "You make the best piece you can to match the stone you picked and then the mayor chooses the one he likes the most."

"What does he like usually?" Ligriv asked.

"This doesn't happen often, boys, so there's not really a pattern to it. I don't think he's chosen the same thing ever. Whatever he picks, that's it."

The competition didn't matter to Nigriv, he just wanted to see Midderbuilt. Knowing it was all about making jewellery meant he wouldn't be the winner anyway.

If it came to it, he knew Ligriv was much better at that than he was. His twin's fine detail work was exceptional. When it came to working the stones or larger metalwork there wasn't a lot between them but jewellery was Ligriv's expertise.

"What did you do?" Ligriv asked.

"A pendant for a necklace. It was a blue sapphire and even I have to say it was stunning. I don't know what inspired it, I'd never made one like it before, but it won me my token."

"What should we do?" Nigriv asked.

"Whatever comes to you, lad."

"I think I'll make a ring." Ligriv seemed more alive than he'd been for days.

"Keep your minds free of choice until the time you have to work it. Wait and see what stone you get."

"How many different types of stones are there?"

"In the pond? Shikes, I couldn't even count them. That's why we say it has to be magical, boys, there's so many different gems that show up there over time you can never know what's going to be there."

"But which one is most valuable? Surely…"

"Value has nothing to do with this, Ligriv. It's whatever the mayor picks and what he picked last time has no bearing on the next time. Besides, it's been a long time since he's had to choose, who knows what his thing might be now?"

"But there must be stones that are more likely to appeal?"

"Those gems are all high quality, there's no difference in that, except..."

"What?" Nigriv asked.

"There's a gem, if you can call it that, which shows up occasionally. It's not the same as any of the others."

"How?"

"It's a strange stone, very plain. You'd know it if you saw it, white and dull, at least when you see it in the pond. Once I went to pick one up to look at it..."

"What happened?"

"Somehow I just couldn't do it. Every time I tried to reach in for it my arm wouldn't work right and pains would run down it. In the end I chose the sapphire and I'm glad for it. No one I know of has ever chosen it, in a competition or not."

Nigriv thought about the stone he carried. It sounded much like the one Berrell was describing, and how they'd been told other people couldn't touch it. He'd never shown his gem to their mentor and even now he didn't want to speak about it.

His brother had given him a quick look, like he was thinking about the very same thing. Nigriv shook his head ever so slightly, he didn't know why but they weren't meant to discuss it.

"So, we should avoid it?"

"I would, Ligriv, but then it's not me who'll be competing. But if I was picking something to work on when I get there, I wouldn't choose that one."

"This place sounds strange."

"It's definitely unlike anything you'll see anywhere else. It sits on a flat spot up in the mountains, with a ridge that pushes out over a spot of desert below. There's only one way up to it, a narrow path cut into the cliff face. At the top is the heavily guarded gate. It's impossible to assault just because of that. The few buildings that exist up there all sit below the spire that reaches up so high you cannot see the top."

A gust of wind whipped around their canvas, tossing sand as it came, stinging Nigriv's face and eyes. He had to spit some out of his mouth once it had passed.

"I'll be glad to get out of this sand."

"That's not going to happen. We'll be sleeping down in the camp, which is sheltered from above but there's still plenty of sand. If I could I'd take you up to my hut."

"You have a place there?"

"It comes with the token…" He paused and sat there saying nothing for several minutes. "The camp will be where we stay."

"What is it for?"

"Anyone who comes to trade, those without tokens, have to stay there. Some stay longer. It's like a makeshift village, but mostly it's just a transit point. The town plateau extends out over part of the desert below, a massive ledge that creates a cover. While it keeps the sun out it doesn't protect from the sand and winds, so there's a permanent camp down there."

"Do we have to do anything to enter?"

"No, Ligriv, but… I'm not sure what they'll have to say about the two of you."

"What do you mean?" Nigriv asked.

"The mayor still gets to choose whether an apprentice can enter or not. And with there being two of you, I don't know… there's usually just one."

"Isn't that why we're here?" Ligriv sounded angry to Nigriv.

"Easy, boy. It is. Just because it's not been done before doesn't mean it can't happen."

"Then this walk would have been for nothing."

"I'm not concerned, it's just that it's never happened before so I don't know."

"I'll sit out if need be." Nigriv was comfortable with not competing. He didn't have any desire to be judged by anyone, he already knew what he could and couldn't do well.

He knew his brother wouldn't fight with him to compete but if anyone was going to, it needed to be Ligriv.

"I shouldn't have said anything. We're not there and all will be fine, you'll see. I'm turning in. We'll know more when we get there."

Nigriv lay down and listened to the whispers of the desert, while his brother sat to the side, the connection still blocked, staring out the side of the canvas into the night.

* * *

IF THEY'D EXPECTED the spire to be spectacular, they were disappointed. Later the next afternoon it came into view, albeit way off in the distance -- a narrow peak that disappeared into the group of clouds that surrounded it.

Step by step it grew, the closer they got, but nothing about it changed Nigriv's impression of it. He was drawn to it, as much by the story as anything else, but seeing it now he wondered how much of the tale was really true.

The closer they got he felt a strange connection to the spire. It took up much of his day, looking at it instead of the desert. He felt as though he knew it already, like he'd been to it before, even though he knew he hadn't.

Ligriv seemed to have no interest in it and was still withdrawn.

"Not long now, El."

His brother shrugged, and Nigriv worried about what was wrong with him. He knew his brother was competitive, much more than Nigriv was, and wondered if it was that which was holding his tongue.

He hated that there was a rift between them, it had never happened before. Nigriv wanted to discuss it with his brother but that wasn't something to be done around Master Berrell.

They camped that last night without anyone having much to say. The next day they reached the fence of the camp lying beneath the huge rock ledge.

"Traveller's Rest. We're here. We'll have to walk around to the gate on the other side though."

As close as they were, it took them another hour or more to reach the opposite side. Once through the guards they headed to the only hut.

"We'll need a tent, thanks."

The man behind the counter took his money and pointed to where theirs was located. "Supply stalls are almost closed for the day, best you hurry."

Once they'd purchased much needed food and water, Master Berrell dropped his things in the tent. "I'm going to head up to the town and see when it starts."

There wasn't much for the boys to do except rest their legs and chew on the last of their stale food. When Berrell returned he carried a jug of ale. He sat with them and poured out three cups.

"We made it in time, the competition starts in two days." He took a long drink from his cup.

"For both of us?" Ligriv asked.

Master Berrell nodded. "Yes, no problems there."

"Great." Ligriv turned to his brother, a broad smile across his face.

Nigriv was relieved that his twin seemed happier than he'd been and that they'd both be able to see the gem pool inside the town. He didn't care much for the competition, but something about this place was pulling at him.

LIGRIV

Not needing to get up and walk at dawn suited Ligriv. He lay inside the tent alone in no rush to move. The trip had been tedious and given him far too much time to himself.

For no reason he could work out, he'd not been overly interested in talking much at all. Only half of him was excited to finally get to Midderbuilt.

It had only been him that had ever asked about the town, always remembering what Hembleth had told them as boys. Yet now they were here there was something else that conflicted with that desire.

He wasn't sure if it was the competition making him anxious or something else that dampened the excitement. Whatever it was, it was messing with his stomach and his thoughts.

Ligriv knew his work was good. He could make great jewellery, he didn't need to be told, and yet he had been. Perhaps the thought that he was going to have to prove it was the problem.

Up until now it had only been a small world of people that had admired what he could do, whereas here they were at the centre of the trade on the whole continent and to win he was going to have to beat other people he didn't know.

Nigriv wasn't going to be a problem, both boys knew that Ligriv's work was better than his. Nor did his brother want the accolades and recognition.

That was one thing that was quite different between them. At least up until now he'd never expressed any desire to win anything. If his twin didn't even compete then it would be one less person to worry about.

Maybe I can talk him out of it, he doesn't care about it anyway.

He pulled on his boots and stepped outside the tent.

"Morning, sleepyhead." Master Berrell was sitting outside on a log bench.

"Where's Nigriv?"

"I sent him to get us something to eat from the stalls, he'll be back shortly."

"What do we do today?"

"Not much, son. You'll just have to explore the camp and rest, tomorrow will be a big day."

"Do you know who else is here?"

The older man shook his head. "Some will arrive today, no doubt, we'll know by sunset who else is competing."

A loud voice caused them both to turn. "There you are, I couldn't believe it when I heard!"

A short portly man, with no hair on his head but a dark black beard from ear to ear, was headed their way.

"I could do without this," Master Berrell muttered only loud enough for Ligriv to hear. "Erllog, what a nice surprise." Berrell stood and the two men shook hands vigorously. "Care to join us?"

"Why not?" The man sat down opposite Master Berrell. "I thought you were dead, man. No one's seen you in a decade."

Master Berrell simply nodded.

"But you're back. Is this your boy?"

"One of them. Ligriv, meet Master Erllog, he's one of the token holders."

"Nice to meet you, sir."

The man looked at Ligriv but didn't acknowledge him. "One of them. You have more than one?"

"Two boys, both apprentices."

"You didn't care to bring the other? Not good enough, hey?" The man laughed coarsely at his own words.

Ligriv wanted to say something but saw Master Berrell give him a dark look and chose to stay quiet. He already didn't like this man and understood why his mentor didn't either.

At that moment his twin arrived back carrying some bacon and bread.

"Here's the other. Nigriv, this is Master Erllog, one of my peers."

"Sweet Seth, they're the same."

"Twins, yes."

"And both competing?"

Master Berrell nodded.

"Well, no doubt you'll need two to give you a chance, Berrell. My lad, he's a gem." Again the man laughed at his own words. "See what I did there?"

"Where is he?"

"Preparing his tools, getting ready, like the professional he is."

"Where did he do his trade?"

"Watersend, where else? When I wasn't there he worked under Master Urith, you remember him don't you, Berrell?"

"You know I do, Erllog. He will be well taught then, if he listened properly, unlike you."

Erllog laughed hard. "Good to see you still have some bite in you, old dog. He's well trained alright, I just had to get him up to my level. He's ready, that's for sure. Where did these lads train?"

"With me."

"The whole time?"

Master Berrell nodded.

"Don't you feel they need someone else's touch? I guess they'll get to see what the best can do here, be time to get them down to Urith if you want them to be real masters."

"They're just fine, Erllog. Now we need to eat if you don't mind. No doubt I'll see you in town later."

"Indeed you will, I need to go stock up before all this gets underway. Best you clean up your place, old man, before the spiders take it over." With that he stood and wandered off.

"Mule." Master Berrell shook his head. "He's always been one, foolish to think time would change that."

Neither boy said a word. Nigriv knelt at the fire and started cooking the bacon.

"Don't worry about what he said, lads, you're as well trained as anyone from down there. But he's right, I should be getting you to work with others."

"Why?"

"To get a new perspective, Ligriv, learn new ways of doing things."

"I thought we did just fine."

"You do… you do. Anyway, we don't need to worry about that now. It's your choice, you're good enough to be masters that's for sure."

Ligriv was still smarting from Erllog's words. The other master didn't even know what they could do and yet he was talking them down like they didn't matter.

Foolishly he'd thought this would be a friendly group but that didn't seem to be the case. "Are they all like that?"

"Like what?"

"False friends."

"That's a good observation, son. He's the worst of them as far as I'm concerned, but none are true friends. Not one ever sent word to see how I was doing, or where I was. They're peers, colleagues, but that's all. None are as ugly about it as he is, but they'll all want their apprentices to win, don't worry about that. No love lost now, you can guarantee that."

All three ate in silence. Once they were done, Master Berrell stood.

"I'm going to go back up to town today. He's right about one thing, I need to take a look at my place and see what state it's in. There's little for you to do but look around the camp, just don't go getting into any fights."

"Us?" Ligriv smirked.

"I know it's been a long time, but there'll be people like Erllog that'll do anything to get an advantage. Having you disqualified for any reason would be just up his alley."

Once Master Berrell had left, the twins cleaned up the few items Nigriv had cooked with.

"Shall we take a look around?"

"If you want," Nigriv replied.

"What's eating you?"

"Nothing, why?"

"You're not saying much."

His brother paused as though he was going to say something but then didn't. "Just tired from the walk, El. Nothing else."

The pair set off walking the perimeter of the camp, taking in the sites. There were just as many tents empty as there were occupied. Ligriv couldn't help but stare at some of the people they passed, he'd never seen such a wide range of races before.

"This town must be important."

"Why?"

"People from all over coming here. It's not like it's easy to get to."

"I guess you're right."

A little later they saw Erllog talking to a man probably a half-dozen years older than themselves. It looked to be a serious discussion with Erllog pointing and prodding the other man as he spoke.

"He seems very serious about it."

"Aren't you?" Ligriv asked.

Nigriv shrugged. "Like I told you, I'm happy for you to win. I don't care for it at all, I just want to see up in town."

"Why?"

"Just do. And I want to see what you can make, brother, you'll show them."

"You think?" Ligriv liked his brother's words.

"You know it, I know it. Doesn't matter where you train."

"I want to see this gem pond. I can't believe it's like Berrell said."

"I do too, that's the thing I am here for."

By the time they'd finished their walking the day was still not even halfway through. It was several more hours until Master Berrell returned.

"Well, that's set."

"What?"

"Everyone is here, you've got five others to contend with."

Ligriv felt his stomach tighten. He really was beginning to get bothered by the competition now, and as much as he tried to relax, he couldn't. He just wished it was tomorrow already.

The afternoon passed too slowly for his liking and having done nothing all day, he struggled to sleep. For much of the night he sat outside rubbing his orange stone.

Ever since they'd got within a day's walk of Midderbuilt the small stone had become very warm, so much so that he couldn't keep it in his pocket. As much as he wanted to win this competition, he got a strong sense that this stone didn't want to be here.

I wonder if there'll be one like it in the pond. I'd choose that if there was.

As if in reaction to his thoughts the stone in his hand heated up so much he had to drop it. It took some time for him to be able to touch it again and he put it away in his bag and lay down to sleep, or pretend at least.

22

———————

LIGRIV

When Master Berrell rose just before dawn Ligriv waited until he'd woken Nigriv before getting out of bed. Outside the tent their mentor sat both boys down.

"It's going to be a long two days, lads. I'm confident you're up to the work, but being a competition it's always different. And you can't collaborate, you'll be working on your own for both days."

"What do we need?"

"Just your tools, nothing else. You'll be fed and provided drink as much as you need."

"When will we leave?"

"We should go now if you're ready."

Ligriv went back into the tent and grabbed the bag they'd need. His stomach was still all over the place and he reached into his satchel to grab his stone. It always made him feel more at ease.

The amber stone was still warm to the touch and it didn't make him feel any better at all. If anything it seemed to be resisting his touch. He stuffed it back in his satchel, burying that under their bedding.

They weren't alone as they started up the steep narrow path cut into the cliff face. At best two people could pass each other where the

154

ledge was at its widest, but when it switched back on itself at the corner it was only just enough for one person.

To his right Ligriv could see the edge of the camp, visible under the big rock ledge, surprised at how small it looked. There was a unique beauty to the view including out over the desert as the sun rose.

Daylight brought heat and he began to sweat, as if the climb wasn't hard enough already.

Out of nowhere the memory of the cliff where their father had fallen popped back into his mind. Ligriv briefly braced his left arm on the cliff face as an anchor, focused on Nigriv ahead and took some deeper breaths.

When the top of their climb came into view Ligriv's anxiety began to ease. His attention was grabbed by how odd the wall and gates looked. Two wooden doors, three times their height at a guess, filled an arch, the adjoining walls spanning ten feet or so on either side of the path.

That there was no more wall gave it the appearance of being unfinished, yet it wasn't difficult to see why it was built that way. Having just dragged himself up here, he couldn't imagine attackers climbing the cliffs to get past the short walls.

Although a wall might stop folk falling off. He wanted to laugh but didn't have the energy for it.

A guard standing in the one open gate smiled at Master Berrell.

The older man pulled his token out from his tunic and showed it to the guard. "These two are competing."

"Two apprentices, Berrell. One not enough for you?"

"Such is the way of things, Vorn."

"You know the rules, they must stay with you at all times and leave when instructed."

"Right you are."

Master Berrell had told them it wasn't a big town, which was true, but it was unlike anything Ligriv had ever seen. The small plateau that held Midderbuilt was encased by the steep rock faces of the mountains.

Buildings had been constructed haphazardly throughout the plateau, some jutting out of the mountains, others plonked wherever they sat throughout the hard surface at their feet.

The rock ledge stuck out into the air, with a crane and large platform on the southern edge of it. No buildings had been built out there which made Ligriv wonder how safe it was to be camped underneath.

What stood out more than anything else was the spire which overshadowed the town and everything else beside. Its peaks couldn't be seen it was so tall, piercing a cluster of clouds above and disappearing.

The spire, unlike the surrounding mountains, was rock which had a distinctive blue hue flecked with white spots throughout it.

"Wow!"

"It's something else isn't it?" Master Berrell stood beside him looking up.

"You had said it was tall but…"

"No matter what I could have said it wouldn't have matched seeing it. You'll see more of it, but let's get you both signed in."

He led them to the vacant space that was as close to the centre of the town as you could be. They were the second group to arrive. Berrell went and spoke to the other man, shaking hands before he returned to the twins.

A familiar face headed their way from behind the table where they'd registered for the competition.

"Berrell, I was glad to see you had come."

"Wasn't much choice now was there, Orthtan?"

The soldier shrugged and embraced Master Berrell.

"You caused a stir."

"How?"

"No one expected you to come. All of the others rate you… you should know that, so they would have preferred your apprentice wasn't here… and instead you bring two."

Ligriv liked that the discussion was friendly between the two men, it was clear they had a long relationship. He also liked the idea that their presence was worrying other competitors.

He and Nigriv watched as the others arrived over the next short while. When Erllog appeared with his serious companion, Ligriv had hoped he'd stay clear but instead he walked over, a big grin on his face.

"I didn't scare you off then, Berrell?"

Master Berrell greeted him but ignored his comments.

"Boys, this is Xevean, you'll get to see what a true aspiring master works like. Perhaps he can teach you a few things while you're here."

The younger man, still half a dozen or more years older than the twins, stood there looking the two boys over with a sneer.

Ligriv wanted to do what his twin usually did and go punch the man in the face, but heeded Master Berrell's warning. Instead he looked past him to the other competitors and their masters.

If anyone else was going to come speak with their master they got no chance as the sound of a bell rang out. The mayor stepped forward toward them and raised his voice.

"You're all here and so we will begin things."

He paused and slowly looked over the entire group.

"Seth protect Ullia who now lives in the sands. His passing leaves us with a vacancy which must be filled. A new token will be handed out to the winner of this competition, granting access to the town and its rewards."

Again he stopped, letting his words settle over everyone.

"One at a time you'll go the pond at the base of the spire to select one gem. A bell will tell you when to go, and another when your time is up. You each get two minutes. You can choose any gem from the pond, it matters not which type nor size. It will be what you do with it that matters. When that is done, I will tell you the rest of the rules. Understood?"

The competitors murmured their acknowledgement.

"You'll go in the order of your master's last name. Which means, Berrell, your lads are first."

Master Berrell pulled Ligriv and his brother close and spoke at not much more than a whisper.

"Best that you get to choose early, boys, that's a boon, for sure.

Who knows what gems will be there. Try to let your heart tell you which one. Now who will go first?"

Ligriv wasn't ready for this. It all had begun to feel too much, he needed time to get ready, so he pointed his finger at Nigriv. "You go, brother."

His twin scrunched his face as though questioning him.

"It's fine, you go, I'll prepare myself."

"Fair enough."

Ligriv watched his brother walk over to the base of the spire and then a bell rang. He could see Nigriv reaching into the pond, water swooshing as he sought out his gem.

Through the connection between them he could sense when Nigriv had found something that he liked. He stood up holding his gem and turned back to the group.

Shortly after, the second bell rang, and he returned. Ligriv was able to see the white stone that he'd chosen, surprised at how dull it looked.

"Next."

Ligriv's anxiety was flooding his chest and stomach and he struggled to take a step. *Get a grip!* He took a deep breath and through sheer will pushed himself toward the rock pool.

Within his chest his heart pounded, he was sure everyone else would be able to hear it. *It's just picking a gem, get over it.*

Vaguely Ligriv heard the sound of the first bell, his hearing muted by the sound of the pulse throbbing in his ears. He knelt at the edge of the pond and began scooping gems in his hands, lifting them to let the water run through his fingers and inspecting the stones.

Whatever it was he was supposed to feel when he handled the gems nothing came. He ran his fingers over as many as he could, picked up some of the bigger ones, but nothing.

Ligriv looked to see if there were any orange gems like his stone but there were none. Every moment that passed made him more anxious, surely the time was about to run out soon.

Every handful he scooped up all looked perfectly fine but none called out to him. As the sound of the second bell rang he looked at two larger gems in his hand, one blood red the other a light green.

The blood red one stood out because it was the biggest. He had to choose so he let all but the red one fall through his fingers and stood up. As he walked back to his brother and Master Berrell he wondered if he'd done something wrong.

It's too late now.

Ligriv was too distracted to pay any attention to what the other contestants chose. He was lost in his thoughts when the mayor called out to everyone again, startling him.

"Now that is done, the rest is simple. There are only six rooms that you will work in, which means the twins will have to share."

He turned and stared directly at Ligriv.

"You work on your own item only and stay away from each other. A guard will be present in each workroom to ensure there's no assistance or interference. Any breach of a rule and you'll be disqualified immediately."

With those words he paused and let everyone take them in.

"Worry not about your competitors, there's nothing about them that will help you win the token. What and how I choose the winner, you couldn't influence anyway, so just do good work."

Ligriv could feel the tension amongst the competitors.

"You have two days. At sundown today a bell will ring, you all gather back here to be escorted to the camp by your mentors. Tomorrow be back here at sunup to begin again. Tomorrow's final bell will ring while there is still enough light for me to judge your work, at which point tools go down and you bring your pieces here and I will make my choice."

Ligriv wanted to get away from everyone. He couldn't take much more of how he felt, and the mayor's words weren't helping. He wanted to win but he didn't like all of these rules.

"Once my decision is made it is final. No debate, no recourse, and anyone that causes a disturbance or disputes my decision will never be allowed to compete again."

He held up a token on a leather cord. "This is what you're

competing for. The token and right to live in Midderbuilt. As a lapidarist with a token your work will be sought after throughout Dharatan, you'll never want for coin again."

Everyone's eyes were on the token. Slowly he lowered it and put it away. Then a guard directed each competitor to their workshops, then shortly after a bell rang signalling it was time to start.

Neither brother said a word. Ligriv had never felt pressure like this on him to produce something but was happier the talking was done. He quickly unwrapped his tool bag and laid out his tools.

Here we go.

23

LIGRIV

For the first time in his life Ligriv was competing against his brother. More than that, he couldn't remember any time before where he desperately wanted to win like he did now.

His whole body was locked into the need to win, he could feel it like a compulsion that cried out to him to win this -- so much so that his stomach felt sick from it and he struggled to get control of his thoughts.

His brother didn't seem to be bothered by it at all. Nigriv seemed calm and unphased, as though they were simply back in Barrack working away. Ligriv looked up at him, wishing he could speak to his twin to help calm himself down.

That wasn't allowed here, so Ligriv turned back to his gem and studied it again. The deep red colour throughout it was intense, all except for a spot at one end. A discolouration there represented damage or a flaw.

At first he was concerned that he'd picked a dud gem, but slowly he began to see the beauty it held. He was glad he'd picked the biggest one; there was more than enough stone to work with.

While he inspected the ruby again a vision came to him. He could see a woman, her face obscured, tall and elegantly dressed, wearing an intricate amulet and within it was a shining red stone. This stone.

There it is, the intuition Master Berrell told me I'd get.

And in that moment a wave of relief swept through his body, and with it the anxiety he'd been feeling dropped away. Now he knew exactly what he was going to create.

His first step was to grind away the part he wasn't going to use. This was the part that their mentor had repeated so many times it had driven Ligriv crazy, but right at this moment he was happy for all the practice.

He needed to get this right, or he'd damage the rest of his stone and not have enough to fit the amulet he wanted to create. There was only one grinding wheel in the workshop and Nigriv wasn't using it but he needed to mark his stone up first.

Ligriv used a charcoal stick to draw out the amulet on his benchtop. With that drawn correctly on the tabletop he placed the stone over it, marking the gem to match where in the drawing it would go.

With the stone in hand he went to the grinding wheel. It was different to the one they used in Barrack but the principle was the same -- a stand with a wooden spindle held a round granite disc, several inches thick.

The spindle was connected to a wheel, which was connected by twine to another wheel near his foot. A pedal beside that, when pressed with his right foot, spun the bottom wheel and then the upper one, making the spindle turn.

It took some practice to get the speed at the pace he needed and hold it steady. Ligriv clamped the ruby in some pincers and then slowed his breathing and focused completely on the spinning granite.

Slowly he pushed the ruby forward until the flawed end came in contact with the stone wheel. This was done in the smallest of movements so the stone only just touched it.

A box below caught the dust fragments as they ground off the stone, but Ligriv only focused on what was in his hand. Little by little he worked the ruby closer to the wheel, shaping the grind as he did so.

The light in the workshop was bright enough to help him see

when he'd ground away the flaw and he removed the stone before lifting his foot from the pedal.

When the stone had stopped, he smiled, grabbed the box of grindings and took it back to his workbench. He'd need them for the polishing he'd be doing next.

He wandered to a window and held his stone up to the outside light, checking every part of it before nodding to himself. *That will do nicely.*

After the pressure of this first phase he needed a break, and went to a side table where food and drink and been left for them. He passed his brother who was setting up his polishing wheel for use.

Nigriv looked much calmer than Ligriv felt, which didn't surprise him. His twin had always been the pragmatic one. He worked hard on his tasks but didn't seem to care about them to the same degree Ligriv did.

"As long as it makes the owner happy, El, that's good enough for me," Nigriv had once said. For Ligriv it was the opposite: while he loved the praise from those who purchased his work, a part of each piece remained with him.

Ligriv could remember every item he'd made and what he could do better the next time. He was never fully satisfied with them, believing there was always something he could improve upon.

That desire for perfection was why he believed that being a lapidarist really was his calling. Hembleth had been right, this was what he was meant to do. But Ligriv did wonder if that was true for his brother, and if not, what was he meant to be doing?

He finished drinking the ale he'd taken back to his bench and began to test out the wheel he would use for polishing. It was a hand wheel where he'd need to crank the handle until the plate on the left would be spinning.

Once he was happy with how much he could get the wheel spinning, he got to work. With the grindings and some water, as well as some emery from the side pot, he began to polish his rough cuts.

Using the same pincers he held the stone firmly in his left hand, and then took turns adding the paste into the plate, and cranking the handle. Each time he'd push the ruby into the plate and let the motion and the grit work against the side of the gem.

It was a time-consuming process but one of the most important. By the time middle day had passed he stopped, washed the stone and again checked it in the light.

Ligriv was very happy with how beautiful the ruby looked, the light letting him check that he'd removed the large scratches and grinding marks.

He washed the plate clean of the remaining grit before settling down to a finer paste of emery and water to finish off the polishing. By the time he'd spent an hour on it the gem was just the way he'd imagined it.

One thing Ligriv was sure about, was that this stone was as well cut and polished as any that would be presented in this competition. He could see why being here was so coveted, the quality of the gem was outstanding.

He set the ruby to the side of his bench and sought out the silver that had been provided. To pull off the amulet design he would need to use two different techniques.

The back of the amulet was the easiest, requiring silver pressed to shape and cut, but the intricate elements around it would need him to create cables of silver, intertwining them and then drilling and filing the gaps.

Heating the back of the amulet wouldn't be needed but he'd need to carefully hammer a cut of silver to the thickness he wanted. That was the task he set to next.

The bell signalling the end of the day's work surprised him and Ligriv put his tools down. He couldn't believe how quickly the day had passed, and a little of the anxiety grew inside him again as he thought about what he'd need to do tomorrow.

Once he picked up the ruby to pack it away that eased a little as he smiled at how good it looked. He'd done enough, he had his design and the stone was ready.

This amulet was going to be exquisite and inside he felt proud of what he was doing. His confidence was high as he placed all of his things into the lockable cupboard they'd been provided with.

He gave his key to the guard at the door and he and his brother met Master Berrell back in the town centre. There was a sombre mood amongst all the competitors and their mentors.

"You can get back into your workshops at sunup tomorrow. Until then you must go back to Traveller's Rest."

There was no need for any discussion and one after the other the groups headed to the gate then down the precarious path to the camp below. Ligriv was glad for what little light remained in the day, as he'd forgotten how dangerous the walk was.

NIGRIV

Being in Midderbuilt just felt right to Nigriv. That's as well as he could explain it. There was a happiness within him that wasn't caused by someone else, or him doing anything in particular, it was just there.

It had begun yesterday when they'd entered Midderbuilt and then increased when he'd picked the gem out of the pond. Master Berrell had been correct, he had known exactly which one to choose.

He'd not needed to touch it to know, just seeing it was enough, which was surprising. Compared to all the others it was plain. Every other gem in the pond was rich in colour and many were larger.

The plainness of it appealed to Nigriv as did the contrast to all the others. He liked that it was totally unique, that was enough, and yet something else drew him to it that he couldn't explain.

When he had picked it up a sense of comfort flooded through him, putting him completely at ease. At that moment he knew he'd picked correctly but also what to make with it.

It wasn't until last night that he'd had time to think through the day and it had only been then that he'd recognised how similar it was to the stone Hembleth had given him.

Even how that stone made him feel was similar, just not as intense.

The words that the old man had told them had been true. Nigriv was meant to be in Midderbuilt, at this moment, working on this piece and absorbing how it felt to be here, even if he didn't win anything and couldn't ever get back.

He did wonder what it would be like living here all the time, feeling the mountain, the stones, this sensation every day. Yet that was never going to be his life, he could never leave his brother, nor would he want to.

Today had begun early. Master Berrell had made sure they were on the move before sunrise. Not that it mattered too much, Nigriv hadn't slept and was pretty sure his brother hadn't either.

Nothing had been said by anyone last night, they'd all ate in silence and retired to their bedding. Nigriv hadn't been worried about the competition; he just couldn't stop thinking about how good he felt in the town.

Standing in the workshop, back in the town, he had been soaking up the sensations from being up here but knew he needed to get on with his work. He wasn't worried about the deadline, there was more than enough time for what he had left to do.

On his bench lay the cut and polished stone, the ring and the twisted silver threads he would need to encase the stone and set it. Of everything, this would test his skills the most, but he was ready.

It was going to be a fine ring, something that he hoped its owner would love to wear but it was not extravagant.

Winning wasn't the goal for Nigriv. He'd not come expecting a token. If he could carry how he felt here home with him then that was the best prize he could ever imagine.

As pragmatic as he felt about everything, he was concerned about how his plain work might reflect on Master Berrell. Their mentor was as excited as Ligriv to be taking part in this, but this was all Nigriv could muster up.

Not long after middle day Nirigiv sat back and let out a sigh of relief. He held the ring up to the light, twisting it around and around, inspecting it all.

The moonstone was now held in place by three fine silver strands that criss-crossed each other. Flecks of blue twinkled from it as he turned it and a small smile formed on his face.

There was nothing else he could do to make it any better and while there was plenty of time left, it was daft to stay here pretending to work.

Nigriv packed up his things and then walked to the door, whispering to the guard, "I'm done."

"No coming back if you leave."

Nigriv nodded his acknowledgement and stepped outside, staring up at the spire for a moment before walking back to the centre of town. One guard waited by the mayor's table, surprised to see him approaching.

"I'm finished."

"Wait here."

Shortly after, the guard returned with the mayor by his side.

"He said you're finished?"

"Yes." Nigriv began to hold out his ring.

The mayor turned his head and held a hand up toward Nigriv. "Don't show me, I'll see it later. Do you realise that once it goes into the box, you can't do anything more to it?"

Nigriv nodded. "Yes."

"There's still three more hours, are you sure you don't want to keep working on it?"

"It's done."

"As long as you're sure." He looked at the guard. "Open the box for him."

Nigriv placed it in the box and watched the guard close the lid before locking it.

"You will have to wait here until we ring the bell to end the competition."

"Can I sit by the pond?"

"I will allow that, but do not remove anything from it."

Nigriv nodded.

"And no walking around, the rules still apply to you as they do to the others."

Nigriv was happy enough with that and made his way over to the pond. It was difficult to look up at the spire from where he sat but that didn't matter. He wanted to soak up the feeling being here provided for these last few hours.

As he waited he began to sense the tiniest of vibrations emanating from the rock he sat on. There was an occasional shimmer to the top of the water as well.

For such a tiny sensation the more he thought about it the smaller it made him feel. Like it was coming from the spire itself, a huge thing with the power to move rock.

Indeed.

Nigriv looked around expecting to find someone close by that had spoken, but he was alone. He shook his head, he was imagining things now. He closed his eyes and let the vibration become his only focus, and let the happiness run through him.

A bell rang, startling him, and Nigriv opened his eyes to see that all of the contestants and their sponsors were gathered in the town centre. Unsure how so much time could have passed when it felt like just a few minutes, he stood and hurried over to be with his brother and Master Berrell.

Ligriv gave him a curious look but said nothing before the mayor called out.

"I will begin my judging. While I do that, please keep your thoughts to yourself. When I am ready I will pick one, and only one, and that decision will be final."

No one replied, not even a murmur, and Nigriv could feel the tension in the air, in stark contrast to the peace he'd felt all day.

One of the guards moved the box to the end of the table and opened the lid while the mayor reached in and took out the first piece. He began inspecting it, using a handheld eyepiece to examine it up close.

After he reviewed each item he would place it onto the velvet runner in front of him and move on to the next. The third item he pulled out was an amulet which by the colour of the stone Nigriv knew was his brother's. Even from this distance it looked remarkable, which didn't surprise Nigriv as he knew how talented his brother was.

A few murmurs came from the group, causing the mayor to raise his eyes and look toward them. Everyone went silent. Nigriv could see a small smirk on Ligriv's face; his brother liked the reaction to his work.

Then the mayor lifted Nigriv's ring and spent equally as much time reviewing it as he had the others. Nigriv knew it paled in comparison to Ligriv's, as expected.

When the mayor had placed the last item on the table he took his time to pocket his eyepiece and look back along the table one last time. Nigriv felt as though all of the air around them had been removed and everyone was gasping for a breath, waiting on him to speak.

"All seven of these are very good work, which doesn't surprise me. You should all be very proud of what you have made."

And with that Nigriv was able to breathe. He'd been caught up in everyone else's tension and lost his calm. He and his brother shared a look and he could see that Ligriv was still very uptight, waiting to hear the result.

"My decision is made." The mayor looked across the table as though second-guessing himself, or simply confirming his decision, before he reached out and picked up his winner.

He help up the ring that Nigriv had made and moved it left to right in front of the group. "This is the winner and earns the token. Can the creator please step forward."

Nigriv felt the ground beneath him move, at least that's how it seemed at the time. His ring had been chosen.

Yes.

Again he heard a voice but had no idea where it was coming from. Slowly he walked up toward the table.

"Nigriv… a very nice piece, well done, lad." The mayor held out his hand and vigorously shook Nigriv's hand. "We'll engrave the token now with your name, then you're free to access Midderbuilt and ply your craft here."

Nigriv didn't know what to say. He looked at the other items on the table and wondered how on Dharatan his could have been chosen when the others looked so much better.

"This is a great honour, young man, ensure you treat it as such."

Nigriv nodded and had no words to say. Inside he could feel two conflicting sensations. The deep calm was there, with a touch of pride, but equally across the bond with his brother he could feel Ligriv's dismay, surprising him at how strong that sensation was.

As he turned back to the group Nigriv knew that everything had changed. Master Berrell's face was alight with a big grin, while the other competitors looked more like his brother, disappointed.

Then the other token bearers stepped forward and began to clap, followed by the rest of the group, albeit a little reluctantly. Nigriv walked up and each of the other men shook his hand.

"Welcome, Nigriv."

He couldn't remember anyone's name as his mind was almost entirely focused on the sensations coming from his twin, none of which were happy.

Nigriv wanted to enjoy the moment. He'd not expected it, and he was shocked to be the winner, but the level of discontent from his brother unsettled him.

They'd always been a pair, nothing had ever come between them. Admittedly these last few years the relationship had changed -- Ligriv still wouldn't argue with him, not in any meaningful way -- but his desire to be the best had become evident.

Ligriv wanted recognition and reward, that was his thing. Nigriv didn't care for it, and even now he'd give up the token if it could be done. He didn't want this to come between them, he couldn't stand that.

"Well done, lad." Master Berrell was happy, that much Nigriv could tell.

The mayor began to speak again and the group stopped talking and turned back to face him.

"Of course for the other competitors I know you will be disappointed, that's natural. The work you've completed here is exquisite, and tomorrow at the market I am sure each of you will be well rewarded."

Nigriv wasn't sure what he meant, but before he could ask Master Berrell the mayor continued.

"Remember to represent yourself well down in the camp. You will see many people have arrived for tomorrow, and anyone down there could be your next employer or patron. Your careers will only be boosted from this competition."

He was done and signalled to the guard to lock the jewellery back in the box.

"All but the token holders must now leave, and the rules of access go back to normal. I will see you all in the morning. Nigriv, you will wait until your token is ready and we will discuss your piece at that time."

The mayor and his guards left the town centre and the main group began to disperse toward the gates back down.

"What does he mean about my piece?" Nigriv asked Master Berrell.

"Only the winner gets to decide what happens to their jewellery. Everyone else's gets sold -- that's what we do, make things to sell to others. Whatever each piece sells for is given to the person who made it, except a small fee to the town. That's why he said you'll be well rewarded, Ligriv. Your amulet was a beautiful piece and the colour in that ruby, even from a distance, was amazing."

"Then why didn't he win?"

"No one knows why the mayor chooses what he does. When I won mine I didn't think it was as good as another's but that's how it goes. I warned you that it's not just about what looks great."

Ligriv finally spoke. "Well done, brother."

Nigriv knew that the words didn't reflect how his twin was really feeling.

"So what about mine?"

"You get to choose."

"What do you mean?"

"You get to choose whether you keep it or put it in the sale."

"Why would I keep it?"

"I can't tell you that, but maybe you'd want to sell it elsewhere."

"Did you keep yours?"

Master Berrell shook his head. "No."

"What would I do with a ring like that?"

It wasn't a question he expected an answer to nor did he get one.

"We best be going, Ligriv, you must leave now."

Nigriv watched the two of them go, suddenly feeling very alone, standing by himself in the middle of this odd town. A tap on his shoulder startled him.

It was Orthtan. "Let me show you to your new home."

Nigriv had completely forgotten he would have a home here as part of his token. They walked over to the southern side of the town where a stone building backed to the mountain.

"Was this his?"

Orthtan nodded. "His things are still in there. You can do with them what you will. No one else is allowed in another person's place unless invited here in Midderbuilt, it's part of the rules, so nothing has been cleaned out."

"I understand."

"Come back to the centre in half an hour, your token will be ready and the mayor will give you your choice."

Nigriv went inside and found a dusty and untidy house and workshop, filled with clutter. Nothing about it felt like a home, and he couldn't imagine living there.

It might be his, but at this point in time, it was very much the reminder of someone else. He doubted he could live here for any length of time, no matter how good the town made him feel.

He stepped outside and looked around, taking in how stark and harsh the environment really was. With the sun almost down the cold evening was already taking hold.

Nigriv took a stroll around the town, taking in as much as he could. As he walked he wondered whether his brother would feel the same if he'd been the winner. Would he choose Midderbuilt over being together?

Maybe he'd stay and cut us in half.

When the mayor arrived back with his token, Nigriv was ready to get back down to the camp and be with his twin and Master Berrell. He was exhausted from the competition and all the conflicting thoughts.

Hanging the token around his own neck felt an anti-climax, with no one around to see it.

"It's a big responsibility, Nigriv, but also a great reward. Your future is your own now. As long as you abide by the rules, you are free here to make your life and use the resources."

"And I can't bring my brother in?"

"Never. Unless he can earn a token he can never come in here, except for a competition, and only while his mentor is still a token holder."

Nigriv nodded.

"Now you also have to choose what to do with your ring."

The mayor handed it back to Nigriv. Instantly Nigriv felt more at ease.

"Do you want to keep it or sell it?"

He'd thought he was going to have it sold right up until he touched it again, but now he wasn't so sure.

"I have to choose now?"

"No, just before the sale starts."

"Very well. Then I think I need the night to decide."

"Best you stay in your hut, it's getting dark and that path…"

"I want to go down."

"Then I'll hang onto that until the morning. And congratulations."

"Thank you."

Nigriv handed the ring back to the mayor, turned and headed to the gate. He wasn't sure why but he needed time to decide about what to do, he didn't want to rush that. And he didn't want to spend the night up here. He wanted to be with his brother.

LIGRIV

He'd wanted to be chosen, Ligriv knew that, and it bothered him that he hadn't been. His amulet was amazing and stood out amongst all of the pieces, even Nigriv's.

During the walk down from Midderbuilt Ligriv tried to figure out why he hadn't won. *What was the point of putting all that effort in if they didn't reward the best?*

He was conflicted. He knew he should be happy that his brother won the token but he wasn't. For the first time in his life he felt ill feelings toward Nigriv. *The token should have been mine.*

Ligriv noticed how much fuller Traveller's Rest was than two days before. Arriving back at their tent without his brother just highlighted that there was now a difference between them. Nigriv could go into Midderbuilt and he couldn't.

He had no desire to speak to anyone and decided a walk wouldn't be a bad idea. He could check out all the new people to take his mind off things.

The noise and smells of the camp were amplified with so many people and his head was filled with all of the life bustling about. Laughter burst from some groups, clanging of pots and tins in others, and smoke regularly drifted past him from fires or those enjoying a pipe.

Near the centre of the campground a section was roped off and guarded. Inside were larger and more luxurious tents. One tent stood bigger than most others. It wasn't just its size that made it stand out but the colour as well. He'd never seen such a black fabric before. When looking at it it almost seemed to shimmer.

Ligriv headed toward it, fascinated to see it up close. Four guards stood around the tent, dressed in a similar black fabric, and if it wasn't for their very white faces they'd have blended into the tent they protected.

Something about their attire seemed familiar but he couldn't recall what. He was about to continue his walk when a woman stepped out through the door flap. She was very tall, but when she turned in his direction it was her face that made him go breathless.

Her skin was very white, uniquely so compared to what he was used to. It was as white as the snow and ice he'd grown up around. Her dark brown eyes briefly glanced his way and he could have sworn he saw flecks of orange sparkle from within them.

And her hair was… golden… now the memory returned. *Is it her?* Ligriv's breath caught in his chest and he wanted to call out. Was she the same woman he'd seen in Ubico?

She smiled at him before continuing on her way, accompanied by several of her guards.

Sweet Thenis she's beautiful.

Ligriv was stunned by how attractive she was. While several young women in Barrack had previously caught his attention none compared to this woman's looks.

He watched as she disappeared amongst the other tents… even her clothing was cut differently and he could tell she was wealthy, everything about her spoke it.

Is she a merchant? Surely not. But why would she be here otherwise? Of all the places.

Ligriv wanted to follow her and ask her but was scared to. He was frightened by her guards and unsettled by the possibility that she was the same woman he'd seen before.

By the time he got back to their tent he'd lost the anger he'd felt earlier about losing. If anything, now he was curious and a little excited, both about the woman but also the auction tomorrow.

By the time Nigriv arrived most of his angst had subsided, thankfully. He didn't want the awkwardness he'd created with his brother to continue.

"You did well, brother."

"Thanks, El. I'm sorry for you."

Ligriv shrugged. "It was out of our control and you were picked."

His brother looked at him without saying anything. Both knew part of him was still bothered by it.

"I'd say you'll be a wealthy lad tomorrow, Ligriv."

Ligriv turned to Master Berrell. "Why's that?"

"Even a blind person couldn't help but see how many merchants are here. This camp is as full as it's ever been. The mayor might have chosen Nigriv's ring but your amulet will be hotly fought over. It's a beauty!"

Ligriv wanted to scream. *Why didn't it win then?* But he kept his thoughts to himself and nodded. "We'll see."

* * *

He didn't sleep well that night and was glad for daylight, which signified it wouldn't be long until the auction began.

Master Berrell was sitting outside their tents. "Today is the first day of you being craftsmen in your own right, I'm looking forward to this."

Nigriv joined them and they headed to an area outside the campground set up for the event. Plenty of people were already there and it took some time for the boys to get to the area where they would wait as competitors.

A dozen guards stood around the stall that had been prepared, and plenty more were stationed throughout the growing crowd. Another group was coming from the base of the Midderbuilt path and Ligriv could see the mayor amongst them, carrying his locked box.

Off to the side of the crowd Ligriv spotted the woman he'd seen yesterday, accompanied by two of her guards keeping her separate from anyone else. Everything about her radiated class, and her green dress seemed to match the stones on Xevean's brooch.

The woman and one of her guards approached the mayor's group, causing some tension between the town guards and the man in black. Words were spoken between the woman and the mayor which he couldn't hear, then she returned to where she'd been standing before.

Once the mayor reached the stall he opened the box and laid out each of the pieces, bringing the crowd to silence. He signalled Nigriv over and his brother went and spoke with him.

At the end of it, the mayor handed Nigriv his ring, which his brother pocketed before walking back to join them. Ligriv noticed the mayor turn to the woman in green and gave a slight nod.

What's that about?

Before he could spend any more time pondering, the mayor spoke. "As you might have worked out, the winning ring will not be available to purchase today."

Murmurs came from the gathered audience.

"It's the winner's right to choose. Which means there will only be six items on sale today. That said, you will not be disappointed," the mayor continued. "The work that's been done this year is quite simply outstanding."

Get on with it. Ligriv was eager to get this done, he wanted to know what he was going to earn from it.

"Payment for each item is due on winning the bid. Once settled, we'll progress to the next item, and so I shall begin."

Ligriv could feel his heart rate speed up and he felt much better than he had earlier, the excitement lifting his mood. And then the bidding began and he became caught up in the bids from the crowd and the calls of the mayor.

The amount of silver coin being offered surprised Ligriv -- ten and twenty for the first two pieces. One by one, each item sold and Ligriv's nervousness grew.

There were only two left, his and a large leaf-shaped brooch. Xevean, Ellorg's apprentice, had placed emeralds along the leaf which stood out in the sunlight.

Ligriv kept his eye on the woman in the green dress but she hadn't bid on anything. *Will she buy that? The colour is almost an exact match to her dress.*

She didn't bid on the leaf either. *Why is she here if she's not going to buy anything?* By the time the mayor declared the winner for the brooch an elderly man had spent four gold coins for it, an amount far beyond what Ligriv could even comprehend.

Xevean was grinning from ear to ear, which Ligriv couldn't blame him for, he had just made a small fortune. Which meant he'd probably beaten Ligriv which grated on him.

"And now to the last item for this year."

Silence fell over the crowd. Ligriv felt his chest tighten, wondering if anyone would bid for it. He saw the mayor look again to the woman in green and like he had earlier gave the smallest of nods.

"Do I have an opening bid?"

No one spoke and Ligriv closed his eyes. Nothing could be worse than not even getting a bid. He couldn't imagine another person spending what the old man had just done.

Maybe my piece isn't as good as I think it is.

"Ten silver pieces," a voice called out, giving some relief to Ligriv.

"Thirty!" another added moments later, stirring up the crowd.

"One gold coin." The man's voice quietened most of the chatter.

"Twenty gold coins," a gentle but commanding female voice called out.

Ligriv opened his eyes, looking for an indication of who had made the bid. Everyone was staring toward the woman in green, no one making a sound.

"Did I hear you correctly, ma'am? Your bid is twenty gold coins?" The mayor stumbled over his words.

She nodded.

"Twenty it is then… twenty gold coins, is there anyone who wishes to bid higher than that?"

None of the previous bidders said a word, nor anyone else in the crowd.

"Then we are done. Our last piece for this year's competition has been sold for twenty gold coins."

Ligriv was stunned. He looked at his brother and Master Berrell, both of whom beamed at him. Master Berrell had said he'd get rich from this but he wouldn't have thought this rich.

What on Dharatan will I do with all that gold?

The lady and her guards settled up with the mayor, one of the guards securing the jewel in a small case he carried. The lady was in a lengthy discussion with the mayor, who nodded multiple times.

"Yes, yes, I'll arrange it."

The contestants were told to remain while the crowd slowly broke up and returned inside the campsite. When everyone was gone the mayor beckoned the contestants to the stall.

"My my, everyone, what a successful auction. What prices!"

He worked his way along in the order the pieces had been sold dealing, out the earnings from each sale to the recipients. Each left once they'd were handed their coin.

"Xevean, what a price, you must be happy with that?"

Xevean's face beamed with pride at the price his brooch had fetched. "A lot more than I thought, that's for sure." He looked at Ligriv, a sneer to his tone. "Not as much as yours, don't let that go to your head."

With that he tucked his pouch into his jacket and hurried away. "And as for you, Ligriv, what a remarkable bid."

"I don't know what to say."

"It's quite a piece, but that price… my word, I've never sold something for that much. What say you, Berrell?"

"Surprised the pants off of me, Mayor, that's a silly price." He looked at Ligriv with a grin. "Just saying. Not that it's not a beautiful piece, lad, but I'm surprised at how much she paid." He looked back at the mayor. "Who is she?"

"That I do not know, Berrell. All I could tell you is that she's from the east, not that you couldn't work that out for yourself. She wants to meet Ligriv later which I said should be possible."

Berrell looked at Ligriv.

Ligriv shrugged. "Of course, it's the least I can do." The idea of getting to speak to her excited him and his stomach flipped.

"Good, good. She'll send one of her guards later."

"Fine."

With that the three of them headed back to their tent, Ligriv very conscious of the gold he had stashed in a pouch under his tunic.

"We'll need to secure that, lad. It'll be tempting to any number of fools."

"What can we do?"

"We'll probably want to hire some guards to get us home. I need to think on it."

Ligriv nodded. "Right."

"Don't worry, I'll sort it. Wait till Esphe hears about this." He smiled with pride.

Ligriv looked at his brother, "You didn't want to sell yours?"

Nigriv shook his head. "No, besides it was never going to match yours. I'm happy yours sold like it did, El. It's been a great day."

It had been a great day and was only going to get better if he was going to meet and speak with the noble lady who'd bought his amulet.

Then he laughed out loud. "Who could have imagined the pair of us like this?"

NIGRIV

Nigriv looked down and saw he was scratching at his arm unconsciously. Something was bothering him and he had no idea what it was. He shoved his hands into his pocket and stared across the camp in an attempt to distract himself.

He still couldn't make sense of how he'd become the token bearer but that wasn't the issue. As best he could make out it was his brother's reaction.

After the auction he could sense the pride Ligriv felt at being paid so much coin for his piece. It had been the highest amount ever paid for a single piece out of Midderbuilt. That fed his twin's need for recognition, at least for a while.

It should have been enough to know he'd be the one with that record holder, and the pouch of gold coins... but it wasn't. Nigriv could sense the discontent through their connection.

There was a tinge of jealousy, coupled with disappointment. He couldn't reconcile any of that, such feelings just didn't exist in Nigriv. Nor did he really care much for what had happened.

He didn't care for the amount of gold his brother had made nor what the other competitors had earned. He'd evaluated his ring against all the other pieces and he knew exactly where his sat in quality and craftsmanship.

At best he was third but more likely the worst of the lot. And that didn't matter to him either. All he'd wanted from this was to be able to see inside Midderbuilt.

And now he could, whenever he wanted.

He was able to stay there if he wanted, but more importantly he could sit by the pond and soak up the sense of comfort he felt there. He had never felt more at ease.

Nigriv wanted to feel that again. He stood up.

"Going somewhere?" Master Berrell asked.

"I'm going up to town, I want to have another look around."

His mentor smiled. "Very well, I'll stay here with your brother. I don't think he should be left alone with all that gold."

"Is it that risky?"

"Where there's coin there's always those who'd like to take it off you without having to earn it. Who knows who might be in this camp for nefarious reasons."

"I won't be too long, then I'll stay with him so you can go look for some help."

"That will work. I'd like to be off tomorrow or the day after if we can. There's that contract with Aarin to deliver."

"Suits me, I'll be glad to get home."

Master Berrell nodded but said nothing else.

No one else was on the path up to Midderbuilt and Nigriv was glad for the solitude as he climbed. As he approached the gate the guard greeted him by name and opened it without pause.

Nigriv liked that.

Without all the people gathered in one spot the town felt empty and quiet. The odd person wandered around doing tasks but it was so unlike Barrack or anywhere else he'd been.

As he wandered over to the pond he craned his neck to take in the size of the spire. He felt less unrest inside just from being in the town but when he sat on the edge all his concerns melted away.

Nigriv got a sudden desire to put his ring on which was odd.

While he was happy with the workmanship it was too much for him, a simple trapper's son, to wear. He didn't care for jewellery at all.

The thought quickly became more of a compulsion, much like his scratching, and he pulled the ring out of his pocket. The stone seemed to be alive, a tiny blue flame inside.

Just like my other stone.

He couldn't believe he'd not made the connection before, but the events of the competition had been all-consuming. Taking that out and holding them together he saw they were as he'd thought, the same stone.

Nigriv saw little harm in wearing it here, besides there was no one around. But as he slid it onto his finger everything around him faded into a blur.

There you are.

Nigriv spun his head around looking for who had spoken. "What?"

I'm not out there, I'm in your head.

"How? Why?"

If you keep speaking out loud like that people will think you've lost your mind.

There was no one around to be bothered by him talking but he spoke in his head anyway.

"I am losing my mind if I can hear voices."

No you're not.

"This isn't normal."

No it is not.

"What do you want?"

You.

"Why?"

That's hard to tell, but you were part of a foretelling and...

"Someone else said that to us."

One of my brothers.

"Hembleth?"

Yes.

"He never spoke in my head, where are you?"

He could have if he wished, but he chose not to. I'm spread a little too thin to be able to show my face where you are, plus there's some complications.

"What?"

Never mind. That ring, it has a special purpose.

"What?"

"You don't need to know right now, but you must keep it."

"Why?"

Because I told you to. Now that it is in ring form others can bear it, but none can touch the stone except for you.

"My brother can."

Not in the same way he can't. Just as you cannot handle the amber as well as he can.

"Why is that?"

There's things I cannot or will not tell you. This is one of those. Just know it's true, but that's of no consequence. You must keep the ring safe until the right person comes for it.

"Who?"

That is not yet determined.

"I don't understand."

There are things which haven't happened yet. Just as we knew that you'd show up, it wasn't until Hembleth found you that we knew who you were.

"So how am I meant to know who to give it to if you don't even know?"

When it happens you will know.

"How?"

The stone will light up and shine blue around them. Even brighter when they touch the stone. If and when that happens you'll be able to give it away.

"If?"

Many things can happen, Nigriv, there's no telling how it will all play out.

"This is a bit much."

To Nigriv it felt as though the woman speaking to him chuckled but he couldn't be sure.

One more thing.

"What's that?"

Your brother cannot know about this conversation.

"Why not?"

It's not a request. He just cannot, nor anyone else.

"People might wonder why I am not selling it."

Deal with it. You must keep it safe until the time is right. Many will want to steal it from you, seeking their fortunes, but it must never happen, not even your brother.

"He wouldn't."

Who can say what someone will and won't do when driven to it? Best you come up with a good story.

"I doubt they'll buy it."

Be convincing, Nigriv, everyone's life depends on it.

"What do you mean?"

What I said, Nigriv. It's not just you and your brother at risk, but your entire world.

"I don't want that responsibility!"

Destiny isn't a choice, Nigriv, it simply asks if you're willing to fulfil it. But it comes nonetheless. Protect the ring and tell no one.

* * *

AND WITH THAT the pond came back into focus and she was gone. He looked around incredulously, seeking out this woman, but she was nowhere to be seen.

I had to have dreamed that.

The calm he'd felt moments before had been replaced with a tightness in his chest. That he'd just had a conversation in his head with someone he couldn't see was pure craziness.

He was no one, none of this made any sense. Nor could he imagine how he'd hide something like this from his twin. As they'd developed, the differences in them had grown, but not anything that was significant -- personality and some physical things, but their deep connection still existed.

Much of that had changed since they'd come here and not all of it good. That the competition had already come between them, even if just in a small way, bothered Nigriv.

He didn't want to keep a secret from his brother, nor did he want Ligriv to keep any from him. Or was this just the beginning of how things would be different now they were becoming men?

Will there come a time when we're more different than we are alike?

That idea upset him. Nigriv couldn't fathom a time when that might happen, or any circumstance that might cause it. He'd come up here seeking peace and instead felt worse.

Nigriv hurried out of the gate and down the path back to the camp. In one way he was happy -- if he'd imagined the town was luring him to stay, that thought was gone now.

All he sensed was the weight of what the woman had told him, the seriousness that his silly ring was part of something so big that he had to hide it from everyone.

He sought out his brother and couldn't feel him. Maybe it was because he was already uptight, but a wave of concern swept over him.

Has something happened to Ligriv?

He hurried down the path as fast as he dared until he reached the bottom and rushed into the camp. When he got back to their tents he saw Master Berrell sitting calmly outside them.

"Good, you're back."

"Why?"

"I want to go and find some muscle that can travel with us home."

" Where's Ligriv?"

"He's with that woman."

"Who is she?"

"No idea. Some noble is about all I can say, they all behave the same."

"What do you mean?"

"Thinks she's superior to everyone else. Just because she has all that coin, somehow they think it makes them better."

"Why does she want to see him then?"

"If she's got spare money then it will be greed, simple as that. She'll want to get more work from him. No doubt she's looking for pieces that no one else at her home would have."

"What for?"

"It's all show, Nigriv. The nobles have nothing but time and coin, so to them it's all about looking better than each other. So finding something unique and valuable has to be why she's here."

"Seems pretty stupid."

"Welcome to the world of being a lapidarist. You'll make many fine pieces but you're doing it for them, don't mistake that. You're only as good as who is willing to purchase what you make."

"I'll be glad to get home."

"How was the town?"

Nigriv shrugged. "Quiet."

"Did you get any gems?"

"No, why?" Nigriv snapped back.

Master Berrell's face looked confused by Nigriv's response. "To take back with us, to work with."

"I didn't even think about that."

"It's too far to come here often, lad, it would be good to carry some back with us to work with."

"When are we going?"

"As soon as I can find a guard or two."

"Good."

"You won't want to be wearing that ring, just another attractor for anyone with ill intent."

Nigriv looked down at his hand having completely forgotten he was still wearing it, and yanked it off, tucking it in his pocket.

"How long has Ligriv been gone?"

"Since not long after you left. Like I said, he'll be fine. I need to go see if there's any muscle for hire."

While he sat on his own Nigriv felt more bothered than before he'd gone up into town. Instead of it making him feel calmer, now he was concerned for what he'd learned and about his brother.

In some ways he now wished they'd never come.

2 7

LIGRIV

When Ligriv stepped inside the tent he was taken aback by what he saw. Unlike the simple one that his group was sleeping in this was massive, split into two rooms, the second closed off by a thin curtain.

Rugs lined the floor, ornaments hung everywhere and incense was burning above a small fire. While there wasn't a lot of furniture it still felt more like a house than a tent.

The curtain opened and the woman stepped through.

"This is Ligriv, Lady Tarna."

She nodded at the guard and he departed leaving Ligriv to feel even more nervous. He was already uncomfortable being in these surroundings, but he'd never been alone with a beautiful woman like her before and had no idea what he should do.

"Would you like something to drink?" Her voice was soft and yet still commanding.

"Yes… please." He almost stuttered.

"Wine is all I have, will that suffice?"

"Yes." He struggled to say much more than single words.

Ligriv couldn't not look at her, she captivated him from head to toe. He could have sworn her hazel eyes had orange twinkles in them.

Her silk gown was a deep purple colour, reaching from her throat all the way to the ground, covering her feet completely, and swept over the rug as she moved.

"Come and sit."

Ligriv did so and was happy to have a goblet to hold onto, sipping the wine while he waited for her to speak.

Lady Tarna reached over to a box on the side of the table and pulled it to her, opening the lid. She picked out his amulet and held it alongside her gown.

"It's exquisite, Ligriv, thank you so much." Her face began to smile at him.

"Thank you, I'm glad you like it. I..."

"What?"

"I'm surprised at how much you paid for it." It was true but he felt inadequate saying it out loud.

Her grin expanded. "Surely you understand the value of work like this, Ligriv?"

"That's the first time I've made something of that style."

Her eyes opened widely. "No, surely not? This is the work of a seasoned craftsman."

"I've made many things before but that was the first time I've combined them together in such a way."

"Even more exciting." She clapped her hands. "What else could you do?"

It was then he noticed the pendant hanging on her chest, a heart-shaped orange stone of amber set in gold. She looked down at where his eyes were directed.

"You like this?" She lifted it.

"It's amber, right?"

"You know of amber?" She seemed much more focused on him now.

"A little..." he had never mentioned his stone to anyone before.

"What?"

"Just it's very rare."

"Only here on Dharatan, but where I am from it is everywhere. It's my favourite stone."

"I wish I could have made your amulet with it then."

"Don't be foolish, the ruby you chose is magnificent and you didn't have any amber anyway."

Ligriv felt an urge to talk about the stone he'd found all those years ago. That she'd said it was rare on Dharatan explained why he'd never seen another like it... until now.

"What is wrong?"

"Nothing. Could I see the others?"

Lady Tarna looked at him curiously but nodded. She stood and went into the other room before coming back out with a larger box. She laid all of its contents out on the small table.

There was a wide range of rings, brooches and more pendants. He'd never known anyone to have such a collection of jewellery. She obviously liked them but he was proud there was nothing like what he'd made for her.

Individually none of the items stood out but collectively all of the orange gems gleamed in sync with each other, lighting up the room.

"They are lovely."

"Aren't they?" Then she placed his amulet down beside them all. "And yet for all of them and how many jewellers I have, none match the skill of your piece. Can you see now why I paid what I did?"

Ligriv nodded and a small smile formed on his face. He knew that his was better. He'd always had a special touch when working jewellery, which was why not winning the token still stung.

Having this wealthy, beautiful woman tell him how good he was and how much she liked his piece over everything else she owned removed any angst he'd had about not winning. He liked the way her words made him feel.

"I could make you one with amber in it." He just blurted it out not knowing why.

"Sorry?"

"I have a stone... I found it."

In an instant her smile dropped and her eyes bored in on him as though he was the only person in the world and his heart skipped a beat.

"Tell me." It was no more than a whisper and rolled over him like a gentle wave but he couldn't have resisted if he'd wanted to.

"Years ago… in the north, I found it."

"Where is it?"

"In my tent."

"It's like these?"

"Bigger."

"Bigger?"

"Yes, but it's raw, I've not cut or polished it."

"But you could?"

"Yes. Why couldn't I?"

"Well…" she stumbled over her words briefly, "it is a different type of stone, many can't work well with it."

Ligriv remembered how even his brother didn't like the feel of it and nodded. "I understand. my brother didn't like holding it, but it feels perfect to me. I've just not known what to do with it before."

She said nothing for what felt like minutes but her gaze held its lock on him and Ligriv struggled to breathe.

"You'd do that for me?"

"What?"

"Give up your stone to make me another amulet?"

Ligriv nodded.

Her eyes lit up and he felt his heart ache just at the look of her.

"Well, that answers that."

"What?"

She didn't reply immediately, as though she'd spoken out loud by mistake. "Oh… that you're definitely the one."

"One what?"

Again she didn't answer immediately. "To make me more jewellery. If you're so willing to do that and your work is so much better then I must have you work on more for me."

Ligriv couldn't help but smile. "I would love to."

"Then it's settled…"

"But I can't."

"Why not?"

"Well, not here. I can't access the town and there's nowhere to make anything down here."

"You have your tools?"

"Only the small things, not enough to do what I would need."

"Then you could come to Watersend and work there."

"Watersend?"

"Yes, that's the way we came from and we'll be returning that way on our way home."

"Where is home?"

"A long way to the east."

Ligriv sensed she didn't want to say any more so he didn't push any further. "I need to be heading back with my brother and Master Berrell."

"To where?"

"Barrack… north, following the mountains then toward the ocean."

She reached into a pouch and turned her hand over. "Don't you want to earn more gold coins, Ligriv?"

Her open palm was filled with coins and her eyes were boring in on his again. The coins excited him but more than that, he wanted to go with her.

"Yes, but…"

"You don't like me?" Her face seemed to break as though she would burst into tears.

"No, it's not that at all. I just need to get home."

"You like that more than me?"

He wasn't sure what she meant but he didn't like her being upset. "This is all a bit of a surprise. Maybe I could go there then come back… or maybe they'll come too. My brother is good too."

"I only need one person, Ligriv." Her tone had changed dramatically, there was a sharpness to it which released the hold her look had on him.

The space in the tent suddenly seemed very small and Ligriv didn't feel as good. He wanted to leave but didn't want to offend her.

"I should go, I need to speak to them."

"Of course, that makes a lot of sense. I'm sorry to pressure you like that, you must think me silly. I just love your work, you're so good, Ligriv, it's amazing."

The tension eased and she stood with him and walked him to the flap in the tent.

"Can I see your stone?"

Ligriv was confused for a moment. "The one I found? Of course."

"How about now?"

"Now?"

It was all a bit rushed and he couldn't believe he'd told her about it, but he couldn't walk that back now.

"Only if you don't mind."

"It's alright."

They started walking, followed a little way back by one of her guards. Ligriv felt very conspicuous walking alongside her through the camp with her flowing silk gown and guard.

As they approached his tent he saw Nigriv sat outside.

"Brother."

"El, you're back… with company."

"This is Lady Tarna and this is my brother, Nigriv."

"A pleasure to meet you, Nigriv."

"Me too." His brother said a little awkwardly as he stood.

"Let me get it." Ligriv left her with his brother and went into their tent. When he got back out Master Berrell had returned.

"Master Berrell, this is Lady Tarna."

"She was just introducing herself." He didn't seem very pleased that she was here.

Ligriv held out his hand to her with his stone in it. "This is it."

"Oh my!" She reached out for it. "May I?"

For the first time since he'd owned it Ligriv didn't pull back when someone reached for it. "Of course." He could see his brother and Master Berrell looking at his stone and her curiously.

"This is quite amazing. Where did you say you found it?"

"Malamig, far in the north. A long way from here."

Her head nodded several times while she turned the stone over in her hands. Then she placed it back in his palm, her fingers delicately brushing his skin, causing his stomach to flip.

"Thank you for showing me, it is a beautiful stone. I should get going, you have lots to discuss with your family."

She turned abruptly and swept away, her guard following closely behind.

"What's that all about?" Master Berrell asked.

"She wanted to see my amber, she has a lot of it."

"Where on Dharatan did you get that from?"

"Like I said, back home… where we grew up. Why?"

"Amber is rare, Ligriv, very rare, I've never seen a piece not already set, and never as big as that. I never knew…"

"I've always had it, it was never a big deal."

Master Berrell stared at him for a while, thinking about something.

"So she is from Enderk then."

"Where?"

"Enderk. She doesn't look like one, but her guard sure does." Master Berrell was almost sneering as he spoke.

"Where's Enderk?"

"Far to the east across a land bridge, it's a continent in its own right."

"Why are you so sure?"

"The amber. That's the only place you find it, and for her to have a lot of it means she really is some noble. Explains all the gold coin too."

Ligriv shrugged. It was just a stone to him, except now that it was being talked about he felt protective of it and stuck it in his pocket. He only now realised she'd handled it without any issue.

"What do you need to talk to us about?" Nigriv asked.

Ligriv wasn't so sure he wanted to discuss it any more given how annoyed the others seemed with him.

"Come on, lad, spit it out." Master Berrell was definitely annoyed.

"She wants me to go to Watersend to make her some more pieces."

"Watersend? There's no time for that, we have to be getting home."

Ligriv always knew that would be the answer but he'd been hoping for something different. While he wouldn't argue with his brother he didn't feel so concerned with Master Berrell.

"But she wants me to make more pieces for her... for more of her gold coin. Isn't that a good thing?"

"I told you what happened to me, boy. See, you're already caught up chasing coin and this is just the beginning."

"When will a chance like this come around again?"

"It's all about the coin then? That's what matters most to you?"

"Why not?"

Master Berrell shook his head and went into the tent.

Nigriv had been quiet but shook his head as well.

"We can't go to Watersend, we have to get back for the contract."

"It's his contract, not mine."

"I can't believe you'd say that after all he's done for us. He didn't even want to come here. If he hadn't gone against his own rules you wouldn't have any of that coin."

It was the first time the two boys had ever really argued about anything and Ligriv didn't like it.

He wanted to snap back at his brother, *And you'd not have your stupid token either*, but he didn't. Instead Ligriv checked his feelings and simply nodded.

What was so wrong with him wanting to make more coin from his ability? Wasn't that why Berrell had apprenticed them in the first place? It seemed so stupid that now he had a chance to do something with it the old man didn't want him to.

There was more to it than that and Ligriv knew it. He'd only spent such a short time with Lady Tarna and he wanted more of it. He wanted to be around her, to have her praise him.

But his brother was right, they did need to get home.

"Sorry."

"It's fine, El, I understand. Maybe she can come to Barrack?"

"I don't know."

"Maybe tomorrow you can ask her?"

"Maybe."

Ligriv sat down by their smouldering fire and watched his brother retire into the tent. He knew he was being silly to be so attached to the idea of this woman already when he knew nothing about her.

She was way above his station and was only interested in him for his workmanship, but he could dream couldn't he? There was something about her that made his heart jump and words stick in his throat.

And she seemed familiar to him, not that he could think why, but there was something that just connected with him. Ligriv let out a big sigh, these last few days had all been a lot to handle.

2 8

LIGRIV

*M*orning didn't bring any relief from the conflict that Ligriv felt. He knew they had to get home and that he was being selfish but he also felt like this was a special opportunity.

Master Berrell and Nigriv were already up and busy outside the tent when he stepped out.

"Good, you're awake, now we can get going."

"We're leaving today?" Ligriv hadn't known it was happening so soon.

"We can't lie around here, lad. The competition is over, it's time to get home."

"But..."

"But what?"

"What about my arrangement with Lady Tarna?"

"What arrangement? You don't have one, nor do you know anything about her, Ligriv! How do you know she isn't just stringing you along?"

"How?"

"What if you get to Watersend and she won't pay, or offers you a lot less?"

"Why would she?"

"Why wouldn't she? She already has your main piece... what's in it for her?"

Ligriv couldn't answer and was annoyed at Master Berrell's words and his tone.

"You're just jealous!"

The older man stopped packing his bag, and stood, a smirk on his face. "Jealous am I? Son, I've always known you were great at this, both of you are good and you're turning into a better craftsman than I ever was." He grew serious. "I'm happy for you both but my life isn't here, and I need to get home. I don't trust her or people like her. Seen 'em before and in the end they're all only interested in one thing."

"What's that?"

"Themselves. I can't make you come with us, lad, but we're going today... soon as we're packed. I have enough supplies to get us to Darkside. Help us get ready and come with us, or get out of our way and go where you want. But you'll be making the journey back to Barrack from Watersend on your own. You ready for that?"

Berrell went back to packing his bag and cleaning up the camp site. Ligriv was angry, partly from how blunt Berrell had been but also because he knew the older man was right.

Ligriv had become infatuated with her, and her coins, from just one meeting. He didn't know anything about her and while he would love to have more of her gold coin he didn't need it, he already had a pouchful.

"Did you find us guards?"

Master Berrell turned back toward Ligriv. "There was no one interested. I even asked the mayor if he'd lend us a guard but he wouldn't."

"Will we be safe?"

"We'll have to be. There's three of us and I know you two can use your bows. We just need to get going without making a big deal about it. Before anyone knows it we'll be long gone."

Ligriv nodded. He knew that they needed to be back for the

contract Berrell had committed to it and in truth Ligriv wanted to be home as well. He missed Esphe, the only mother he'd ever known, and slowly went into the tent and gathered his own things, preparing his bag.

Nigriv came in and picked up his own things. "You coming?"

Ligriv took a last look around their campsite before all three headed for the gate. At the market area they split up the skins and food sacks and tied them on their backs as well.

Outside Traveller's Rest they had to walk the external fence all the way around to the northern side. Ligriv stared back into the camp, his eyes firmly on Lady Tarna's tent, which was easy to make out amongst the others.

I should have told her.

He felt a pull to head back, at least to tell her he was going, but he couldn't. Besides, he knew Berrell was right, she was only interested in herself, not him, and he needed to put her out of his mind,

Several hours later, with Midderbuilt well behind, the length of the walk sunk in and Ligriv felt glum about the distance they had to cover.

As much as he could, Ligriv distracted himself daydreaming about Lady Tarna and her collection of amber gems which helped for a bit, but even that wore off.

They'd expected trouble on their journey but it was the weather that became their biggest adversary. The respite they'd had under the rock ledge, from the relentless sun, was gone now and Ligriv's skin already felt dry and parched.

Late in the second week, around middle day, Master Berrell turned to look behind several times.

"What is it?" Ligriv asked.

"I don't know, just an inkling, as though we're being followed."

Nigriv looked behind them. "There's nothing there."

Master Berrell shook his head and kept walking. "Let's just stay alert."

A few hours later he turned again. "There's someone coming."

Ligriv could see what looked like a horseman, or more, off in the distance. "What should we do?"

"Keep walking. We don't know who they are or what they want, but it wouldn't hurt to be prepared."

All three stopped to reposition their bags and supplies, and to prepare their weapons. Ligriv and his brother now held their bows ready to use if needed as they set off again.

They'll not get my gold coins or my stone.

When the horses got close the three of them took a break.

"We might as well be facing them when they come," Berrell said.

There were two of them and the nearest man called out, "Ho, travellers."

"Hi there. Where you heading?" Master Berrell replied.

"Around to the coast then north."

"To Vaelin?"

The man paused briefly. "Yeah, and then onward. You seen others on the trail?"

"Few, it's an uncommon route this one."

"Agreed. Well, we'll be on our way. Safe travels."

The two men kicked their horses and kept riding. Once they were out of earshot, Master Berrell spoke.

"They're trouble."

"How do you know?"

"There's no such place as Vaelin, I wanted to see if they knew where they were heading. They're here for us, boys, no doubt about it."

"Why didn't they just attack us now?"

"Too obvious and they wanted to check us out. That's why he asked if there were others around. They'll wait until dusk or near dawn to catch us unawares."

"What do we do?"

"Just what we have been doing, we keep walking."

"Toward them?"

"There's nowhere else to be going. We're closer to home now than

Midderbuilt. Besides, we just need to make it to Darkside. Stay alert and we'll be fine."

That night all three of them were uptight. Few words were spoken, and Master Berrell took the first watch. Not that Ligriv was able to sleep; when it was his turn he was already awake.

"Anything?"

"No, but there's no light to help. Listen for trouble with your ears more than looking."

Ligriv heard and saw nothing and when he swapped with his brother he did fall asleep. Dawn arrived without incident and all of them got up.

"Let's get moving, we're better on the move than standing still."

Both boys didn't need much convincing and they set off. By the third day Ligriv wasn't convinced they were going to be attacked. He knew Master Berrell had more experience than them but they'd not seen the riders again.

"Less than two days and we'll be in Darkside. I'll be glad for a roof and a cot, plus some of Lunnie's ale." Master Berrell's voice sounded lighter and more optimistic than he had all week.

On their way south the small inn in Darkside had simply been a stopping point to replenish, but now Ligriv couldn't wait to get there and see the keeper, Lunnie, again as well.

That night Ligriv struggled to stay awake while on watch, and felt happy when the tiniest sliver of sunlight appeared to the east. It was only because he stood to stretch that he saw a shape moving alongside the rock ledge up ahead.

"Someone's coming." He kicked Master Berrell as he grabbed his bow and began to nock an arrow.

The older man was on his feet immediately which was just as well, as two men rushed forward.

"Hand over the coin and no one need get hurt."

"You'd be best to turn and run, scum, the only thing you'll be getting from us is steel."

Master Berrell moved ahead of Ligriv, while Nigriv came alongside with his hand axe ready. The second attacker began sweeping out to their right.

"You two watch him." The boys did as Master Berrell told them.

The man watched as Ligriv raised his bow and let the arrow fly, ducking to his left at the last moment. The arrow missed and Ligriv fumbled with his attempt to load another.

To his back Ligriv could hear the clash of metal and grunts as Master Berrell fought with the other attacker. His heart was pounding in his chest and his hands were trembling.

"Hurry up!" Nigirv called to him as he moved toward the nearest man whose attention was now fully on Ligriv's brother.

Finally Ligriv had the arrow ready and it flew truer, hitting the man in his right thigh. The man hardly paused, quickly grabbing the shaft with one hand and hacking it off with his blade, growling as he did so. By the time he looked back up at the boys, Nigriv was almost on him.

Just like he'd done in Ubico, Nigriv let the hand axe fly, hitting the man in the centre of his chest. The attacker teetered where he stood for a moment, his eyes staring at Nigriv in surprise, before he fell to the ground with a thud.

Nigriv reached him and placed a foot beside the axe before yanking it free. Ligriv turned at the sound of a loud gasp from the other fight.

"NO!" Ligriv yelled, as he saw the blade poking through Master Berrell's back.

He quickly loaded another arrow and sent it flying, hitting the other attacker in the shoulder of his free arm. The man yanked his sword free of Berrell and turned to face the boys.

Nigriv was much closer to the attacker now, but Ligriv didn't wait, he nocked another arrow and sent it flying, hitting the man in the centre of his chest.

He fell down in a seated position, one hand on the arrow. His other, loosely on top of his sword, lay beside him. He was about to say something when Nigriv reached him and drove his axe into the man's head.

In a rage Ligriv's brother hacked at him several times, making Ligriv turn away. He hurried to Master Berrell who had propped himself up on the rocks.

"How do you feel?"

"Not good, son."

Ligriv couldn't believe it. He wasn't sure what to do. "You'll be alright… we'll get you to Darkside."

"I'm not going to make it, Ligriv."

Nigriv hurried over, covered in blood. "You'll make it, we'll get you there."

"I can't walk, boys, and it's a long haul."

"Their horses!" Nigriv blurted out.

"What?" Ligriv asked.

"They had horses, they must be nearby. I'll go get them. We'll get him to Darkside. Wrap him tight with something, I'll be back."

Ligriv set to work on Master Berrell, fumbling his way through tearing a spare tunic into lengths to wrap around the older man's middle. He finally got it tight enough to help stem some of the bleeding.

"That'll have to do."

Nigriv returned shortly after, dragging two horses by their reins. Neither of them had ever ridden before so they loaded up Berrell and tied him onto the saddle of one, the bags on the other, and set off jogging beside the horses, holding their reins.

"He's not well, Nigriv."

"I know, El. Let's just get him there."

The dread Ligriv felt wouldn't go away. He just ran as hard as he could, hoping they wouldn't be too late.

* * *

THEY REACHED the gully by late afternoon and Darkside not long after sundown. Lunnie's tavern was the only place they knew so they headed straight there.

"We need help!" Ligriv shouted as he ran inside.

"What's wrong, lad?"

"We got attacked on the road. Berrell's hurt."

All the men in the bar leapt to their feet and rushed outside. In a matter of minutes they had Master Berrell off the horse and into a room while someone went for the only person in the town who had healing knowledge.

"You boys need to get cleaned up. I'll put you in a separate room. Go get washed and fed while we deal with this." Lunnie led them there and left them to it.

It took Nigriv an age to wash and clean himself and he said nothing when he came back. Once Ligriv was washed up both boys waited in the main room, only picking at their food and ale.

Lunnie came out, his face looking grim. "He's not in good shape."

"Will he make it?"

The man shrugged. "It's up to him and Seth now. You boys did good to get him here, he's a much better chance than he would have had out there."

Lunnie asked all the details of what had happened while the boys sat glumly at the bar. There was no frivolity in the inn today, everyone sat quietly and spoke in hushed tones.

That night everyone took turns by Berrell's side, including the twins, despite Lunnie trying to get them to rest. Ligriv couldn't sleep, and struggled to accept that Berrell had been hurt so badly, all because of his coin.

* * *

LIGRIV SAT LOOKING at the plate of breakfast that had been prepared for him but had no desire to eat. His brother was across the table scratching at his arm, which was beginning to annoy Ligriv.

Lunnie came into the main room.

"How is he?" Ligriv asked.

When the innkeeper shook his head, Ligriv's heart dropped in his chest, and his stomach swirled as though he'd throw up what little it held.

"What?" Even Nigriv seemed upset.

"Sorry, boys, he didn't make it."

"You should have come got us!" Nigriv sounded angry.

"He's just passed, there was nothing anyone could have done, lad. Either he was going to fight it or..." Lunnie never finished what he was saying.

"Where is he?"

"In the room."

Ligriv followed his brother into the room where their mentor lay, still and pale on the bed. Tears rolled down Ligriv's face. The man had been as much a father to them as anyone and now he was gone. *This isn't fair.*

The bedroom smelled of old blood and something else -- Ligriv could only think it was death. That it carried its own odour when it took someone. He wanted to shake the older man, to wake him, but he knew it was pointless.

Nigriv stood quietly staring at the body in the bed, before turning and leaving the room. Ligriv went after him. He went into the main room and grabbed an ale and swallowed the whole lot.

There were no tears on his brother's face, not that Ligriv expected any, he didn't work like that. Then Nigriv went outside. Ligriv thought about following him but needed his own space and went to the room they'd been given.

He lay down on his bed and sobbed until he fell asleep. Sometime later his brother came into the room and shook him awake. Nigriv turned to him, "We have to get his body home, to Esphe."

"How?"

"We'll use the horses."

"We don't know how to ride."

"Lunnie said he'll show us enough to get us moving."

Ligriv wasn't going to argue with his brother, not now, not about this. If that's what was needed then he'd do it. "When?"

"Now, Ligriv. We need to get going."

The lessons weren't of much help, but it was going to have to do.

The boys set off with an extra horse to carry the body, that had been wrapped to keep vermin away from it.

"As fast as we can, El." Nigriv nodded with his head for him to go first.

"I guess I'm leading then?"

There was no laughter or smiles, nor did his brother reply.

* * *

As they reached the end of the gully Ligriv slowed his horse to a walk. When Nigriv rode alongside, the third horse on a rope behind him, Ligriv pointed ahead.

"There's a carriage."

"We don't need another fight."

"How many attackers come in carriages?"

Nigriv shrugged and they rode cautiously toward it.

Ligriv knew who it was as soon as he saw the men dressed entirely in black, the clothing appearing to shimmer in the sunlight, making them hard to focus on.

One of the guards opened the door and out stepped Lady Tarna. Ligriv's stomach flipped a little and inside he was pleased to see her, albeit very surprised.

She looked at the third horse. "Ligriv, what's happened?"

"We were attacked. Master Berrell didn't survive."

"I am so sorry."

"Why are you here?" Nigriv's tone wasn't friendly.

She looked at him coldly. "I was seeking Ligriv." She turned back to him. "You left without saying goodbye or discussing my offer."

"Sorry, but we needed to get going… Master Berrell…" Tears filled his eyes again and he choked up.

"It's alright, I just wanted to find you. Now isn't the time. How can we help?"

"You can't, we need to get going. Come on, brother." Nigriv kicked at his horse and pulled ahead.

"I'm sorry, I need to get going."

"Where to?"

"Barrack, our home."

"We'll follow."

"Just keep the mountains to your left and close to you, it's the only town before the ocean."

"We'll talk there."

Ligriv was more confused than ever. He wanted to be excited she was here, that she was following, but his concern was about Esphe and getting Master Berrell's body to her. It was not going to be the happy homecoming he would have liked.

NIGRIV

*E*very part of Nigriv's lower body hurt. The insides of his thighs were raw, all of his muscles ached, even his knees and ankles were burning from the days of riding the horses.

Neither he nor his brother had ever spent any time on a horse and he wasn't sure he'd ever want to again. He kept having to reposition his lower back to ease how much it hurt, but they had no choice other than to keep going.

The three days it had taken them, while much quicker than on foot, were more difficult than anything he'd ever faced. Neither he nor Ligriv spoke a word, there was nothing to be said.

All Nigriv could think about was Esphe. He could only guess at what the news would do to her. It was not something he could relate to, all he knew was that her husband had died.

He was very aware that he'd been rubbing and scratching at the underside of his forearm and that there was a connection to the concern he was thinking of but that was as close as he got to the sadness others expressed.

What was bothering him though was that even though he and Ligriv were riding close together, the connection between them was mostly absent. It flickered on and off from time to time, which made its absence only more noticeable.

His twin was visibly upset and Niriv knew he couldn't appease him, at times like this Ligriv preferred to be left alone. Then he'd flip completely and need to talk until Nigriv's head hurt, but that was his way.

The sight of Barrack in the distance jolted Nigriv out of his reverie and he slowed the horse to a stop. Ligriv did the same and they sat staring toward it.

Barrack was home, Nigriv could feel that as he looked toward it. He would have been glad to be back if he didn't know what was about to come next. At least he was able to confirm that this was home for him.

"We might as well get this over with." The words probably sounded cold to his brother which he didn't mean, he just wanted to get to the other side of delivering the news.

They rode at a walk all the way to the outskirts of town, only dismounting as they approached the house. Esphe was in the front garden, her back to them, and only turned as they entered the yard.

"My boys!" she exclaimed in surprise, a massive grin on her face.

She turned and hurried to them, stopping in her tracks when she realised that there was only two of them.

"Where's...?" Her words froze in her throat.

Ligriv hurried to her and wrapped her in a hug.

"NO!" She wailed. "No! No! No!"

The tears came next and then sobs. Nigriv stepped in and wrapped his arms around the pair of them as best he could, the whole thing making him very uncomfortable, but he knew enough to know it would make her feel better, or at least add some comfort.

After several minutes she pushed her way out of their embraces. "What happened?"

"Later, Esphe. Not now."

She was about to argue when several of the neighbours came closer, including Yommo hobbling on his crutch.

"What's going on?"

There was no need to answer. Everyone saw the wrapped body on the third horse and the two boys, which told them all the needed to know.

Madame Ayla, the town healer from two houses down, grabbed Esphe and led her back into the house.

Once she was out of earshot Yommo grabbed both boys by the shoulder. "What happened?"

"Thieves came for us, before Darkside. We killed them both but only after they had injured Berrell." Nigriv had to take a breath, just saying it tightened his chest.

"We got him there but he didn't make it."

"Thieves… what did they want?"

"Gold…"

"It doesn't matter, not now. We need to do something with his body."

The men of the town led the horse away leaving the two boys standing there alone. Nigriv knew this was only the beginning of things but wished it was the end.

He headed inside and Ligriv followed him, expecting to see Esphe in the kitchen, but she wasn't there. Her wails could be heard coming from her and Berrell's room accompanied by the soft voice of Madame Ayla.

Nigriv fetched ale for both himself and his brother and sat at the table, staring at the wall. So much had happened and little of it made him feel good. One thing he was sure of was he'd give back both the token and Ligriv's gold just to go back to how they were before.

Eventually he washed and went up to his room and lay on his bed. At some point his twin came in and did the same. Ligriv would speak when he wanted to, so Nigriv just lay there in silence.

While he lay there his mind drifted to the ring he'd made back in Midderbuilt. He pulled it out and slid it onto his finger. There was no voice speaking to him like had happened in that town but it made him feel better for wearing it, much like the stone Hembleth had given him.

He and Ligriv had never had any time to discuss that he'd kept the ring, nor had his brother asked. Ligriv had been completely consumed with his winnings and that strange woman.

That was another thing that Nigriv wished had never happened. He didn't like her, he couldn't explain why, he just didn't. Too many things had changed, including this distance between him and his brother, and Nigriv didn't care for it at all.

Before he knew it he'd drifted off to sleep, the ring still on his finger.

* * *

HE CAME AWAKE in what seemed like how he'd imagined a cloud to be. Everything was bright white around him, but there was nothing but air holding him in place. He tried to grasp at something to hold onto but there was nothing there.

Somewhere around him he could hear voices but in what direction he couldn't tell.

"What's she up to?"

"I don't know, she seems to like living as one of them."

"Her time must be running out, she will have to come back soon enough, we can ask her then."

"Not that she's ever been one to tell us what she's doing."

"Messing with their world isn't good."

"And yet isn't that what we've been doing?"

"Who's that?"

"What?"

"There's someone here."

"Who?"

"How odd, it's the boy. I best take care of it."

* * *

WHEN HE DID WAKE, Nigriv had a shocking headache, struggling to even open his eyes. He'd been dreaming, he knew that, but the pain behind his eyes made it hard to remember all of the details.

His finger was hurting and after opening his eyes against the morning light he could see that he still wore the ring and it had cut into his skin.

Forgot to take it off, I shouldn't do that.

Ligriv was still asleep in the other bed, and Nigriv put the ring away, still confused by what he could remember of the dream.

3 0

LIGRIV

The kitchen felt cold as Ligriv descended the stairs. Neither his brother nor Esphe was there. Before the attack he'd been looking forward to getting home, now he wondered if it would ever be the same again.

With no reason to stay there Ligriv set off for his workshop, hoping that would feel more welcoming. Outside the house he heard banging from Berrell's shed.

Nigriv was inside cleaning out ash from the fire. "You're up."

"How is she?"

"Asleep. Madame Ayla has been dosing her with something to keep her calm."

Ligriv shook his head. He didn't know what else to say.

"I'm going to work from here." It was typical Nigriv, just a statement without any explanation.

"Why?"

"I want to be around her… and… I don't know, it just seems right."

"Very well." Ligriv knew it would be strange to always work apart from his brother, but also they were their own people now. Both were craftsmen and didn't need to hold each other's hands.

"You can too if you want." It wasn't a question, just a statement.

"No, I like Yommo's old shop, I'll stay there."

Nigriv nodded and began shovelling again.

Ligriv knew his brother wasn't going to have a deep discussion with him about what was happening. Nigriv just handled things practically, it had always been his way and this wouldn't be any different.

That wasn't the only thing where they were different, although to the casual observer they were still very similar. Ligriv knew that things were changing between them and they had different opinions about many things.

His workshop was only several streets over and several buildings along but it was the hardest walk he'd taken. Every step reminded him of something about Master Berrell, each building, an event or discussion that they'd had in that particular spot.

They were connected to this town because of him and every memory of it was filled with the man. For the first time ever Ligriv considered how maybe it might be better to not be here.

But where?

Tabt was an obvious choice, it was still close. *Close enough for what?* He couldn't leave his twin and the pair couldn't abandon Esphe now. They were anchored here now, or at least while she still lived.

He could work away temporarily, which wouldn't be so bad. It would be a change of scenery for a period. But he wasn't sure he could leave his brother even for such a short stint.

And Watersend was too far to go and of course he couldn't work in Midderbuilt. Then it hit him like he'd run into a wall. *I'll never be able to win a token... our mentor is gone.*

Instead of sadness Ligriv felt angry, not at Berrell, but at the unfairness of it all. His amulet had been by far the best piece in the competition but the stupid mayor had chosen his brother's ring.

It was nice enough, but that was it, it wasn't in the same class as what he'd built. He'd been inspired to make it, it wasn't just a random idea, and he'd made it exactly as he'd seen it in his mind.

As he'd told Lady Tarna, while he'd done each of the elements in one way or another before, that was the very first time he'd created an amulet like that. And it was, like she said, an exquisite piece.

But still I didn't win... and now I never can.

Ligriv was angry when he opened his workshop doors, angry as he emptied his own fire, and angry up until he had the fire burning. As he stared into the orange flames, little by little the fire inside him dampened and the colour reminded him of his stone.

He pulled it from his bag and remembered how calming the touch of it had been previously. All of the angst he'd been feeling subsided but behind it came the frustration and sadness of recent events.

Tears filled his eyes before rolling down his face. Ligriv slumped to the floor and let them flow as he began to sob. It lasted for the better part of an hour.

Slowly he stood and resumed the cleaning of his workspace. There were layers of dust, cobwebs and other things to sweep away while he continued to stoke the fire. It was going to take a good while to get enough heat and the coals dried out.

He left the amber stone on his bench, occasionally looking back at it. It had been with him a long time now, the only other constant apart from his brother, that had never changed.

After he'd done most of the tidying he emptied out the bag of tools he'd taken on the trip, setting them back where they would normally live. Inside his workbag was a pouch of thirty-odd gems that Nigriv and Master Berrell had collected for them to bring back.

When he was still alive...

They were meant to give them a leg up, to speed up their income by not needing to spend as much time fossicking in the mountains. Not that Aarin's contract needed any gems.

It was all silver work and engraving. Repetitive and a little dull but Berrell had promised it to the man, so it would get done. Inside his bag was also the pouch that held his gold coins.

Ligriv had nowhere else to put it, at least while they'd been on the road, now he needed to be more practical. In theory they were safe in Barrack, but if one set of thieves had come then maybe others might follow. And who knew what a few of the locals might consider if they found out about it.

Ligriv walked around the workshop collecting a few things that he'd need. There were some steel bands he could reshape and fashion, and a dirty wooden box that held some old leather aprons and fabric.

It was enough, he could secure the box with the steel bands around it and add a solid lock. Being locked it would draw attention if anyone saw it, but he had an idea to stop it being carried off.

For now he put both pouches in a drawer in his bench and dragged the box over to his bench. It was heavy enough that it couldn't just be picked up easily, but he still would need to secure it to one of the thick wooden posts.

The first thing was to measure everything out and then he'd need the fire, which wouldn't be hot enough until tomorrow. As he was preparing the pieces of steel he sensed the presence of someone and turned to the door.

Lady Tarna was standing just outside with one of her guards.

"You're here."

"Yes, Ligriv, I am. How are you?"

He didn't know what to say. He knew she was coming to Barrack and that he was the reason why, but the loss of Master Berrell was still too fresh.

"Is it better if I come back another time?"

"I'm fine, it's just all very raw."

"So this is your home town?"

Ligriv nodded.

"It's very small."

He suddenly felt very embarrassed. Up until that point he'd not judged it. It was simply Barrack, but to this woman who was some noble from the east, it was exactly as she'd said -- small. Not only that but it was a simple place, nothing fancy about it at all.

"Where are you staying?"

A sly grin crossed her face. "The mayor has graciously lent us his house... it will do, for now."

The superior tone was something he'd not experienced from her back at the camp and he couldn't help but feel it was directed at him as much as at the town. *You followed me, I didn't make you come here.*

Lady Tarna's eyes switched back to look directly at him and bored in on his as if she knew what he was thinking. Ligriv looked back at his bench; anything to avoid her focus.

"That's good." He still had no idea what to say to her and unlike his first meeting with her, she seemed peevish.

"Did you not want to work on more jewellery for me?"

"Sorry?"

"Back at Midderbuilt that's what we were discussing, that you might head to Watersend with us and produce more work."

"It wasn't possible."

"And yet look at what happened, such a terrible thing. Perhaps it would have been much better if you'd taken my suggestion."

As much as he found her stunning and extremely captivating, right now the loss of Master Berrell wasn't something to hypothesise over. Maybe it never would be. He could feel himself becoming angry inside.

"That was very insensitive of me, my apologies." Her voice had changed, there was a softness to it, and her eyes weren't boring in on his, but expressed sadness, which Ligriv couldn't resist.

"It's alright."

"Maybe I could invite you to dinner this evening and we could discuss it then?"

His concerns from earlier had all but melted away and he recalled how he'd felt about her the first time they met. Here she was asking simple him to eat with her.

"I'd like that."

"So will I, I will look forward to it."

"Should I bring anything?"

She smiled. It was friendly but still a little patronising. "No need, Ligriv, I'll cater for everything."

With that she twirled and left and he couldn't take his eyes off her. Then she was gone from sight and his senses came back to him and he looked about the workshop.

He was done for now and walked out, locking the door and heading back home, his mind completely distracted by the evening ahead.

3 1

LIGRIV

igriv was still in Berrell's workshed when Ligriv got back home and he didn't bother to disturb him. He went up to his room and tried to find something clean enough to wear to dinner.

He had only one other tunic that hadn't gone on the trip south, because it was already well worn and patched. He'd never needed anything more than what he had, until now.

Ligriv hated that he felt inferior because of it and wished he could buy something, but there were no stores that sold clothes in Barrack, only a seamstress.

While he had plenty of coin now to afford something in Tabt he didn't have enough time. He wondered if perhaps there might be something he could find amongst Master Berrell's things.

He went downstairs and quietly slipped into Esphe's room. She was still fast asleep, as was Madame Ayla, who was propped up in the chair beside the bed, snoring ever so slightly.

From the open rack on the far wall he grabbed the first tunic he could find and slipped out of the room, with mixed feelings. He was happy to have something better than any of his, but less so that he'd gone in and taken it without asking.

It didn't fit perfectly either but it would do. Next came a wash. By the time he was clean he felt uptight. Ligriv was excited to meet her again and what work she might have for him to do but there was more to it than that.

She was the most glamorous, attractive and powerful woman he'd ever met and that appealed to him. He fancied her but knew he was nowhere close to being at her level, which made these feelings even more ludicrous.

There was no ambiguity about why she had followed, nor that she saw him as a worker to help her get what she needed. Ligriv needed to put everything else out of his mind and enjoy the opportunity.

On his way out he passed Nigriv coming back into the house.

"Going somewhere?"

"Dinner with Lady Tarna."

"What does she want?"

"She wants me to make more pieces for her."

"So why dinner?"

Ligriv shrugged. It was a good question, not that it mattered really. He was happy to eat with her.

"Don't forget we need to get started on the contract, just because..." there was no need for him to say it "... doesn't stop the agreement that was made. It's up to us now."

"I know." Ligriv walked off. he didn't need to think about that now, his day was over.

The mayor's house was nothing particularly spectacular nor extravagant but some of the items from Lady Tarna's tents had been laid out inside. Several rugs brightened up the main floor and he could smell more incense burning.

Ligriv sat nervously in a chair watched by a guard waiting for Lady Tarna to appear. When she did, his heart jumped into his throat. She was wearing an emerald green gown and her hair was tied into a bun, but what excited him the most was the ruby amulet pinned on her chest.

She saw his eyes lock on it. "Do you like it?"

"Well, of course, but on its own it doesn't look anywhere as impressive as you make it."

A small smile formed on her face. "How sweet, Ligriv."

What she said was such a simple thing but it made him feel light and very much alive.

"Come, let's go and sit at the table. I'm sorry that there's not much to this place, but we have made do."

He felt awkward again, sat opposite her, and was grateful when she offered him a drink of wine. She waved the only guard out of the room without a word.

"Tell me more about this place, Ligriv."

"There's not much to tell. You've probably seen the whole town already."

That partial smile formed again on her face but she said nothing.

"Is there something you would like to know?"

"You were born here?"

"No."

"So where were you born then?"

"In Malamig, way to the north."

"I remember, that's where you found the stone isn't it?"

Suddenly Ligriv's mind darted off to recall where his stone was. He patted his pocket but already knew it wasn't there.

"What's wrong?"

"It's nothing."

"Come on now, you can tell me."

He looked into her hazel eyes that were locked on him, and any thought of not answering disappeared.

"The stone, I'm not sure where I left it."

"That's not good." Her face had hardened, the smile wiped from it.

"It's alright, I just don't have it on me."

"That's no ordinary stone, Ligriv."

"What do you mean?"

"Exactly what I said."

"I know it's rare but…"

"Is that not enough?" she snapped. "Others might try to take it from you, that would not be good."

Ligriv was confused at her change in mood. It was just a stone, albeit not the usual ones, and he knew that Nigriv didn't like to touch it, but that was all.

As though nothing had happened, her smile came back, her eyes softened and the atmosphere changed. "We should talk about your work."

"What did you want me to make?"

"Perhaps it would be better if you made me something that you think will suit me best? You did such a wonderful job of this amulet."

"I didn't know it was for you at the time."

The smile broadened. "Of course, but it was very inspired. Do you think you can find the same inspiration?"

Right at that moment a woman appeared carrying bowls of food. For the next hour they were served food in several stages and the rest of the conversation, as little as there was, centred on that.

"I have quite a few stones I brought back from Midderbuilt. Maybe you could pick one to make it easier?"

She wiped her face with a small cloth and stared back into his eyes. "If you wish."

"Then I can come up with a design for it to show you."

"No need for me to be so involved, Ligriv, that's what you're here for. Where are these stones?"

He paused for a moment, thinking back over his day. "In my workshop… that's where the amber is as well, I remember now."

"You've just left them there?"

"It's Barrack, no one will bother them there."

"What about the thieves that attacked you? Were you not warned about that as well?"

He dropped his eyes from hers. She was right, he knew that, but despite it he didn't want to revisit that topic.

"Maybe we should go and check on it… on them, I mean, just to be safe. I could choose one right now and be done with it."

"There's no need, I'll do it on the way back."

"I think I'd prefer if one of my men accompanied you and besides, now that you've awakened my curiosity about which gem to pick, I would like to do that."

"It's dark, choosing a stone is best in the light."

Again her face hardened and she stared at him. "We should go." It wasn't a question and much more than a statement. Her words came out as a command and he bristled a little at them.

"Sorry, Ligriv, that came out far too harshly. You can tell I've been travelling with just my guards for such a long time now, I've lost all my manners. I'm happy to go with you, even a little excited in fact."

And again her eyes changed and he felt much more comfortable about her suggestion. He was ready to go if she wanted.

"Now?"

"Why not?"

Two of the guards, in their full black clothing, walked behind the pair as Ligriv led Lady Tarna back to his workshop. Despite changing he still wore the key to the door's padlock around his neck, on a leather cord.

One of the guards rushed ahead of them as they approached the building, seeing what Ligriv only just noticed now: the doors had been prised open, breaking the section of wood that the padlock secured and creating an opening wide enough for a person.

He hurried after the guard and fumbled hurriedly through unlocking the padlock so the door could be properly opened. It took him another minute to get a lantern lit and brought to where the others had gathered.

A man, unknown to Ligriv, lay flat on his back. His eyes were wide open, staring up at the ceiling, but he wasn't seeing anything, he appeared to be dead.

The fingers of his left hand cradled Ligriv's orange stone.

"You were saying?" Lady Tarna looked at Ligriv.

"Who is he?"

She shook her head.

"Why is he dead, there's nothing wrong with him."

Footsteps behind them caused everyone to turn.

"What's happening?"

It was the mayor and several of the other townsmen.

"Someone broke into my workshop." Ligriv was still shocked.

"Who?"

"I don't know." Ligriv pointed to the man on the ground.

"What happened to him?"

Lady Tarna and her guards had stepped back a little.

"Why is she here?"

"We were coming to look at some things I brought back from Midderbuilt."

"Did one of you attack this man?"

"We found him like this," the lady replied calmly, "just as Ligriv said, when all of us arrived together."

The mayor looked back at Ligriv. "Is that true?"

Ligriv nodded, still staring down at the man lying on the ground.

"What's he holding?" The mayor moved closer to see in the dim light.

"It's one of my stones."

"Let me see..." he leaned in to pick it up.

"Don't do that!" Lady Tarna's voice was sharp. "Ligriv, you should retrieve it, no one else. Remember how your brother didn't like it!"

He felt something like a push, although it came from no one, and moved past the mayor and pulled the dead man's fingers apart before taking back the amber stone.

"May I?" The mayor was looking curiously at both him and Lady Tarna.

"I'd don't think you should."

The mayor looked at him but said nothing.

"El, are you alright?"

Ligriv turned to see his brother coming into the workshop followed by others. It looked like half the Single Fiddler inn had arrived, including Yommo, Sillamone the keeper and her daughter Gantcy.

"Yes, but..." He pointed at the body.

Nigriv came alongside him and looked down. "What happened?"

"That's still to be determined," the mayor answered. "But on first glance it would look like he was in here trying to steal Ligriv's things."

"You're alright?" Nigriv asked.

Ligriv nodded.

"I don't think we'll find out anything more tonight, perhaps we can try and figure out who he is in the morning."

"You're not leaving him here are you?" Ligriv asked.

"No, son. But we'll want to look about tomorrow." He turned to Yommo and some of the others. "Let's get this out of here."

They lifted the dead man and walked him out. Slowly others left as well leaving Lady Tarna, her guards and the twins.

"He had my stone."

"Which stone?"

Ligriv opened his fist and showed his brother.

"I've never liked that. What's she doing here?"

"We came to look at the gems I have."

"Hello, Nigriv." Lady Tarna stepped out of the shadows and approached them.

Nigriv turned to her but said nothing.

Ligriv didn't know why his brother was being rude to her but he was in no mood to discuss it with him now.

"I'm going home. Are you coming, El?"

Ligriv looked at him, then at her, before nodding. "In a minute, I just need to secure things here."

"Want a hand?"

"I can manage."

He went to the drawer and pulled out the two pouches containing the gems and the gold, glad they were still there, and pocketed them. "Maybe we can look at stones tomorrow?"

"Of course, Ligriv. But keep the amber on you at all times, you must not let others touch it again."

"Why not?"

"It's not for others, Ligriv. Do you understand?"

He didn't, not really, but she waited until he nodded.

"We should go." She said to her guards. And just like that they left the workshop. He locked the door as best he could, not as bothered about it now that he had his valuables with him.

His twin was waiting just off to the side. "Shall we go home now?"

Ligriv nodded and started walking. He was still trying to work out what had killed the man and why Lady Tarna was so uptight about the amber. All this talk about it being special, and the boys' marks seemed to be less of a tall tale than he'd believed.

He held it tight the entire way home, and even when he lay down in bed. There'd been too many dead bodies recently for his liking.

3 2

LIGRIV

*I*n his dreams, Ligiv saw dead men everywhere. They were at his workshop, throughout the house, out in the roads, anywhere he went there were dead bodies.

When he got up he felt just as exhausted as he had when he'd lain down last night. He stumbled down to the empty kitchen rubbing his eyes. The heart of the house was never going to be the same while Esphe wasn't in it.

Feeling guilty for taking Berrell's tunic yesterday he carefully opened the door to see if the women were awake. Esphe was partially sat up, staring at him as he poked his head through the door.

"Good, someone to take over from me." Madame Ayla leapt out of the chair beside the bed, surprisingly energetic for someone her age.

"I have to…"

"I've been here the last few days non-stop, I have things to take care of. You should watch over her until I'm back."

"I am more than capable of looking after myself, Ayla." Esphe's voice was flat but at least she was speaking.

"You need to rest."

"Lying here isn't rest."

"Do as I say."

The healer gathered up her things and hurried past Ligriv toward the front door. "I'll be back later. Make sure she eats."

He didn't know what to do and stood there awkwardly for a minute or so. Eventually he went and sat in the chair beside the bed.

"How do you feel?"

Esphe turned to look at him slowly. "Dead."

His heart ached for her. He knew she would be upset but this was more than that, she looked like the life in her had faded.

"He wasn't meant to be in that place... I should never have made him take you boys."

"It wasn't your fault, Esphe."

"He'd never have gone if Orthtan had left him well alone. My Berrell would still be here."

Silence fell over the room as she slumped back down again. Neither moved or spoke until Nigriv appeared in the doorway.

"You're awake?" His voice was more animated than anything else in the room.

Esphe looked up at him but said nothing.

He turned to look at Ligriv. "We should get her up, she needs to eat something."

"Madame Ayla said she needs rest."

"I can make up my own mind about what I want."

Both boys looked at her.

Then suddenly she clambered off the bed and brushed past them into the kitchen. Ligriv followed after his brother. Esphe set to work in her kitchen without saying a word.

Ligriv knew better than to get in her way and waited at the table beside his brother. There would be no oats this morning; the fire had gone out the day they'd returned and it would take too long to get it ready.

After a short while she placed cut bread, butter and a jam from her store on the table and sat down with the boys.

Ligriv ate several slices and was glad for it, but the kitchen was devoid of the warm feelings that he was used to there. The atmosphere was so cold that he was glad to finish eating and head to his workshop.

What surprised him as he left their property was that one of Lady Tarna's guards was outside waiting for him.

"What are you doing here?"

"My mistress wanted to make sure no harm would come to you."

"Why, is there something you know I am not aware of?"

The man rolled his eyes as though Ligriv should know why. "Someone tried to steal from you… you have a lot of gold coin and the stone."

"Did you know the thief?"

The guard shook his head and pointed down the road, indicating they should get going. Ligriv didn't need a guard in Barrack, it was silly, but he wasn't going to argue with the man.

Dealing with Esphe had stopped him thinking about what had happened last night, but now he could think of nothing else. Almost nothing else.

That Lady Tarna was concerned enough to send a guard for his protection, even though it was unnecessary, pleased him and he couldn't help smiling a little bit. Thankfully he was in front of the man in black who was none the wiser.

Even more pleasing was that she was waiting at his workshop when they arrived. He'd not expected to see her this morning and was happy for it. Perhaps she might be more forthcoming about the stone and what was said last night.

"Good morning, Ligriv."

"Lady Tarna. I wasn't expecting you, or your guard."

"There is much to discuss, and I wanted to make sure you were safe."

He looked at his workshop's entrance. The door was going to be one of the first things he needed to fix -- the fact he'd padlocked it last night was almost laughable, it wasn't stopping anyone.

When he'd dragged both doors open they went inside. Ligriv tended to his fire, adding fuel and stoking it, using the bellows until he had it burning strongly.

Then he joined Lady Tarna who had sat herself on a stool beside his workbench.

"There really isn't much to be worried about, I'm a big boy."

"And yet you were attacked on your way home to Barrack and now someone broke into your workshop. I think that's more than enough to cause alarm." She wasn't asking for his opinion. "There are men who would cut another man's throat for a single gold coin, even less, and I'll not have that happen to you, dear Ligriv."

The way she was speaking so affectionately to him made his heart flutter a little, causing his face to flush.

"Don't be embarrassed, I am serious. There's many reasons that I want you safe, including what we were planning last night when we came here."

Ligriv had to think about it for a few moments. "Choosing the gemstone you'd like me to work on?"

"Yes, but overnight I wondered if perhaps there's not a better option."

"Such as?"

Her eyes bored into his in a way he couldn't resist, and his adoration for her rose with it. "I'm very interested in your stone."

"In what way?" Her focus on the amber gem didn't bother him like it did with other people.

"You should work on that."

"For you? I…"

"No, silly." Again the lightness and familiarity of her tone pleased Ligriv. "I just think you should work on it, I want to see what you can do with the amber. I think you'll be amazed at what it looks like after you've spent time on it."

"But what about your jewellery?"

"You'll have enough days to make me some more things, Ligriv, but I think this… this is what I'd like to see."

"It's important to you isn't it?"

She let a broader smile form on her face. "Oh, you're so sensitive, you can read my emotions already."

They sat quietly for a minute or two, Ligriv unsure what he should say.

"Like I said, I'm very excited to see what you can do." Lady Tarna stood abruptly, stepped closer to him and leaned in to kiss Ligriv on the cheek, taking him by complete surprise. And then she twirled quickly and left without saying another word.

Everything in his workshop felt different. He wanted to jump up and yell out at the top of his lungs. The light in the room seemed different and he felt his heart beating fast in his chest.

Her impact on him was significant, he'd never felt so much for someone before. *She can't really be interested in me, surely. It's just my work she loves.*

There was so much he didn't know about her but none of it mattered anymore, not after that kiss or the way her voice had risen excitedly as she spoke about him.

That this wealthy noblewoman would show interest in him, a simple lapidarist… he'd never expected that. All he could think about now was living up to her desire and creating something special from the stone.

He set up his bench so he could roughly mark up some ideas on the top of it with a charcoal stick. But his mind wouldn't bring him any inspiration, every piece of jewellery he tried to sketch felt wrong.

In truth he'd hoped it would be just like in Midderbuilt where the ruby and the idea simply came to him, but nothing was happening. To have to live up to his own work was something he'd never experienced before, and now the pressure to please her made it even harder.

He was becoming more and more frustrated and put down the charcoal and placed his elbows on the bench ready to sink his head into his hands.

And then he saw it.

In the middle of his palm was the mark he and his twin both had, ever since their birth. The shape of a teardrop. Exactly like the white stone Hembleth had given to his brother, that was what he was going to cut the amber into.

Why it made sense to replicate that, he didn't know, but in his bones he could feel that it was what the gem wanted him to do. Somewhere in his memories he knew that the strange old man had told them something about the two stones, but Ligriv couldn't recall what it was.

He didn't want to waste any more time and took the stone to his polishing wheel. The outside was very rough and he was going to need to gently grind the surface away to form the basic shape he'd need.

For hours he sat on the stool, holding the stone with pincers, cranking the handle to keep the wheel spinning and taking away only slivers of it. Little-by-little he cut back the outer edges.

His focus was entirely on his work, made easier by the fact he could see the shape of the teardrop within the stone and all he was doing was just freeing it. With all his cutting done Ligriv cleaned his equipment and then, using a much softer paste, began to polish his stone, feeling excited about what he'd made.

Hours later he realised he was done, the stone was finished. He held it up to check out his handiwork and saw how late it was getting. The sun was dipping down on the western side of town and he'd need his lanterns lit before long.

It's perfect.

"You're still working?"

Ligriv jumped in fright at the voice.

"Easy, brother, it's just me."

He turned to Nigriv, surprised at his own reaction to the voice he knew so well.

"Sorry, I was miles away."

"So it seems. You alright?" Nigriv walked up to the bench.

"Yes... I was absorbed on this."

"It's just like mine!"

Ligriv nodded. He couldn't explain the inspiration to copy the shape but he was very happy with how it had turned out. Now it wasn't just the touch of the stone that set him at ease, he could see the magnificence of the stone as well.

"Why did you cut it now after all this time?"

Ligriv explained to his brother about Lady Tarna's wish to see it and her love of the stone. He even talked a little about her affection toward him.

"Careful, brother, sounds like she's snared you." His brother's face had a big grin on it.

Ligriv quickly changed the topic. "How's Esphe?"

"She's doing things but not like she used to."

"Nor would you expect her to."

Ligriv could tell from Nigriv's look that he didn't understand what Ligriv meant.

"She's making us dinner. You coming to eat?"

"Yes."

In truth he wanted to go to Lady Tarna and show her what he'd made, but she'd not asked him to dinner so he didn't think he should turn up uninvited. He could show her tomorrow and he was concerned about Esphe.

It would be good if they could get back to something resembling normality. He wished he could help her but knew that it would take time, even if his brother couldn't understand that.

The walk back with his twin felt like older times. He felt safe alongside his brother, he always had, and he was glad for that part of their connection. He couldn't imagine it not being there.

NIGRIV

Nigriv had been working through the pile of work that had built up for them while they'd been away. From some small jewellery items to mostly smithy-type work, as well as the contract with Aarin.

That was who was standing in front of him now.

"I thought we had a deal, Nigriv?"

"We do, Aarin, but we've only just got back and then..." He didn't need to say it, the man already knew.

"I understand and I have sympathies, I do, but I paid a deposit and I need to get that back one way or another."

"You'll get the bracelets, I promise. I've already started on them, I just need to clear some of these other things off my plate as well, then it's all you."

"What about your brother?"

"He'll help, we'll get them done. Just give me some time."

"Alright but not long, you hear me? We had a deal and I expect it delivered."

It wasn't like Nigriv wasn't trying but at least he'd consoled the trader, for now at least. He needed his brother's help but Ligriv had only been working on the rich woman's pieces the whole time.

Nigriv needed to talk to him about it and loaded up the barrow with items that would be easier to work in Yommo's workshop. As he pushed them toward the workshop his mind mulled over all the things bothering him.

The biggest of them all was the missing connection to his brother. It had been gone all week and Nigriv didn't understand why.

Nigriv needed to understand things, he sought out the reasons behind events and why people did what they did, unlike his brother. Not that it made sense to him very often but he still pursued it anyway.

The break in their connection had happened several times before and he couldn't find a pattern to it. He'd noticed it on the walk to Midderbuilt, especially the closer they had gotten, and now again this past week.

When Nigriv rolled the barrow into the shed Ligriv was sat at his workbench. His brother looked up at him.

"What's this?"

"Work that needs doing, El. You're not helping and there's all this needing smithing plus the contract."

"I've got my own work to do, brother, you know that."

"And we have to deliver the contract for Aarin, that Master Berrell agreed to."

Ligriv didn't say anything and Nigriv assumed he was just going to accept what he said like always.

"Why is it our problem anyway? Master Berrell made the agreement, I sure didn't."

"Don't start that again. He made it with us, for us, we've already had money for some of it."

"Then I'll pay him back, why does it matter?"

"That's your solution to everything now? I've got coin!" Nigriv noticed he was annoyed with his brother, which was unusual in itself. Even stranger was Ligriv arguing back.

"I have the coin… and more with these pieces, she's paying me a gold coin per completed piece, two for some."

"It's about what's right, have you forgotten that? Berrell made a deal, it's ours to stick to."

"You're such a stickler for silly rules, what does it matter?"

"It matters because long after your mistress has gone we'll need customers to work with and our reputation is how we'll get them."

"She's not my mistress. And she pays a lot better than that merchant does for those stupid bracelets."

Nigriv shook his head, feeling angry at his brother.

"You can't see what's going on, you're blinded by her."

"And what is going on, mister seer?" Ligriv's tone was snarkier than Nigriv had ever heard from him before.

"She's using you, pretending to like you so she can get what she wants from you... Mark my words, she'll be gone soon and you'll never hear from her again."

Ligriv's face had become angry. It was one thing he had learned to recognise in his brother.

"You're jealous, aren't you?"

"Of what?"

"Her and me. How much she paid me."

Nigriv could see he wasn't going to get through to his brother and shook his head. "I don't have time for this nonsense. These need smithing, you can do it when you're finished fawning around like a puppy."

He turned and left the workshop not understanding his brother at all. They'd always stuck to their word and done the right thing before, he didn't get why this would be different to him.

As he walked he began scratching at his arm without realising it, distracted by how silly he thought his brother was being. He didn't know what to do with him, to help him see the truth.

Ligriv was putting this woman first over what was the right thing to do. She was to blame, Nigriv was sure of that. He thought about what his brother had said, about him being jealous, but it wasn't that at all.

Inside he felt there was something off about that woman, about her being here, and what she was using her brother for, but that was all that it was and he didn't know how else to explain it.

Having seen how his brother reacted just now he knew it wouldn't matter what was said to him. Ligriv was infatuated with her and was going to do whatever she bid of him.

What will happen when she goes? He's going to be devastated.

It was bad enough watching what had happened to Esphe since Berrell had gone, he wasn't sure he could handle her and his brother as well.

His brother was so absorbed with Lady Tarna that he wouldn't even realise the impact. But it did explain the lack of connection between the two boys.

Nigriv had always assumed the way they understood each other was inbuilt and unique, but now he was having to accept that it was about affections or something similar. When the two boys were together he could feel it come back but it didn't last, and when Ligriv was with her then Nigriv could sense nothing.

His life was feeling very empty at the moment. When he wasn't working he was caring for Esphe who, at best, was going through the motions of living.

She hardly ate and said little. The house felt empty much of the time, and now when he thought about the relationship with his brother he had a similar hollow feeling inside.

Not for the first time Nigriv wished they'd never gone to Midder-built. He didn't need his token and he wished his brother had never made that amulet or met this woman.

It was true what he'd said about Lady Tarna, he didn't trust her even if he couldn't say why. Just being around her rubbed him the wrong way. Worse was how pleasant to him she always was.

Nigriv didn't find her genuine at all, but it was much more than just her falseness. It was a gut instinct he had, but that wasn't going to change his brother's mind.

I've got to stop this.

If he pursued it with Ligriv it would become a bigger wedge

between them and Nigriv didn't want that at all. He'd already said too much, that was obvious.

The last thing he wanted was to have his brother avoiding him. As he entered the house he could smell the meal Esphe was cooking which was a positive.

"Where is your brother?" Esphe asked, a hint of sadness in her voice.

"Same place he always is," Nigriv answered.

Normally that would be about all she said, but when she placed their food on the table she started up again. Her face was brighter than it had been, and her tone seemed different, as though she was talking to Berrell.

"I worry about him and that woman. I don't trust her..."

Nigriv looked at her, not sure if he should answer or not. Esphe's eyes were a little glassy and she seemed to be speaking to the empty space on his left.

"She's no girl, that's the problem!" Esphe's words were as sharp as Nigriv had ever heard them.

There was a gap just as there would be if she was listening to someone speaking. Nigriv was worried about her, this wasn't normal.

"What woman her age wants a boy of his? It's not right, that's what I'm saying. What happens when she goes? It will break him."

Nigriv had to speak up. "It's alright, Esphe, we've been through worse." He knew it was different when their father had died and that his brother would be upset, but deep down he didn't mind that at all.

Across the table Esphe's face changed. She turned to look at him, then back to the empty seat and then her face broke. Whatever she'd been seeing before was gone and the realisation about her husband being gone flooded back.

She collapsed on the table, sobbing and wailing, and Nigriv had no idea what to do. After a while he lifted her up and walked her back to her room and covered her with a blanket, sitting there until she fell asleep.

He cleaned up the kitchen but didn't know what to do next. It was too early to go to sleep and the house was feeling too small. After checking Esphe was still asleep he headed over to the Single Fiddler for an ale, hoping the noise and people might make a difference.

Nothing stays the same.

At the bar he was served by Gantcy, the keeper's daughter. At least she had a smile for him.

"Where's your brother?"

Nigriv shrugged, not wanting to say anything bad.

"Always the man of few words."

"Is that wrong?"

She smiled at him and shook her head. That was about as much as the pair of them had ever said to each other. Part of him wanted a conversation with someone, except it was his brother that he missed, nor did he know what to say to her anyway.

Someone else called her over and she walked off, the moment passing. Nigriv sipped his ale and then took it to a side table, not so sure this was such a good idea after all.

Everywhere seemed to have a different atmosphere these days, ever since they'd got back. Usually he'd be here with Ligriv and Berrell. That wasn't going to happen again. He could only hope that the noblewoman would leave soon and he and his brother could go back to how things used to be.

When he got home he poked his head into the bedroom downstairs. As best he could tell in the dark, Esphe was still asleep. Ligriv wasn't back which wasn't unusual, Nigriv was surprised his brother was still sleeping here at all these days.

Nigriv lay down and stared up in the dark, wondering what was going to help make things right again. He rubbed at his arm for a while before turning on his side and falling asleep.

3 4

LIGRIV

*L*igriv had been too annoyed to go home or visit Lady Tarna last night after the argument with his brother. They'd never had a disagreement like that before, and it wasn't something he enjoyed.

For much of their life Ligriv had always avoided letting anything come between them, he'd found it much easier to just let his brother make decisions.

But Nigriv's words against Lady Tarna weren't something he could let slide by. As far as Ligriv could tell, his twin was jealous of him and his relationship and was trying to get between them.

That's how it felt and he'd let him know he wasn't going to accept it. Nor did he care much for the work Nigriv was so worried about. But that was just a mask for what really bothered his brother, he was sure of that.

After spending much of the evening at his workshop, eventually he went home and thankfully his brother had been asleep. Ligriv was up and gone early and back at his workshop but still the disagreement was bubbling away under his skin.

He pulled the teardop-shaped amber from his pocket and polished it with a cloth again, trying to find any imperfections in it.

There were none and he knew there was nothing more he could do with it.

A sense of calm came over him, washing away the thoughts of his brother and their argument. Inside he felt great and excited about what Lady Tarna would think of it.

She had said it was her favourite stone and he wanted more of it so he could craft her the jewellery she wanted. But he had none other than his teardrop to use; he needed to get some of what she had.

Unable to think about anything else he decided to chance turning up to see her uninvited. He pocketed the teardrop, locked the workshop and headed over to the mayor's home.

The guard outside the front gate let him through but the one at the front door made him wait while they went inside. Ligriv was nervous standing there, unsure how he'd be received.

After several minutes the guard reappeared and beckoned him inside the house to a large waiting room. A minute later Lady Tarna arrived.

"Ligriv, I wasn't expecting you." Her tone was clam, neither frosty nor warm.

"I wasn't sure about turning up unannounced but…" He paused.

"What is it?"

"The stone… I wanted to show you what I did with it."

She stepped closer, an expectant look on her face. "You've finished already?"

He nodded and reached into his pocket. Ligriv didn't have the patience or will to delay this and held it up in between them.

Lady Tarna's eyes and mouth opened in surprise, causing Ligriv to wonder if she didn't like what he'd made.

"Oh, Ligriv, this is… something else."

He felt his cheeks redden and smiled.

"Why this shape?"

"You don't like it?"

"Oh, I do… I do very much. I am curious though, why this shape?"

Ligriv felt silly telling her but she held her gaze firmly on his eyes. "It's this." He held up his palm.

She saw the dark red mark on his hand and gasped.

"What's wrong?"

Lady Tarna reached out and placed a hand on his shoulder. "Nothing, Ligriv, nothing at all. I was just… it doesn't matter."

"So you like it?"

"Yes. It confirms to me that I made the right choice. Can I hold it?"

Ligriv let her take it from him and roll it around in her hands. He could have sworn he saw flickers of light within it, like a tiny flame, but when she handed it back there was nothing inside.

"This is amazing."

"What is?"

"I've been looking for someone who can work amber like this, for the longest time."

"There aren't lapidarists back in…"

"Enderk, dear."

"That's it… Enderk."

"There are, but not like you, Ligriv, no one quite like you."

"Do you have any more with you that I could work on?"

"Nothing like that, unfortunately. I wish I did, but it's all back home."

"Oh."

"What's wrong?"

"I…" Ligriv wasn't sure he wanted to say anything, but went on anyway. "I wanted to make you something in amber given it's your favourite stone."

"You are such a sweet one, Ligriv, always thinking about me." She leaned in again and kissed his cheek and he felt like time just stopped.

When she pulled away his face was flushed and he was sweating.

"I should go, it was just important to me to show you."

"You were right to do so. Please come any time, I love having you by my side."

"Really?"

"Of course I do… you don't think I came all this way just for some jewellery do you?" She winked at him and before he could say anything continued, "Now go back and do your things and I'll see you later tonight."

Still elated from the kiss and her words, Ligriv wasn't bothered by her sending him away and was lost in his thoughts the whole way back to his workshop.

He was certain now he needed to make her something special, something that wasn't for coins, despite her previously saying she wanted to pay for his time.

This was different now, she'd said it was, and he unlocked his storage box and pulled out the pouch of gems he still had from Midderbuilt. Ligriv laid them all out on his bench and cast his eyes over them seeking inspiration.

In the end it was easy: the ruby he chose would match the one in the amulet she already had. He put the others away and set to work on the gem.

* * *

It took him three days to complete everything exactly the way he wanted. As he held up the earrings to the light he felt pride in how good his work was. The silver settings were as identical as he could get them without having the amulet to work off.

He was sure that his memory was good enough and despite how delicate and tiny the settings were, he knew they would look exquisite alongside the amulet.

Ligriv just wanted Tarna to love them as much as he did. They were his gift to her, for what she'd already done for him, the coin he'd earned that would take him an age to spend.

It was all hidden, where no one would find it. Not that it mattered, all he wanted was her to be happy… and to be with her. Almost on cue he looked up and there she was, standing in the doorway.

"What is that, Ligriv?"

"These are my latest work for you, my dear."

She marched across to him and he held them out so she could see.

Her eyes lit up and she smiled. "They are beautiful, a perfect match to my amulet."

"Which was my intention. I wanted to make you something special, something from me to you, to thank you for everything you've done, and..." he stumbled over the next words, "...my affection."

If he'd been worried about how she'd reply he hadn't needed to be. She smiled warmly, her cheeks flushing a little. "You're so kind and sweet, Ligriv."

Neither said anything for what seemed to be minutes as her eyes peered deep into his. He felt as though she could see deep inside, into his thoughts and heart, and he had no way of escaping... not that he wanted to.

Tarna looked back at the earrings on the workbench. "May I?"

"Of course, they are yours." He handed them to her.

"They are quite lovely, Ligriv." She leaned in and kissed him on the lips. "I'll see you later?"

"Of course."

She turned and wandered out of the workshop, her guards joining her outside. Ligriv watched her as she walked away, taking in every last part of her.

He felt they were now much closer than ever and he beamed from it. His whole body was alive and warm, as if he was standing out in the middle day sun.

His whole life had been flipped on its head, ever since Midderbuilt. A laugh burst out of him as he thought about how upset he'd been at not winning the token.

That mattered nothing to him anymore, in fact it had been the best thing. His work was clearly the best, he knew that, it had been confirmed by her and she wanted to be with him.

Compared to his brother who might have the token he'd rather be where he was than that. It took Ligriv a moment to accept his thoughts. For the first time he felt very separate to his twin, not just because he couldn't feel the connection like he used to, but in his mind they had very different goals.

Ligriv liked working for Tarna, and he'd like to work for other nobles as well. He liked their respect and the price they'd pay for quality work. He could imagine himself travelling from place to place earning rich rewards.

Or they could come to me, perhaps in Watersend or...

That would mean leaving his brother, unless Nigriv would come with him. That would never happen. Ligriv wondered if he really could go his own way.

He had noticed their connection had been replaced. He felt close to Tarna, there was something between them, particularly when she stared into his eyes. As though they were meant to be together.

There was nothing else to be done today but clean up from his work, and as he busied himself doing so his mind drifted off to places only in his imagination where he might go and sell his skills.

It might only be a dream but Ligriv enjoyed every bit of it.

35

LIGRIV

The mayor's house that Lady Tarna was using for her time in Barrack wasn't huge but it was private, which is what she had told Ligriv mattered most.

During these past few weeks Ligriv's whole life had been turned on its head. He wasn't sure if he was the only guest that visited her in the house; he'd never seen anyone else when he'd come. He wasn't even sure if he was a guest or not. Everything about their relationship confused him, she was quite unlike any other female he'd ever been around.

Tarna was sitting in the main room when he arrived.

"There you are."

"Were you expecting me earlier?" She wasn't smiling like she normally would.

"No, but there's something I need to talk to you about."

Ligriv wasn't sure what he'd expected when he arrived -- he never did with her -- but this sounded serious and he felt nervous.

Tarna patted the couch and Ligriv sat there, a small gap between them.

"What is it?"

She didn't answer immediately but looked deep into his eyes like she had done earlier. All of his anxiety began to melt away.

"The time has come when I need to be getting back home."

Ligriv could feel tightness forming in his chest. This wasn't what he was expecting. "When?"

"Soon, Ligriv, very soon."

"I'll be sorry to see you go." He didn't know what else to say.

She let out a soft chuckle. "You mean my gold."

He felt his face redden. "No! I mean you…"

Tarna placed her hand on top of his and a tingle ran up his arm. "I'm jesting, Ligriv. You know you're special to me, don't you?"

He nodded.

"I have a proposition for you."

"Yes?"

"What you showed me today highlighted that you're so much more than I expected, that you could help me in ways no one else could."

"With your amber?"

She smiled again. "That's what I like about you, Ligriv. Well, one of the things. You're smart and direct."

He felt his face flush again.

"I can't stay here, nor do I have the amber you would need, but…"

Ligriv wondered what she was going to say.

"…you could come with me. It's a long journey but worth it to see the splendour of Enderk."

"Me?"

"Yes you, us, together." She leaned in toward him and placed her lips on his.

Ligriv became lost in the moment and as they kissed deeply he thought of nothing but that moment. When they separated he could still feel her on his lips, as though they were connected.

"I… what does it mean?"

"It means you would be my partner and of course my lapidarist. You can be both things can you not?"

"Of course."

"And you would love it, Ligriv. En Carta, the capital, is the most amazing place."

He was stunned and couldn't say a word.

"And what you've done with that stone, I just know there are many great things we can do together, Ligriv."

He brought his racing mind under some control. "My brother."

"What about him?"

"I don't know if I can leave him."

"There is no space for another in my affections, Ligriv."

"I didn't mean that!"

She laughed. "It was another jest, Ligriv, you need to be less serious."

"I've never been away from him, ever. There's…" Ligriv wanted to say there was a link between them that was always there, but he now knew that wasn't true, but they were still close.

Could I actually leave him? What would Nigriv say?

"I understand it would be hard to leave your family, but I cannot stay here either, Ligriv. You'll need to decide."

He looked back into her eyes and his mind flitted back to the touch of her lips and the feelings he had for her. Now his chest had tightened again at the ridiculous choice he had to make, between his love of this woman and Nigriv.

How has it come to this?

"Stay with me tonight, no need to rush your decision. I will be here for two more days but then I must be gone."

Ligriv nodded and she slid over to him, leaning against his side as they had done many times before. The thought of how they would come together later excited him in ways he couldn't not think about.

Eventually they went upstairs to her room and he became lost in their lovemaking, unsure how long it lasted. Afterward, while she slept, he lay awake with the question of what to do rattling around in his mind.

As the sun rose he slipped out of her bed, dressed and left the guest house, heading for his workshop. He was tired, his head felt muddled, and he hoped his workshop would give him space to work out what to do.

There was no one he could ask for advice either. Had Berrell still been around, Ligriv would have sought out their mentor's opinion. He certainly couldn't ask his brother, not after their recent argument, and because it involved him.

Ligriv stoked the fire and pottered around the workshop trying to let the familiarity of it ease his angst. There was little for him to do, he always left it spotless, unlike his twin.

It wasn't the only difference. There were probably as many things different as there were the same. None of that mattered, he'd never been apart from Nigriv. Never… and the thought of it brought tears to his eyes.

Enderk?

All he knew was that it was a long way away, far off to the east. How would they stay in touch? Would they visit? Nigriv wasn't keen on travel, he was more than happy living here in Barrack.

I'll have to be the one to visit, to stay in touch.

Would they though? Or would he be splitting them forever?

Tarna was important to him, so very important, and he loved her desperately. *She does love me, doesn't she? That's why she wants me to go.*

Ligriv wrestled with the thoughts and the cynicism he had that she just wanted his skill, but then he remembered last night and the other nights between them. He couldn't believe she didn't, she…

Enough!

He wandered back and forth in the workshop, staring into the flames of his fire for hours repeating the same questions and answers until his head hurt.

The whole time he held the amber stone in his hand, letting it help ease his angst, until he decided on what he would do.

He had his answer and it wasn't going to please everybody, he knew that. But some things were more important than others and he couldn't argue with that. He didn't really want to argue at all.

Ligriv locked the workshop and slowly walked back home, his heart feeling very heavy and an immense sadness filling his body.

36

NIGRIV

Nigriv was stunned.

"I'm in love with her."

He and Ligriv were sat across from each other while his brother told him he was leaving. While the connection wasn't like it had been Nigriv had never expected that they'd ever be apart. Living in different houses, yes, but this… this was something different.

"I'm going to go with her to Enderk, her homeland."

"I know nothing about it."

"I only know a little, but that's about to change."

Nigriv wanted to say something, to talk his brother out of it, but he couldn't. This time it was he who wouldn't argue. It wasn't that he couldn't but he had nothing to say.

He didn't expect to feel any emotions, that wasn't how he worked. Even when their father had died in front of him, Nigriv only saw the practical side of it.

Losing Berrell had felt strange to him but he hadn't brooded over it and struggled to understand how destroyed Esphe was by that. This was different though, this was his twin, his brother, they'd been together always.

It was completely nonsensical that Ligriv would leave him… them.

There was nothing he could relate it to. The only feeling he could ever reach was anger, but he couldn't even find that inside. Not today.

There was something else, a sense of someone or something, almost like words being spoken out of range of his hearing. He couldn't hear anything but he felt its intent, that that he shouldn't let Ligriv go with this woman.

Yet he couldn't say a thing, he couldn't have his brother go and they be at odds. There was nothing he could say or do to make him see through the facade that Nigriv believed Tarna had.

If only I had proof.

But he didn't have any and all it would sound like was jealousy. It was clear he didn't like the woman despite not knowing her well. He didn't want to know her, he just wanted her to go and leave his brother alone.

He wished he'd paid more attention to that instinct and sought out some way to help Ligriv see it too. But he'd just expected her to up and move on, to leave and upset his brother.

Not take him with her!

"When?"

"Within a few days."

"That quick?"

Ligriv nodded.

"And when will you come back?"

"I don't know."

They might only be across the table from each other but a gulf had formed between them that Nigriv couldn't cross. A chill ran down his spine at Ligriv's words, a warning perhaps. Nigriv opened his mouth to say something but didn't.

Later he'd ask himself if it would have made a difference, if it would have kept him there, but by then it wouldn't matter.

"You don't seem upset."

"What do you want from me, brother? I don't want you to go, you're part of me, but… why would I try and stop you?"

"I don't know…"

"Do you want me to try and stop you?"

"No."

"So then we should not fight about something that doesn't matter. We're brothers, nothing changes that, no matter where you are."

Ligriv's eyes were moist. Nigriv knew this was not easy on his brother either, he wouldn't know what he'd do in the same position. Not that Nigriv needed to make such a decision, there was no one else in his life except his brother.

And Esphe.

"You'll have to tell her!"

"What?"

"Esphe, you'll have to tell her you're going."

"Will she even know?"

"Of course she will."

Nigriv thought his brother was going to argue with him again but he didn't. He just nodded his head.

"I'll speak to you tomorrow when I know more, then I'll tell her."

"Fair enough."

Ligriv got up and went out, leaving Nigriv alone in the kitchen. There was a chance that Esphe had heard them from her room, but he hoped not. She was a handful as it was and Nigriv didn't want her any more upset.

For the first time, he was having to contemplate what his future was going to be. Prior to Midderbuilt there was nothing he'd have changed, but now it had all changed around him.

He wished they'd never gone. He wished his brother was just upstairs and they were going about their lives like they had before.

The anger began to surface now and all of it was directed toward Lady Tarna. Nigriv didn't want to be angry; the only times he really got angry people normally got hurt, and he wouldn't do that to his brother.

He walked slowly up the old stairs to his room and dug into his things to pull out the stone Hembleth had given him all those years ago. It always made him feel better.

As he pulled it out, the small pouch he'd forgotten about came with it. He pulled out the ring and placed it on his finger, with the teardrop in the same hand.

His anger eased but that other sensation was much stronger now. It wasn't his imagination, he could almost hear something. The feeling he was getting was all about Ligriv and Tarna, that he shouldn't let it happen.

But he couldn't… he wouldn't. It wasn't his job to stop his brother. His unease grew again. Annoyed that he couldn't find peace holding the stone, he put it and the ring away again and returned downstairs.

Hours passed with him sat in the kitchen unable to find peace with his thoughts about Ligriv's love and why the wealthy woman wanted him. None of it made any sense. Not that his brother wasn't a great person, but they weren't the same.

She wanted something else or wanted to use him, and all Nigriv could see was problems.

* * *

Two days later Nigriv found himself hugging his brother outside the house as they said their goodbyes. He felt detached, almost cold, to what was happening, in contrast to the obvious emotion Ligriv was exhibiting.

"It's time."

"Be well, brother. Come back soon."

"And maybe you can come visit."

"Of course." As he said the words Nigriv knew it was a lie. Wherever his brother was going, Nigriv would never go there to see him. He didn't know how he knew that but he did.

"I will send word when I arrive."

Nigriv nodded and they lapsed into a long silence. Ligriv appeared to be struggling to take that first step that would mark the point of no return. When he did, Nigriv's vision blurred and he became detached from the scene around him.

He was aware of the carriage leaving, he could hear it more than see it, and he remained where he was. Esphe hadn't come out; when Ligriv had told her, she had screamed and cried.

She refused to accept it. Nigriv had gotten Madame Ayla back to give her some herbs to make her sleep, which she was still doing.

The next few hours passed without him even realising. At some point he made his way back inside and sat in the empty kitchen. A numbness had invaded his entire being and he couldn't escape it.

As night fell and the light ran out he didn't light a lamp but stumbled up to his room and collapsed on his bed, not even removing his boots. Nigriv lay facing Ligriv's empty bed, thinking of nothing, feeling nothing.

At some point sleep enveloped him. He couldn't remember, but he woke as sunlight shone through the unshuttered window. He was still facing the empty bed in this silent house.

There was nothing calling him to get up, no one to speak to, so he lay there until he needed to relieve himself, with no choice but to move. As he sat up Nigriv noticed a piece of folded parchment on Ligriv's bed.

When he opened it he saw Ligriv's scratchy handwriting.

I will miss you more than you can understand.

There is no need for me to take the gold.

It's in the woodshed roof.

Nigriv shook his head. *I don't want your gold, brother, it can't replace you.* He took the paper downstairs with him and laid it on the table. As he shuffled around getting food and something to drink he thought about the note. It was the only thing Ligriv had ever written to him but he knew he couldn't keep it.

That information was worth too much to the wrong people. As much as Nigriv wanted to keep it as a reminder of his brother he took it over to the fireplace and spent a minute starting a fire. Once it was burning he watched until the paper was all ash.

Now what?

37

NIGRIV

Days turned into weeks where all Nigriv knew was an eternal numbness. If it wasn't bad enough for him to endure the loss of his twin, Ligriv leaving undid the remaining threads that had kept Esphe sane.

The herbs that Madame Ayla used were only effective for a short time before she became a mumbling mess of a person. No full words came out of her mouth and she had to be cared for constantly.

A group of ladies in the town took turns watching her during the day while Nigriv went about a routine of working before he returned home each night to care for her.

He didn't have any capacity to interrogate what he was experiencing, all he could manage was simply existing. Not that he had any desire to get out of it. Part of him had been ripped away, at least that's how it felt, and he had no way to deal with it.

It was morning and he lay on his side staring at the empty bed opposite him. Every day since Ligriv had gone had begun with the same choice running through his head.

Get up or stay here?

Once again Nigriv rose, dressed and went downstairs. Out of habit he went through the motions of preparing basic food, nothing much, but enough to keep him going and a little for Esphe.

He wanted to be there more for her, like she'd always been for them, but he wasn't sure she even knew who he was. Nor did he know how to break free of the shackles of what his mind and body were behaving like.

The wooden bowl looked ridiculous with two small spoons of porridge in it, but that was as much as he could ever feed Esphe. It was enough to keep her alive, just.

Reluctantly he went to her door, knocked gently on it and opened it, not expecting a reply. The room smelled sweaty and stale like it always did, and before attempting to feed her he placed the bowl on the bedside table and opened the curtain and window.

Even the outside air seemed reluctant to enter so thick was the air of defeat that hung within this room. Esphe was turned away from him and he stepped closer to wake her gently.

She didn't respond to his hand on her shoulder and he had to shake her more forcefully.

"It's me, Esphe, Nigriv... time to have something to eat. Esphe!"

Her body felt more rigid than normal and he pulled her more forcefully, turning her body over, her head following hesitantly. In that moment he knew she had gone.

Nigriv stood there, bowl in hand, looking down at the only mother he'd ever known. The underside of his forearm began to burn, and if it weren't that his other hand was full he'd be scratching it.

That urge to scratch was the only thing pulling at his mind that wasn't numb, but the longer he stood over her the greater the numbness grew until he couldn't even sense his arm.

How long he stood there he couldn't tell, but he was startled back to the present moment by a distant voice then a hand on his shoulder. As he turned he saw Madame Ayla in the room.

"Come, Nigriv, let me deal with this." She led him into the kitchen and took the bowl from his hand. "Head to your work, lad, I've got this."

One foot in front of the other he did exactly that until he arrived at Ligriv's old workshop, that he'd now taken over. For the last few weeks that had been how he got through each day, moment by moment. People would come to collect work he'd finished or to ask for something new, and he was aware of all of that, but it occurred in a daze for him.

Now he truly was alone, in this town without anyone. He managed to get through the day. A few of the ladies came to visit him and they had arranged for a small gathering to bury Esphe.

The mayor came and took him there. He watched throughout the whole event, completely numb to everything that was happening. Several people shed tears and everyone looked at him but there wasn't anything he could offer them.

He retired to his bed that night and at some point slept, wishing that he might not wake from this nightmare he was living in.

* * *

WEEKS PASSED where he rose each morning and made his way to the workshop. Somehow he completed some of the work he was meant to, even Aarin gave him extra time and space on the contract.

Nothing seemed real anymore. The life around him happened but he wasn't an active participant. He preferred living inside his head where he was still connected to his brother and they were together.

It wasn't real and he knew it, but he wished it was. Ever since Ligriv had left he couldn't sense his brother at all. That void where he'd once always been able to touch his brother was where the numbness had come from and Nigriv was glad for it.

Darkness had arrived outside, a trigger for him to return to his empty home. He shuttered his fire, trying to avoid thinking about how little meaning there was in his life. Why was he even here now? The house was his but it no longer felt like a home.

There had been no word from Ligriv, and he was frozen in time, stuck in this place while all of his connections to it were gone. He shrugged and continued with what he was doing, not noticing the arrival of someone.

When he was done he turned and stepped back in shock. The fright of seeing a person in the doorway broke him free of his endless thought loop.

"Hello, Nigriv."

"Gantcy? What are you doing here?"

"Mother sent me."

"Why?"

"She told me to make you come to the inn tonight."

Nigriv looked at her. She was probably around his age, he'd never really thought about her much.

Gantcy stood there with a concerned look on her face but stayed quiet.

"I was just going to go home."

"She told me to get you, don't make me drag you."

For the first time in as long as he could remember Nigriv almost laughed. Gantcy's face remained unchanged. While he was sure she couldn't actually enforce what she'd just told him, she did believe in her task, or at least what her mother had sent her to do.

I'll not embarrass her.

She stepped out of his way as he closed and locked the door, then she turned and headed in the direction of her mother's inn. Nigriv walked alongside her, happy she didn't speak but also strangely happy for the company.

At the door to the inn, she led him in, turned and said, "I need to get back to work," then walked away.

Nigriv looked inside to the main room where all the noise came from and turned back. He didn't want to be around others, he'd rather be at home. The shroud that had been wrapped around his mind began to close again.

"No you don't. Look at the state of you!"

Nigriv turned to see Sillamone standing in the door to the main room, with her hands on her hips. While he might have questioned her daughter's ability to make him do anything he felt the opposite about this broad and physically imposing woman.

"What do you mean?"

"You've near faded into a shadow, boy! When was the last time you had a real meal? I near lost my breath when I saw you this morning. It's been months, boy, you'll die if you keep up like this."

He wasn't sure what she was on about, but she didn't stop.

"Get inside, now! I'll get you a meal and some ale, go and find some of your friends in there. They might all be letting you fade away, but I won't."

She shifted enough that he could squeeze past. Sillamone was not quite as tall as he was and her eyes never left him as he moved inside. He half expected her to grab him by his ear lobe and drag him along.

The main room was filled with chatter and smoke and the mixed smells of ale, cooked meat, fat and sweat. A stool sat off to the side of the main bar area and he headed there until he felt his sleeve grabbed.

"Nigriv, join us son." The voice was deep and familiar.

It belonged to Tharen, one of the farmers on the edge of the town, who had been good friends with Master Berrell. He was sat with a group of the older men that Nigriv knew well.

They made a space for him and before he knew what happened he had a mug of ale in his hand and the warm embrace of companionship to lift his spirits.

Questions began to fly about why he hadn't been in lately, had he heard from his brother and more. Whether he wanted to or not he was forced to talk, and as promised a meal showed up, bigger than he had eaten in weeks.

By the time Sillamone was kicking everyone out he felt like a different person. Some of that was the amount of ale he'd drunk, but the rest was the interest of the people around him.

They were people and friends whose company he enjoyed, he'd just shut himself off from them. As he stood his legs felt a little unstable.

"Woah boy, take it easy."

"I'm fine, good to see you all."

Everyone stood and began to file out of the inn. Nigriv turned to look at Sillamone who stood behind the bar. He nodded and she returned it to him, a small smile on her face.

For the first time since Ligriv had left, Nigriv felt normal, a little too normal for his liking. He still had enough awareness to know he was going to have a sore head in the morning.

NIGRIV

As anticipated Nigriv woke with the sort of headache no one ever wished for but often created for themselves. His head felt as though it was being crushed between two large rocks.

His mouth was dry, his tongue coated with something foul-tasting, and he desperately needed a drink of something to wash it away. But that required Nigriv to move, to get out of bed and find his way downstairs.

He knew a meal would fix it, that and a light ale, but it meant he needed to move and then make something. Slowly he swung himself upright and waited until his head stopped swimming.

As his head cleared a little he heard someone downstairs and recognised the smell of cooking. Despite his mind being heavily impaired he was able to rationalise that if there was a thief in the house, they were highly unlikely to be making him food.

Is Ligriv back?

His spirits lifted at the thought and he hurried his way down the creaky stairs, surprised to see Gantcy fussing over something on the stove.

"Gantcy?"

She turned and looked at him. He didn't think she smiled but she wasn't scowling.

"I thought I'd come back this morning and fix you something, you were not really with it when I put you to bed last night."

"You… what?"

"You don't remember?"

Bits of it flashed across his mind causing the headache to worsen. "Sort of, although I'm sure I would have made it."

"Maybe, or you'd be waking on someone's doorstep." She turned away from him and got back to what she was doing.

"You didn't have to do this, Gantcy."

"I know, but what else did I have to do?"

Nigriv wasn't sure if he should be offended or flattered at her comment. It was nice to have someone here in the house doing something for him.

"Go and clean up, you look a mess. I'm not eating breakfast with you like that. It'll be ready in just a few."

He held his hand up, not wanting to nod, and took a quick drink from a mug she'd filled on the table. With some fluid on board he did as she said. When he returned she was sat at the table with breakfast plated for them both.

She'd fried up beef, smashed potatoes and bacon and once he started he couldn't stop until it was all done. He was a little surprised to see she ate as much as he did. With the food and more light ale on board his head and stomach had settled.

"That's magic, Gantcy, I feel much better. Thank you."

She shrugged. "Can't have you hiding away from everyone, Nigriv. It's not good for you."

"Now you sound like your mother."

She blushed a little at that. It was probably the first time he'd ever seen her show anything remotely like an emotion.

"What's wrong with that?" He didn't understand her reaction.

"You think me old?"

He shook his head as much as it could handle. "No, I didn't mean that at all. You're not old. It's just... never mind, you know what I mean."

She smiled at him, teasingly. "Go do whatever it is you do, I'll clean up here before I go home."

"I can clean up."

"Like it was before?" She was the one shaking her head this time. "I don't think so, you've let everything go, Nigriv. Off with you, it's no bother."

He got up to follow her instructions. "You're sure?"

"Yes!" She had a strength in her voice that he liked. Then she spoke much more meekly. "Will I see you at the inn tonight?"

Nigriv never planned anything these days but felt a little beholden to her for her help. He nodded without thinking about what he was agreeing to, and she smiled at his response.

As he walked toward his workshop he couldn't not think about what had just happened. There had been nothing physical between them, at least not that he could remember.

No, she wouldn't have put up with anything like that, I was clearly far too drunk.

But it felt as though her being there was quite deliberate. She and her mother had inserted themselves in his business without him having any say. Nigriv wasn't sure if he was happy about that or not.

While the breakfast had made a difference it only lasted a few hours and he found it hard to focus. As the morning wore on, his headache grew progressively worse and his attempts to work on his current project, a tin box, were futile.

The job itself was simple, certainly within his abilities, but it required him to hammer the tin. Any noise just made his head hurt more and the heat of the workshop just compounded how he felt.

It was close enough to middle day and Nigriv reasoned that if one meal had helped then an early lunch might be the best option. The only other inn in Barrack, the Wagon Wheel, was slightly further away but he headed that way.

"Haven't seen you here in some time, lad."

"Been busy, Layall."

For an innkeeper Layall didn't feel the need to speak a lot, which suited Nigriv today. He took his jug over to a table in the corner where he could be left to himself. He smiled a few times at familiar people as they came and went but avoided conversations as best he could.

The meal and ale did improve how he felt and as he sat there he found himself thinking about Gantcy. By the time he was done and walking back to the workshop he shook his head, laughing to himself that he might as well have been at her inn, he'd thought about nothing else.

He liked that he could see the humour in it, he'd not had such thoughts in quite some time. *Why does she want me to go back tonight?*

Nigriv knew he wasn't great company and she was right, he hadn't been looking after himself at all. And despite feeling a little better now he wasn't sure that company was what he wanted right now. Not the people in the inn, nor her.

Or do I?

It was relieving that for the first time in weeks his mind was consumed by something other than Esphe, Ligriv and how empty his life felt. Those ever-repeating thoughts about how he'd been left on his own had been pushed to the back of his head.

While he was still overthinking, at least it was about something more pleasant and not negative. Back in his workshop he couldn't find any extra focus for his work and gave up on attempting to be productive.

Feeling called out about his tidiness in the house, Nigriv decided to use the remaining daylight to organise the shop until he was happy enough with what he'd done.

I should just go home, get some sleep and get my head straight.

But he didn't and found himself walking toward Sillamone's place and feeling a hint of anticipation for the first time in ages.

39

LIGRIV

The idea of travelling had always appealed to Ligriv but after days in the carriage he was so bored he wanted to scream. The hours rolled by at a crawl and neither he nor Tarna could fill all that time with talk.

From time to time he would walk alongside to get some exercise and for space. He'd never spent so much time with any one person, except his brother, but that was different.

He regularly thought about Nigriv, wondering what he was doing. Ligriv missed him, missed the deep connection they used to have. He knew that they would have ended up living separate lives but this was much more extreme than he ever imagined.

The loneliness of it surprised him. He'd left to be with his lover but at times he felt more alone than ever. Coupled with the anticipation for where they were going, Ligriv was more confused than he'd ever been.

Seeing such a plethora of new places was his respite from the drudgery of the travel. Unfortunately they never stayed anywhere more than one night, Tarna always pushing to get back as quickly as they could.

The carriage came to a stop, shaking him from his reverie. One of the guards opened the door and waited for Lady Tarna to acknowledge him. She nodded.

"We are here, mistress."

She looked back toward Ligriv. "We'll stay here a few days."

That appealed to him. "Where are we?"

Tarna turned back to her guard and raised her eyebrows. More and more he noticed how authoritative she was to them and at times others.

"The city is called Nkuku, mistress."

She simply nodded and looked at Ligriv.

He waited for the guard to back away from the open door and climbed out, holding his hand out for Tarna. They were outside a large building, the carriage parked on the driveway that circled in from the gates.

It was the biggest and fanciest inn that Ligriv had ever seen. "An inn?"

She chuckled, almost mockingly. "No, Ligriv, it's a private boarding house. We only stay at inns in small towns, where we have no choice."

"Where are we?"

"You heard him."

"Yes, but where is that?"

"A realm called Morska, we're on the border of it."

"How far do we still have to go?"

"Many weeks yet, but we need to replenish supplies and I need to refresh myself." He began to feel that she was tired of his questions.

Two servants hurried out of the building and helped to carry the boxes and bags that filled the back of the carriage.

"I think I will wash and rest some."

Ligriv had no desire to be inside. "I think I might investigate the city."

She looked to her guards. "One of you… accompany him!" It was an order not a question.

"I'll be fine."

"We've had these discussions before, Ligriv. While I appreciate you feel capable of looking after yourself, you're far too valuable to me to have anything happen. Cities like this are quite different from your home town."

As much as what she said, and how, stung his pride, Ligriv didn't feel inclined to argue with her. "Of course."

Once she'd entered the accommodation and was out of sight he spun on his heels and headed to the gate, the presence of other footsteps confirming he had a babysitter.

Ligriv was fascinated with how big everything was, especially the city wall. It enveloped the city as far as he could see and towered above all the buildings, despite them also being multiple storeys high.

Pairs of armed soldiers patrolled the main roadways, all of them sporting the same serious, unfriendly scowl on their face. As they marched along he made sure to stay out of their way.

He wandered aimlessly, enjoying the sights and sounds, stopping occasionally to take in the different people and settings. Ligriv had lost all sense of direction and hoped his guard would remember the way back. By pure chance he found himself on a road filled with jewellers and other craftsmen.

It amazed Ligriv to see so many together in one place. There were two silversmiths side by side. He wondered how on Dharatan they could all survive with so much competition, but each of the stores were well kept and inviting.

The jeweller's nearest to him looked as good as any other and he went in. Rows of different pieces were displayed in a series of glass-topped boxes on top of the counter.

The jeweller looked up at him as he entered and appeared to frown as he took in Ligriv's travel-weary appearance. Not the wealthy customer he might have hoped for.

"Help you?"

"I'm passing through from the south, sir, interested to see how others of the craft operate."

The man, stood behind the counter, perked up a little and removed the glasses he had been wearing while cleaning a pendant. "A jeweller?"

"I am."

"Where from?"

"A town on the western coast, a long way from here."

"What brings you to Nkuku?"

"Just a stop before we head east."

"A long journey; for work or pleasure?"

"A little of both, friend, but enough about me. I've not really seen so many stores all together before, doesn't it hurt your business?"

The man chuckled. "You didn't have any competition where you were from?"

"Only my brother and our mentor. But we all had to lay our hand to all types of work as it came in, less so after my brother won his token."

"What?"

"Sorry, what's wrong?"

"A token… you mean from Midderbuilt?"

Ligriv felt a little embarrassed, and his face flushed, "Yes, sorry, why?"

"Oh, just that we rarely get token masters through these parts. I've always wanted to go to Midderbuilt and see the place or even Watersend."

"But you haven't?"

"It's such a long way, and I have this place." He waved his hand in a small circle. "Can I see it?"

"You misheard me, it was my brother that won the token, not I, although I will say I think my piece was worthy of it."

"So sorry. Well, it would be hard to compete against a token holder surely?"

"Not just one, but two."

"Two?"

"Our mentor was one as well."

"But you didn't live in Midderbuilt?"

"No, he couldn't take his wife in there so he chose to live in his home town."

The man looked Ligriv up and down for a moment, as though

considering something. "Oh Maymum, to have two together like that. You must have had slim pickings to have to work behind their shadow."

Ligriv didn't like the way it sounded to this man, that his work was nothing like theirs. "It wasn't like that. In fact, my competition piece fetched the highest price ever, which is why I am traveling this way. My patron has me making many more pieces for her."

The jeweller looked at Ligriv carefully as if studying him.

"The ruby amulet?"

Ligriv's face flushed a little. "You've heard of it?"

"So is it true then?"

"What?"

"That a lot of gold coin was paid for it?"

Ligriv nodded, feeling awkward now, but also a little proud that his feats had been heard about all the way over here.

"I never thought to meet such a man and here you are in our city."

Ligriv wasn't sure what to say, but he did feel happy that his work was known so far away.

"Could you give me a moment?"

"Of course."

The man turned and stepped through a curtain over the doorway into the back of the shop. He was gone a few minutes which allowed Ligriv to examine what was in the display cases better.

When the man returned he wasn't alone and two men quickly moved around each end of the counter on either side of Ligriv.

"Perhaps you shouldn't be bragging so much about your gold, lad, especially in a foreign city like this."

The two men pulled out blades but before they could attack the sound of the front door crashing open caught them all by surprise. Ligriv spun around expecting the worst.

Instead he saw Tarna's guard burst into the shop. Before the thieves had time to react the guard had disarmed the one on Ligriv's left, then elbowed him to the side of his head causing him to slump to the floor. His companion charged toward the guard, his blade sweeping side to side. The guard stepped back avoiding it before swiping his own knife forward, slicing the man's forearm.

The cut was deep, making the attacker drop his blade and grasp the cut as he grimaced in pain. He took several steps back, constantly watching the guard.

"Come!"

Ligriv didn't hesitate and quickly followed the guard outside onto the street.

"Enough looking, we'll go back now."

Ligriv wasn't going to argue and hurried away at the man's side, his hands shaking from what had just happened.

I should have kept my mouth shut.

LIGRIV

That he'd got himself into such a situation made Ligriv feel foolish and Tarna's tone with him was doing nothing to resolve it.

"We're leaving this morning," she said sharply.

"But I thought you wished to spend several days here."

"Plans change, especially..." She didn't finish but walked away, ending any further discussion.

Ligriv had observed her speak like this to others several times but not really to him and he didn't like it. He was both annoyed at her and upset that he'd caused this problem.

They didn't converse until they had been back on the road for several hours.

"What were you thinking?"

Ligriv wasn't sure there was a good answer to her question and didn't want to argue with her so he said nothing.

"You can't bring such attention to yourself. What if something had happened to you? Who would do the work..." She stopped abruptly.

He was about to ask what she meant but she quickly started again.

"I couldn't live with myself if harm came to you."

"Nothing happened."

Tarna turned and looked directly into his eyes. "But it would have if it wasn't for my guard."

He knew she was right and knew he couldn't win this argument, not that he was trying to. That one sentence she'd not completed stood out in the back of his mind.

"I'm fine." Ligriv felt uneasy about what she'd said. "What do you mean about the work?"

She waved her hand at him. "I'm sorry. It was meaningless, it's unimportant. I just don't want us followed by every fool thinking they'll rob us. And I don't want anything bad to happen to you."

Ligriv sat there looking back at her. Her eyes were not as engaging as they often were, there was a hardness about them that made her feel distant. She wasn't telling him the whole truth, that much he knew. What she'd started to say was important.

There was a truth in that she was concerned about what happened to him, but for the first time since they'd left he wondered how much of her concern was about his abilities versus their relationship.

For several hours she continued to give him the cold shoulder which only served to make him feel more like one of her minions and less like her partner.

By the day's end her frostiness toward him had thawed. They talked about unimportant things and Ligriv could sense her affection toward him again.

For days they drove harder than normal cutting a path northeast, weaving across the border between Malamig and Ngahere, staying out of the forests but using them as their guide.

Day by day Ligriv began to detect a change in Tarna and her guards. They were getting closer to somewhere that was significant to them all. It wasn't excitement per se but a happiness that he could recognise people showed when they were going home.

They stopped on a hilltop with a view across the open lands leading to a city surrounded by a wall of dark stone. Tarna's mood was definitely buoyant and he could tell she was impatient to be there already.

Ligriv did not understand why as the place did not appear attractive at all. To him the darkness of the stone seemed to be more than just a colour, it was a feeling that hung over the city, coating it in a near invisible layer. It gave him no such warm feelings or desire to be there, but he had little choice.

Once inside the city walls those feelings were amplified. The physical manifestation of what he could sense was like thousands of insects crawling across your skin, biting as they went.

Ligriv wanted to swat his arms and legs, scratch his stomach and scalp. It was all he could do to behave normally, clenching his fists and focusing all his will on appearing normal.

Every building was made of the same dark stone. He'd never seen such a place that reeked of ill will from its pores. The stone absorbed any light that fell upon it, and were it not for the millions of lamps and torches lining every road and wall it would be like night.

Several times he looked up to check it wasn't so and while he could see the clear sky above, little of that light made any impact down at street level.

On every road there seemed to be another temple, more than he'd seen in any town or city they'd passed through. Unlike Nkuku where soldiers were ever-present, Comerc was populated with an army of priests.

The carriage arrived at a large house within a walled compound. Based on the way the servants and local guards responded to Tarna, Ligriv guess that if it wasn't hers then she came here often. It didn't surprise him that she'd own such a property, given the nearly endless supply of gold she possessed.

After a bath and changing into fresh clothes that had been left for him, Ligriv joined her in a dining room. The table was covered with a wide array of food options, the biggest selection he'd had access to since they'd left Barrack.

"Welcome to Enderk, Ligriv." He liked how much warmer her voice sounded, opposite to how the place made him feel.

"We're here?"

"Comerc is the westernmost city in the realm, the only one on this side of the steps."

"Steps?"

She chuckled. "I forget you are not widely travelled. The mainland of Enderk is across the ocean." She pointed to her left. "There are six islands between here and there with a narrow land bridge that connects them all."

"Oh."

"We will be crossing tomorrow, it's quite a spectacle."

"How much further?"

"Our destination is En Carta, the capital, which is still many days' ride. Are you tired of travelling?"

Ligriv nodded. "Somewhat. I've never travelled so much before, I'd not considered how much time it would take."

"The majority is behind us, my dear. Let's enjoy this meal, it feels good to be home." She smiled as she began to eat.

By the time he'd finished Ligriv knew he had overeaten. His stomach ached and pressed against his tights.

"I think I'd like to walk a little to let that meal settle. Is it safe to do so?"

Tarna looked at him, appearing to be considering her response.

"It is very safe in this city, however a… foreigner… would be most strange seen alone here."

He slumped back in his chair, disappointed that he was going to be stuck indoors.

"However, were you accompanied I think it would be fine, as long as it's only a relatively brief stroll. One of the guards can escort you."

While it wasn't ideal it was definitely better than being cooped up inside. He'd not been able to walk since Nkuku, they'd travelled too fast to allow it and his legs needed to move.

Any thoughts that he'd feel better about Comerc disappeared as soon as he and his escort left the compound. Night did nothing to improve the perspective of the city, if anything it made it worse.

What few people were out hurried about their business with their heads down. No one peered at him, the stranger, as he expected, all giving him a wide berth.

There was no avoiding the temples that were everywhere but he didn't go into any nor look their way, as something about them unsettled him even more. Ligriv was drawn to the dominating sound he could hear, that of the ocean.

Once they'd reached the eastern side of the city he stopped, surprised to see there were no walls there at all. The cliffs fell away below at such a height that he took a step back.

While he could see no one could use the cliffs to gain access, the lack of a barrier to stop anyone from falling concerned him. Far below the water thumped against the rocks, the sound carrying up and over him.

Ligriv couldn't hear anything else and enjoyed the sounds as a light spray blew on his face and arms in the breeze. He enjoyed the freshness of it as though it was the only thing able to wash away the ill feeling Comerc gave him.

He didn't like this place at all and hoped the capital they were heading to didn't feel like this. Ligriv couldn't stand to live in such a place.

Staring out across the ocean he thought about the last time he'd been near the see, when he and his brother had first approached Barrack. He thought about his home there and how different that small town was to this place, causing his unease to expand.

How is Nigriv?

Over the weeks of travel he'd wondered about his brother and how he was doing, also Esphe. He hadn't been able to sense his brother at all, that connection they'd had when they were younger just didn't seem to exist anymore.

He did miss Barrack, and Berrell. The man had been another father to them and wanted only the best for them. Ligriv hadn't even spent any time mourning the man's death. He'd been so infatuated when Tarna had shown up, he'd hardly let any of his feelings out.

Have I done the right thing?

Ever since the incident in Nkuku that idea had bubbled up more than once, not just because of the threat he'd faced but because how Tarna had changed toward him.

She had softened in the last two days but there was a change that had come across her... across their relationship which bothered him. She was colder, if that was the right way to describe it.

Not her words, she was good at saying the right things, but in a way he couldn't describe. He could just feel it. Ligriv shook his head and just looked out across the ocean with speckles of moonlight on it.

I'm overthinking everything.

He let it go and just listened to the sound of the waves below. When he felt more at ease he began to walk again, his guard a few steps behind. He took another road back and as he reached what he guessed to be the middle of the city he saw an orange light emanating from a large building in the centre.

It was faint and only stood out because of the night darkness, but it caused him to pause. As he looked up he sensed a physical sensation against his right leg.

Ligriv reached in and pulled out the stone he always carried which was wrapped in a cloth. Even through the fabric he could feel a warmth coming from it that he'd not noticed before.

He unwrapped the stone and held it out between himself and what was clearly the largest temple in the city. The glimmer of orange from within the large temple seemed to reach out and touch his stone.

Right back when he'd first found the amber stone he'd noticed the tiniest of glimmers within it, but this was different. He couldn't mistake the glow that it had, albeit still small but larger than ever before.

If he didn't know any better he'd say that the light from that temple was feeding his stone.

How strange.

His guard tapped his shoulder and when Ligriv looked the man was pointing off to their right. He put the stone away in his pocket, and as he followed the man Ligriv kept turning to his left to look at the temple.

Whatever was in there giving off that glow had to be similar to what he carried. He remembered that Tarna had mentioned the stone was unique and rare, now he was intrigued. He just wasn't sure if she should bring it up with her or not, he didn't want to lose the softening in her manner with him.

Any thoughts about his past disappeared with his curiosity about his stone and why she'd brought him back here.

41

LIGRIV

*L*igriv had spent hours lying awake in his room, holding his amber stone and watching the change that occurred within it. He hadn't been mistaken, there was more light within it, almost like a fire.

Eventually he was able to put it away, but he was still too intrigued to go to sleep. The way it had reacted to the temple, or what was within it -- there seemed to be more to this stone than Tarna had let on.

While he'd been focused on it he'd lost all thoughts about his brother, Esphe and home. With it put away again and as he lay unable to sleep, the conflicting thoughts returned.

Am I doing the right thing?

On top of that he couldn't ignore the idea that had popped up about Tarna's reasons for wanting him. Her recent manner toward him and even her tone of voice at times felt as if he was simply a worker for her. That and his immediate dislike of Comerc added to his worries.

The closer they got to their destination the more he was questioning whether this was the life he wanted. This city was the first time he'd seen how very different his future might be.

As he lay in the dark Ligriv tried to reach out to his brother again, to find their connection. He'd thought when he was in Barrack that it was the closeness to Tarna that had severed their ability to connect, but he wasn't feeling that close to her right now and he still couldn't find it.

He'd never had to force it before, it was just something that existed. As he tried to regain the way it had felt he got a sense that somehow it was being blocked rather than replaced.

Is it some form of magic? Does she have something to do with it?

Ligriv didn't like that he was questioning Tarna in his mind any more than he liked not being able to sense his brother. But he had to think it through as much as it upset him.

Their connection had been there up until... *It was before Midderbuilt...* that realisation made Ligriv feel better. He couldn't understand why she would block it, if she could.

She had no reason to, Nigriv was no threat to her or her world, apart from his relationship to Ligriv. Thankfully he'd been able to separate that out in his mind, and yet he still didn't know what was causing the block.

The more he continued to ponder all of it, the more he felt alone. There was no one he could talk to; no Berrell or Esphe, no Nigriv. Everything had happened so quickly... Ligriv was about to travel over the ocean all by himself. *I miss you, brother.*

Dawn didn't come with the expected bright light he was used to, instead it was a murky, lacklustre breaking of the dark unlike anything he'd seen before.

Ligriv rose with it, tired and unsettled, and decided that a walk might help shake these gloomy thoughts. He wanted to feel that ocean spray again and to look across the vast sea.

A guard stood outside his door which surprised him, but he had no desire to comment and brushed by him and headed down to the front of the building.

Two men stood guarding the inside of the front door, which Ligriv found odd. Weren't guards meant to be on the outside to stop intruders coming in?

As he approached them he spoke quietly. "I wish to go for a walk again. Who will come with me?"

Neither guard said anything, both just stood there. It was the one from outside his room who was following him that spoke. "You cannot go out."

Ligriv turned. "Why not?"

"It's our orders."

"I went out last night."

The guard shrugged and added nothing else. Cranky from his lack of sleep, Ligriv was in no mood for this. It felt as though he was a captive here and he didn't appreciate that at all.

Belligerently he turned back to the front door and stepped forward. The two guards crossed their staffs over each other to block his path.

"Let me past."

Neither of the guards spoke to him but the sound of the man behind him rushing away was easily heard.

"I want to go outside, let me past." Ligriv was stocky and strong and while not quite as tall as these guards he wasn't intimidated by them.

They paid him no heed, and their staffs still locked together didn't budge as he pushed against them. The idea of being blocked by these men bothered him more than it should and he felt his anger rising quickly.

He stepped forward again and was met with the same reaction.

"Let me past!" he shouted.

"What's going on?"

Ligriv turned to see Tarna, wrapped in a robe, hurrying down the stairs followed by the other guard. Her voice was as sharp as he felt.

"These men won't let me past. I wish to go outside."

"That's not a good idea, Ligriv." Her tone was a little softer but he could still sense annoyance behind it.

"Why not?" Normally he avoided arguments with anyone, at least until recently, but situations like this were forcing him to change his approach. Being blocked from simply wanting to go outside was a step too far for him and he wasn't going to accept it.

Tarna raised her head and stared at him. "Excuse me?"

"Excuse you what?" Ligriv wasn't in the mood to play games and looking at Tarna he saw she wasn't showing any affection either.

"I am not sure I care for your tone."

"I'm not sure I care to be unable to go outside."

"It's for your own safety."

"Safety? From what?"

She stared at him for a moment before waving the guard behind her away and speaking in a more gentle and friendly tone. "Come with me, Ligriv, and I'll try to explain."

Reluctantly he followed her into a sitting room off to the side.

"I went out last night, what's the difference?"

"It was dark then, few people were about to notice a stranger, a foreigner in our city."

"Stranger?"

"You're no fool, Ligriv, you can see how different you look to the people of Enderk."

He knew she was right but didn't see why that mattered.

"This is a very closed and conservative city, Ligriv. Comerc is extremely religious and to have a non-believer in here will upset many people."

"Non-believer in who?"

She held his gaze for several moments, her eyes probing his, and he could feel his resistance to her soften. "You don't need to worry about that, Ligriv, just trust me that I'm doing this in your best interests."

"I just want to go for a walk."

"It's not safe."

"Safe from what?"

"Those that see you as a threat, that may want to harm you."

"Why didn't you warn me about this before?"

"I hoped it wouldn't matter, not for now at least. I didn't expect you would need to go outside."

"Why the guard outside my door?"

"The same reason."

Ligriv was struggling to believe what she was saying. Why should he be a threat to anyone here? Why was he even here then?

"What about where we're going?"

"What do you mean?"

"En... En..."

"En Carta?"

"Yes, that. Will it be the same there?" Her lack of answer told him everything he needed to know. "I'll not be able to walk on my own there as well?"

"It will be difficult for a little while, Ligriv. Everyone will adjust to it, but it is a very different place."

"Is it like here?"

She shook her head. "No, there's nowhere like Comerc. But you'll be a mystery to everyone, someone quite unique. That will make you..."

"Unsafe?"

"Not the word I would use. You'll be a curiosity and that isn't always a good thing."

"How is it that we've not discussed this up until now?"

"You've not asked."

"Maybe I should have. I am not sure I like the sound of living there. This isn't what I expected."

Her face hardened, the speed of her transformation surprised Ligriv. "You don't want to go?"

The hostility in her voice wasn't hidden at all, making him feel very unsettled. Ligriv didn't like fighting with her but this was important, it was about his future.

"I didn't say that, but..."

"But what? After all this time you don't want to be with me." In an instant her appearance changed again, the hardness gone and she looked as though she would burst into tears.

Ligriv's emotions flipped just as quickly at the sight. His chest ached and guilt flooded him for causing her pain. "No, that's not what I meant."

"Then what?"

Ligriv was all at sea. The part of him that knew he needed to be strong was being overrun by his desire to make Tarna happy, something he'd never experienced before. "I… I just need to understand what I'm going into."

"You'll be with me, isn't that enough?" She got up and looked down at him. "Maybe you should go back to your room and make up your mind about what you want."

Taran stormed off and Ligriv felt as though she'd reached into his chest and taken his heart with her. Everything felt cold and it took all of his will to do as she said, trudging up to his room and locking himself inside.

What shall I do?

LIGRIV

*B*eing blocked from going outside and sent to his room like a scolded child was making Ligriv feel angrier if that was possible. If she'd thought he'd be bullied into making up his mind she was greatly mistaken.

Perhaps if they'd remained talking he might have been able to see around the issues… but not like this. It was another instance of that change in how she spoke to him.

Ligriv had no desire to be cooped up inside any building indefinitely until such time as curiosity about him waned. How would he learn anything about where he was going to live if he couldn't go outside?

He knew nothing about Enderk, it's people or how they lived. *What deity do they worship over here? Is it not Thenis or the other gods?*

Of course he should have thought more about what might happen before he left Barrack, but he'd been so obsessed with her that he'd thought of little but her affections.

He'd been blinded by love, he knew that, and the idea of losing her had been too much to consider, so he'd made the only other choice there was. And yet now he was in that very same position.

When she'd stormed off earlier he felt as though his chest might explode. He couldn't bear the thought of her not loving him which mattered much more than her tone.

He was now faced with a choice: going with them, or heading back across Dharatan. They had been planning to begin the crossing of the land bridge today.

Was he prepared to continue on with them or not? If he said no, would she try to convince him? Was she worried about him, or only about the work he could do?

Will they let me go? Of course they will, I'm not really a prisoner.

Ligriv believed he could say no and be allowed to leave. He guessed they'd escort him to outside the gates and set him loose. He'd be walking his way back home, across the vast lands he'd already travelled with nothing to his name.

Is that what will happen? Is that what I want?

He was peering through the closed window unable to see much more than the nearest buildings. With a little effort he found the window opened which was better than nothing.

The air that came in was cold and damp, like fog but dirty. It smelled of people, animals and old rotted food. He gagged on it until his nose and mouth were able to filter it out.

If I can't go out maybe I can go up, I just want to be outside. Without any further thought he climbed out onto the windowsill. Above him he was able to grab onto the edge of the roof and with the strength in his arms pulled his body upward.

To his right there was a ledge in the stonework which he was able to get his foot onto. Walking his hands in that direction he was then able to climb up onto the roof.

He was alone up there and could see no other obvious ways for any of the guards, or anyone else, to get up to stop him. For the first time since arriving here he felt a sense of freedom, even if only small.

Using his feet and hands he pushed himself backward up the steep roofline until he was perched on the peak. Sitting up there he had a much more comprehensive view of Comerc.

The layer that appeared to block the light was much more apparent up here, like a blanket of dust that held everything out. *Or perhaps in.* The ocean was visible off in the distance and at this height he caught faint traces of its taste on the breeze.

The main temple was easy to spot in the centre of the city. It was taller than any other building and any thoughts it might be grander or more attractive were false.

Like everything else in this repugnant city the building appeared to absorb any light that reached it. The outside light had little chance of brightening this dull place.

Despite its appearance he still found himself drawn to the building. He wished he could go inside and see what had given off the glow he'd seen last night.

He pulled the amber stone from his pocket and held it up in line with the temple. Just like last night his stone seemed to respond to the temple.

The teardrop gem had been with him all these years and while he'd only shaped it recently, he still knew what it looked like inside. That glow had been only tiny before and had grown recently.

It warmed as he held it out and he thought he sensed a subtle throbbing within it. The longer he held it the more his own heartbeat fell into sync with that pulse, and as he sat there his angst began to drop away.

Comerc felt less oppressive to him and he didn't feel as bad being there, or as bothered about not being allowed outside as he had earlier.

He almost believed he could hear subtle whispers speaking to him, comforting him. This city was just a city, one he was passing through, that was all. Why was he letting it bother him so much?

Ligriv lowered his arm but kept the stone out, letting it warm him, and soaked in the city without judging it. He noticed how well designed it was, all roads lined up perfectly with each other. Buildings and temples placed in exact positions so that he imagined from above it would look very symmetrical. The longer he looked, the more impressed he was, and little by little he relaxed until he could feel a smile on his face.

For the first time in days he felt very happy and comfortable.

Everything was going to be alright, he'd be happy in En Carta, he just knew it.

It was enough for him. He pocketed the stone and carefully clambered back down and in through his window. As he swung into his room he heard knocking on the door.

"Ligriv, are you in there? Please let me in." Tarna sounded concerned, not angry.

Quietly he closed the window before opening the door.

"I'm here, it's fine. What's the matter?"

"I just wanted to see you, to make sure you were alright. Especially after our words, I have been most upset."

Despite how good he felt there was a niggle in the back of his mind that found her sudden remorse a little too easy, that his stone and her were somehow connected, that she knew he'd been doing something with it.

But he couldn't hold the thought and as she stared into his eyes the smile on her face filled his heart to the extent that that rogue thought was pushed so far away he couldn't hear it at all.

"As have I, but there's nothing to be worried about."

"There isn't?"

"No, Tarna, I want to be with you and can't wait until we get to your home."

Her smile grew and a look came across her face that he couldn't explain. He'd remember much later how different that look had felt, but for now all he could do was smile back and then pull her into his arms.

Today they'd cross the water and what was done would be done.

43

NIGRIV

hy do people always need to talk? It was something Nigriv struggled with. His brother and he could go days without saying much at all, they knew how the other was… or he used to.

Gantcy was similar in that way, she also had no need to constantly say something for no other reason than she could. Everyone else felt like they needed to speak to him, more so since he'd begun going out again.

Being able to sit in silence mattered to him, it was what he needed to be at his best. Which was why he was sitting on a rock ledge high above the town, a gentle breeze ruffling his scruffy mop of hair.

It was warm enough that he had taken off his tunic and was enjoying the way the sun baked his skin. No one would bother him here, it was too high up and difficult for most people to climb.

Nigriv watched as a bearded vulture swept over his spot, eyeing him to determine whether he was a threat or not, before it swooped away. *I need to come up here more often, I'd forgotten how heavenly this is.*

No noise, no people, just the mountain, and the sun warming his bare chest as he lay back on the rock. As he lay there he thought he could hear sounds within the mountain, the shifting of rock within the very mountain itself.

He laughed, it was such a stupid thought. As if the mountain moved! It was solid and stable, a quality he liked about rock. He smiled at how silly he was being.

Usually when they'd come up here it had been in search of gems or to mine the silver vein that Berrell had shown them. Even though they'd often been working, Nigriv had still felt good on this mountain.

Life was very different now to how it had been. He was slowly finding a new normal. Previously things all just happened around him and he'd never thought much past the next day.

But now, whether because of his age or all the recent trauma, he'd begun to wonder what his purpose really was. What did his life mean?

Even that was a little daft. No one else in Barrack seemed to think much, although he had a sneaking suspicion Gantcy had thoughts about more than just being friendly.

Barrack was a community where they all looked out for each other, in good times and bad, as he'd learned recently. He liked that, he appreciated what others had done for him.

With the darkness he'd succumbed to, mostly in the past, there was an itch inside that he wasn't used to. Something he couldn't scratch, even more irritating than the burn in his forearm.

He was in this part of Dharatan because of what seemed random events and the words of Hembleth, who'd told them they would learn to work with gems.

Which they had. He wondered if they wouldn't have been better as simple trappers back where they'd been born. Sure, he had a token and was a master of his craft but he didn't know if all of that even mattered.

Hembleth had said there was some prophecy, which sounded ridiculous at the time, and yet here he was. *Was this what it meant? Why this, why did Ligriv have to go?*

The more he thought about Hembleth, the more he felt a desire to hold the stone that old man had given him. *The same shape as the one Ligriv cut.* Nigriv sat up and pulled the white stone out of his pocket.

He enjoyed holding it, it always felt comforting and now it seemed to draw in sunlight and warm his hand. *This started it all. Maybe if I got rid of it he'll come home?*

Nigriv could almost hear a response -- a whisper that had no words was as best as he could describe it. It felt like the words were arguing with him or the idea of throwing the stone away.

An image of his ring popped into his mind. He didn't really understand why but he pulled that out as well. Such a coincidence, as he'd felt an odd urge to bring it with him today rather than leave it at home.

He slipped the ring onto his finger and that vague whisper came into focus, a voice he'd heard before.

* * *

IT WON'T HELP.

"What won't?"

Throwing the stone away.

"Why not?"

You cannot destroy it, Nigriv. And it's not at fault.

"How do you know?"

It is not a harmful thing.

"It's just a stone."

Well, if that's so then it's another reason why it cannot harm you.

Nigriv scoffed out loud, she'd used his own logic against him.

"How are you here?"

You're on this mountain range and of course the stones.

"Stones?"

The one you hold and that ring, combined with all the rocks around you, help connect you to me. It's harder than when you were in Midderbuilt but still possible.

"Can others speak to you?"

Not like this, no.

"Why not?"

There is a block in the minds of normal people, Nigriv, that stops them being able to do this.

"Who put it there?"

It's just the way they are. Their minds don't allow it, or at least they avoid it.

"But I can communicate with you?"

Yes, and more easily with the stones.

"Why could Ligriv and I do it?"

Do what?

"Communicate in our heads."

Speaking?

"Not really, but I could sense him and impressions. Like danger or happiness."

She didn't reply and Nigriv thought she had gone. That bothered him more than her being able to speak to him. He didn't like that she'd just turn up then disappear like that.

I was thinking about what you said. I believe it's part of what makes you both so important and why I can do this more easily with you.

"So why would it stop?"

What do you mean?

Nigriv explained the way he had rarely been able to connect to Ligriv since Midderbuilt and he wondered if somehow they were being blocked, until he decided it was his brother's love for Tarna that caused it.

Tell me more about this woman.

"What do you want to know?"

What did she look like? What was her name?

HE DID his best to answer her questions while she made concerning sounds, none of which comforted him.

I wish I'd known this before.

"Why?"

She isn't who she made herself out to be.

"Is he in danger?"

I can't say.

"Can't or won't?"

The voice in his head stayed quiet for longer than made Nigriv comfortable.

Can't, because I don't have an answer.

"I should go after him."

And do what?

"Protect him?"

Do you even know where he is?

"Enderk... somewhere."

Exactly, somewhere. And if you found him, what would you say? Why would he believe you and suddenly leave and come back?

* * *

NIGRIV WAS ANNOYED, she was making far too much sense, and he felt foolish.

* * *

"WHO ARE YOU?"

A friend.

"I wish I could believe that..."

That stone in your hand, how does it make you feel?

"Good."

And who gave it to you?

"Hembleth."

Yes, my brother. Do you trust him?

"I guess."
I'll take that as a yes. Then trust me, I'm on your side.

* * *

NIGRIV WASN'T SO sure he believed that, but her reasoning did ease the concern about Ligriv she'd created.

* * *

FOR NOW STAY PUT in that town, Nigriv.
   "You can read my mind?"
   No, but I could sense your unease.
   "Oh."
   "You don't have to be alone all the time. Not everyone will leave."

* * *

AND WITH THAT he felt her presence go. Her words about him being alone stung him. He did like being alone in moments like this, but she'd touched on something that had been eating away at him.

These last few weeks all his thoughts about what to do were hiding something else. He was experiencing an emptiness that he'd never felt before.

He realised this was what others called emotions and he didn't like it at all. So far he'd been able to push it down and keep it at bay. If this voice hadn't just disappeared perhaps he might have asked her about it, but she'd gone.

She's wrong, everyone goes.

Ligriv had gone, leaving him without his other half… and Esphe and Berrell, they were gone. Even his mother and father had left him. He knew that was irrational but the thoughts, the feelings inside were sweeping through him and he couldn't control them.

Sobs came up and burst out of him uncontrollably, racking his body with their severity. Tears flowed down his face and he did nothing to stop them.

I am all alone.

LIGRIV

*L*igriv rubbed his eyes as he struggled to waken. He had been woken rudely as their party readied for what he'd been told would be several difficult days of travel.

Outside their accommodation Lady Tarna's carriage waited for her as did everyone including himself. Noticeably, to Ligriv at least, was how large their travelling party had become.

Lined up in two columns behind the carriage were twenty guards, in their customary black outfit. An equal number was stood in front of the carriage.

A little further behind was a line of mules and servants.

She really is important!

When Lady Tarna exited the building she was wrapped in a heavy coat much like the one Ligriv had been given. He joined her and climbed into the carriage.

Nothing was said as they rolled toward the cliffs. Ligriv had seen the bridge on his first day as well as when he'd been up on the roof.

"How long will it take to cross?"

"Days, none of them pleasant."

"Why?"

"When we cross you'll feel how windy it gets. During the night those winds increase and become intolerable, dangerous even."

"Doesn't sound enjoyable."

"It is not, and while I will put up with staying in a tent where there is no other choice, out there the only place I will stay is in this carriage."

She turned away from him and closed her eyes, something he couldn't do, especially as they reached the edge of the land. It felt surreal and frightening to be inside the carriage yet he couldn't not peek around the edge of the curtain on the window.

There seemed only ten feet or so on his side of the carriage to the edge of the land they were travelling over. That edge was loosely marked by mid-sized stones placed every six feet or so.

Not that you could miss the edge.

The carriage began to rock from side to side as they moved across the bridge.

"I do not like this part at all."

Ligriv didn't say anything as it was clear she was not going to enjoy this ride.

He had to admit when the view of land outside the window expanded as they reached Step One, at the end of the first day, Ligriv was grateful for it. His stomach was unsure about what had just happened and he was feeling a little uneasy.

Tarna hadn't been exaggerating when she'd said how bad the winds were at night. Ligriv didn't sleep for more than a few minutes at a time due to the incessant howling.

By morning he was more than willing to be moving again, wishing this trip was over already. When the procession set off, he chose to walk this time, wanting to feel the ground beneath his feet.

A gust of wind whipped around him and Ligriv pulled his coat tightly around him, pushing his hands into the large pockets. His eyes were watering and he wondered if this was such a great idea after all.

It took several hours from their camp before they approached the next land bridge. At best this one was only forty paces across.

The edges were nothing more than crumbling earth and stones

affording him no confidence in the strength of what they were about to cross. He could only imagine they were very thick.

There were no barriers on either side so their group proceeded down the middle. The guards had closed on him, one either side and others behind, not so close that he couldn't see but if he veered from the centre, he was nudged back to the middle.

Walking behind Lady Tarna's carriage he could see why riding in it was so unpleasant; the body of it rocked constantly as wind whipped around it.

No one spoke. Not that the soldiers had shown any inclination to converse with him, but the roar of the wind and the sounds of the ocean far below made it pointless to even try.

Eventually Ligriv wished he was back in the carriage. The wind had eaten through any warmth his coat offered and seeped into his bones, the exposed skin on his face felt sore and any awe at the view had long since worn off.

The following days passed at a crawl, the temperature had stayed low with the wind easily cutting through any barrier and chilling Ligriv to the bone.

At Step Four the procession halted without warning and the two who had always been with Lady Tarna gathered by her carriage door. Ligriv stepped forward to listen when they spoke to her.

"The bridge is crumbling, mistress."

"What do you mean?"

"This one has been degrading for some time, but it is much worse than when we left."

"How bad?"

The guard said nothing but in that he answered her plenty.

"We must be across there, Eleven. I cannot be delayed any longer."

"May I suggest you walk?"

There was a long silence.

"It is that bad?"

"I fear what the carriage might do to it."

"The carriage is needed, Eleven!"

"We will walk you over, then everything from the carriage to reduce its weight, and last the carriage itself."

"Will that work?"

The guard again did not answer.

"If we must, although I am not happy to have to view the drop."

"You can cover your eyes, if that suits you best."

Her reply was sharp. "I will not walk like I am afraid, Eleven. Let's get this over with."

She climbed out holding the man she had called Eleven's hand and then summoned Ligriv with a nod of her head. He approached her and she placed her arm through his and began to walk.

As they approached this land bridge Ligriv saw easily why the guards had been so concerned. Where the previous ones were roughly forty paces across, this was at best fifteen or less in places.

While none of the edges had looked secure this one was visibly crumbling and ragged. In front a single line of the men in black walked a few paces apart.

On either side of Lady Tarna and himself were Eleven and the other primary guard from Midderbuilt.

It was impossible not to be buffeted by the wind and Ligriv felt like the ground beneath them was moving with it. No matter what, he'd never felt so afraid in his life.

The length of this bridge seemed longer than the previous ones and every step felt dangerous. If Tarna had been looking for him to be stoic then she would be disappointed.

Halfway across the line stopped suddenly. Everyone watched as a piece of the bridge fell away on their left.

"Faster, Eleven, we cannot wait here."

Everyone picked up the pace and Ligriv couldn't help but stare at that spot as they passed it. Even the steadfast guards seemed to be apprehensive, but perhaps that was for the care of their charge.

When they reached the next step Ligriv was sure he heard a collective sigh and had never been happier. Tarna continued walking past the guards until they were well onto the large land mass.

All of the guards then hurried back across in single file to the other side and returned carrying boxes and bags until everything from the carriage and their supply mules was across.

Then everyone watched one of the drivers as he steered the carriage over the bridge. There was only a half-dozen paces at best either side of it and it rocked precariously side to side.

Ligriv could see that if the horses or the carriage were blown off course then it would be pushed right to the crumbling edge. He couldn't but hold his breath as he watched the drama unfold before him.

Slowly it crept across the bridge with the horses placing their feet carefully. As it came to the narrowest section Ligriv waited for the worst to happen, but miraculously the driver navigated his way straight through. Once he reached Step Five everyone sprang into action loading the carriage again.

Lady Tarna climbed back into her seat and this time Ligriv joined her. He'd had more than enough excitement for the day.

Over the next few days, he stayed put inside the carriage desperate to be on Enderk. By the time they reached the far side Ligriv was exhausted.

The city on the other side was called Ponte and Ligriv was glad to be there and to rest overnight from the disconcerting trip across the land bridges.

Once again they set off early the next day to continue their journey east, now on mainland Enderk. His spirits were improved from the short stop in Ponte, as it had appeared to be much more like cities on Dharatan than Comerc had been.

Their entourage was again accompanied by a full squad of soldiers, cooks and attendants for Lady Tarna.

Each night they slept in elaborate tents that were carried in additional wagons, servants setting them up and then packing them away each morning.

As much as Ligriv was intrigued by the land around him, in the end there were only so many trees one person could show interest in. Hills looked like hills and wild grasses were grasses.

The most interesting part was when they entered what Tarna

called the Great Plains. They had passed through a gorge in a mountain range that opened into this vast plain of grasslands, surrounded on all sides by more mountains.

To the south lay a huge city stretching out from the massive cliffs behind and directly ahead, far to the east, was another pass. Midway between the two passes was what looked to be a single building.

It took a quarter of a day to reach what turned out to be a temple sitting alone at the junction of the roadway they had come along and another leading to En Carta.

"We're nearly there, Ligriv."

* * *

It was mid-afternoon by the time their carriage finally came to its final stop.

"We're here."

Tarna had perked up the closer they had come, whereas Ligriv was more anxious than at any time previously. *I hope I like it.*

The door opened on Tarna'a side and she was escorted out, not by her guards but by what appeared to be a priest.

"You're back, my lady."

"Clearly, Uksod."

The young priest's flinch was barely noticeable but Ligriv detected it. There was a look to him that reminded him of Tarna when she snapped at him, but on his face it seemed permanent.

"You have company?"

She waited until Ligriv was out of the carriage as well. "Ligriv, meet Uksod, he's the head of our church throughout all of Enderk."

Ligriv wasn't sure how to address the man who appeared to be of a similar age to himself. Thankfully the priest spoke up.

"It is my pleasure, Ligriv." He dipped his shaved head before looking back up at Tarna.

"Come see me in the morning, Uksod, there's much to catch you up on."

"Of course, Ya..." He stopped abrubtly and Ligriv thought he caught a scowl on the face of Lady Tarna. "...Lady Tarna."

"Let's go inside, Ligriv, I am sure you'll find the baths here quite splendid."

Ligriv held out his arm, she looped hers through it and they climbed the stairs to the large building before them. When they reached the top he turned to take in their surroundings.

On their left was a large temple, bigger than this significantly-sized house, and Ligriv assumed it was the home of the tall priest he'd just met. Next to that was an even bigger building which dominated everything around it.

"That is the High Prince's palace, Ligriv."

"It's impressive."

"Come, I'm desperate to wash and find something different to wear. You'll meet him soon enough."

"I will?" He walked with her through the doors into her home as servants hurried to open and close doors as they moved through the building.

"Of course, he'll be keen to learn about my travels."

Ligriv knew he shouldn't be surprised that someone of such great wealth was well connected, but he'd not considered her position within this realm. Nor why the priest appeared to be beholden to her as well.

Who is she really?

He felt foolish that he had never learned much about her, although she was very adept at avoiding the questions he had asked. She was very wealthy, which he knew, but as to how or why he was clueless.

At times he felt ordinary around her, or simple, but now that he might be meeting a ruler now he felt much more uncomfortable.

He was a simple lapidarist -- what right did he have to meet a High Prince? *Maybe my work is for him and not her after all.*

Tarna pointed to some servants. "Take him to his room and show him the baths." With that she left, followed by the remaining servants.

A woman beckoned him to follow her and Ligriv did. She took him to a large room and pointed at some clothing hung in an open closet. She said nothing but used her hand to direct him along a narrow corridor that ended at a large room filled with steam and a large bath.

The servant stepped up to him and began to undo his clothing.

"I can do it."

She stepped back, her head pointing downward.

"I'll be fine."

The servant went and stood near to a pile of towels and other cloths. Ligriv was embarrassed to be undressing in front of her but had little choice as she wasn't going anywhere.

He hurriedly got out of his tunic and tights and slipped into the massive pool before hiding himself in the steamy water. Footsteps behind him caused his head to turn and the servant scooped up his clothing and hurried away.

They really do need a clean.

In surprise he turned when he felt a wet cloth on his back and saw the woman that had taken his clothes away stood behind him in the water, naked and carrying a bar of soap and a cloth.

He awkwardly stood there in the hot water while this stranger washed him completely. It felt good to be clean, cleaner than perhaps he'd ever been, the hot water making everything feel good, too good.

The woman left him and he climbed out of the pool, put on the robe she had left for him and walked back to his room. As he entered he heard the slightest sound of a door closing but saw no one.

Alone in there he was confused as to why he had rooms of his own. On the table he found a platter of breads and fruit, dried meats and various nuts as well as a carafe of wine.

As much as he wanted to meet up with Lady Tarna, after all the travel and the heat of the bath he was happy with the wine and food. After consuming a small amount of each offering he climbed into the massive bed and fell asleep.

4 5

NIGRIV

*N*ever before had Nigriv experienced any such emotions. They had consumed him, he'd been unable to think straight for hours. Nor had he ever cried so much, he couldn't remember the last time he'd cried at all.

By the time the episode had subsided he was exhausted mentally and physically. The barrier that had cracked left him flooded with these feelings and he didn't like it.

Shaken and confused, he'd been unwilling to move. The sun dipped and he lay there shaking from the cold all night, lost inside himself, missing his brother, feeling very alone despite what the voice had said.

Eventually he coaxed himself to leave, slowly climbing down off the mountain, not even fully aware of where he was or why. The depth of the feelings he'd been exposed to, frightened him.

Some were those he wished had never surfaced, including the memory of his father dying in front of him. Whatever his connection to the voice had done, he wished he could go back as he preferred how he'd been before.

In a daze he stumbled back toward town, where Gantcy found him. She stayed with him that night. The next day he began drinking ale early and continued throughout the day until early evening when he fell asleep, head down, on the table in the kitchen.

When he woke he was in his bed unsure how he'd made it there, nor caring. Days turned to weeks and he hardly left the house nor went to his workshop.

Each day blurred into the next and he had vague recollections of Gantcy's presence, despite him being no company at all. She cleaned up after him, and often must have put him to bed because he couldn't remember ever getting himself there.

Then it stopped. Whatever melancholy had absorbed him ran dry and something shifted inside. He looked about and could see that he wasn't meant to be living inside his head like this.

He took stock of what a mess he was; unshaven, dirty and thin again, and knew he had to change. The house was empty -- if Gantcy had been staying some nights in Ligriv's bed, she hadn't this night.

It wasn't easy but he went outside, stripped his dirty clothes off and scrubbed himself from the cold water in a barrel. The soap bar he used did a decent enough job to clean off the unseen dirt he felt on himself.

Once he'd dried off and dressed in fresher clothes he addressed his face, clipping it before shaving. Surprisingly he found enough fresh food to make himself something to eat.

By the time that was all complete, Nigriv felt much better than he had for a good while. His head and heart were still affected by what he'd gone through but despite his reluctance he went outside and headed for the workshop.

It needed a lot of willpower; his arms felt weak, his legs heavy, and Nigriv had to fight the urge to turn around at every step.

His workshop was cold and dusty, but just being there he knew was a step in the right direction. He opened the windows and began rebuilding a fire which would need a day or so before it had a good base.

Other than that all he had managed was a little cleaning but he returned the next day and again each day thereafter. Slowly he clawed his way out of the funk he'd been in, until he found life beginning to feel normal again.

Gantcy had remained by his side the whole time and they were sharing a bed together often, she just wasn't staying over. He liked her company and even more the fact that she didn't need to be talking all the time. They could be sitting somewhere, just taking in a view without a single word said.

Then there were the times when she was like the complete opposite of herself. If she got excited over something then there was no talking her down, almost as if someone had filled her with a jug of energy.

Nigriv tried his best at those times to ride along with her excitement, as much to support her as she had him. He needed to give her that as she'd helped him more than she might ever know, and he was glad to not be alone.

Today she rushed into the workshop, brimming with animation, but this time she wore concern on her face.

"He's back."

Nigriv had no idea what she meant. "Who?"

"That trader… from Tabt."

And now he knew why she was concerned. There was a deal that Nigriv was meant to be fulfilling but he hadn't been working much recently. Aarin wouldn't be pleased at his lack of progress.

"How do you know?"

"He arrived just before and took a room."

"Then he'll be here soon enough."

Half an hour later the tall man about the same age as Master Berrell stepped into the doorway of Nigriv's workshop.

"Nigriv!"

Nigriv wiped his hands on his apron and walked over to the man to shake his hand. "Aarin, how are you?"

"I'm good, lad, how about you?"

Nigriv didn't know how to answer. So much had happened, he couldn't even recall the last time they'd met. So much of his recent memory was a blur.

"It's alright, if what I hear is true, you've had a lot to deal with."

Nigriv nodded.

"I've been delayed a bit getting back here, I had some business further north which took longer than I expected."

"Is that so?" Nigriv wasn't looking forward to telling him he hadn't got much to show him but anything to delay that was good.

"Why don't we talk about that later? What have you got for me?"

This wasn't how Nigriv had expected his day to go but he was still pragmatic, he had to face up to his failings.

He went to the lock box that his brother had made some time back and pulled the key over his neck and undid the padlock. After lifting the lid he grabbed the bag that held the work he'd been doing for Aarin.

Slowly he walked back to the workbench and placed it down. "I've not gotten much done."

The older man looked at him with a furrowed brow. Nigriv emptied the bag onto the bench to show the bracelets he'd made for the trader.

Aarin looked at them but didn't say anything. He picked several up, one at a time, and eyed them before looking at the next. An awkward silence hung in the workshop. Gantcy was stood off to the side watching.

He counted them out then looked at Nigriv. "You're right."

"What's that?"

"That's not a lot given how long I've been gone. We had a deal, son, and you're not delivering on it, but we're square."

"What do you mean?"

"Back at the beginning I gave Berrell a deposit and what you've made here covers all of that. So while I'd like to have plenty more you don't owe me anything."

It felt like a poor win from the situation to Nigriv but at least the man wasn't angry.

"Why don't we start again?"

"How?"

"Do you want to continue making them for me?"

Nigriv nodded.

"Good, because where I've just been is a sizeable market for such items. And a while back you mentioned making something with stones. If you could do that then I'd take them."

"What are you thinking?"

"Pendants and bracelets with stones as well as what you've already been making."

Nigriv didn't see any issue with it. "I can do that. What sort of numbers are you wanting?"

"Thirty, as a start. Can you do it or get help?"

"I don't trust my work to anyone else, and I've no desire to take on an apprentice at this stage. So it's just me and as many as I can make."

"Can you do it in four weeks?"

Nigriv did some quick calculations in his head. "It would be tight."

"You have to stick to this deal, Nigriv, or we're done. I've been lenient with you, partly because it wasn't you that made the original deal. I know you've had some obstacles but if we shake on this, there'll be no deposit and you have to deliver if you want to get paid. I'll only buy the whole batch or none."

Nigriv felt like this was all going one way, he'd not received any more coin for what he'd just delivered and now the man wanted him to create all of this work with nothing up front.

"What price? You're asking me to do nothing else for four weeks, it needs to be worth my while."

A sly grin formed on the man's face. "Good to see you're not an easy mark, son."

They went back and forth for a few more minutes negotiating the price until both men were happy and shook hands.

"It'll work both ways though, Aarin. I'll allow you up to six weeks to be back, if not then they go to another buyer, or I'll head up there and sell them."

"You're smart, I'll give you that. Don't worry, Nigriv, I'll be back. This is too good a haul to miss out on."

Nigriv looked over at Gantcy and she had a grin on her face. He could see the excitement in her eyes and she nodded at him.

Aarin turned and left, saying his goodbyes to Gantcy as he went.

She couldn't hide her joy at what had happened.

"You'll have lots of coin from this."

"Work is work."

She seemed ridiculously happy about it and he let the joy that she exuded soak into him. Being around her made him feel good and he appreciated that. The work wasn't going to be difficult, it's what he was trained to do.

As he saw how happy she was for him without asking for anything in return, an idea popped into his head. He tucked it away for now and let her wrap herself around him in a massive hug.

There was a feeling deep down that came out when she was like this, he didn't know what it was, but it made his chest ache a little. It wasn't a bad thing but he wasn't sure he wanted to let it completely out. He might have changed a little, but he wasn't ready for that... not now.

46

LIGRIV

Foolishly Ligriv had expected they'd spend more than a half hour touring the city. Surrounded by guards, they went for a short stroll in the roads close to the palace compound and that was all.

He felt much better after the night's sleep and was keen to stretch his legs and take in as much of this city as he could. His face must have shown how he was feeling.

"Another time you can explore more."

He looked at Tarna, who never looked anything other than pristine.

Instead of returning to the house they went into the neighbouring temple. As they entered through the massive stone doors and made their way into the main chamber of the temple Ligriv saw that the interior was filled with an orange hue similar to the one in Comerc but much stronger.

While lanterns and candles lined every wall it wasn't them that created the light. A column stood in the middle of the chamber taller than any person could reach upon which the largest egg-shaped gemstone was set.

This was the source of the orange light which was illuminating the temple. Ligriv felt himself drawn to the stone, sensing a subtle vibration that ran up through his feet filling his whole body.

He took his stone out and wasn't surprised to see it too was completely full of light now, glowing like the large one across the chamber.

"It's home."

Ligriv turned to Tarna. "Home?"

"It comes from here, Ligriv."

He was a little confused. If it came from here, why had he found it in the creek bed in Malamig?

She gently laid her hand on his arm. "I'll explain later."

Any further questions he had dissolved as her eyes looked deeply into his. She took him by the arm and led him toward the stone. He could feel his stone pulsing in his hand, getting stronger the closer they got to the column.

"It's..." He couldn't find the word.

"Yes it is, isn't it? There's even more to it than what you see." She had a large grin on her face -- or was it a smirk, Ligriv wondered briefly.

He was about to ask what she meant when the priest, Uksod, appeared to their left.

"Highness." He dipped his head to Tarna.

Ligriv again noticed how he referred to her as Highness. He would have to ask her about that. Several times the question had come up, but he kept forgetting to ask her more about herself. Hopefully they'd get some time alone soon.

"Uksod." It was all she said, but it was done with authority and this priest deferred to it. That he treated her as his superior was very clear to Ligriv.

"Will you be heading down?" the man asked.

"Soon, but first, his Highness wishes to meet our visitor."

Ligriv knew she meant him but felt a little annoyed at her description. After all they had been through she was referring to him like he wasn't even there.

The stone in his hand warmed suddenly, drawing his attention, and then what irritation he had been feeling melted away. Tarna flashed him a quick look that made him feel as though she was aware what he was thinking… as if she… he lost his train of thought again.

"Let's go meet the High Prince, Ligriv."

"Now?"

A small smile formed on her face. "Yes, why not?"

"I don't need to change my clothing for him?" Ligriv felt a little flustered by the news.

"He's quite a practical man, no need for pomp and ceremony in such a meeting."

Feeling very out of his depth, Ligriv followed along as she walked ahead of him, into a corridor that led directly from the temple into the palace complex.

Tarna kept a quick pace and he struggled to keep up. If he thought the temple was impressive he found the palace even more so. They came into a massive room filled with outside light. He looked up and stopped, staring at the ceiling which was all glass.

Unlike the temple which was shut off from the outside, all of its light coming from the amber egg, this room shone with sunlight that lifted his spirits and stopped him in his tracks.

Gems inlaid in the stone around the walls and pillars gleamed a rainbow of colours, sparkling like millions of stars.

"Keep up, Ligriv." Tarna's tone was sharp, and commanding, breaking his fascination with the atrium. Without even thinking, he did as she commanded and hurried after her, toward the back of the palace.

She led him into a large sitting room. No sooner had they taken their seats than a door opened and guards led in a man dressed in a dark green gown.

He was tall, but not imposing, or at least not in the way Ligriv had expected. His manner was no different to anyone else Ligriv had ever met, although his brow was creased with lines as if he was always in deep thought.

The High Prince waved to his guards to stay at the door and he walked over in a smooth and unhurried manner.

"My Lady, I am so pleased that you are back."

"Your Highness, it is good to be back. You look well."

"I am."

"Have I missed anything?"

"Nothing of any import, things tend to remain fairly stable around here."

Ligriv could have sworn he heard Tarna mutter *for now* under her breath and looked at her but she only had eyes for the Derk leader.

"And who have we here?"

"High Prince Schevenal, I would like to introduce my lapidarist, Ligriv."

Ligriv hadn't known what to expect when being introduced but he'd expected more than just his skill. She'd said he was to be her partner but he was referenced simply as a worker. It took all of his concentration to grab control of his emotions and hold a welcoming smile.

"Your Highness."

Suprisingly the High Prince reached his hand out, which Ligriv took and shook. There was no strength in it at all, he wasn't trying to prove his position, he was simply greeting Ligriv who was mindful to reciprocate.

"Welcome to our lands, Ligriv. Where do you hail from?"

"A town on the western coast of Dharatan called Barrack, Highness."

"You're a long way from home." He looked at Tarna. "So he's the one?"

"Yes."

Ligriv wanted to know what was not being said but held his tongue, unsure of protocol in such a place.

"Good. I have to admit I was getting anxious with you being away so long. There's only a few months before I will need to leave."

"I am aware, Schevenal." While Ligriv was surprised at her tone and familiarity, the High Prince appeared to have no issue with it. "Ligriv's work is second to none, I am very confident in what he will be able to do."

The High Prince looked back at him, his eyes staring at Ligriv's face. "Is that so?"

Ligriv felt his face redden a little, but her praise improved his mood. "I am proud of the work I do, Highness." He had no idea what it was they were planning, but his earlier instinct that the work wasn't for Tarna sounded like it was correct.

They stood in silence for a minute. Schevenal seemed to have disconnected from the conversation, his mind elsewhere. Tarna gave a small cough, which brought his focus back to his guests.

"I shan't keep you from getting settled into En Carta, Ligriv, and I cannot wait to see what you can do."

Ligriv bowed slightly as the man turned and walked away, his guards opening the doors for him automatically and closing them as they left. He noticed that Tarna had not bowed when the High Prince had arrived or left. *More questions.*

"I'm going to guess you want to know what that's all about?"

Ligriv looked at Tarna and raised his eyes interrogatively.

"How much do you know about the rulers of Dharatan?"

"Very little, I've never had any reason to know."

"You're from Morksa, or at least that's where you live."

He nodded, that much he knew.

"Barrack was on a loose border between Morska and Sahro, another realm, which contains Midderbuilt. In total there are ten."

"Ten?"

"Realms, Ligriv, keep up."

He felt his face flush. "How many are there over here?"

"Only one; Enderk is both the realm and the entire land mass."

Another thing he'd not thought to ask.

"On Dharatan there's an event known as the Great Fair. It's a significant event that happens, in Sahro, once every four years."

He was about to ask why but sensed she wanted to carry on uninterrupted.

"Each of Dharatan's rulers attend and it's there that any disputes are settled, trade agreements made and many social events take place including large sporting contests. Very important. However, Enderk has never been invited to it."

"Oh?"

"Until now."

"Why not?"

"Ancient animosity, fear of the unknown and other reasons no doubt. Historically Enderk hasn't had much to do with Dharatan and vice versa, up until people needed the goods we have."

Ligriv nodded. It made sense why that would change things.

"That's the role of Comerc, it provides a place for trade to occur, a point to conduct that. Which has led to a changing approach to how we're dealt with. And after many years, an invitation to this year's fair."

"And I fit into this how?"

"The High Prince wants to make sure this isn't just a one-off event. He is very keen to get full trade occurring between Enderk and the other realms."

He still didn't know what that meant for him.

"And he wishes to bestow a gift on each of the rulers. Something they will not be able to forget."

"And those gifts will be something I make."

"Yes, but not just any gift, something no one else could give them."

"Such as?"

"I think to answer that question I need to show you something."

"What?"

"Like I said, you need to see it, then what I am going to ask will make more sense."

While his doubts about Tarna's motivations for her affection toward him weren't settled, his ego was intrigued. To be able to work on something that she said was unique excited his desires to be the very best. He couldn't wait to learn what it was.

4 7

———

LIGRIV

*H*e was speechless.

Ligriv stood at the bottom of the stairs that had taken them the better part of an hour to walk down. His attention was fixed completely on the largest gem he'd ever seen.

The stone filled over half of the cave they were in, reaching up far out of sight. If the egg in the temple had impressed him, this was unbelievable.

Orange light flooded the cavern at this level and shone into every nook and crevice above. As he stood there in awe, Ligriv detected a vibration that had to come from the stone itself, accompanied by the faintest of hums.

He felt more alive than he had in some time and he recognised the underlying feeling came from that vibration. He didn't even need to think about it but took the small stone out of his pocket.

It was ridiculously small in comparison but matched this stone in colour and shape.

"The Debrua."

Ligriv was stunned by Tarna's voice, he'd forgotten she was even there. "Sorry?"

"It's the Debrua Stone."

He nodded but had nothing to say. Ligriv could hardly even think, he was in so much awe. The stone in his hand was being pulled toward the large stone and Ligriv moved with it. Step by step he walked over to the base of the massive Debrua Stone.

At its base he was able to see the way it swept upward in a massive version of the tiny stone he held, the teardrop shape. His eyes were drawn to a dark spot that wasn't the vibrant orange.

It was an odd shape, much as if someone had carved a small chunk out of it. As he held his stone out the dark spot shrank and morphed into one that resembled the stone he held.

Without thinking Ligriv reached out and placed his stone into it. At first it was a little small for the space but within seconds the gaps filled and he could no longer see where his stone ended and the Debrua began, it had been completely absorbed into the larger.

The Debrua Stone's glow pulsed briefly and the hum changed to a soft high note that played ever so briefly before reverting to the original.

"It is pleased its baby is back."

"Baby?"

"That stone you had, it was taken from here a long, long time ago. The Debrua is glad that it's back."

"You're talking about this stone as though it has feelings."

"You felt it, Ligriv, don't be a fool."

The sharpness in her voice and the rebuke stung him. It was becoming more common since they'd crossed the land bridge and he didn't like it. As quickly as his annoyance rose though, it softened and slipped out of him just like it had in the temple.

"This is your project."

"What?"

"The Debrua has accepted your gift, and, all being well, will allow you to take some new gems from it."

"I get to work with this?"

"Only if it lets you."

"Why me?"

"You bear the mark and the cutting allowed you to work with it."

It had been a long time since he'd even noticed the mark on his hand. He held it up in the glow; the teardrop shape matched his stone and the Debrua.

I've been marked for this all my life.

It wasn't a voice, but Ligriv felt a confirmation in the vibration from the stone. *What about my brother, what does his mark mean?* The warmth from the stone chilled a little and he could sense the hint of a negative vibration from the stone.

He didn't know what it meant that both of them had the same mark, albeit on different hands. Staring at that spot broke through his fascination with the Debrua and sadness crept over him, the sadness of missing his brother and wondering if he'd made the right decision.

At that thought a jolt of pain stung his right eye then the back of his head and started down his back. Ligriv had never felt such a pain and dropped to his knee, his face twisting in pain.

"What have you done, Ligriv? What were you thinking about just then?"

Tarna's voice and the pain broke any thoughts of his past, or his twin, and he looked up at her. The pain subsided as quickly as it had come.

"I'm alright."

"Whatever you were doing, don't do that again. You must understand the power of this stone. We've waited too long to find someone like you…"

She stopped abruptly and Ligriv tried to think through what she was saying. *Someone like me… has she just been using me?*

Before he could consider it any further a wave of warmth and love washed over him and he stopped thinking about much at all. He stared at this beautiful woman before him who he'd followed all the way here.

Tarna was the love of his life, that was all he could think of, and he'd do whatever she wanted. Ligriv agreed he would get to work with this stone if it would let him, and turned to it, placing both his hands firmly on its side.

All at once an immense power run through his hands into his arms and through them filling him with such love and inspiration he thought he might burst.

Tarna also placed her hands on the stone and in a way they became connected, to the stone and each other, and in that moment he could see parts of her that he'd never seen before.

She wasn't just a noblewoman from this place, in truth she wasn't from here at all. There was so much more to her and a power which resembled that of the stone in many ways.

Tears flowed from his eyes to run down his cheeks and he lost himself in a sea of orange, merging deeper into the stone toward the pulsing heart that was part of it.

His past seemed to disappear and he could see himself only as belonging to this stone, shaping and moulding little pieces of it, doing its work and being blessed for doing so.

And then everything went black.

48

YANTARNAYA

That didn't go exactly as I had planned.

Yantarnaya looked at Ligriv collapsed beside the Debrua Stone and waited. These people were so fragile at times it frustrated her, but her plans needed this one.

Time was short and now she had him here ready to begin she hoped he wasn't permanently harmed by what had just happened to him. The Debrua had shown him much more than she would have, too much.

His adoration for her was cute but of little consequence to what she needed him for. As long as he felt these emotions for her he'd be supplicant enough to follow her directions. She just needed to control him until the work was done.

Ligriv wouldn't have felt a similar emotion back from her because she held none. She had him here to do a job and she'd used her physical form to help get the task done.

Yantarnaya was tired of this form she'd taken. She was unused to staying in the world of men like this for so long. She and her siblings were normally limited in how long they could stay, based on the numbers and devotion of their followers.

That the Debrua Stone connected her to a whole realm of people allowed her to stay indefinitely. Its power seeped out into Enderk through the amber everywhere and the people worshipped her, the face of their religion and the stone's power, through it.

Mentally it was hard to be with all these people for so long a time. They were so simple and small-minded, which made them easy to manipulate but also tiresome. Like this man, he was so needy.

That said, being here was easier than putting up with the demands of her siblings who were exhausting and irksome. They were so consumed with what they thought was right, they wouldn't see what she was up to until it was too late.

Compared to what she felt when connected to the Debrua, all of them bored her. *I just need to stay here and get this task done, then none of that will matter. And besides, having a pet is enjoyable.*

"Mistress, should I help?"

Completely surprised by the man's voice, she turned abruptly. "Don't creep up on me, Uksod." *My other plaything.*

"What can I do?"

"Do you think you can move him back up to his room without help?"

"If that's what is needed."

"No one else should be down here, Uksod, you know that. It is better that way."

"I will manage, mistress."

Tarna looked at the tall, lean man, so young and full of hope, but doubted he'd be able to get it done so easily.

"As you wish."

She was a little shocked when he was able to leverage Ligriv's limp body up onto and across his shoulders, wrapped around his neck so that his legs were on one side and his head and arms the other.

Uksod didn't seem to be struggling with the weight at all and Tarna admired a new side of the man she'd placed at the head of her religion to serve her needs.

Without further talk he walked off, a little awkwardly to begin with, shifting the dead weight on his back until he seemed more settled. A few minutes later he was gone from sight, up the stairs hidden behind the sidewall.

Alone again she laid her hands on the stone letting the power of it flood through her. Ever since she'd first found it, the strength within enthralled her.

It was completely different to the Citadel Stone, the one her siblings knew about. That was indifferent to much of this world and stayed out of the ways of men.

The Debrua Stone was opposite to that other power, like a counterweight and it welcomed her as she did it. Up until this point the faint sense of a greater power had seemed out of reach until she'd discovered this portal to it on this world of Scurra.

Now with its power they could achieve many things. She was its conduit into the world and it sucked on the people around it to fuel what it needed to give her that strength.

Her only limit to accessing it was distance, which is why they'd begun to place beacons, the egg-shaped stones, within temples like that in Comerc, which relayed its strength.

The people worshipped those eggs as though they were her, and in return the stone nudged them in the directions it needed, their minds completely in thrall to the Debrua without knowing it directly.

Only she, Uksod, and now this gem-cutter knew of the scope of the stone and its existence here beneath En Carta. That was the way it wanted to keep things, which was safer for everyone.

A single touch of the stone would kill normal people, which was why finding Ligriv was so important. The mark he carried was the sign that he was different and he'd proven that with the work he'd done on his cute little stone.

Even Uksod couldn't touch the stone, she'd had to make that very clear using examples. He was allowed to know, the stone allowed it, but there was a price he would have to pay... he just didn't know it yet.

The stone wasn't happy Yantarnaya could sense that and she laid her hands upon its surface, seeking more immediate answers than the subtle impressions it would feed her when unconnected.

She'd expected it would be happy to have the small off-cut returned, which it was, but there was something else disturbing its peace. Its concern was Ligriv's brother.

He'd been thinking about him and another small stone, one which Hembleth was involved in. *I wonder what that's all about?* She would need to spend some time investigating what her brother was up to.

That she'd brought this man here and he'd laid his hands upon her had made the stone displeased. Yantarnaya sensed it was due to what was going to have to happen.

As she stood there impressions of what would need to happen came to her. The stone would give up parts of itself for Ligriv to work with but it wasn't going to like it.

Will he be alright?

The stone cared little for his wellbeing, only for the results of what he was here to do. Yantarnaya knew that once that was done he wouldn't be needed, but she'd known that from the beginning.

He now knew too much and this would be the last place he would know. *He just needs to make us these gifts and quickly.* She removed her hands and looked around the cavern, then at the stairs.

It was the part she hated the most, the climb back to the top, but there was a price for anything worthwhile and this was what she wanted. By the time she'd arrived back in the temple Uksod was waiting for her there.

"He's asleep in his quarters, mistress."

"Good. I was impressed, Uksod."

"With what?"

"Your strength, I didn't know you had it in you."

His face flushed a little. It was one of the things these Derks couldn't hide, their pale skin so easily reddened in the cold or when they were embarrassed.

She looked at him, her other fawning subject, and his discomfort at her words. It amused her.

"What does he know?"

"A lot more now. I wouldn't have bothered but the stone had other ideas. Maybe it was necessary but I don't see why."

"So what do we do with him?"

"Hopefully he will recover quickly, then we'll keep him out of sight and get him to work. There's little time and there's only one other option who will be much less willing."

Uksod nodded his understanding. She liked that generally he didn't prattle on with endless conversation, most of the time at least.

"Is that all? I am feeling exhausted."

"Sorry, mistress."

"Don't be, Uksod, I appreciate your help."

And with that she turned and left for her home. She had no idea how her plaything would respond when he recovered, but she would be able to handle him. He was easy enough to manipulate when she wanted to. She smiled. Such little games amused her.

NIGRIV

It took Nigriv five weeks to make the batch of bracelets which didn't bother Aarin, once he saw what had been produced. He was very happy with the jewellery, paid Nigriv what they'd agreed, and headed off north.

For his part Nigriv had promised he wouldn't make anything similar for at least three months. He doubted that anyone knew where Aarin got them from anyway, but his word was one of the few things Nigriv could control and when he gave it, he stuck to it.

Just like he had with the ring he'd made in Midderbuilt. He'd agreed to protect that ring and keep it out of others' hands and so far he had. As far as he was aware, no one else knew he had it, not even Gantcy.

How will I know it goes blue if I never show it to anyone?

Maybe he should have asked the voice that but Nigriv had no desire to speak to her again. The last time had caused him so much distress, he wasn't sure he ever wanted to repeat that.

He'd been so absorbed with the deadline he'd not thought about much else for the last two months. As he pottered around in the house he discovered a letter that he'd seen previously but paid no attention to.

The seal on it indicated it was from Midderbuilt which triggered Nigriv, he was expecting it would carry bad news -- nothing good seemed to come from that place. It was from the mayor and dated many weeks ago.

We have already received many orders for the coming Great Fair from across multiple realms. Traders have filled Traveller's Rest, camped out to bid on everything that is made.

There is also a special commission being offered for a unique gift that will be bestowed on the High Prince of Enderk, from all of the other rulers, as he has been invited to his first Fair.

It's my obligation to advise you of this so you have an opportunity to participate. The prestige, and the price, will be high for the chosen craftsman.

All of the other token holders are here and working day and night to take advantage of this once-in-four-year opportunity, as well as the special chance to create a one-off piece.

Nigriv shook his head, of all the things that could have been asked of him, this was too much. To return to Midderbuilt, where everything had gone wrong, to make something for the ruler of the realm where his brother had gone to, was of no interest.

"What's that?"

Nigriv spun around to see Gantcy.

"Just a letter."

"A letter from where?"

He hesitated. He didn't want to discuss this at all. "Midderbuilt."

She looked at the letter in his hand, then back up at him. "What about?"

"Nothing." He shook his head and folded the paper up, threw it into the fire and watched it burn.

"Can't be nothing, I can see it bothers you."

"Just a message about what's happening down there, nothing of interest to me."

She eyeballed him for a minute. "You sure? You seemed bothered about something."

"I'm good, just brining back memories."

"Oh."

"What did you want?"

"I just wanted to see if you're coming to the inn for lunch?"

Nigriv shook his head. "I don't think so."

"I'll come see you later then." She smiled and left.

He felt bad for lying to her, but despite being intrigued about what he'd just read, he wasn't going anywhere. Midderbuilt wasn't a place he was in any rush to return to, nor did he want to leave her.

Gantcy was the one good thing in his life and Nigriv didn't want to take her for granted. Apart from keeping him company she was always looking after him, even now, not just before when he'd not been at his best.

She never asked for anything in return, and often he wondered why she hung around given what poor company he could be. He preferred to sit in silence as much as talk, but that didn't bother her at all.

If anything it suited her too. He had to guess she was comfortable with the relationship as well, but his idea from earlier seemed like a good thing to do. He wanted to do it for her.

Up until the episode on the mountain he had no connection with any emotions, but since then that had shifted. Only a little but he did feel things, and he knew he felt better for Gantcy's company.

What he was planning was as good a way as any to take his mind off the letter, his brother and all the things he couldn't control. For the first time in ages he was excited about working on something.

Nigriv gathered the left-over silver from the recent work and got started. His brother would have made something even more extravagant, but late in the day when he was done Nigrv was more than pleased with the small brooch he'd made.

He held it up to the waning daylight coming in the window. The emerald stone sparkled with the light and green streaks ran across his hand.

I hope she likes it.

Out of nowhere everything in his workshop changed. He was surrounded by a smokey orange haze, that had no smell and wasn't moving. Nigriv tried to reach out to touch it but felt nothing.

Nothing around him moved and the air seemed to have stopped in place. He couldn't work out what was happening at all and he began to feel anxious.

Suddenly he could see Ligriv in the haze, distant and out of reach, but it was clearly him. Nigriv tried to call out but no sound came from his mouth.

His twin brother was stood with his hands on something large that Nigriv couldn't see, but Ligriv's face appeared blissfully happy. Then his brother appeared to slide down out of Nigriv's view and then the image disappeared.

The workshop came back into view and Nigriv found himself stretching forward as though trying to reach something invisible and almost lost his balance. A snigger came from behind him and he turned to see Gantcy standing at the doorway.

"What are you doing?"

Nigriv felt his face redden. He struggled to grasp what had just happened and felt silly as he recovered. "I… I had a… nothing."

There was no specific reason he didn't want to explain what had happened, but he decided to keep it to himself. "Nothing, I think I was daydreaming."

She laughed. "It sure looked funny."

Nigriv didn't enjoy her making fun of him but her smile brightened the dull workshop and he knew she was laughing as much with him as at him. He turned back to his bench and looked at the brooch still in his hand, closing his fingers around it.

Gantcy walked up behind him and he felt her arms slip under his and wrap around his midriff. "What you been working on?"

"A gift."

"Did you get another customer already?"

"No, silly, a gift."

He wriggled out of her arms and turned to face her and saw confusion on her face. Nigriv held his hand out to her and opened his palm.

"Ohhhh! That is beautiful, who is it for?"

This time it was he that smiled, enjoying being able to tease her.

"Tell me! Who is it for?"

Nigriv said nothing but popped its clip and pinned it to her top. "I made it for you... 'Silly'!"

Gantcy's eyes opened wide with surprise. It was one of the things he enjoyed about her, the uncomplicated way she responded to life and how expressive she was. There were no games played or twisted words, she was exactly who you saw in front of you.

"No, really?"

"Yes, Gantcy. You do so much for me, and I never say thank you enough. I wanted to make this, as my way of..."

He couldn't finish what he was saying as she leaned forward and kissed him passionately. When she finally pulled away he had to take a deep breath.

"So you like it then?"

"I love it!"

Nigriv felt his chest tighten, not in apprehension but pleasure. What had seemed such a simple act for him to do brought her such joy. Seeing her happy like this triggered sensations he didn't understand.

All thought of the vision and his twin slipped from his mind and he soaked up Gantcy and the happiness in her eyes.

This isn't so bad at all.

5 0

LIGRIV

*S*tanding at the window in his room, Ligriv could see very little. Outside was dark and there appeared to be no lanterns in the outer grounds. Since he'd awoken he'd been standing here trying to understand everything that had happened with the Debrua Stone.

It was much more than just an inanimate object. Ligriv had felt the life force inside of it and what it had communicated to him. Despite it having no voice he had still been able to understand.

Yantarnaya. That was her full name, not just Tarna. And she wasn't one like him and his brother. He'd been sleeping with a goddess.

"A goddess."

Saying it out loud didn't make it any easier to come to terms with. Ligriv wasn't even sure what that meant. Neither he nor Nigriv had ever spent any time with priests or learning about religion.

Never before had he heard the name Yantarnaya spoken, which was perfectly reasonable if she only existed for the Derks. He'd never been to Enderk before either.

That she also looked different to the Derks made a lot more sense as well, as did the authority she bore here. *Do they all know? Surely not. While they defer to her in many situations they don't bow to her.*

Suddenly the realisation that the man she called her brother, Hembleth, was also a god, hit Ligriv. *And Rainbow.* So all along they'd been manipulated into what they were doing by gods.

Why us?

She wanted him here because of the mark on his hand and he was to help craft stones from the Debrua. But he had no idea why.

He liked that he was so special that he was the one to do this, that they couldn't do it without him. That mark had pulsed when it was on the stone and even now he could see a taint of orange in it.

With his hands on that massive, magical stone Ligriv had felt that he was being tested. Once that was over he felt that it had accepted him as the person it would work with.

Me. Out of everyone!

That he was so unique that a power even greater than the goddess chose him touched the parts of Ligriv that craved recognition. He felt excited and very happy about that.

While he could sense much about the stone there was a lot he couldn't grasp, especially the vast power that lay behind it. It left him feeling very small despite being unique.

He had no idea what he would be designing yet, but he had a feeling that it was going to be something very special. It would take everything he could muster, all his skill and imagination, but what better test of his capabilities could there be?

That he hadn't won the token now seemed meaningless compared to what he would get to do. His only wish was that others would get to see it and know it had been made by him.

The door to his bedroom opened quietly and he sensed someone enter. Ligriv turned and in the darkness could make out the shape of Lady Tarna -- Yantarnaya -- slipping into the room.

"You're awake?"

"I am."

"And how do you feel?"

"Great."

Ligriv wasn't sure what would happen now that he knew all of the extra information. Yartarnaya stood across the room from him, just a silhouette, before approaching and standing beside him, looking out the window.

"So now you know."

"What does it mean?"

A pause. "The same as it did before, Ligriv. You're here to make some jewellery, in fact the most amazing jewellery the world will ever see."

"You seem very confident."

"I've been looking for you for quite some time. It's been something the stone and I have been working on."

He laughed.

"What?"

"I'm still struggling to comprehend that the stone isn't just a stone."

"Many wouldn't grasp the significance, Ligriv, don't let it bog you down. It's also important you understand that what you have learned cannot be shared."

He nodded.

"I mean it, no one can know about it, ever. The Debrua chooses to stay out of sight for its own reasons. But as you've learned, others cannot touch the stone without it harming them. Such knowledge is best kept hidden."

Ligriv heard her words and wasn't concerned about them. Deep down he did wish he could tell his brother, not that it was possible in this moment.

"Perhaps you can understand why I could never explain it to you before. You had to be here, to see it and then to… be tested."

He nodded.

"And you passed the test, which could only be done by the stone itself. It would not give up any of itself for just anyone."

"What of my original stone, how did that come to be in Malamig?"

"That's a story for another time, and also before my involvement."

They stood there saying nothing for a few moments. Ligriv had many questions but the one he asked was practical.

"What is it you want me to make?"

"Eight identical amulets."

"What for?"

"For each of the rulers of this world, including the High Prince. They are to be gifts at the Great Fair."

"And then?"

"That isn't enough? Your work will be worn by every ruler across Enderk and Dharatan. You will be famous, Ligriv."

Her words touched that part of him that craved acknowledgement, what he'd been thinking about only moments before. He wanted to be recognised as the best at what he did.

Now he would be.

And the Mayor of Midderbuilt and all the token holders would know. Their tokens didn't mean the best, it wasn't a competition of quality. He was a master already and now he would be the greatest lapidarist there ever was.

"So now the real question."

"Which is?"

"Will you do this, Ligriv?"

"It's a valid question. The task will be arduous, it might seem simple but I can guarantee you it will not be."

He had turned toward her but still could see little of her except for perhaps those tiny flecks of orange in her eyes. Even those he understood better now.

"What choice do I have?"

"What do you mean?" Her tone sharpened.

"I'm here aren't I? Who could not take on such a task?"

"I see what you mean. Still, you need to accept the task, Ligriv. It's not enough that you just undertake the work, you have to be willing, the stone will require it."

"I am."

"Say it."

"I accept this task, I will do it."

"Good."

"When do I start?"

"Tomorrow."

"Very well."

"You get one day to prepare yourself, to rest, before you must start. There is a timeline."

"Which is when?"

"Several months until the Great Fair commences. High Prince Schevenal has to get there though and it's a long journey, which is why we needed to get back as quickly as we did."

"No pressure then?"

This time it was her that laughed. "You'll be fine, Ligriv."

"I will need things, a workshop, and…"

"Don't worry, all of that will be taken care of for you."

"Where?"

"You will be working down in the cavern, by the stone."

"Down there?"

"Yes, Ligriv, there's no other option, only the three of us can know about the stone."

"Three?"

"Uksod, you and I."

"Of course… I forgot."

"He will be the one that brings you whatever you need."

Ligriv was too consumed by the whole idea to recognise that she'd alluded to her absence.

"I see."

"You should rest, you have a lot to do."

"After what you've told me, I won't be able to."

Yantarnaya said nothing else and stood beside him. He wasn't sure how long it was before she turned and left his room not even saying goodbye. At first he was disappointed that she hadn't stayed with him, that they hadn't gone to bed, but then his mind drifted back to an image of the Debrua Stone and how it had felt.

How will I cut from it?

It was going to be a very unique experience for him, something he would one day be able to tell his brother, despite what she said. But right now he had to think about what these amulets would look like, and he let his mind soften as he sought out inspiration for their design.

5 1

LIGRIV

True to what he expected Ligriv didn't sleep a wink. By the time morning came he wasn't exhausted, far from it. He was desperate to begin, his excitement bubbling away inside him.

Standing out on the balcony staring out at this foreign city he heard his door open and turned to see Tarna -- he still found it easier to call her by that name -- march into the room.

"You're already up?"

"After what we discussed any chance of sleep was going to be slim."

"I hope you'll be able to do your best work." She didn't sound happy. He'd seen how much more curtly and sharply she spoke since their arrival in Enderk and now he understood why.

The sense of superiority she had was real, she was a goddess.

How much of her being nice to me was real? "You seem angry?"

"I am not, Ligriv, but there are things to be done and you need to be at your best."

"I will be fine."

"Then let's get to it."

"Shall I not eat first?"

"We'll bring you everything you need, food, drink, everything."

334

She might not be angry but Ligriv could sense how uptight she was for this to begin.

"As you wish."

She studied him closely. "Thank you."

Ligriv grabbed his bag containing the tools he'd brought with him and slung it over his shoulder. They walked in silence and entered the temple.

No one else was around and Ligriv stared at the glowing orb in the centre as they headed into the caves where the door down to the Debrua was hidden. The priest, Uksod, was waiting for them.

"Mistress."

"Make sure he has everything he needs, Uksod, the deadline must be met."

"Yes, mistress."

The priest still felt cold to Ligriv. While he came across as pleasant, it felt forced. There was no warmth about him and he certainly wasn't welcoming.

Maybe it was the almost blue hue to his pale skin that disturbed Ligriv, or his intense eyes, but he felt badness within him.

"Follow me." The priest turned and went through the door.

Ligriv turned to Tarna. "You're not coming?"

"Not yet. I will be down later, but you don't need me, I'm not sure I'd be much help."

Ligriv hadn't really considered the practicality of him working in the cave and she was right, he didn't need anyone to hold his hand, but it still disappointed him a little.

He turned and followed Uksod as they began the long descent to the bottom. Neither had anything to say and Ligriv spent the walk paying more attention to the cavern they were descending to than he had accorded it the first time.

He noticed the stench that filled the air. An unpleasant, foul smell that had to come from animals. Everywhere he looked he could see bats hung from rocks throughout the enormous cavern that the stone lived in. *It must be them.*

The vibration he'd felt previously was still there and step by step he began to fall in sync with it. With it came the memory of what it felt like when he'd placed his hands on it, how it had communicated with him.

Ligriv craved its touch again, more than he did Tarna's touch. He knew that was odd but he didn't really care, the desire for it was much stronger than his will.

He was just as awe-filled when he reached the bottom as he had been the day before. The light was so bright he may as well have been out in sunlight.

"What will you need to work?"

Ligriv remembered Uksod and turned to him. "A bench for starters."

The priest pointed to a space back behind the stairs they had come down. A long stone bench was built into the rock wall, and beside it were shelves filled with tools and miscellaneous objects.

"If you need light directly on the bench, light the lanterns hung above it."

"Right."

Uksod walked to the left and beckoned Ligriv to follow him. As they approached, Ligriv could see a round table which had a platter of food and jugs on it.

"I'll keep this topped up for you. If you need me, there's a cord beside your bench. If you pull it a bell will ring in my quarters. Assuming I am there I will come down when I can."

"Understood."

Ligriv didn't think to ask about what he should do when he was done working for the day, his mind was already elsewhere.

Uksod said his goodbyes and left. Ligriv went over to the stone, walking around the base very slowly, reviewing its shape and edges, trying to think how best to carve his gems from it.

A sadness filled him every time he imagined using his tools on it and, despite not touching the stone, he could feel its influence over his thoughts.

How will I be able to work on you if you don't want me to cut?

Once he'd completed a full lap of the base Ligriv inspected everything that had been provided for him. There was even a makeshift fireplace where he'd be able to work the silver that he'd need to set the stones and finish the amulets.

Without the sun to guide him Ligriv had no idea what time it was or how long he worked. He began designing what he was planning to make, sketching it on the bench as best he could.

He began thinking about using gold -- they'd said they would get him whatever he wanted -- but the more he looked at the amber he knew it needed a contrast.

It would be best to be set in silver. That was the right metal for this stone, the rest would be all about the actual style. He had the original amulet he made for Tarna in his mind. It was good but it was the first one, and if he improved on that they would be even more amazing.

Ligriv felt a little weary from his lack of sleep and all this thinking. He stood and stared in awe at the Debrua, feeling drawn toward it. With a deep inhale he placed both hands onto it and felt the rush of power flow into him.

A smile formed on his face. Every part of him felt stronger and purged of any aches or pains, his mind clearer. All he could think of was the stone.

Her. The stone was not an it, but a she.

"How will I work on you? I cannot carve something from the side of you, I couldn't." His angst was washed away by a feeling of calmness.

As he did so his body seemed to relax more than it ever had, to the point that if he weren't propped against the stone he would have fallen down.

Then he felt himself moving forward... into the stone. Fear gripped his chest and he tried to pull back before a blast of peacefulness rushed up his arms and he relaxed again.

Inch by inch he slid forward, unable to exert any control over what was happening as his arms moved into the stone. Ligriv closed his eyes, feeling the difference in his skin between the parts inside the stone and those outside.

She was telling him, in her own way, to trust her, and he tried his best to do so, but he couldn't watch.

It took several minutes before he could no longer sense the outside air against him. There was no sound, he was in some form of cocoon that felt gooey.

Ligriv opened his eyes and saw he was in a bubble in the center of the Debrua, able to see out into the cavern. He could move but it wasn't easy and he had no problem breathing. *What on Dharatan?*

Then he began to see images in his mind from the Debrua Stone, and he now understood why he was inside her. He held out his hands and a shape bulged out of the substance around him into his palms.

He pushed his hands together, shrinking the object, and as he did so the excess of it flowed back along its connection to its mother. Once he had what he needed he could sense the sadness again before the thin thread between the object and the main stone broke where it joined with the smaller piece.

In his hands he held what would be the stone of the first amulet. His chest was filled with emotion, not his own, but flowing through him from the mother stone.

The bubble he was in began to move back toward the outside of the stone. As they inched their way forward he got an overwhelming sense from the stone… *Look after my child.*

It was only when he was fully outside the stone again, with the gemstone in his hand, that he was able to properly breathe. He looked back and could still feel the sadness in the vibration from the stone.

He headed over to his workbench speechless but invigorated to begin.

LIGRIV

*L*igriv had no concept of time. The orange glow that lit the cavern floor never rose or set like the sun and he didn't know how long he'd been at his work.

His entire being was focused on this single task of working this beautiful stone. Every tool he used felt substandard to use on such a gem but he had to make do with what he had.

Enthralled and a little terrified he slowly cut off the smallest of slivers using the wheel that had been set up for him. Ligriv wasn't sure if he imagined it or not but as he made each tiny cut he thought he could feel the Debrua's pain.

Not wanting to do any more than was needed, he was glad once that was completed and moved on to polishing the stone to remove any of the cut marks and finalise the shape.

Every time he held it up to the light he noticed new colour and flows within it and things he wanted to adjust. *I don't think I can ever do it justice.*

The energy he'd begun with after exiting the Debrua faded and occasionally, when his tiredness became too much, Ligriv lay down on the cot nearby to rest.

It was never for long and he wasn't sure how much rest he actually got, his mind completely obsessed with what he was creating. He was being driven by a compulsion he couldn't control, nor did he want to.

Ligriv needed to make the stone as perfect as any person could, to do it justice. Holding it up he saw he'd reached the point where he could do nothing more to the stone.

That is it.

One last wipe with a cloth and then he put it down and forced himself to step back, and to breathe. As difficult as that might have been, the setting would be even harder.

His mouth was so dry that he struggled to moisten his tongue. The wine jug was empty on his supply table as was everything else. He'd been so busy he'd paid no attention nor pulled the rope to alert the priest.

Ligriv pulled at the rope multiple times hoping Uksod was there to bring him food and drink. Now that stage was done he realised how hungry he really was.

After pacing about the cavern for a short while as he waited, Ligriv decided to get back to work instead, as a way to distract himself. He had already pictured the setting in his mind and was confident he could pull it off.

The gem had to be the centrepiece and to stand out, not be overpowered by heavy metalwork around it. What he intended would be intricate, delicate and yet, he hoped, support the stone it carried.

Creating the base of the amulet was the easy part and he shaped it by cuts and working the silver as he heated it before creating the rim that would ultimately hold the gem in place.

Then he had to form the thin strands that would be needed to create the interweaved lace effect. Several times he twisted one of them too much or over-heated another.

At one point while he was doing this he heard the priest arrive and thirstily drank from the jug of ale that he'd brought down. It wasn't going to last long but it was enough.

Once he had enough of the strands needed he began to tease them into shape, gently cursing himself for how difficult he'd made his plan.

The hardest part was heating them enough to twist before they hardened but not too much.

It took every ounce of focus he had. At times his eyes blurred by a layer of moisture from sweat and the dirt from his sleeve as he tried to wipe them clear.

When the last strand was in place he waited for it to harden, wolfing down scraps of bread and meat that had been left for him. His patience was thin, he was so desperate to move on to placing the stone, but forced himself to wait.

If he'd maintained the shape correctly then it would fit perfectly but it was now that he'd find out for sure. His confidence was always tested in these moments when he reached this critical stage.

Thankfully the stone fitted exactly as it should, his exactness in the detail and how he marked up the setting, coming to the fore now.

With several deep breaths he moved on to securing it. He had left just enough silver to allow it to be folded in on the bottom of the stone to hold it in place.

Little by little Ligriv had to fold the rim onto the stone to hold it in place. If he'd weakened the silver it could crack and he couldn't afford to press too hard in any spot and flatten that spot.

By the time he was finished Ligriv felt exhausted but he wasn't done yet. Through the small gaps in the silver weave, Ligriv passed a wire which he used to cut out the exact shapes he needed. Then he needed to polish everything until it was smooth and looked perfect.

While many wouldn't notice that level of detail, he would. He'd drained all the jugs by the time he knew he was finished. He was so exhausted that he could hardly stand where he was but lifted the amulet to the lanterns above his workbench and let out a cry of joy.

It is truly done!

Ligriv was in awe of what he'd made, proud of his abilities, knowing that this was by far the best work he'd ever made.

"Is it complete?" Her voice startled him and he pulled the amulet close to his body, his hands wrapping completely around it.

Ligriv didn't know how long she'd been there but this moment felt ruined by the interruption. When he turned Yantarnaya was standing at the base of the stairs.

"Yes."

She approached him, her eyes looking to his hands and back up to his eyes.

"May I?" She held out her hands.

Ligriv was conflicted. He wanted to protect his baby, the stone's child, but it was her he was making these for. He was so tired that his emotions were playing games with his mind. Slowly he unravelled his fingers and passed her the amulet.

"Amazing."

Ligriv knew that it was, he didn't need her praise, but it was still nice to hear it from another.

"This is perfect."

Ligriv smiled. Her approval was nice but he was most happy simply knowing how good his work was.

She carried the amulet to the Debrua Stone and held it up. "Do you approve?"

Ligriv was certain he could feel the stone's approval coming through the vibration, and the smile on Yantarnaya's face confirmed it. "I told you he was the one."

She returned to Ligriv and handed him back the jewel.

"How long have I been down here?"

"Four days."

His eyes opened in amazement. "Really?" He cradled the amulet like it was his own.

"Do you think it will be quicker now?"

For the first time since he'd started Ligriv remembered that this was but the first of eight he needed to make. His heart sank at the thought. This had taken so much out of him he didn't know how he could replicate it.

"What's wrong?"

"I..." The whole idea sucked any remnants of his energy out of him and Ligriv had to brace himself on the table. "It took so much... I cannot think how I will repeat it."

"But you must, Ligriv." She was very direct.

"I know."

"And they must all be identical, lest one of the leaders think theirs is lesser than the others… that cannot happen."

Ligriv had nothing to say. At this moment, the whole idea seemed ridiculous. All he wanted to do was to go to the cot and lie down and sleep for days.

"At this rate we hardly have enough time to complete them before the High Prince must leave. You must push on."

It wasn't quite an order but it felt close. He placed the amulet on the shelf beside his workbench, no longer excited for what he had done. That feeling had been replaced with dread.

"I'll be back again in a day or two, don't let me distract you." With that Tantarnaya turned and left him alone, in the depths of this rock cavern.

As he stood there feeling distraught he realised that he wasn't alone down here, and the other entity was trying to communicate with him, the vibration becoming more noticeable again.

He could feel the Debrua beckoning to him, calling him in its own strange way. Ligriv took off his dirty apron and shuffled over to the stone, placing his hands upon its skin again.

Any worries he might have had disappeared immediately. Energy flowed up his arms and throughout his body, replenishing his strength and his will.

His heart swelled and the love and warmth he'd felt before returned. Ligriv could feel his hands being drawn into the stone. He wasn't going to watch what happened but he couldn't wait to be back inside.

5 3

———

LIGRIV

The row of completed amulets now counted six and Ligriv couldn't help but stare at them from time to time. He was amazed at his ability to perfectly replicate each one.

And it wasn't just the stones, none of which he could tell from the others, but also the silver settings. They were all identical, silver thread by silver thread.

It was the hardest work he'd ever done but the results were spectacular. If he'd been enamoured by his skill after creating the first, he now truly believed that he would be considered unequalled out in the world.

He rubbed his eyes with his hands and noticed the mark on his palm, the thing that had brought him here, one way or another. Ligriv massaged it gently with his right thumb.

For the first time in weeks his mind broke free of the hold that working down here had on him. He continued rubbing his palm as he paced about the space where he slept, worked and ate, stretching out his shoulders and neck as he did so.

It all felt claustrophobic, he'd been stuck here for too long. Ligriv needed some fresh air, a break from all of this before he went about creating the last two amulets.

Perhaps Yantarnaya might spend some time with me up there.

She'd not been back in several amulets, not that he was as bothered by that. He'd like to see her, to speak to her -- not as her lover, but to understand more about what she and the Debrua were planning with these gifts.

There was something about them he couldn't quite get his head around, a contradiction about the stone and sending these out into the world. As he rubbed at his palm the thoughts came more to the fore but he just couldn't grab hold of them long enough to work through them.

He was so tired, so worn down by it all. Every time he entered the stone to bring out a 'baby' he faced the deep sadness, even a reluctance to let go, before the final separation.

I need air, just for a while...

Ligriv pulled the cord for Uksod but rather than waiting for him, he climbed the stairs, one slow step at a time, hoping to get to the top before the priest came down.

As he climbed he noticed a small difference in the power of the vibration of the Debrua. The further he climbed, the weaker that connection became; only in the tiniest of amounts, but having been down there all this time he was very in tune with it.

Also the higher he got, the more he noticed the stench of the cavern which he'd become oblivious to at the bottom. His legs were tired and the foul air took its toll on his breathing.

By the time he reached the closed stone door at the top he was sweating profusely and puffing heavily. Ligriv leaned on the door trying to gain some composure, hoping that the priest was aware he'd pulled the cord and would come soon. He didn't want to have to go back down and reclimb these stairs.

A short while later the door moved inward, just a small amount, and Ligriv stood back. It opened away from him and a surprised Uksod stood on the inside of it.

"What on Enderk are you doing here, Ligriv?"

"I need fresh air."

A thin smile formed on the priest's face but he stood there unmoved for half a minute.

"Come with me."

Ligriv was pleased to be out of the cavern. The priest led them through a series of corridors and stairs, an endless maze that Ligriv would never be able to remember.

They climbed even further, Ligriv feeling better for the cleaner air but struggling to keep up behind the gangly priest as he hurried forward. Just as he thought he'd have to stop they came to a door at the end of a long corridor. Uksod opened it inward and directed Ligriv in with a nod of his head.

"You can spend some time here. I'll get a meal delivered, then perhaps you might like to wash and change?" It was said with a sneer.

"I'd like that."

The priest turned and left, closing the door behind him ending the brief conversation. Ligriv didn't move and was able to hear the key turning on the outside of the wooden door.

He hadn't expected to be locked away. Ligriv had assumed he'd be taken back to the room he'd stayed in when he first arrived. When the priest came back he'd have to find out why.

The far side of his room was an open balcony, or as he discovered when he went out, a ledge cut into the side of the mountain, surrounded by sheer rock faces on both sides.

He was high up in the mountain looking down on the city, the cliff below him unclimbable. The sheer drop made him realise how much they'd climbed, much more than he would have thought.

Ligriv closed his eyes and took multiple slow deep breaths, feeling immeasurably better for the outside light and clean air. Standing there staring across these strange lands, he let it all soak in.

He struggled to feel any of the vibration of the Debrua at all up here and that saddened him. He'd become so accustomed to it, to the love it exuded to him, that he felt empty now.

After a short while he regained a little of his composure and his normal self. Unconsciously he began rubbing at his palm again as he thought about how different things had turned out to what he'd expected.

Being locked in this room only exacerbated his sense of feeling trapped, like a prisoner.

For the first time in ages he thought of his brother and wondered what he'd make of all this. Nigriv had never been one to show jealousy. He would probably praise him for his work. Perhaps. Although, he'd probably be concerned about the situation Ligriv had found himself in.

Am I actually a prisoner?

That he was working on something special was a reason to keep him hidden, perhaps, or safe from harm. There was no one else that could do what he was doing, he knew that.

Shouldn't that make them want to treat me more special, not lock me away?

But there was a hint of something else that worried him now he was up here away from the Debrua. How were these amulets going to work? He'd seen first-hand what happened when someone touched his stone in Barrack.

What will happen when these amulets are handed out to the rulers? Are they planning to kill them?

It seemed such a simple idea now he was up here, but that hadn't been the way Tarna had explained it to him. They were meant to be special gifts that the rulers would be grateful for.

Why would they kill them with the amulets? Why have me go to all this trouble? And everyone would know who had done it.

Was that why he was locked away here? That he might understand this was a threat to the rulers of Dharatan?

If that was the case then they would never let him go, he'd never be able to leave Enderk. He shivered and not just from the cool night air. Nothing about this trip was turning out how he might have imagined.

It can't be true. Surely.

Ligriv tried to rationalise everything in his mind. His relationship with Tarna -- Yantarnaya -- was almost non-existent since he'd learned who she really was. It was a stretch to imagine that it would continue past this point, not when he'd finished what she wanted from him.

Unless. Unless she and the Debrua have more plans for me? I am the only one that the Debrua trusts to do this.

That idea was a little comforting even if he wasn't that convinced by his own reasoning.

"I've been such a fool."

His words drifted off into the open air and he stared up at the sky above, unsure about what came next. *What would happen if I refused to finish them?*

If there was no one else that could do it, then it was at least something he could use to his advantage.

The door to the room opened and another younger priest brought in food and drink before quickly exiting. Ligrv didn't even have time to speak with him and once again heard the key turning in the lock.

He sat down and ate, that at least comforted him. There was a flask of something they hadn't given him before. A brandy that tasted sweet and once he'd had a sip he found he couldn't not drink more, it made him feel so good.

By the time it was finished and he'd finished eating, those thoughts about not finishing the amulets had dwindled and he felt good inside, refreshed.

That's why I needed to get out of the cavern, just to breathe some fresh air and to replenish myself.

Once he was full, Ligriv lay down and fell asleep, a deeper sleep than he'd had in a very long time.

LIGRIV

*L*ight cut into his eyes from the open doorway out to the ledge, making him wake reluctantly. Ligriv's head hurt. He lay on his side staring at the table beside him and saw the empty brandy jug.

I should have known better.

Whatever that was Ligriv had liked it at the time, whether because it was more intoxicating than the wine or because of its taste, but there was something about it he couldn't resist.

All he wanted right now was more of it, certain it would ease the pain in his head and bring back how good he'd felt while he was drinking it. It had been a poor substitute at first to the way the Debrua felt, but then he enjoyed it more.

Ligriv was happier in this room, he could breathe fresh air and pretend everything was normal. Even though it wasn't. That was much clearer to him out of the cavern.

Slowly he forced himself upright on the sofa, his head swimming and stomach nauseous. No one had been into the room that he could tell. Part of him had hoped Tarna would visit him here, she would have known about his whereabouts, but she hadn't come.

That annoyed him… she'd lied to him, manipulated him to get him to Enderk and it was looking even more likely they weren't going to be a couple like she'd promised him they'd be.

Maybe he should have known it was all too good to be true, listened to his brother, but at the time he couldn't think straight. She'd ensnared him through his feelings and he'd been led so easily.

Around the Debrua such thoughts didn't take as much hold, or perhaps he didn't let them. Much like he'd chosen to believe everything about her, he was letting that stone control every part of him.

Ligriv looked down and saw he was rubbing that mark on his palm again. It almost relieved the pain in his head as he massaged it over and over again.

He felt angry at her. She'd played on his feelings, still was, and it was all a game to get him here, to do this work. She'd known how to manipulate him by his ego and it had worked.

That hurt his pride.

But he couldn't see any way out of his predicament. He was under their protection, if he could call it that -- it felt more like he was a prisoner. He had no support here and no real option to get back home.

Nor did he even feel valued, this had all come down to him being the person that could do this work. He knew it now; the question was, could he do anything about it.

Very cautiously he stood and went into the side room, where a bath of cool water sat. It was difficult to submerge into but afterward his head felt better and he used some of the oils and soaps to scrub himself clean.

There was no fire in the room and he felt the chill even more after the bath. He ate what food and ale was left slowly, making sure it all stayed down.

His head still ached, albeit less, and he was annoyed at his situation and also how he'd just been left alone like this. The sound of a key turning in the door grabbed his attention and Ligriv stood to observe Uksod coming into the room.

"Sorry to have left you here so long, I had some other matters to attend to and they took longer than expected. Do you feel better?"

"Not so much." Ligriv wanted to be angry at this man but everything felt difficult at the moment.

The priest looked to the empty jug on the table and nodded.

"Let's get you back downstairs, perhaps that will help."

The walk back was as confusing as it had been coming up. Ligriv wasn't sure he could find his way through all these corridors on his own even if could get out of the cavern.

Uksod opened the door to the staircase down to the Debrua but didn't step through after him.

"You know your way, I'll leave you to your work."

Before Ligriv could reply or argue with him Uksod closed the door. There was no handle on this side and when he pushed against it the stone door didn't move.

If he wanted back out he'd have to go down and pull the rope and then trudge back up here, hoping the priest would show up, just like he'd done earlier.

With little option, Ligriv began to descend back to where he'd been working these past weeks. When he reached the bottom he could see that his supplies had been replenished.

He walked over to the workbench and admired the six amulets he'd already produced. "Two more, then it's done."

Then what? It wasn't a question he could answer. His options were limited right now, he needed to find a way to leverage his skills to help him get free of here.

The vibration was there just like before but wasn't changing his feelings like it had before. *Why is that?* He approached it and walked around the base, trying to understand what was really happening here with these amulets and to him.

Again he noticed that he was franticly rubbing his hand, on the mark, over and over. *Is that it?* Ligriv forced himself to stop and went back to his workbench.

His angst was relieved being down here, little by little he felt it subsiding. His headache and that sour taste in his mouth and gut were also disappearing.

The work he still needed to do felt colossal at this point and his mindset wasn't helping his motivation. That part of him that wanted to be rewarded for his skill knew he had to finish the set so that they could be gifted, but he was struggling to get started.

He picked up each of the existing amulets and inspected them. Their touch improved his mood and he felt good looking at his work, being able to hold these unique gems.

Needing to go back into the stone was part of his reluctance to get started. It was an amazing thing to do but also impacted his emotions. To be intimately connected to such a power and to feel its sadness took a major toll on him.

Hesitantly he walked over to the Debrua Stone and laid his hands on it. As though it could sense his uncertainty the connection was cooler than previously.

Ligriv had to relax and let the warmth build from its touch before he felt less conflicted and more aligned with it. Then with a rush the power of it flowed up through his hands and into his body and all his concerns disappeared.

By the time he was pushed back out of the stone with the next gem baby in his hands his mind was solely on what he needed to do. He wasn't sure how many days passed before he was able to place the finished amulet on the shelf with the others.

The task was almost complete. Ligriv sat and ate and quenched his thirst taking in his surroundings. He laughed out loud at the absurdity of it.

Who could have thought finding one gem like I did would lead to all of this?

A memory of the funny old man, Hembleth, and his visit to see them in Malamig entered his head. Words that the man had said struggled to come back into his mind but he could loosely remember them.

It has a unique value. *He was right about that, what he said about my stone. How did he know all of that?*

And he'd given Nigriv his stone, the teardrop one, what was it he said about that? A child of something larger. *Does that mean Nigriv's belongs to a stone like this?*

Ligriv looked down as he thought about his brother and found himself again rubbing at his hand. It was like that mark on his hand allowed him to separate his thoughts from the vibration down here. At least in part.

Maybe our fate was sealed long before I knew it. Hembleth told us that there was a foretelling, was it this? That I'd be here and stuck with no control over my future?

That being true meant that not only just he, but his brother as well, had been manipulated for most of their lives. *But why? What did we do to deserve this?*

He wondered what might have happened if they'd not run that day. Would they have lived their lives out in Geler? Or was this future always going to come their way?

Another memory came into his head about that time. There'd been a woman who'd hired those men to seek out the boys. *Was it Tarna? Was she on our tail even back then?*

For the first time in an age he could see the past in his mind and things he'd missed connecting. *It was her in Ubico, I am sure of it.*

Why hadn't she come to them herself? Or perhaps she'd not known who they were, just where the stone was. She must have been able to track the stone but not directly.

He really hadn't had much control at all, that much Ligriv could see now. It didn't change anything. If this was what he was meant to do then who was he to fight it?

Let's get this over with.

With that he stood and returned to the Debrua to get the last gem. The massive stone was just as sad for this stone as it had been for the first. He struggled to keep his feelings separate, her sadness merging with his own and his concerns.

As he stepped free of it his emotions were in turmoil, and Ligriv struggled to regain the composure that he usually had after leaving the stone.

I've done it too many times.

That, and what he'd been thinking about earlier which had unsettled him. Despite all of that he still had an underlying need to great work and he tried to find his focus.

But he couldn't settle. He simply couldn't let go of how Tarna had used him and kept him down in this stinky dungeon. He walked around the cavern staring into the massive stone, seeking a way to relax.

It didn't work, nor did sitting and trying to calm himself through deep breaths. The fact was he would be kept in Enderk for the rest of his life, there was no being set free.

There was no going back, no more seeing his brother. He'd be kept somewhere, not with her, alone in this foreign place just to do their bidding whenever they needed someone to work on this stone.

Ligriv couldn't think how he would get out of Enderk. First he'd have to find his way out of these caverns, probably by hurting Uksod, and somehow out of the maze above… then what?

He looked very different to the Derks. There was no way he could avoid people and the soldiers in this city, or cross those vast plains unseen, especially on foot.

When he'd had an opportunity to leave in Comerc, he hadn't acted on it. He should have taken her up on it, not that he was sure she'd have actually let him go.

She was putting on a performance back then to manipulate him, not that it mattered now. It was all too late. He replayed all her words and actions in his mind, and it just made him angrier.

Bubbling away underneath his concerns was a deep unhappiness about being tricked, but mostly just anger. It was typically his brother who couldn't control that emotion, but now it was eating away at himself.

Ligriv looked at the amber gem in his hand and slung it onto the workbench harder than he had intended and it bounced on the stone surface before dropping off the end and landing on the hard floor.

He didn't care, right at that moment. Ligriv rubbed at his palm and screamed out loud. He was angry, angry at Tarna, angry at the priest and this huge stone, but more than all of that he was angry at himself.

All of this had happened because of his ego, because he felt inferior to his brother and wanted to prove he was better.

"I'm a fool!"

The vibration from the Debrua was pulsing around him. The stone had sensed his feelings and knew what he'd done with its baby. It wasn't trying to soothe him and the feeling of it was grating against Ligriv's nerves.

He stooped down and picked up the gem. As he stood up and held it to the light he saw the smallest of cracks in it. Instead of being upset he smiled.

"Serves you right."

His thought was stupid, he knew that, but against all of the power of the Debrua, that he could do this felt good. He'd been everyone's pawn, including the stone, and he hated it.

The vibration continued to irritate Ligriv, he was no longer in sync with it at all. Nor did he care, but whatever it was trying to do wasn't easing his pain, it was compounding his resentment.

What would Nigriv do? He'd know what to do, I wish he was here! What would his stone do?

A burst of clarity hit Ligriv. Nigriv was the only person that mattered to him, that loved him unconditionally, and Ligriv had left him, chasing a false prize.

Tears began to flow and built until Ligriv was sobbing. His whole body was locked into this immense sadness and anger now, he hardly felt the vibration at all.

"I hate you!" he shouted over the hum that filled the cavern. "I hate it here, all you wanted was to make these stupid amulets. I won't do it, no more."

He held up the cracked gem and knew what he had to do. She needed eight of them but only seven were made. This one was already damaged, he doubted he could save it either, not that he wanted to.

In a rush of blood an idea came to him and he put the stone on the work bench and took up his tools. He found the crack and placed a thin chisel above it, then taking a mallet, he took a big breath and pounded down on the chisel.

When the chisel split into the amber gemstone, a loud screeching exploded in the cavern, piercing his ears and making his head feel like it would burst from the pain.

Fighting against all the pain and noise, Ligriv did it again, and this time he heard nothing, not even the hammering he was doing. All of his anger flowed out through his arm, into the mallet and broke the stone apart.

The cut was crude and didn't just break the gem in half but it split into several small pieces. There was no undoing that now, not that the stone wasn't damaged already.

In the silence without any hearing Ligriv slumped to the floor, exhausted. He'd had no idea how much anger had built up in him, and having just let it all out like that left him feeling flat.

Now what?

55

LIGRIV

It took a long while but slowly Ligriv's hearing returned. At first it was heavily muted but little by little he could hear more. For the first time since he'd entered this cavern he heard sounds he'd ignored before.

The noise air made as it blew through parts of the cavern high above. Flapping wings, scratches and squeals, somewhere up there out of sight. The hum of the Debrua pulsed away, different now, definitely not in sync with him, but still influencing his mind.

Ligriv had been able to weaken what it was doing by rubbing the mark on his palm. He didn't know if it was simply a mental thing, a way to reconnect with thoughts of his brother, or if it was a real link.

It wasn't going to undo what he'd done. He'd broken the last child, and it wasn't hard to sense how angry the stone was with him. What would it do now, what would Tarna do?

Perhaps the Debrua could meld it back together again, or make a new one. That didn't matter to Ligriv, no matter how much Yantar-naya pleaded he wouldn't help her any more.

That would leave them at an impasse; she needed the whole set, he wouldn't make another amulet, it might be enough to bargain his way free. An idea formed in his head.

I'll make one but only back on Dharatan. Tarna wouldn't like it at all but it gave him better odds of breaking free. Much better than here. *It's something at least.*

As he stood there rubbing his palm these thoughts of freedom felt as fresh as the air he'd breathed previously when they'd let him out. It made him feel better and like he had some control over what was happening.

Somehow the simple action -- or was it that the mark had its own power? -- helped him think, helped him remember. Ligriv wished his brother was with him... not here, but somewhere far away from this place, together.

With his eyes closed he could almost imagine himself in Barrack laughing together at some silly joke. *I guess you'll lead, brother.*

His daydream was broken by her voice. "What have you done, Ligriv?"

Ligriv opened his eyes and saw Tarna standing at the bottom of the stairs. He didn't respond. What could he say?

"Answer me. Why is she so upset?"

He turned and pointed at the pieces of stone on his bench.

"What did you do?"

"What did you expect, that I'd just be your pet and do all your bidding? You've left me in this dungeon alone for weeks... you're keeping me prisoner!"

Her tone was angry. "I left you so I didn't distract you, you fool."

Ligriv didn't believe her, she'd made it clear he was here for this task, not her.

Tarna shook her head furiously as she walked over to the Debrua and cautiously laid her hands on its side, flinching a little at the touch. Ligriv heard a change in the vibration but was blocked from sensing its emotion.

Many minutes later her hands came free and she walked toward him, her head shaking. "How could you?"

"I'm not your puppet, not any longer."

"Is that so?" Her eyes were hard and bored in on his. He struggled to keep his thoughts clear.

"Can she not take them in and fix them?" He wanted to distract her.

"She will not, they are tarnished by you now."

"Then what?"

"I do not know. She has not decided."

Tarna looked away. "You can wait here while we figure out a solution." She said nothing else and stormed away up the stairs leaving Ligriv alone in the cavern with the angry stone.

Some time later Uksod appeared carrying supplies, avoiding looking at Ligriv or coming near him. He placed several jugs and fresh food on the table then left again.

Ligriv was bored but at least they weren't starving him. He sat at the table and poured himself a drink. As the amber liquid flowed into his mug he recognised the brandy he'd had days before.

His mind instantly craved it and despite being wary of how he'd felt after it, Ligriv took a sip. He smiled. The flavour was just as good as he recalled and it made him more relaxed immediately.

I needed this.

By the time that mug was empty Ligriv was feeling much less angry. As he went to refill his mug he paused. Last time he'd drunk it all too fast and suffered for it. *I should keep my wits about me.*

To distract himself from his desire to drink the sweet liquor, Ligriv went back to his workbench, admiring his handiwork. Everything seemed so much better now than earlier. He struggled to understand why he'd been so angry, why he'd damaged the stone.

They're only broken when they haven't been finished. It was something Berrell had taught him the first time he'd learned to cut gems. An idea came to him and with nothing else to do he began to work on the gem fragments.

Ligriv couldn't help himself. His desire to be the best wouldn't let him just leave these gems as they were. Not when he had idle hands and time to use.

He set the grinding wheel in motion and began to shape the stone to fit the picture in his mind, before swapping to polishing it. An hour or more must have passed and still no one came but it didn't stop him, he was completely absorbed in the work.

Once again he used silver and began to shape out a circlet, hammering sections of it before engraving a pattern of leaves along the outer edges. Each cut was made precisely so both sides matched perfectly.

Then he set the amber stone in the centre and fixed it firmly in place. As he held it up to the light he noticed a glimmer in its small stone as though even the Debrua admired what he'd done.

Ligriv knew it was a fine piece of work even if made under unusual circumstances. His head felt a little heavy now and he was tired and he took a break, filling his mug again and sipping on the brandy without thinking.

Once again his spirits soared and he felt driven back to his bench. This time he worked the remaining pieces into three rings and an arm bracelet. Each carried a perfectly crafted stone set within them.

He became so lost in the work he wasn't even fully conscious of what he was doing, his mind lost in a state of happiness that made everything seem effortless.

The one thing he was in control of was his skill and what he could make. He couldn't rest until he'd fixed what he had done to the best of his ability.

"What's that?"

Tarna's voice frightened him and he spun around.

"A gesture of goodwill."

"Fat lot of good that will do."

"I couldn't leave them as they were."

She walked over and inspected what he had done. "At any other time, Ligriv, I'd be pleased."

Tarna took the items and walked over to the Debrua, showing them to the stone. She put her hands on the side of it and stood there for a while.

"This doesn't solve my problem though."

"What problem?"

"I need another amulet."

Ligriv said nothing. He wasn't going back in the Debrua and while he'd made these other items he was still against making the amulet, at least here.

"Will you complete it?"

"You don't have a stone… I'm not going back in there."

"She wouldn't have you anyway."

"Then how?"

"Leave that to me. Can you be trusted to not do this again?"

"It depends."

"On what?"

"Getting out of here."

"What do you mean?" She approached him and her eyes stared into his again.

Ligriv could feel her probing at his mind, trying to control him. "I'll do it but not here."

"What do you mean?"

"Take me back to Dharatan and I'll finish it there. You'll be on your way to the Fair and you'll have the set of amulets, you can't lose."

A sinister grin formed on her face. "Clever, and what happens after?"

"You let me go."

"You're not a prisoner, Ligriv." Her eyes softened and her face changed.

He'd seen this before, she was trying to attract him. He pressed his thumb into his palm as he tried to resist her. "Aren't I? I could walk out of here now?"

Her look changed again, her eyes colder. "Sit and have a drink, Ligriv, I think there's lots to discuss." She moved to the table and sat pouring out two mugs of the brandy.

Once again her eyes locked in on his and he felt his resolve weaken. He sipped the brandy and everything changed. He felt his affections for her growing and less anger. *What's happening?*

"You need to know something."

"Yes?"

"You will make the amulet, and it will be here."

He shook his head, this wasn't what he was going to do. Ligriv put the mug down and pushed at his palm. It helped a little but not as much as before.

"Oh you will, or your brother will pay the price."

"What do you mean?"

The grin on her face was more sneer than anything else. Tarna reached out and placed her hand on his head. "Close your eyes."

As soon as he did, Ligriv could see Barrack, as if he was walking along the road to their house, and in the yard he could see Nigriv. He called out but his brother couldn't hear him.

Out of the corner of his eye Ligriv saw a man dressed entirely in black lurking in the shadows of the workshop, a blade in his hand. "Nigriv, Nigriv, watch out" he called, but his brother saw nothing.

Everything went dark and Ligriv opened his eyes. Tarna had removed her hand.

"What was that?"

"A picture of your brother, being watched by my men."

"Why?"

"In case you choose not to do what I want. Security if you like."

"You wouldn't!" Ligriv felt frightened. His brother had no idea what was happening, what threat he was under.

"Nothing need happen, Ligriv, that's entirely up to you."

"Then what? I never get out of here."

"Your life here can be as good as you wish, Ligriv, maybe not quite what you imagined but very good. There will always be things for you to do."

He felt deflated. Ligriv had thought he could outsmart them, give himself a chance, but she'd outsmarted him. *Was that vision real? Was that really Nigriv or just another trick?*

There was no way he could take that risk. Whatever happened he was trapped here, but he didn't need to bring his brother into it.

Tarna was still staring into his eyes and a smile formed on her face. She must have sensed his resolve disappear. "Good, then she will give us another."

"How?" Ligriv felt frightened, he didn't want to have to go inside the Debrua.

"I have come to an agreement with her."

"What sort of an agreement?"

"None of your concern, just do not mess this up. You've done enough damage."

Tarna went over to the stone and placed her hands onto the side of the Debrua then slowly began to slide into the stone like he had done. Ligriv struggled to watch; doing it yourself was one thing but watching it happen to someone else made him nauseous.

Tarna reached the middle, then a ball formed in her hands, before she inched her way back to the outside. Her hands came out then she stopped. Her words came through the stone. "Take it, Ligriv."

He walked over, confused as to why she wasn't bringing it to him.

"This is the deal, me for it. She doesn't trust you. Do not let me down or it will be your brother that pays."

Ligriv took it from her, holding it as though it was the most fragile thing ever, and watched as Tarna slid back into the stone. His mind and heart were conflicted.

He still cared for her even after everything she'd done. Foolishly he wanted to be around her, not have her in there. In his head he knew it kept her away from him but if, like she said, he could live his life here, then maybe they could still be together.

Her eyes were locked on his, almost pleading with him, before he turned back toward his bench carefully carrying the gemstone, ready to make the last amulet.

5 6

NIGRIV

Nigriv woke suddenly. It was still dark and despite the coolness in the bedroom sweat covered his skin, enough that he had to wipe his forehead to keep it from his eyes.

What was that?

He'd been dreaming about his brother... Ligriv was angry, so very angry, and had shrieked about something. Nigriv could almost remember what he'd seen in the dream... almost, but it was so fragile, slipping from the front of his mind as soon as he got close to it.

Why are you so mad, brother?

"What is it?" Gantcy had woken and placed a hand on his shoulder.

"Just a dream."

"You alright?" Her voice was more asleep than awake.

"Yes, go back to sleep."

Her hand slipped away and he could hear her breathing settle as she drifted off. *Ligriv always was the emotional one but he seemed extremely upset.*

Nigriv tossed and turned for an hour, unable to get back to sleep again, before slipping out of the bed. After grabbing all the clothing he needed he quietly made his way down to the main table and dressed himself.

Something about the dream hadn't felt normal at all and Nigriv was worried. He couldn't just ignore it. While he'd been lying in bed he'd decided that there was someone that might be able to give him more information about his twin, even if he was reluctant to speak to them.

It was so early in the morning that there was no one else on the streets and he left town unnoticed. Once at the bottom of the mountains he found the pathway he would normally use to climb up. With limited light he had to be more cautious, but then he wasn't in any hurry.

He reached the outcrop where he would often come to sit and contemplate just as the sun crept over the horizon. Nigriv sat and watched the orange ball of light in awe.

It wasn't lost on him that the colour reminded him of the stone his brother had found and that it came from far off to the east. *Where are you, brother?... Are you alright?*

Nigriv breathed deeply and let his mind calm. He knew it was silly to have let a fleeting dream bother him so much, but then nothing about his brother leaving was normal.

Up on this ledge he could hear the occasional animal moving, the wind when it chose to brush over something and the sound of the mountain. It was a subtle and almost imperceptible sound… a vibration or hum more than anything, but Nigriv noticed it whenever he was up here.

As the sun lifted above the land he took out the teardrop and his ring, which he slipped onto his finger. He focused on the stones, letting the rest of the world fall into the background.

* * *

Hello Nigriv.

"I wondered if you would come."

I don't have to come, Nigriv, I am simply here.

He didn't want to have discussions about her or her state of being, he wanted to only know one thing.

"Do you know where my brother is?"

Of a sort.

"What does that mean?"

Only that I know he is not on Dharatan.

"He's not dead is he?"

That's not what I meant, I meant he isn't on this continent, but then you knew he was heading to Enderk.

"Can't you sense him there?"

Ever since she wrapped her spirit around him we cannot detect him.

"I don't understand. Who? Tarna? What do you mean wrapped her spirit around him?"

There was a period of silence.

She is one of us. Her name is Yantarnaya, she used a short version to keep her full name hidden.

"One of you?"

Yes.

"What does she want with Ligriv?"

I thought that was obvious.

"Why would she be interested in him... like that?"

The voice chuckled.

Not like that, Nigriv, it is the mark on your hands. That was what Hembleth explained to you when he first met you. Both of you bear that mark, they link you to the stones.

"How, why?"

We still don't know the all of that, Nigriv.

"What about the prophecy Hembleth mentioned, doesn't that tell you?"

If only it was that easy. It points to things but is not so clear. All we know is that she must want him to work on her stone.

"Her stone? I don't understand."

Those stones you hold in your hand link you to something much bigger, but... she has become linked with a powerful alternate to our stone. An amber one.

"And that's why she took him?"

It's the only logical reason we can determine.

"Can't you just ask her?"

I can't really tell you much more than that. What is it that you really want to know, Nigriv?

"Is he alright? Will I see him again?"

I cannot sense him so as to his welfare I cannot say. As for seeing him again, that will be up to him and her. For reasons I do not know, few people ever come from Enderk to this land. Whether he can return or not I cannot say.

"Why would he go if he couldn't come back?"

He might not have been thinking about the long-term when he decided to follow her.

"Or she had him muddled with magic or something."

The voice didn't answer.

"If you won't help him, or me, I'll have to go and find him, there's no other choice."

You cannot do that, Nigriv. Of all of the things you can do, that is one you must never do!

"Why not? You can't stop me."

If we had to...

She paused for some time.

You would leave Gantcy and head off possibly to never come back yourself?

Nigriv paused. He'd not given any of this much thought. If his brother needed help then nothing in this world could stop him, he'd go no matter what.

This woman wasn't helping his unease; if anything she was making it worse.

"I am not sure. He is my brother, if he isn't safe... I want him back."

Perhaps you need to let him make decisions for himself.

"What if he can't?... What if he can't leave."

And you would fight off an entire nation and make it back, just the two of you?

"It sounds stupid when you put it like that."

Not my intention, Nigriv.

Another lengthy pause.

Be patient, for a little longer. I feel that there's a time coming when all of this will be clearer.

"For you maybe."

* * *

NIGRIV WAS DONE TALKING. It hadn't helped. He'd hoped coming here might ease his concerns, but now he was more worried than ever. He slid the ring off and placed both jewels in his pocket, then sat staring out across the desert for a while longer.

Slowly he started back down the mountain. The way was easier with daylight, but he felt no less unsettled.

He hadn't liked the voice's responses. Would she really intervene if he was to head off to find his brother? How? Deep down his instinct told him that Ligriv needed him, or at least he wanted to believe that.

"I'll not wait forever. I have to go find him if he won't come to me."

5 7

LIGRIV

igriv simply couldn't focus enough to work on the amulet. He feared for his brother's safety and what might happen to him. *Will they harm him anyway? Can I still bargain with them?*

He dared not look toward Tarna, floating inside the Debrua, for fear she might be able to read his mind. He'd promised he'd make the amulet and he knew that was the only answer, yet still he couldn't settle.

Stupidly he still had feelings for her, even after all of this. He wanted to free her, he struggled to see her stuck inside the stone like an insect. Nothing about it was natural. It might not have been more than that, but it was enough.

And yet as soon as he began to feel ready to begin work he'd think about the threat to Nigriv and become annoyed. She must have planned to use this threat all along. To have left someone in Barrack, or close by, required a lot of advanced thought.

The anger wasn't as strong as when he'd broken the last gem, but he still felt some. Nothing about any of this was good. He'd backed himself into a corner, all he could do at this point in time was to finish the work.

It tormented him that she could drive him to such anger while he still loved her deeply. More than that, he needed her attention and love. When she turned her gaze on him and praised his work, he felt good.

Yes, he knew she'd manipulated him to get him to Enderk and to do this work. But he still believed that she had to have some feelings toward him. What had she hinted at earlier... that he could choose what he wanted and would have a good life here?

Would that include with her? He was sure he'd felt something from her when they'd been together. To accept anything else hurt too much.

Finish the amulet.

Then she would be out of the Debrua, Nigriv would be safe and he could discuss with her what happened next, what future they might have.

Ligriv carefully picked up the gem baby, sensing the mother through the vibration within it. He held it and put his mind to how that vibration felt, letting his body and it become more in sync.

All of his concerns dropped away and he inspected his previous seven amulets. They made him happy, he could see the beauty in what he'd created. He was very good at his craft.

The best!

The final resistance slid away and he began his work on the final gemstone. There wouldn't be another, that he was certain of, this one was what he had to convert to the final replica of the other amulets.

All his focus was now on cutting and polishing the amber stone. The key to the quality of his work, he believed, was that he left something of himself in every piece he made. Every gem he cut, every piece of jewellery had a sliver of his being within.

With the other amulets he'd been so lost in the work that it happened without even thinking. Today there was a slight disconnect, only minute but it bugged him.

He wanted his work to be perfect. No matter what happened moving forward, these amulets would be out in the world, admired and envied. *Focus!*

With the shape completed, all he could do was polish it. There was little tolerance left at this point. When he held the stone up to the light he spotted a flaw in its base, the tiniest of chunks was missing.

What?

Ligriv didn't know how it had happened. He'd been as careful with this as all the others, taking only the tiniest of slivers when he cut. He wanted to scream but that would only let her know something was wrong.

No one could know. She'd said they all had to be identical, else one of the rulers felt slighted. He looked the rest of the stone over, looking for anything else wrong with it.

Finding nothing else he placed it flat down on the bench letting the light pierce into it. The flaw wasn't noticeable, thankfully on the back of it, which would be sitting on the silver base.

Quickly he began on the setting, wanting to get it placed so no one would ever see it. He wiped his brow with his sleeve and carried on. It would still look exactly the same, he was sure of it.

Hours and hours passed as he crafted the strands of silver into the identical weave he'd made for the others. He had practised this process so much, it was much easier than the first time.

When the amulet was done he held it up, relieved that it looked perfect, just like the others. *To the eye at least.*

He was done, he'd fulfilled their agreement. Maybe he could find a way out of his situation, or at least find a compromise that worked for them both.

How do I guarantee Nigriv's safety? What about mine?

Like he'd done earlier he rubbed the mark on his hand, as much for comfort as anything else, but it didn't seem to change his thought patterns. *What can I do?*

Ligriv looked at the Debrua. None of what he could see made any sense to him -- the stone, a goddess, being inside the stone… he'd think it was all madness if he hadn't experienced it himself.

Without the energy boost he'd received from touching the Debrua previously this had left him exhausted. *If only I could put my hands on it, and soak up that power, I'd feel much better.*

It was a crazy thought, enticing, but crazy. Ligriv couldn't trust what might happen. Tarna was faced away from him and he wondered why it was holding her inside.

Out of curiosity he laid his hand onto the face of the amulet he held, seeking out the smaller vibration that came through it. Slowly he allowed the rhythm of it to alter his feelings until he could sense the larger stone through it.

For the first time he intuited that it wasn't a single vibration but the combination of many. They were layered on top of each other while some twisted around each other.

He was able to detect sensations from within it, much like when he'd been inside. Some were like words, others more emotions. There was a familiarity about the words, to the voice, and he focused on that.

Tarna was speaking in her head to the Debrua. It was muted and distant but if he let it come to him rather than chase it he was able to understand it.

* * *

WE ARE ALMOST THERE, *with this last one I can begin.*

* * *

HE COULDN'T DETECT any response from the stone but it was as if she was having a conversation.

* * *

THEN I HAVE *no need for him.*

* * *

WHY? *All of the amulets are made, what use could he be?*

* * *

KEEPING him under control will not be easy. He'll have to stay hidden from everyone. Perhaps in here?

* * *

EVEN IF HE'D wanted to listen in anymore, Ligriv couldn't. He spun out of the connection, dropping the amulet on the workbench, afraid to touch it again.

The sound he made caused Tarna to turn and look his way. She stared toward him but he averted his eyes, seeking out the comfort of rubbing his palm.

There was never going to be a happy ever after for him, she'd been playing with him when she'd hinted at more. Deep down he'd known it but his heart, his dreams, had latched on to her words… hoping.

But she was just trying to manipulate him to finish the work.

You're a fool. Ligriv's heart ached thinking about his brother. *What would Nigriv say?*

"You're done?"

He nodded.

"Show me."

He held up the amulet, careful not to let his skin come in contact with the orange stone. Even so he could feel the vibration and it trying to reach him.

Ligriv began to repeat his brother's name in his head, like a mantra, as he squeezed his fingernails into his other palm.

"Bring it closer, I'd like to see it."

"It's identical to the others, you've already seen them."

Yantarnaya looked at him, moving toward the outer edge slowly. "What's the matter?"

"Nothing. I'm tired and my work is done."

"They are amazing, Ligriv, I am so pleased. They will be the most perfect gifts."

Despite not looking at her eyes Ligriv could still feel her, or the Debrua, reaching out to him, trying to probe his mind.

373

It was like tiny threads, or tendrils, that tried to wiggle their way inside. *Nigriv, Nigriv, Nigriv...* It helped, he just had to stay strong.

"I need you to come here to help me get out of the stone."

"Why?"

"What do you mean, why? Because I asked you."

"I never needed help to do that, it just pushed me out."

"Look at me, Ligriv. I need your help." Her voice sounded angrier now.

Ligriv still wouldn't look at her eyes, as tempted as he was. "I am sure someone of your power has no need for my help."

"It will not let me out on my own."

That was interesting. Why wouldn't the stone let her free... or was she lying to get him to touch it so it could control him? *Nigriv, Nigriv, Nigriv.* On and on he repeated it, cutting his nails into his hand until it hurt.

"I know what you are trying to do, I'm not going back in there."

"What?" It was almost a shriek and his spine shivered listening to it.

"Come and help me out of here, Ligriv, now!" Her anger wasn't masked now.

Of all the possibilities of what was going to happen next, he knew he wasn't going to touch the stone.

"Let me out of here, I'll get him and bring him to you!" She was shrieking, not to him but at the stone.

He wanted to be free from here, back in Barrack with his brother. A tear formed in his eye and ran down his cheek. *This is all my doing.* Ligriv turned away from the stone and placed the last amulet up with the others.

He wasn't sure if she could harm Nigriv or not, he no longer had any say in that. He wasn't going back into that stone, not for anyone.

I have to escape... somehow.

Quickly he gathered his tools into his bag and headed toward the stairs. If nothing else some of them were handy weapons, which he didn't doubt he'd need if he was to get free.

"Where are you going? Come here, Ligriv, help me... please." She had changed her voice now to sound victim-like. She was good, he had to admit, trying everything she could to capture him.

It tugged at his heart but he kept repeating his brother's name and refused to look her way. Then the screeching sound returned, but this time it was more controlled.

Slowly the level rose until it stung his ears and the inside of his head began to throb. It got louder and louder and he stumbled against the side wall.

His legs were struggling to function from the pain in his head and ears. It was all Ligriv could do to stay upright and shuffle sideways.

Nigriv... Nigriv... Nigriv... Almost there. Ligriv was sure his palm must be bleeding now he'd cut into it so much. He just needed to get away from the stone, the bigger the distance the better for him.

Another step.

His eyes flickered closed and open, he felt liquid run from his ears and then he couldn't hear anything at all. It was only his stubbornness that kept him on his feet.

Nigriv... Nigriv... Help me get out of here.

He shuffled right and dragged his left foot there. It wasn't even about willpower now, he was almost numb. She'd betrayed him, he'd loved her and yet she hadn't cared for him at all.

All his life he'd wanted a female to love him, it had only been recently he really understood why -- the lack of a mother. At its best his life in Barrack with Esphe and Berrell had been near perfect, but he'd always been seeking more.

I should have appreciated what I had, it was all I really needed.

At the bottom of the stairs he paused briefly.

I've made it.

As Ligriv looked up his heart dropped. There was no brother coming to save him, only hundreds and hundreds of stairs. And then he saw the shape of the priest, Uksod, hurrying down from above, hands pressed against his ears.

58

LIGRIV

*P*ain on Uksod's face let Ligriv know he wasn't the only one suffering from the noise and vibration. At least the screeching was lessened by the damage it had already done to his ears.

The priest was struggling as he stumbled to the bottom of the stairs, looking toward the Debrua and seeing where Tarna was. His eyes opened in alarm and his mouth moved, but Ligriv couldn't hear what was said.

He didn't hesitate and used the distraction to attack the priest, punching him in the stomach. One thing Ligriv had going for him was his natural strength. Uksod doubled over in pain, still blocking the way upstairs.

Ligriv could see something hung on a cord around the man's neck. *A key.* He would need that to open the door at the top. Ligriv grabbed the priest by the scruff of his robe and pulled him closer, tossing him down on the ground.

Quickly he knelt on Uksod's chest, pinning him where he was. He didn't expect the man would give in easily and now Ligriv could see he was angry. He yanked the cord over the priest's head, taking the key, and pushed upward before punching him in the stomach again.

Uksod winced at the hit and began to roll away, then got to his feet, pulling a knife out from under his robe. That left Ligriv at a disadvantage and he kept his eyes only on his opponent.

At this point Ligriv's only plan was to get up the stairs, but he was going to have to deal with Uksod first. Whatever happened after that he'd worry about then.

Uksod turned to the Debrua and nodded. All Ligriv could hear was the muted screeching from the stone. The priest lowered his knife to his side, but hadn't put it away. *She doesn't want him to harm me, that's something at least.*

But ultimately Ligriv needed a way to get out of here without having to fight everyone to do so. *The amulets! They'll do anything to protect them... that's my best leverage.* If he took them, then he could trade his way out… or use them.

He remembered what had happened to the man in his workshop who'd tried to take his first stone. It had killed him where he stood. *Would that happen to Uksod as well?*

It wasn't his worst idea, and he'd prefer to use his head and not his weapons to get free. But he'd have to go back to his workbench, and it had been hard enough getting this far away from it.

Without turning his back on Uksod, Ligriv began stepping sideways toward the amulets. Another thought occurred to him -- if he did kill Uksod, then no one would know she was down here.

It might buy him enough time to get away. He remembered now, she had been the one that said only Uksod came down here. It might just work in his favour.

While he moved, he hung the key over his head and kept digging his fingers against the mark on his palm. It didn't stop the pain in his head or the heavily muted screeching but it made him feel that he wasn't alone.

Once he had the first amulet in his hand he held it out, directly in front of his body at Uksod who'd followed him. If the man attacked he'd press it against him, assuming the priest wouldn't know what would happen.

Uksod stopped and turned toward his mistress, nodding and stepping back another pace. Ligriv couldn't tell if she'd told him about the danger or not but the priest was being more cautious now.

While there was more space between them, Ligriv dragged his satchel around from his back and dropped the amulet in it, quickly picking up another to hold out in front.

He watched Uksod, making sure the priest didn't try to rush him, then repeated the action, again and again until all but the one in his hand were in the bag.

He was only hoping, or guessing, that the amulet's gem would harm the priest. In case it wouldn't he needed a weapon, but the only ones he had were also in the bag.

The choice was go for one of his tools or keep hold of the amulet. He didn't like that his hand was on the amulet -- if he let his fingers touch the stone he could be more easily controlled.

In the end that concern was enough for him to put his hand into the bag for anything he could use. Uksod had been waiting for any chance to move in, and took it, rushing forward. Ligriv immediately pulled his hand free and punched at his attacker.

The priest ducked under the swinging fist and swiped his blade across Ligriv's thigh. It wasn't deep but the pain gave Ligriv pause. Uksod didn't hesitate and kicked out at Ligriv's leg, connecting with the wound.

Pain shot up Ligriv's leg causing him to drop to his knee. He looked up just in time to see Uksod's fist as it slammed into the side of his head. The strength of the punch surprised Ligriv just before he blacked out.

He came around to feel his back scraping on the floor, the bag dragging behind his head and his good leg being pulled by the ankle. Uksod was dragging him toward the stone. Ligriv couldn't let that happen.

With a flick of his injured leg Ligriv twisted his body and broke free of Uksod's grip. Despite the pain that shot up his leg, he pushed himself up from the ground, his eyes firmly on his opponent. He wouldn't underestimate the lanky priest again.

There was a dark, malevolent grin on the other man's face. Again he held his blade out in front, and stepped toward Ligriv. Ligriv fumbled around in his bag and pulled out a hammer.

It would have to do. He turned back and held it at the ready. His head was less groggy from the punch and he was as ready as he could be. There were no options now, it was him or the priest.

Ligriv stepped sideways trying to create some space between him and Uksod. Blood dripped down his leg, the leg aching from his injury, but he could do nothing to help that right now.

Uksod feinted forward, waving the blade. Ligriv pulled back instinctively, and stumbled as his foot tripped on something. As he looked down to steady himself the priest moved in.

Ligriv felt the blade cut through his tunic and into the bicep on his right arm. Struggling to keep hold of the hammer he moved forward instinctively and punched with his cut arm, using the flat of his hand straight into Uksod's chest.

The priest stumbled back but didn't appear bothered in the least. If anything the smirk on his face had grown and he regathered himself blocking Ligriv's path to the stairs.

With all the pressure in his head from the stone and the blood loss, Ligriv could feel his body weakening. He needed to end this quickly. He was going to have to try one of the amulets unless he got lucky.

He couldn't afford to take his eyes off Uksod again and cautiously reached into his bag, trying to feel for the back of one of the amulets. His fingers touched something but he couldn't tell what it was.

Suddenly a pain shot into Ligriv's hand and up his arm. Part of his hand must be touching one of the amber stones giving the Debrua and Tarna direct access to him.

The pain increased, causing him to drop to his knees and the hammer fell free. He dug his left fingers inward again and desperately repeated his brother's name.

His fingers in his bag came free and he grabbed the hammer again, expecting Uksod to attack. The man must have been held back by his mistress; if it had been the other way around, Ligriv would have seized on that opportunity.

Once more on his feet, he shuffled back toward the stairs. Uksod darted forward without warning, but kept his knife hand low. Ligriv had no choice but to keep his eyes on that.

As the man got almost within reach, Ligriv swung his arm and hammer to hit him, but the priest ducked back a step as quickly as he'd attacked. The hammer found only air but worse, Ligriv overbalanced as he followed through.

Uksod was ready for that and kicked out again at Ligriv's wounded leg. More pain shot up the leg and Ligriv grimaced backing away, not needing to look to know that the blood was flowing fast again. *Think smarter!*

Ligriv dropped to one knee, forcing his face to appear even more pained than it really was. Then he dropped his head toward the ground as if he was resigned to defeat.

It was a desperate ploy to try and turn the tables on Uksod. He had to lure him closer, hoping that the man's instructions were only to injure him not kill him.

He waited, using every breath as an opportunity to ready himself and recover, even just slightly. The priest's sandals appeared in the top of his vision as the man inched forward.

Closer.

At his next step Ligriv moved as fast as he could, swinging his arm up in a loop from the floor and snapped it downward, smashing the hammer into the man's foot.

Ligriv only wished he could hear the scream. He looked up and watched Uksod's face writhing in pain as he hobbled away. Without hesitation Ligriv jumped to his feet, dropped his hammer and rushed Uksod, grabbing the wrist of his knife hand.

Drawing on all of his remaining strength, Ligriv turned his opponent's hand inward toward his own body. He'd expected the priest would show concern or fear but his dark eyes looked devoid of anything but a desire to harm Ligriv. They were cold and focused.

With a final drive Ligriv pushed the knife into Uksod's side, then again, making sure the blade cut in deep.

Ligriv expected Uksod would loosen his grip, allowing him to take control of the knife. What he didn't expect was the man to knee him in his groin, catching him completely by surprise.

It was enough for Ligriv to let go of the knife and he stumbled backward. As he looked up all he saw was hatred in the priest's face, who pulled the knife out without hesitation and rushed Ligriv.

The last image Ligriv would see as the knife plunged into his own chest was the look of pure evil staring at him, smiling. Uksod twisted it back and forth before Ligriv dropped to the floor.

Breathing became difficult and tears flowed from his eyes. All he could see was his brother's face as the light began to fade and he slipped from the world.

I'm sorry, brother.

59

NIGRIV

*W*ork had been tedious of late for Nigriv. He'd never have thought he'd miss the stress and workload of making all those bracelets for Aarin, but since that commission had ended he was just plodding away at local things.

This meant more smithing than fancy things, which was perhaps part of the issue. While he was not as hung up about his work as his twin, having produced all those pieces and knowing they were in demand was rewarding.

Making horseshoes, hammers and wheel rims wasn't quite the same, but it was all he had right now. He found it funny how at one time he didn't care for all the bracelets and now he missed them.

No doubt when Aarin gets back he'll have another batch he needs, then I'll be sick of them.

Nigriv undid his leather apron and headed over to hang it by the door. Out of nowhere it hit him, a wave of pain burned through his chest and his knees buckled.

His ears were filled with a screeching sound, louder than anything Nigriv could imagine, bringing tears to his eyes as his body flopped to the ground.

Then another wave of pain hit him. Through the ringing in his ears words came to him like a strange whisper...

I'm sorry, brother.

"NOoooooo!"

* * *

"Nigriv! Wake up, Nigriv! Are you alright?"

Thankfully the pain in his chest and ears was gone. Confused, Nigriv opened his eyes and saw Gantcy kneeling beside him on the floor of his workshop.

What happened?

The room was dark, and his mouth had dirt in it. He spat it out and began pushing himself upward. She tried to help him. He got as far as a sitting position before the memory from earlier returned. He wobbled in her grip.

"What is it?"

He could hear the concern in her voice but Nigriv couldn't speak. His brother was dead. He passed out again.

* * *

Nigriv wasn't lying in dirt anymore, it was softer and the air smelled familiar. Slowly he opened his eyes to his bedroom... their bedroom.

Gantcy. She was there.

Somehow she'd got him back home and into his bed. But it didn't matter, Ligriv was dead.

Nothing mattered except that.

He felt an emptiness from his chest down to his navel, like someone had carved a massive hole in him. Were that true he'd be dead, but it wasn't real, it was just a sensation in his body. In one way though he did feel dead.

It can't be true.

Nigriv couldn't face it. He didn't want to feel this void, the pain, or anything else. He didn't want to be awake. He turned over and closed his eyes, succumbing to that thought.

* * *

WHEN HE WOKE AGAIN it was because of sunlight burning through his eyelids. He didn't want to be awake, there was no respite from the pain. Not that sleeping protected him completely, but it was better.

He'd been dreaming about Ligriv; memories of their early years replayed in his mind as he slept, the joy at reliving them destroyed now that his sleep was broken.

He ached for his brother. He needed to know that it was just a bad dream but the sensation inside told him it wasn't so.

"You're awake."

Her gentle voice should have eased his aches but instead it felt like an unwelcome intrusion on his pain.

"Are you unwell? What's happened?"

Slowly Nigriv looked at Gantcy sitting patiently on a stool. Her face was filled with concern. He said nothing.

She took a damp cloth and wiped his brow. "Can I get you something to drink?"

Nigriv just stared at her. He knew she cared for him, that she was concerned about him, but he had nothing to give her. He only cared about his loss and no one, nothing could fix that.

While he had nothing tangible to show him that his brother was dead, Nigriv knew it was true. While their connection might have been muddled or weaker over recent times, it still existed.

That's what this pain showed him: their link had been severed and he doubted he'd ever feel the same again. He stared in her direction for a long time, unmoving and without speaking.

Gantcy, a woman of few words herself, just sat there patiently for hours waiting for him to respond. Even when she got up and left the room Nigriv didn't move.

Later, he couldn't say how long, she returned, but this time she wasn't alone. "I've brought Madame Ayla, maybe she can help."

Nigriv knew the old villager couldn't help him. He didn't need the herbs that she'd used on Esphe. *There's nothing you can heal here, old woman.*

The frail-looking healer sat on the stool beside the bed and looked into his face. Her eyes didn't look frail at all as they stared into his.

"Can you help him?"

Madame Ayla turned to Gantcy. "I do not know what ails him, lass. There's nothing to look at, and your description of what happened to him tells me nothing."

She turned back to Nigriv and felt his forehead and picked up his wrist, holding it for some time.

"Lad, I'd like to lay my hands on you, to find out what ails you. But you're conscious so I'd want your permission before I do."

Nigriv didn't know what she meant nor did he care either way. She couldn't tell what it was and he was in no mind to tell her or anyone else.

"Do it." It was Gantcy.

"I'll not do it when he's awake like this, child. He has to consent."

"Nigriv, let her do it, please."

Nigriv could hear the pain in Gantcy's voice, but it changed nothing.

"If you can't speak, lad, you can nod, or blink if you can manage that. Your eyes open and close, I'll take that as a nod if you can blink for me."

He looked at Madame Ayla and all he could think was how futile their efforts were. *Just leave me be!* She stared into his eyes and they weren't weak at all, there was a resolve in them he'd not noticed before.

"One blink, that's all."

She watched him as he lay there. *Will you leave me in peace then?* He blinked. There was nothing she could do but at least it might make Gantcy happier. *Just do it and be gone... all of you.*

The old woman's hands felt anything but frail. She laid her right on his forehead and had he the will he would have pulled back from the icy coldness of it.

Her other was placed on his chest and he could have sworn it was on fire, from the heat surging into him. Despite how they felt he lay still. Moving wouldn't fix this, nothing could fix this.

Madame Ayla was silent the whole time until she removed her hands. "I see."

"What is it?" Gantcy asked.

"His other half has left this world, child."

There was a silence before Gantcy spoke again. "You mean, Ligriv?"

"Yes."

"Oh my!" Gantcy gasped but she was out of Nigriv's view.

His eyes were fixed on Madame Ayla sat beside his bed. *How does this old woman know?*

"I am surprised you could stand the pain, lad, it must be unbearable."

It is.

"There's nothing I can do for him. He has to want to be here."

"He's not going to die is he?" Gantcy sounded more anxious than before.

"Not from any wounds you can see, child, but if he doesn't want to live, if he has no reason to… I cannot say."

The old woman stood up slowly, then leaned down toward him and in a whisper muttered, "Go with Thenis, my boy."

To Gantcy she said, "Give him this tea," she pulled a pouch out of a bag, "morning and night. It might allow him some rest, but there's no fix apart from time."

The two women left the room. Nigriv thought he could hear their voices in the distance but he cared little for the conversation and was only thankful to be left alone.

His eyes stayed open until dark came. Even Gantcy didn't return, which didn't upset him. He drifted off to sleep again as he had no reason to be awake anymore.

6 0

NIGRIV

There was no breeze up on the rock ledge where Nigriv had been perched for more days than he could remember. He no longer felt hunger and sipped on the last skin that he had brought with him. Others… Gantcy… might wonder where he was, none of which mattered to him.

They hadn't spoken in weeks anyway and while she might still worry for him, he had nothing to give anyone else. She'd moved back to her mother's inn leaving him as he wished to be.

Somewhere within, there was a spot that cared for Gantcy and he'd wondered whether he should have allowed her to comfort him, to open up to her, but he couldn't. That wasn't how he was made.

Nigriv scratched his full beard, more as an activity than for any reason. There were no meaningful reasons for him to do anything, not anymore, not without Ligriv.

It didn't matter that his brother had been gone for months before his death, that they'd already been pulled apart. This was different. There was no coming back from this.

His body was at war with itself. He had scratched the scar on his forearm until it bled, the numbness his only relief from overwhelming feelings he couldn't handle.

387

This ridge let him find a touch of calm, more than he could in town. Down there he was lost. The shock hadn't abated, not in any way that allowed him to be his previous self. Nor did he want to be.

What point is there in being alive without him?

The question wasn't seeking an answer to his own demise but simply putting words to the numbness. In better times he came up here for peace or to talk to the voice.

But there could be no peace up here, not now, not ever. He'd come to confirm the only thought that made sense to him. There was one person that could tell him what he needed to know, perhaps, but he wasn't sure he could even speak to her.

He'd not spoken to a soul since it happened as he couldn't find his voice. At most he used gestures to get by. Talking to the voice didn't need his mouth, but he still had to open his mind and he wasn't sure he could face that.

The middle day sun cooked his already burnt and raw skin. At night the cool air dried it and during the day it split and burnt more. Nigriv welcomed the pain, it was the only relief he could find from what he felt inside.

He checked his satchel again just in case he'd missed another skin, already knowing it was stupid. His fingers brushed against something soft and he pulled out a small pouch.

Nigriv tipped the contents out beside his crossed legs. The ring he'd won the token with and the white teardrop stone that Hembleth had given him all that time ago. *What had he said?* For balance.

What balance, old man, who was balancing to protect Ligriv?

These gods, if that's what they really were, had been involved in this from the beginning. Why hadn't they protected his brother? Why couldn't they have left them both alone?

And this ring, what is this even for? The voice had told him someone would come for it, he'd know them because it would turn blue. *Who? What good is that if they couldn't save Ligriv?*

Nigriv blamed Lady Tarna most of all, but couldn't forgive any of them. Every time he brought Tarna's face into his mind a deep, primal anger bubbled up inside him.

That was the only thing that replaced the numbness. It raged within and gave him focus. It was the only time since Ligriv had gone that he felt a purpose.

I need to find her and make her pay!

Hunting her down was a goal he could pursue. That was why he wanted to speak to the voice -- she knew more than she was letting on and she could tell him exactly where Tarna was, how he could get to her.

Nigriv slid the ring onto his finger and cupped the teardrop in his hands. He could sense a vibration within it, subtle, but it was still there.

She'd said all he had to do was speak, so he did.

* * *

"WHERE ARE YOU?"

Why are you here, Nigriv?

"I need your help."

With what?

"I want to know what happened to my brother..."

I don't know what you mean.

"You must know what she did."

* * *

SHE SAID nothing for many minutes. His anger began to grow and he was about to yell out to her when she answered.

* * *

I AM a little busy at the moment, there is more to this world than just you, Nigriv.

"I want answers!"

* * *

SHE SAID NOTHING ELSE. He waited and waited but she never returned. He waited for an age but nothing. Whatever he'd expected might happen, it wasn't that.

Inside his rage continued to grow. For weeks on end the numbness had kept it in check, a way to manage his loss. Perhaps it was sadness like others spoke of, he didn't know.

But this anger he could feel, and now he wanted to use it. It was too large, too needy to be ignored. She might think she could fob him off but he wasn't going to sit here and wait.

Someone had to pay and if it was going to cost him everything then so be it. Without his brother it no longer mattered. He would find this witch that had ensnared his brother and make her pay.

If it took him raging through Enderk, then that's what he would do. But now he wondered if this voice, this goddess and her brothers weren't to blame as well.

They avoided him now, yet had interfered in their lives whenever it suited them. Where were Hembleth and Rainbow when his brother needed them? *Nowhere.*

Stupidly both of them had been influenced by these goddesses and gods but had never discussed it. *Could I have saved him if we'd just talked?*

Nigriv shrugged. There were no answers, not for the past. *What's done is done. That's what Father would say.*

There was only action, that's what he'd told his twin back when Father had died. They had to move forward and that's what Nigriv knew he had to do now.

In his mind he saw the look on his father's face in his last moments and understood it. It wasn't fear or even worry, it was a strange sort of acceptance that some things were over and that he was moving on.

Nigriv felt that way right now.

No matter what happened, what he thought, Ligriv wasn't coming back. He couldn't make that happen, but he had a choice and only he could make that.

One way or another Nigriv was going to make Lady Tarna and her siblings pay. He stood and gathered his things. A feeling of absolute clarity came over him as he took in the view across the vast plains to the north and the endless desert to his right.

He'd made a decision and now he had to act on it. His time in Barrack was over. Every inch of the place held a memory of his brother and fuelled the sadness within. He couldn't stay here, it would kill him one minute at a time. He would never survive that.

Midderbuilt would be his first stop. One way or another he would get answers from his voice. Maybe her brothers might be there too, that didn't matter.

There was magic there, he'd felt it. One way or another he would tap into it, get answers, and then he would go to Enderk. Live or die, he would seek retribution for his brother, before joining him.

Nigriv's legs were stiff and sore from the time sitting in one spot and it took him longer than normal to climb back down from the mountain. When he got to his house he found it empty and cold. He couldn't even detect the smell of Gantcy that had been there before and it saddened him.

She's better off without me now, I have to leave.

Gantcy knew what was causing him his pain and there was nothing she could do to help him. Nigriv knew there would be no goodbyes, not to her, or anyone else.

He went room to room gathering what he would need for his walk to Midderbuilt. He made sure he still had his token and checked his bow, making sure his favourite weapon wouldn't fail him.

Before he left, Nigriv placed a note on the kitchen table, hoping Gantcy would find it if she came looking for him. It seemed pointless and cold, but it was the best he could do.

Then he headed to his workshop to get tools. He'd need money to make the trip and as a lapidarist, he could work his way to Enderk well enough.

While Hembleth and Rainbow had directed them into this trade, it had been Berrell who'd taught them, and he'd use that man's memory to aid him. He had been a good man who had also been lost for no good reason.

He was ready. As he turned to go, Nigriv stopped, surprised to see

Gantcy standing before him, a bag slung over her back and a long knife strapped to her waist.

"If you think you're leaving on your own, Nigriv, you're fooling yourself."

He wanted to tell her to leave him alone, but he couldn't. He could see in her eyes she was going to follow him. *Your choice.* Nigriv nodded and continued out the door. Gantcy followed and waited for him to lock it closed.

Then the odd pair set off to the eastern edge of town. Nigriv never stopped or looked back, he just kept walking toward the base of the mountain range and his first steps toward Midderbuilt.

6 1

NIGRIV

*N*igriv couldn't remember exactly how long his other trip to Midderbuilt had taken and he tried to avoid thinking about it. That trip was filled with memories he didn't want to face.

"I need a break, Nigriv."

He turned to look at Gantcy and the anger and focus that was driving him eased. It wasn't that he had forgotten she was there, not at all, but whenever he was walking all he could think about was his revenge.

They found a spot with a touch of shade by the edge of the mountains and sat.

"I'm sorry."

"You don't need to keep saying that."

"But this trip… the walk."

"Enough, Nigriv." Her hand brushed over her brooch, a habit she'd acquired ever since he'd given it to her. "I am here because I want to be."

"Me dragging you like this isn't right. It's my anger, my wish…"

She reached up and placed a finger on his mouth, stopping him.

"What is right?" She shrugged. "I chose you and that's the end of it.

Had I planned to leave my home? No, but then I hadn't chosen to stay either. I won't keep having this conversation. It's done."

There was a strength in her that he had always admired. Despite how quiet and fragile she appeared, Gantcy was much more than that. In these moments with her it stirred things inside him that he didn't understand.

"What is it?"

He shook his head, unable to express what he was feeling. No one had ever explained it to him. He held her hand and smiled, occasionally taking a drink from one of the few remaining skins.

I am not alone, even if I try to be.

* * *

FOR THE NEXT two days they continued, covered from head to toe to block the sun, conserving what little water and food they had left. Nigriv felt they were close now, tying to recall his previous journey.

Despite how peaceful the scenery around them was, something wasn't right. Nigriv didn't know how he knew but he sensed something amiss, a vibration or the feel of the air, whatever it was left him totally unsettled.

"Can you see it?" He pointed up into the range of mountains.

"What?"

"Look along my arm. There's a peak there above the others that keeps going into the sky."

As they both looked in that direction a deep rumbling sound rolled back toward them.

"What is it?" Gantcy's voice sounded afraid.

"It sounds like rocks, maybe a large rockfall. We should get away from the cliffs."

Nigriv didn't really know what was going on but they both moved away, looking upward as they did.

"Look!" Gantcy was pointing back toward the spire.

Nigriv couldn't believe what he was seeing. "It's… it's moving."

As sure as he was breathing and walking the peak was spinning.

"Oh Thenis, what is happening?"

To his left his eyes were drawn out into the desert where a cloud of sand was rising up off the floor and heading toward the mountains. When it reached the range the sand spread out and clothed the entire peak in the shape of a spire.

Any doubt that the mountain was spinning was removed the moment the sand encased it, making it much clearer that it was turning. The line of sand still reached out to the greater desert where a bigger cloud had appeared.

It was moving violently in multiple directions, swirling and twisting before it began to spread to the east.

"Hurry, Gantcy. Whatever is happening I think we want to be in shelter."

"You want to go toward it?"

"There's shelter down there, a massive ledge, that has to be better than out here."

Nigriv struggled to make it sound convincing but all he knew was it wasn't safe out here in the open. He just hoped that the camp still existed, that whatever was happening in the mountains hadn't wiped out Midderbuilt.

Winds reached them now, filled with sand, battering them as they struggled south. They tightened their head wraps leaving only a narrow gap to see through but even that was still was blasted by sand.

For the first time ever Nigriv felt truly afraid. He had no idea what had caused all of this but he had never felt less in control than now. He'd dragged Gantcy along with him, he wasn't going to let her die out here.

Holding hands they had returned to the cliff line using it to guide them so they didn't lose their way. Everything was dark from the storm and in the relentless winds they struggled to see anything at all.

Without warning he ploughed straight into a wall of sand. *What is this?*

Nigriv had one hand tightly gripping Gantcy's and with his other he tried to feel how far the sand reached. His best guess was it was only a few feet taller than them.

He pushed his face up to Gantcy's ear and spoke through the scarf wrapped around his mouth. "We need to climb over it."

"What?"

"Climb. Climb over it. UP!"

Pushing her ahead of him, Nigriv dragged himself up the sand hill. He wasn't prepared to leave the rock edge to find a way around the barrier, this was their best chance.

Suddenly he couldn't feel Gantcy's feet above him, his hand swept about frantically seeking her out. *Where is she?*

Desperately he scrambled upward. Still he couldn't find her, then suddenly there was nothing above him and he plunged forward. Nigriv tumbled downward until he stopped with a thud on hard ground.

He couldn't see a thing. It was eerily dark and quiet where he'd fallen but at least the winds were gone. He pulled his scarf from his face and tried to see.

This has to be under the ledge!

At a guess mounds of sand had formed around the outer camp area and they'd found their way inside. "Gantcy? Gantcy, where are you?"

"Here."

Her voice didn't sound strong and he followed it to find her propped against the sand, shaking.

"What's happening?"

"It's alright, we've made it."

He wrapped her in his arms. *We made it.*

6 2

———

NIGRIV

$\mathcal{N}$igriv and Gantcy sat there in silence staring into the darkness under the ledge. With the noise of the storm muted by the sand walls he could hear others in the darkness.

Lights began to appear as people lit lanterns and he stood, taking Gantcy by the hand, and headed toward the nearest cluster of them.

They stumbled into several tents in the dark before reaching a group of people sitting together.

"Where did you come from?"

"We only just made it. We were heading here from the north, just clambered across the..." Nirgriv turned back to where they'd come from. "...the wall there, before it all closed off."

"You're very lucky to have made it, friend."

"Don't we know it, it was horrific out there."

"Here, come join me, you look like you could do with a drink and something to eat."

"You're sure?"

"Of course."

"What about the guards?"

"I don't think anyone will care much for rules today."

Gantcy and he sat and chatted with these people, a group of traders up from Watersend.

"Terrifying it was. When the rumbling began, we all thought the ledge was about to fall." Nigriv could still hear the fear in the man's voice. "But outside the sands were racing in this direction so we had no choice but to shelter under it."

The man looked up but his face didn't show any less concern. He touched his forehead three times before shaking it.

"It seems safe enough now?" Gantcy said timidly.

"Better than outside. We didn't have much choice, lass."

"It was the spire moving that created that noise."

"What?"

Nigriv explained what they'd seen; the spinning peak as well as the line of sand that stretched out to the desert floor.

"Seth is angry." Another of their hosts shook her head. "We're lucky to be alive."

That night many others came and sat around their campfire to hear Nigriv's story until he couldn't repeat it anymore. No one said it but he could tell they didn't really believe him.

He didn't care. They'd made it and were safe for now. He found an empty tent for them to rest in and they both lay hugging tightly together throughout the night.

Nigriv couldn't sleep, worrying that maybe the ledge might collapse on them and disturbed by what had occurred.

The storm continued outside for three more days, winds raging across the desert. As quickly as people could clear a small entrance on the southern side beside the cliff edge, it would fill again.

Finally word spread around the camp that it had stopped. Nigriv and Gantcy joined the queue of people who climbed out of the opening to see the world outside Traveller's Rest.

The sun scorched Nigriv's face and stung his eyes but it felt good to be out from under the rock ledge. Everyone moved out far enough to look up at the town above.

"The mountain... Look! The mountain!"

Everyone stared up and saw exactly what Nigriv had told them about. A spire of sand was spinning slowly around where the mountain had been before. Spreading up from the base, it was a perfect conical shape of many colours, reds, browns, pale colours, all moving in a constant motion, enough that he had to look away.

He looked at Gantcy and saw her arms were wrapped across her chest. Nigriv understood what she was feeling. This wasn't normal and had to have been created by something unnatural. *Or someone.*

Nigriv looked up at the road into Midderbuilt. It was covered completely in sand, the gate at the top blocked. He wanted to be up there but the path wasn't passable.

The sides to their camp reached almost to the top of the ledge. He figured he could probably scramble up and get into town that way but there were people up there trapped in and the gantry was nowhere to be seen.

"We need tools. We need to clear the road." He pointed to the sand-covered twisting path and looked around at the people gathered. Several others took up shovels and picks and following him toward the base.

While they worked on the path others worked on widening the opening to Traveller's Rest. Gantcy came and joined him bringing skins and her own tools.

There was no need to speak, they just got stuck into the task. His anger was returning and this was as good a way to use it as any. They worked all day, collapsing in exhaustion at night.

Everyone rose early again the next day and continued what they'd started. Once the opening in the camp wall was wide enough for wagons to squeeze out, some of the traders set off for Watersend seeking supplies.

Nigriv kept working on the pathway and over the next few days they got closer to the gates at the top. There was no way anyone above could open the gates with a mound piled against them.

Late that afternoon they freed the door on the right, enough that the men inside could force it open. Then guards stepped out and let the workers in.

Nirgriv reached for his token, buried under his drenched and sandy clothing.

"No need for that, friend, everyone gets a free pass until the city is restored. Get inside and take a break."

They sat on a bench ten feet from the gates and watched as four guards took to the remaining sand. An older man with sparse grey hair came over to Nigriv.

"We're grateful for your efforts. Everyone up here watched you toiling to free the path."

"Had to be done, I wanted to be up here as well."

"I recognise you, you carry a token do you not?"

Nigriv nodded.

"I'm the mayor of Midderbuilt, Threnif." The man held out his hand which Nigriv shook. "It's been a while."

"I have questions."

"We all do, son, but no one has any answers. Never in my life have I seen such a storm but compared to that," he pointed up at the spire, "it was nothing."

Nigriv shook his head. "We almost didn't make it. It was ferocious."

"You're here now. Tell all of your fellow campers tonight they eat and stay up here."

With that he walked away and spoke with the guards, before heading back into the town to join the people working up there. Much of Midderbuilt was buried under sand as well and the residents had formed a chain of people out to the edge, passing buckets of sand and tossing it over the side.

It was the strangest of events but there was a tiny silver lining -- Gantcy was going to get to see Midderbuilt, at least for tonight. He looked around the place and shook his head, still finding it impossible to believe.

63

NIGRIV

Anyone that wanted to was allowed to stay up in Midderbuilt that night. While the town had suffered its share of the storm, little damage was done and the centre of town had been cleared.

Cots were set up for anyone that wanted to sleep and small groups had spent much of the night sitting around staring up at the spire for as long as they could.

No one could stomach it for long. Nigriv found he could only spend a couple of minutes before he felt nauseous. But it was too captivating to ignore.

In the starlight it fascinated him. Gantcy was asleep beside him, her exhaustion winning out. Everyone up there was experiencing it all in their own way. Some feared what had happened, others were more curious than frightened.

The last time Nigriv had been here had been the first time he'd spoken to the voice, after he'd made the ring and won the token. Earlier today he'd handed Berrell's token to the mayor and explained what had happened.

He couldn't imagine what their mentor would think were he here now. Berrell had a tortured relationship with the town, something Nigriv could understand, albeit for different reasons.

Unsure if he needed the ring or not, Nigriv took it from his pocket and placed it on one of his fingers. Something shifted within him, subtle but he could sense it.

* * *

WHY ARE YOU HERE?

"To speak to you."

You could have done that back at your home.

"I tried, but you fobbed me off."

That was not my intent, there was a lot going on.

"Well, I'm here now. I need to know why Ligriv was killed."

He's dead?

"Are you pretending you don't know?"

I'm not pretending anything, Nigriv. You are confused as to what you think we do or don't know. There are places we cannot reach, Enderk is one of them. Why do you think he is dead?

"I know. When it happened, a piece of me was ripped away. I can feel it even now."

I am sorry.

Her words meant nothing to him.

I think it would be best if you came to see me.

"Where?"

Inside the mountain.

"Under this thing? You have to be kidding."

You'll be perfectly safe. What is happening out there doesn't affect what's in here.

"What is in there?"

Something I want you to see.

"Why can't we talk as we are?"

Because for you to understand what has happened you need to see something.

* * *

As much as Nigriv wanted answers he didn't know if he could trust her. His anger toward these people hadn't gone away, it was simply muted. Ligriv had trusted one of them and now he was dead.

But if going to her would help him get his revenge then he had to take that chance.

"How?"

I will lead you.

"Lead me?"

Just follow my directions. Turn to your left, now head up that path between the building and the rocks.

That she could tell his exact location bothered him but in comparison to being able to speak inside his head or move a mountain was nothing. He found himself in a small hut without doors or shutters on the windows.

* * *

"Now what?"

Nigriv heard a clunk from the wall on his right and saw a stone door stood slightly ajar.

Make sure you close it behind you.

He did as she asked before considering how he might get back out.

Can you see the light?

"Yes."

Follow it. It will take you some time.

The corridor seemed endless, occasionally veering left or right as he pushed deeper under the mountain. As he walked the light grew until it was almost like daylight.

When he turned the last corner and saw what was before him, he stopped, stunned. The large cavern before him was occupied by an enormous gem shining an intense bluish white light.

He'd seen this before, it came back to him in a flash. A dream, many years before, not long after he'd first been given the stone, but he'd not been able to remember it until now.

Nigriv reached into his pocket and pulled out the stone Hembleth had given him. It was a miniature replica of what he was standing before but inside it a tiny blue flame was getting bigger and pulsing the same colour as the large one.

He could feel the tiny vibration within his stone increasing and running up through his arms. As it spread throughout him he felt more at ease than he had in a long time.

Even the void he'd had since Ligriv's death shrank, his chest feeling full of a warmth and… maybe happiness, he couldn't describe it. Light began to stream into him giving him the most ecstatic experience he'd ever had.

* * *

WELCOME TO THE CITADEL STONE, Nigriv. That stone you have is a baby, if you like, of this one.

It was many minutes before he could gather himself and respond.

"Which means, the one Ligriv had..."

Yes, a baby of another stone.

"What stone?"

It's called the Debrua.

Nigriv stared upward trying to take all of this in.

"Where are you?"

I am there but also not.

"What does that mean?"

At the moment I am not physically with you in that cavern but using the stone to communicate with you.

"Who are you?"

Who I am matters little, Nigriv. I brought you here to show you the stone, so that you might get some relief. Do you feel better?

"Yes. But you're manipulating me."

The stone isn't changing anything about you, Nigriv, it is simply sharing itself with you. You're experiencing it in the way that you best need it.

He had come for answers, not to feel good.

"Why did it kill Ligriv?"

I know nothing about that, Nigriv.

"When you last spoke to me you made it sound like you knew things were coming, like everything was about to change. Like you knew something bad was going to happen."

No, Nigriv. We could sense a shift in this world but no detail. As much as the prophecy exists, its meaning is obscure.

"You should have done something."

What could we have done, Nigriv? Tried to control your brother's feelings? That would make us no different to Tarna. Besides, what you think we might be able to do and actually can are different.

"But the prophecy. Hembleth said he found us because of it. Doesn't that mean you could have stopped it, left us alone?"

His finding you was as much luck as it was anything else. Had your brother not picked up that stone, I doubt we would have noticed you at all.

"How's that?"

That stone should not have been on Dharatan.

"Why?"

It belongs to the Debrua. Why a piece of it was lying where it was we have no answer to, but once Hembleth found your brother with it you both became of interest.

"He made it sound like it was planned."

If only that were true. But while more of the prophecy makes sense now, back then it was much less clear. Maybe we could have stepped in if we had known.

"Maybe?"

Prophecies have a way of fulfilling themselves, Nigriv. They tell of a greater truth, of the powers that lie under all of this, behind these stones. That are at odds with each other.

"This stone and the Debrua?"

Yes. Like night and day, they exist as opposites to create balance.

"That's what Hembleth said when he gave me this."

Nigriv held up the small stone. The voice didn't reply.

"What moved the mountain?"

That was us.

"Why?"

I will explain, but you will forget much of it by the time you leave the mountain.

"A trick?"

Of sorts, but let me explain. Our sister, Yantarnaya, the one you call Tarna, has become partnered with the Debrua. While we don't know her exact intentions it would appear none of it is good. She had your brother fashion a number of amulets, each of which bore a gem carved from the Debrua. These were brought to Dharatan by the ruler of Enderk.

"For what purpose?"

Gifts, it seems. The reasons behind why your peoples do many things confuses us at times, but in this the ruler Schevenal had desires to impress the other rulers.

"What's wrong with that?"

Those stones should not be in the hands of people, Nigriv. That you and your brother were able to touch them is what alerted us to things not being normal.

"I don't understand."

A normal person touching that stone you carry, or even your ring, would cause them great harm. The amber your brother carried would kill instantly.

Nigriv immediately remembered the man they'd found dead in the workshop in Barrack.

That she created amulets is bad enough, but to send them out into the world was very wrong. Which has proven to be true.

"How?"

As soon as they crossed the Stepping Isles we were able to observe their journey to the Great Fair. Then they were gifted to each of the rulers of Dharatan. Everyone was in awe of their beauty, not just from your brother's work but we suspect from the effect of the stones, so many together.

"In what way?"

You know how you feel better around this stone?

"Yes."

How it affects you depends on the stone and its nature. The Debrua is the

Citadel Stone's opposite, Nigriv. The effect would have been very different to how you are feeling now.

With so many of them together its reach would have been significant, even over such a distance. Things went very wrong, people began to turn on each other, realm against realm, ruler against ruler.

Battles began that made no sense, at first just to protect themselves, but before long it was as if they were all possessed. That was when we had to intervene.

"How?"

The storm. My brother Seth used the might of the desert and the power of the Citadel. I doubt he expected the effect on the spire but the storm stopped what was happening before it spread.

"What do you mean, spread?"

There is much we don't know, Nigriv, but the behaviour of everyone was beyond us. Should any of those rulers return to their realms, who knows the results.

"So where are they?"

We have them.

"The amulets?"

Yes, and the rulers.

"What are you going to do with them?"

Keep them away from everyone, at least until we understand the amulets more, or perhaps forever.

"Where?"

You do not need to know, Nigriv. I tell you this to ease your pain about your brother, before you forget.

"Forget what?"

Everything.

"I don't understand. You bring me here to tell me what happened but then I will forget."

Not just you, Nigriv, everyone will forget. It is what we needed to do.

Nigriv didn't understand what she was saying.

The storm killed almost everyone that crossed its path. That wasn't our intention. But that's the problem with us being involved, the world responds in its own way. It is why she should never have set those stones free, or had your brother make them. The cost to people is too great, the knowledge of the amulets cannot exist, there is no telling what they might do.

"What does this mean?"

We've created something to protect you all. A barrier, something that removes the memories leading up to the Fair and what happened. But it is not like a small cut, it is far-reaching.

"Meaning what?"

You will forget him, Nigriv.

Nigriv's calm was shattered by those words and his anger returned. The stone no longer felt comforting in his hand.

"I do not want to forget him, I came here to find out who was involved."

Why?

"She has to pay."

What do you mean?

"I will kill her if she killed him."

That's impossible.

"Why?"

She isn't of this world, you cannot, nor would we let you.

"You're saying I cannot go?"

Even if you could remember him and her it is your free will to choose that we would not alter. But all you will achieve is your death.

"Then I would be with him."

I don't think your life is meant to be thrown away so easily, Nigriv.

"What do you mean?"

The mark you bear.

"I didn't choose it, but what does it matter?"

It is there for a reason.

"What?"

We do not know, not yet at least, but you are important.

"Like he was?"

She didn't respond. Nigriv stood there uncertain what to do. Maybe everything she was saying was just like how Tarna had manipulated his brother.

He had come here to make someone pay. He stuffed the small

stone in his pocket, unwilling to give it up even if it was connected to this one.

"Am I trapped in here?"

No! You can go at any time. I brought you here to help you understand what this was about. I didn't think you could without seeing the Citadel Stone.

"Then I want to go. I want to be back outside."

I understand. I am sorry, Nigriv, I wish I could offer you more.

Nigriv turned and fled the stone and her voice, not believing that he wouldn't remember this. He needed to think through his choices, to plan how to get his revenge for Ligriv.

And then there was Gantcy. He couldn't take her to certain death, somehow he had to send her away, or leave her. She might be willing to follow him but he couldn't allow it.

He needed to be outside, away from whatever this stone was doing to him, away from the voice. Away from this mountain and whatever magic lived within it. Berrell was right, this place was dangerous, they'd all have been better served to have never left Barrack.

6 4

NIGRIV

As soon as he left the hut and looked around Midderbuilt things felt strange to Nigriv. He wasn't sure why but he felt quite at odds with the place.

He'd just come from inside the mountain. *Didn't I?* He couldn't exactly grab hold of what he'd just been doing. It was daytime now but it had been dark before, hadn't it?

Looking around the town he struggled to recognise it. It didn't feel like last time he'd been here. *When was that?* Nigriv knew he'd been here before a long time ago, or so he thought. *I have, I know it.* But he couldn't place when.

He arrived at the town centre expecting to see something -- cots -- where he'd been earlier. Gantcy. *What is wrong with me?* When he got there she wasn't there. It had been cleared out.

"Everyone was sent back to camp, the leniency is over."

Nigriv sort of understood what the guard was saying. There was a reason it didn't affect him and it took a moment for that to come back to him. He reached for the token hanging around his neck.

He hurried to the gates, a strange urgency filling him. She mattered, he needed to find her. As he reached the gate he turned and looked back to the spinning mountain and shook his head.

I would have remembered that.

A conversation passed across his mind fleetingly, he could almost recall it. A brother… his brother, a voice… A pain squeezed his chest just for a moment. *It's important.* He wanted to hear it but it was gone and he turned away to start the walk down.

Nigriv knew he was going to the camp and that was where he lived, but that didn't seem right. While he had this token he could stay in the town – so where had Gantcy come from?

The closer to the bottom he got he saw the wall of sand still surrounding the camp and could remember the storm and why the wall was there. But if he tried to push backward further his memories seemed to be fading. He only vaguely remembered them walking through the storm to find their way here.

Nigriv was glad to see Gantcy, that memory seemed solid.

"What's that look on your face?"

"I'm confused."

"About?"

"Where did I meet you?

She stared at him and he could see she had the same problem as he. "I… I can't… I don't know. What's happening, Nigriv?"

"I don't know."

She came to him and he wrapped his arms around her, and right at this moment it was the best thing in the world to him. As they stood in front of their tent Nigriv tried to fish around in his head for other memories but found nothing.

He knew his name and hers, he remembered the storm and what had happened since then but that was it. He wasn't even sure there was meant to be more than that. It hurt to even try and think about it.

"What have you been doing?"

She pushed free of him. "No one seems to have any idea what to do, so I started organising people into tasks."

Nigriv smiled.

"What?"

"Just you, you hardly say a word but when you want something done… I can't think of anyone better to lead them."

She slapped his arm gently with a smile on her face.

"What shall I do then?"

"We need to open up the eastern end, why don't you lead that?"

"Fair enough." Nigriv went and rounded up some more men to help him and headed off, happy to put his body to work.

The wall of sand on this side was deep and it took them a week to make a hole wide enough for a person to clamber through. Once that happened it seemed to open much quicker.

A man from Thabeng, Crallo, organised them to use some hand carts and carry the sand they excavated hundreds of feet from the wall. "We don't want to make it easy to blow back here with the first wind that comes."

With that others came to help, using the carts to take the sand his group was removing. Every day it widened letting in more light under the ledge, waking everyone earlier and helping them get more done.

It was hard, monotonous, physical work and Nigriv collapsed at the end of every day. But at least they had a purpose.

More openings were being made on the northern and southern sides and with each one fresh air began to circulate, a welcome reprieve from the smells that had been forming in the enclosed space.

Wagons arrived from Watersend with fresh food and ale, lifting everyone's spirits. No one had any more news than what the campers had; if there was anything more than this, no one knew of it.

Nothing was easy in the camp and the longer they stayed, the less cordial some of the occupants became. Small disagreements broke out and a few of the originals took their leave to head back south, away from here and back to the homes they had vague recollections of.

Nigriv knew there was a time before they had arrived, that he and Gantcy had not just been born here together, but as he tried to put his mind to what he knew he should know, nothing came. Whenever he tried he ended up with the worst of headaches.

This doesn't make any sense. Where am I from?

Something was missing from him that he couldn't explain, part of him was empty and as he probed it he began to feel things that he didn't understand.

The anger within him, he had experienced before, and it spoke to him about some great loss but no details. As he focused on that an overwhelming feeling came, like a numbness, that Gantcy explained was how being sad felt.

He'd changed and he didn't know why. This world had changed and he had no more idea about that either. Then there were the two jewels he carried in a pouch in his pocket.

Something about them was important, he could feel it deep inside, but not the reason why. Things were being kept from him, all of them, and it was important.

Why can't I remember?

65

NIGRIV

The fog was thick, thicker than anything Nigriv had ever experienced before. He couldn't even see the fingers on his hand. Someone was calling him, the voice sounded familiar, almost like his own but different.

"Nigriv..."

That was all they said, just his name called over and over again through the fog. At first Nigriv had simply attempted to understand what was happening but now he was chasing after the voice.

Nigriv wasn't sure why but it felt important to get there, to discover who it was calling his name. He kept moving despite his fear of not knowing.

"Nigriv..."

The voice sounded so distant and hollow, but he kept after it, one step then another, unable to see if he was about to stumble into danger.

And yet he still continued and the more he did, the more he knew he had to. It might have been minutes or hours, Nigriv couldn't tell, but he seemed to be getting no closer.

The voice sounded more and more desperate as time went on.

"Don't forget me, Nigriv..."

Forget who? Something told him time was running out and he pushed ahead as fast as he dared, not quite running but close. "Who are you?"

"You're forgetting already, Nigriv... I'm your brother."

Brother... what broth... Then Nigriv shuddered to a stop. It all flooded back and his body filled with rage. All of the anger and pain rushed back. His brother... Ligriv... had died.

How could I have forgotten... what has been happening? With the memories came the insight that it wasn't just him but everyone's memories that were gone. No one could remember their past in any detail at all.

But this was his brother, his twin, how could he forget Ligriv...?

In that moment much of his past came back to him, memories of Ligriv and himself when they were young, far to the north, before Barrack. But it was hard, as though the fog was in his head obscuring everything about his past.

"Don't forget me, brother!"

"Never, brother, never!"

* * *

"Nigriv! Nigriv, what's wrong?"

His eyes opened and he found Gantcy shaking him. "Where is he?"

"Who? You were dreaming."

"But, Ligriv."

"Who?" She looked at him as though he was speaking another language. "What?"

"My brother."

"Your brother?"

"Yes, stop repeating me."

"What are you talking about? You were having a bad dream, Nigriv, it's okay. You're safe."

She doesn't remember. How is it that I can? But even as he thought it he felt the very words turning to air, his mind was losing the name.

NO! I will remember.

Gantcy shook her head and lay back down and in time he could hear she'd fallen back to sleep. Nigriv would do the same if he could get that dream back, but he couldn't even really recall what dream it was.

Instead he got out of bed and slipped out of the tent. *The name, his name... Ligriv. I can remember that, it's like mine. Brother... Ligriv.*

As his mind drained of almost everything that had come up, he thought of the items in his pocket and pulled them out, slipping on the ring and holding the stone.

The voice... she will know. He needed to get to her, and ask her what was happening before he forgot even that.

As quickly as he could he climbed the path up to Midderbuilt in the dark, repeating the name. *Ligriv... Ligriv... Lig...Rilgiv... no... Ligriv...* Nigriv could already feel he was losing it.

He reached the gate without even realising it.

"What do you want at this hour?" a guard asked him.

Nigriv had to break his concentration to deal with the man. He lifted the token hung around his neck and showed it to the man. "I'm coming in."

"It's late."

"Since when is there a limit on entering? The token says I can come in. Let me in!" His voice expressed how angry Nigriv was feeling, even though he couldn't explain why.

The guard let him in with a shake of his head, but he paid him little notice. He desperately tried to find the words he'd been repeating just moments before but they had slipped away. *Get to the voice!*

Recent memories weren't a problem except he wasn't sure how he knew about this odd little hut and even why he'd been there before. There was meant to be a door here, but he couldn't see it.

Nigriv ran his hands over the wall that he was sure he'd been through before but felt nothing. He banged on it frantically. "Open up! Open up!"

Nothing happened, and he put his head against the rock and began to weep. He retrieved the small white stone from his pocket, and held it up toward the rock wall.

"Let me in!"

There's no need to shout, Nigriv, what on Dharatan is wrong?

"I can't remember, I can't even remember what I don't remember. What have you done?"

He heard a loud click come from the rocks and the door popped open. Nigriv pulled it open and slid through. There was a distant light, and he rushed toward it, a familiar sensation creeping through him.

When he turned into the large cavern and saw the huge white stone he stopped. He knew this stone, he'd been here before, it was a safe place, at least that's how he felt right now.

Nigriv walked up to the stone and placed his hands upon it and all his frustrations and anger subsided.

* * *

"Are you there?"

Yes. Why are you so upset, Nigriv?

"Why can't I remember?"

Do you remember being here before?

"I do now, but not minutes ago."

I see.

"What do you see?"

I cannot say.

"Can't or won't?"

It's for the best, Nigriv.

* * *

A name popped back into his head, the name he'd been trying to remember.

* * *

"Why can't I remember my brother, Ligriv?"

It's what we had to do, what I explained to you last time.

"But I don't remember, how can I know if I can't remember?"

I told you this would happen, I shan't repeat it every other week. You just need to give it time, Nigriv.

"Time?"

* * *

HE PULLED his hands free of the huge stone. Inside his anger had surfaced again and he had an inkling that the stone was dampening it, controlling him.

Not me, you won't.

The voice's unwillingness to tell him everything didn't help at all. The ring on his finger shone as did the small stone he always carried. Yet he wasn't sure where he'd got these things from.

Nigriv removed the ring and stuffed it in his pocket and held the teardrop stone up. It was filled with the same bright white light and touches of blue as the big stone he was standing beside.

They were connected, he knew that, but his connection to it all was unclear. Slowly he walked backwards putting distance between himself and the stone.

Now he could see how huge it was, reaching up out of sight into the mountain. That same mountain that spun constantly. He remembered the storm and the mountain beginning to move, but even that felt vague.

It's all them. They're behind all of this.

Holding the stone now felt like he was carrying something poisonous. He looked at it, beginning to believe that the voice was using it against him, against someone else as well.

She never showed her face to him, she was just a voice. Was it the stone itself? He didn't want the stone anymore, he didn't want to be here. He couldn't hold this anymore.

The rage exploded within him. He wasn't even sure why it was so intense, but he hurled the small stone directly at the larger one.

Sparks flew as they collided, and the smaller one crashed to the floor, splitting in two.

A screech sounded in the cavern and he felt a wave of sadness flood through him. Then anger. Nigriv knew it wasn't his and that it was coming from outside of him. He turned and fled.

There was little light and he stumbled his way back along the long corridor, bumping off the walls as he went, until he found himself in the hut. With a shove he slammed the door closed and hurried away, checking over his shoulder as he made his way to the gate.

It wasn't until he reached the desert floor that his heart rate began to settle and he looked back up at the town, trying to remember what he'd just been up there for.

He hadn't been up there to work, it was night, and he'd felt a little angry about something but even that wasn't clear. He clambered back into his tent to find Gantcy sat anxiously waiting for him.

"What's wrong, Nigriv? Where have you been?"

"Up there," he said, still annoyed.

"Why are you upset?"

"I just am!"

She looked wounded by his tone. "What did I do?"

He saw the frown and sadness on her face and it broke his mood. "I'm sorry, you've done nothing. It's not you. There's something I can't remember, something I should be able to remember, but I can't."

"I know."

"Why are our memories going?"

She shook her head and he saw the fear on her face.

"At least it's not just me." He grabbed her and they hugged for a long while, saying nothing, just clinging to each other as if they'd forget themselves if they didn't.

"What will we do?"

"I don't know, Gantcy. I went up to town looking for answers."

"And?"

"I found none."

They sat there as the sunlight rose with the new day and Nigriv wondered what it was that was niggling away deep inside. He felt like there was more he could tell Gantcy but he couldn't remember what that was.

What on Dharatan is happening to us?

66

NIGRIV

*D*ays passed and any remnant of what had angered Nigriv was lost. As he worked alongside the rest of their little community slowly removing more and more sand he didn't even realise there were memories to recall.

Weeks passed as he and his crew widened the gap on the eastern wall until it was nearly half done. No one spoke about anything other than what existed for them in that moment.

People came and went from Watersend bringing supplies and a reminder of what else lay beyond this strange desert residence. People knew there were other cities and places, but could recall few details about them.

Little by little pieces fell into place with the jewellers up in the town getting back to work and trade recommencing. Life moved forward one stage at a time and any discussion of the past within the community disappeared.

Nigriv sat high on the northern sand wall late one afternoon staring along the mountain range tinged with orange from the setting sun behind it. He smiled at the sight of Gantcy clambering up toward him.

She was his everything, and they were as close as anyone could be.

Their whole life wrapped up here. It was almost enough for him. Almost.

Except for something deep inside, small but annoying, gnawing at his mind but he couldn't work out what it was.

Gantcy finally arrived beside him and sat in a puff of sand.

"Can I join you?"

He nodded.

"I have something to ask you."

Nigriv turned and looked at her as she wouldn't usually precede a question with notice.

"Is this it?"

"Is what it?"

"Midderbuilt, this camp."

"Say what you mean, Gantcy."

"We're not from here. It bothers me that I can't remember where we are from and what happened before the storm. Like the people coming from Watersend, we have to be from somewhere too."

Nigriv shrugged. He'd considered the same question but he had no answers to it.

She pointed toward the north. "I look that way and feel like there's something there I should know, but I can't remember."

"I know what you mean, but no matter how hard I try, there's nothing there. It's like my head is empty."

They sat there quietly for a while before she spoke again.

"I want to go somewhere, I don't care where, but I am done with here."

He looked at her carefully. Gantcy rarely demanded anything from him, but right now he knew she was telling him, not asking.

"Where?"

"North, south, east, I don't care, Nigriv, just not here."

He nodded, neither agreeing nor disagreeing with her. She was right, this wasn't their home. It had harboured them at a dangerous moment in time but there was something else for them.

"Let's go eat."

They half slipped, half walked down the sand bank and headed to the communal camp kitchen. Since the storm, residents had banded together to prepare evening meals and while the camp was changing, this habit had remained.

Having familiar faces was settling at a time when nothing made sense. Sharing with others gave everyone security that they would be okay. But Nigriv knew their time here was over.

Gantcy was right, it was time to move on. The pair of them sat mostly in silence watching the camp become rowdier as the group consumed more ale and wine. They slipped away back to their tent. He was tired, tired of all the labour, tired of being here, but more than anything tired of not knowing.

* * *

SOMETHING DISTURBED Nigriv's sleep and he lay there listening to hear what it was. There was no movement from Gantcy and he couldn't sense anyone outside the tent.

Just a dream?

But he couldn't get back to sleep. His mind was fully awake now and he slowly slid out of their bedroll, doing his best not to disturb Gantcy. His nerves were still on edge, expecting danger as he dressed and pulled on his boots.

There was no one outside nor any odd sounds within the sleeping camp. He chose to walk the camp anyway as much to shake off the chill of the desert at night as anything else.

Nigriv found no one else about and stopped at the eastern opening to stare out across the sea of sand in the moonlight.

* * *

THEN HE HEARD HIS NAME.

Nigriv...

The voice, he knew that voice, a woman's but he couldn't place who it was or how he knew it. He looked around but there was no one to be seen. A thought tugged on his mind and he reached into his pocket and pulled out the ring, slipping it on without thinking.

* * *

COME TO US, *Nigriv.*
"*What do you want?*"

* * *

BITS OF MEMORIES FORMED. He could see the hut, the corridor, and the massive stone shining like the sun. And the woman's voice that he knew from the stone.

As he remembered so too his anger resurfaced. They were connected together and even if the depth of it all escaped him, he knew he didn't trust her fully.

* * *

COME TO THE STONE, *Nigriv, it is important.*

* * *

HE DIDN'T KNOW why she was calling him, and he didn't want to find out. All he could remember was that she annoyed him, that he couldn't trust her.

* * *

"*TELL ME WHY.*"

* * *

THERE WAS no response so he began to think the whole thing was another dream. Maybe he was still asleep and this was all happening in his head. But he knew that wasn't true, there was more to this than he could explain.

Whatever it was he couldn't remember, she knew about it, and he needed to follow that thread. He wanted to know what it was he was missing, what was eating away at him and despite his misgivings, in the end that was enough.

67

NIGRIV

There was a moment standing in the hut looking at the open door when Nigriv paused, wondering if this was such a good idea. He had a vague memory of doing this before but not the result of it.

In the end he stepped through the door and headed toward the distant light.

* * *

"WHY ARE YOU IN MY HEAD?"
We needed to speak to you.

* * *

The voice wasn't female anymore and it sounded familiar. # # #

"WE?"
There are several of us, Nigriv.

* * *

WHEN HE ARRIVED at the Citadel Stone he saw a short, elderly man, with a long beard walking toward him.

"Do I know you?" The man felt familiar to Nigriv.

"Place your hand on the stone."

It wasn't an order, merely a statement, and despite his misgivings Nigriv did so. Instantly memories of the man flooded back into his mind.

"Hembleth?"

The man nodded.

"Why couldn't I remember you?" Even as he asked the question the reason for it returned. "Your magic…"

"The Occultation."

Nigriv looked at him, confused.

"It's the name for the blocking of everyone's memories."

"Where is she? Why hasn't she shown herself?"

Hembleth smiled, which in all of the memories Nigriv had of the man was unusual. "She prefers to stay out of sight."

It was then that other memories caught up with him from his past. When he'd been with Hembleth before he'd also been with someone else… a copy of himself. "Ligriv!"

Tears flooded his face and he dropped to the floor, his back to the stone.

"I'm sorry, son, he's gone."

Nigriv hardly heard Hembleth speak such was his grief at feeling the loss of his twin. So many things raced through his head as his past came back to him.

He wasn't sure how long it had been since Hembleth had stopped talking but he realised the cavern was silent, except for the hum of the stone behind him.

"This is too much."

"I have something to ask you."

Nigriv looked up and tried to see into the man's eyes but they were colourless and impossible to focus on. He looked down again while he waited for the man to speak.

"We would like you to carve something for us."

"What? That's all you care about after this?"

"There are many things I care about, Nigriv. You are not the only person in the world that has suffered, but because of what your brother did, now I must ask this of you."

"What do you mean?"

"The amulets that he made, that were brought here, that come from the Debrua, it requires great effort to block them from harming the world."

"And?"

"To maintain the Occultation there are some things we need."

"You can't put this all on him, he wouldn't have done this deliberately."

"That may be true, but I can't change the cause, only the effects. We needed to do what we did."

"You harmed people, so many people, we nearly didn't make it. How are you any better?"

"It wasn't our goal, but we had to intervene, such things are not exact. While we can do a lot using nature it still leaves a lot of room for things to go awry."

"Awry... that's what you call it?" Nigriv felt angry despite the connection to the Citadel Stone. "Why me?"

"Like your brother, the mark on your hand gives you unique capabilities. Yours are for this stone." He looked at the stone beside them.

"You want me to cut from this stone?"

Hembleth nodded.

"You knew this would happen, when you gave me that stone, when you saw the amber one Ligriv found."

Hembleth shook his head. "I did not, all we had was an obscure prophecy and some inklings."

"Inklings? What would have happened if you had left us alone? None of this, he'd still be here!"

"I doubt that, son. Destiny has a habit of fulfilling itself... despite itself. What lies underneath all of this is much greater than us, outside of our control."

"I don't believe you."

The strange man shrugged and stared back at Nigriv. They stood there in silence for a time.

"What if I won't help you?"

"Based on your last visit here I imagined you'd ask that."

"And?"

"And, I can offer you something in return."

"What?"

"Your brother's memory."

"How?"

"If you do what we need, I will ensure you know how to keep his memory alive."

Nigriv's chest felt tight, his heart was pounding and he could feel the pulse in his ears and neck. He didn't even know if this man was trustworthy anymore.

Hembleth had tricked them when they were young and Nigriv wasn't so sure he was as innocent as he made himself out to be. He was a god, even that was incomprehensible.

The pain of Ligriv being lost felt like a bear trying to swallow him whole, but even that felt familiar to him, he'd suffered through this before. Letting him have to feel it all over again was cruel.

And yet despite all of that, Nigriv didn't want to forget him. Not knowing he once had a brother was in some ways worse than him being gone. He didn't want to lose that memory, not again, not ever.

He didn't trust them anymore, not fully. Like the man had said, he had much more to consider than just him and his concerns. What would stop him manipulating Nigriv to get what they wanted?

"What would I have to do?"

"We want you to carve some stones for us, from the Citadel." Hembleth reached out and touched the stone. As his hand came into contact with it a shard of blue light raced from his hand and into the stone, then whirled and circled throughout the stone so fast Nigriv could hardly keep his eyes on it.

Nigriv inadvertently removed his hand. Now that his body was no longer in contact with the stone he could feel things beginning to slip away again. He quickly put his hand on the stone to stop his memories fading.

"As soon as you leave the cavern they will go again."

"But you can stop that happening?"

"I can give you the memories back, Nigriv."

"Why do you want these stones? Why should I do it? You let my brother die."

"We didn't let your brother die, Nigriv. We didn't even know what our sister was up to."

"Your sister." Nigriv remembered the female voice calling Tarna a sibling. "Your sister killed my brother, why should I trust you?"

"Would you let her succeed and kill others?"

"Why can't you just stop her?"

"That's not how it works, Nigriv. We can't harm one of our own. It isn't within our powers."

"Then who can?"

"The stones control the power, Nigriv, which is why the Citadel will allow you to work with it, to create the stones we'll use to protect everyone."

Nigriv was so conflicted he was struggling to think straight. He was angry about their involvement with the death of his brother. He had broken the teardrop-shaped gem Hembleth had given him when he was last here, that memory returned.

Could he put that anger aside and do what they wanted? He wasn't so sure. He wanted everyone to pay for what had happened. He wanted to make Tarna pay, but the voice had talked him out of that. Maybe that wasn't true either.

All the memories of his brother, what had happened and his interactions with that voice, swirled around in his head. As they did he got angrier and angrier.

Suddenly the memories all stopped. Nigriv could see them begin to slip away. He put both hands on the side of the stone and banged them as if that would bring them back.

"No! Not again!"

"There's a price, son."

Nigriv turned to the old man.

"If you won't help then the memories are gone."

As much as this was hurting Nigriv he was too angry to help them. "One I'm not prepared to pay."

He stormed off and back down the tunnel.

"Nigriv, come back."

"I will not!"

He hadn't even reached the gate before he struggled to remember why he'd come up to town. Nigriv stopped and looked back at the spinning spire towering over them all.

There was something he was trying to remember, why he was here, someone, but he couldn't. He just couldn't remember. This place didn't feel friendly to him anymore, there was something here he didn't like.

Gantcy's right, we need to move on, there's nothing good to come from here.

NIGRIV

*N*ow that Nigriv and Gantcy were certain about moving on from Traveller's Rest they needed coin to survive. The only option to earn it was for Nigriv to use his skills and work in Midderbuilt.

Where and when he'd become a lapidarist he couldn't remember. There were hints, tucked away deep in his mind, but mostly they were inaccessible.

As soon as he started to work with his hands and make things it was clear why he held a token, this was work he could do. It all seemed natural and he found solace in it.

From time to time he'd look at the ring he carried and wonder if he'd made it. That seemed the most logical thing and it felt right to think that, but he couldn't understand why he still had it and hadn't sold it.

Several times he considered offering it for sale to the traders coming to Traveller's Rest but each time his body and mind fought against that concept, or he simply forgot the idea before he could action it.

He had a home, if you could call it that, in the town under the spire, but it was barren and he only worked from within it. The mayor had explained that every token holder had a home and it was passed to the new holder when they died.

Nigriv felt no connection to the space, but it sufficed to work from, and he had enough tools and equipment so he could get on with building them some income.

At the end of each day he returned back to the camp and Gantcy. They settled into a routine that he could see was wearing thin on her. Making items wasn't the issue, but there was only a small number of traders coming from Watersend.

"We might need to take what I've made to Watersend and sell it there."

Gantcy looked at him. "Perhaps, but I'd like to finish helping out here, before we go."

"Just saying, whenever you're ready we can go, there'll be more options down there."

Several days later as Nigriv took a break from his work up in the town he saw a group of people gathered in the town centre. He wandered over to see what was going on.

"What's the fuss?" he asked.

"That guy's turned up with a token, but no one knows him, or how he came by it."

He was a strange-looking man, short, and at that moment highly animated in his conversation with the mayor. Nigriv pushed closer to hear what was being said.

"I can see you have that, but I don't understand why I don't know you."

"It's a token, isn't it?" The man's voice was high-pitched and he spoke very quickly.

"So it appears."

"Then it grants me access, does it not?"

The mayor shook his head, not in defiance but clearly confusion. "I need to check the register, something feels wrong here." He walked back to his own home and office leaving two guards to watch over the new arrival.

When he returned the mayor was no happier. "The ledger holds your name, Tingfurlew, as does your token. I apologise for not recognising you, things have been very odd since the storm."

"I understand, that storm was not of this world."

Nigriv flinched a little at the man's words. He could feel there was a truth in them but he didn't know why.

"Everyone can go back to their business, Tingfurlew belongs here just like the rest of you."

A few days later Nigriv bumped into the new man at the gem pool.

The man was much older and he looked up at Nigriv, staring directly into his eyes. "You can't avoid it."

"Sorry?" Nigriv had no idea what the man was talking about.

"Your destiny, you cannot run from it."

"I don't know what you're talking about, you don't even know me."

The man held out his hand. "Tingfurlew."

Nigriv felt oddly comfortable around him and shook his hand. "I'm Nigriv."

"I know."

"How do you know?"

He smiled at Nigriv but was bouncing on his toes and stepping back and forth like he couldn't stand still even if he wanted to.

"Nice to meet you, Nigriv, now I know you." His face twitched as he spoke. "It needs to be done."

Still Nigriv had no idea what the man was talking about. Something about him felt familiar but he didn't know why, he'd only seen him twice now.

"Hello, Tingfurlew."

Nigriv turned and saw another man, even older than Tingfurlew, walking toward them.

"Hembleth!" Tingfurlew almost leapt in surprise.

"No need to make a fuss. Hello, Nigriv."

"I know you?"

"Yes you do."

"How?"

"Because we've met many times."

"Why can't I remember them?"

"If you come with me you will find out."

"Go with you… where?"

"Under the mountain."

That idea caused him to feel unsettled, almost angry even, and Nigriv had no idea why. The man wasn't threatening and was only asking but it was bothering Nigriv.

"Why would I do that?"

The man walked up to him and held out his hand. In it were two pieces of a white-blue stone.

"What is that?"

"Hold it in your hand and all will become clearer." He looked up at Nigriv who suddenly felt much calmer about everything.

Before he could object the man tipped the stones into his hand. As soon as they touched Nigrv's skin something moved in his mind, just a little, but enough that he understood why he recognised the man.

"I remember."

The man brushed the long red hair off of his face and just kept his eyes locked on Nigriv's.

"I won't go back there."

"Why not?"

"I'm not doing anything for you and her. Not after what happened to Ligriv." A tear formed in his eye, he felt all that pain flowing back. *I can't keep doing this.* "Take them back."

Hembleth had tucked his hands in his pockets leaving Nigriv nowhere to place the gems.

"You can't run from your destiny," Tingfurlew repeated to Nigriv who looked back and forth between the two odd, short men. *Is he one of them?*

"Why are you doing this to me?"

"You have a choice, son."

"Which is?"

"Do you want to lose the memory of Ligriv forever, or not?"

"What sort of choice is that?"

"If you stay on this path you will never get to remember him again.

Without the stone and the proximity of it, without touching it, there's only one other way you can keep your memories alive."

"Which is?"

"If you want to learn that then I need something from you first."

"Carve the stones?"

"Yes."

"And if I don't?"

"Then this world becomes a much more dangerous place and everything about Ligriv and your past will be lost to you forever."

Nigriv let the memories roll across his mind -- Barrack, meeting Gantcy, Master Berrell and Esphe, everything all the way back to Malamig. He saw the first time he'd met Hembleth and when he'd gifted him the teardrop stone.

"I broke this." It was a statement not a question.

Hembleth nodded.

This was an impossible choice. Nigriv didn't win either way. Forgetting everything might be best after all, but only if they never came to see him again, he couldn't keep remembering.

Losing Ligriv time and time again was cruel. They were behind all of this, one way or another, they'd put him in this position, and now wanted him to help.

He looked away and felt the anger deep down fighting against the stones in his hand. The woman's voice wasn't there but he could remember it and also Tarna, the one who'd killed Ligriv.

Despite what he'd been told he wanted revenge on her, he wanted her to pay. In the end that was enough. If helping Hembleth would stop Tarna then he had to do it.

He couldn't run from that, even if it wasn't enough for him. Nigriv wanted her dead, that was the only revenge he could accept. But he wanted to know why he felt this way, he wanted to always remember his brother.

Otherwise why had they left Barrack? He and Gantcy could still be there. *If it's even still there.* Nigriv hadn't even thought to ask if anyone knew that.

Having no memories was worse than almost anything. He needed to keep them, otherwise everything was wasted. As much as he loved Gantcy he couldn't not have his brother's memory in his life.

Ligriv. I won't forget you, brother. "I'll do it."

"Good. Then there's no better time than the present."

Tingfurlew clapped his hands and as Nigriv set off following Hembleth toward the hut that led under the mountain he couldn't help but wonder who this other strange chap really was.

69

NIGRIV

Even with all his memories and the anger Nigriv couldn't help but stare in awe once he arrived back at the Citadel Stone.

"Place your hands on it, Nigriv."

Reluctantly he did as Hembleth suggested. This time he was flooded with a lot more information than before. He could see how the memories coming to him through the stones were controlled by this one.

There was a sadness within it about what he'd done to the small teardrop stone, that he'd rejected that gift out of anger. Nigriv was able to sense a deeper truth, that this power wasn't behind what had happened.

Everything changed within him. His own despair and sadness bubbled up but the anger was no longer tied to it. He could see why his help was needed, that it was the only revenge he could take, but the Citadel didn't put it that way.

Nigriv could even sense it didn't like that desire and wanted him to drop it.

* * *

YOU NEED to have a clear mind and heart, otherwise you will taint the work it wants you to do.

He recognised the voice, it was the female one, who never showed herself.

And she asks you don't try to harm her stones again.

"I didn't want to... it just took me over."

She knows that, otherwise you wouldn't be allowed here.

"Where are you? How come you don't show yourself?"

I'm not there like Hembleth, and it's not important. We need you to carve the stones, Nigriv.

"Won't that harm her?"

This is different and necessary.

"And once I am finished then what? How do I keep my memories without standing here forever?"

There is another way, Nigriv, but you'll have to trust me. We will only tell you at the end.

"What are they for?"

What?

"The stones. Why do you need them?"

To protect people from the Debrua Stone. They will help with what we need to do.

"But I thought you had locked the amulets all away?"

We have, but that doesn't stop the Debrua, or our sibling.

"Tarna?"

Yes, and the force behind her. They will still try to harm others.

Nigriv stood there for a while, not because he was changing his mind, but he needed time to soak up the atmosphere to get his inner self more settled.

He'd made his decision to help, he needed to trust that it would all work out in the end. And no matter what he wanted to remember, standing here he could see Ligriv in his mind, and he smiled as a tear ran down his cheek.

I need you to pay attention now, the stone will share what you need to do, and how you will do it.

"Very well."

A series of instructions flooded into his mind, not only of the stones he needed to shape but how he would do it. This was not something he'd ever done before and when the instructions stopped Nigriv was a little nervous about being able to follow them.

"There's tools and materials in the space over there." Hembleth pointed to an alcove in the back of the cavern. "You'll stay here until they're done. Whatever you need, tell me, and I'll get it for you."

"What about Gantcy?"

"What about her?"

"She'll wonder where I am."

"There's nothing we can tell her, son. Get your work done and you can get back to her."

Nigriv didn't like the answer and he knew Gantcy would worry about him, but he had work to do, like the old man had said. More than everything else he wanted to keep his memories.

The alcove was a good-sized space in the cavern with a ceiling well out of Nigriv's reach. An odd fire had been fashioned in one corner so he could do what he needed, and there were metals and tools laid out on a workbench.

He turned back to the older man but Hembleth was nowhere to be seen nor could he sense the woman in his mind either. That didn't bother him, he had always preferred space and not having someone watching over his shoulder when he worked.

Ready or not, Nigriv could sense an underlying urgency from the Citadel stone, which he approached intrepidly. The vision of what he needed to do was clear and he laid a hand on the stone and waited.

A vibration ran up his arm. Then a sense of warmth and power flooded through him. His eyes were drawn to a spot on the stone's surface where a bump had formed.

Nigriv held his free hand below it and watched in amazement as that bump swelled and formed into a long, thin cylindrical shape. The connection to the citadel narrowed until it was too thin to hold the weight and it broke off.

In that moment Nigriv sensed what felt like a shudder from the Citadel Stone and he could feel its anguish. He'd lived through many strange things in his relatively short life but what just happened was definitely one of the oddest.

Nigriv placed the gem on the ground as another began to form on the side of the Citadel Stone.

It was a slow process and took what felt like several hours before he felt a push against his hand from the Citadel Stone. Without any words he knew it was done and began transporting the eleven smaller stones to his alcove, mindful to not damage them.

As much as they looked like exact copies in size this was only the beginning. The instructions he'd been given required him to shape them all identically. They needed to be exact replicas of each other and of the image he'd been shown in his mind.

Nigriv toiled for more hours than he could count, napping when he became tired.

Each stone carried the power of the Citadel within it, he could feel that as he worked on them. When he made a cut on one he sensed it as if he'd cut his own skin.

But to do what was required he had no choice. He had to give each a flat base so it could stand freely, square-cut edges and a pointed top. It was as if each sliver he removed was also cutting something from himself.

And with it he began to feel things that he'd heard others talk of but couldn't understand. He wasn't just working the stones, they were working him as well.

Once the eleventh was done Nigriv had to prop himself against the bench, exhausted physically and emotionally. He was struggling to cope with these feelings that were so new to him.

"Nice work, Nigriv."

He turned to see Hembleth standing behind him. Nigriv had been distracted by his work and not heard the man approach.

"Now the hard work begins. I can see the toll on you is high, but time is of the essence." The man made it sound like the work he'd just completed was easy. "Can you keep going?"

Nigriv knew if he stopped now he'd never be able to start again.

While he was exhausted the Citadel and working these stones was giving him a different type of strength.

He stood tall and nodded, then gathered his thoughts as Hembleth walked away, disappearing around the corner. At least the next task wasn't working on the stone, that was a relief.

He had to make a strange tool out of iron. Memories of Berrell and Yammo came into his head, and how what was needed from him now came from the learnings he'd received making tools and fixing crude objects back then.

Ligriv had never enjoyed the smithy work, always complaining that working with the heavier metals making or fixing farm tools was useless as far as being a jeweller was concerned.

Nigriv hadn't minded, in many ways he found it easier, often struggling with the fine work his brother excelled at. And now he needed those exact skills to do what was required.

By the time he'd finished it, Nigriv still had no idea what this was for, he'd never made anything like it before. It was a tube with a strong handle on the top and sharp cutting teeth on the bottom.

The inside circumference was roughly double that of the stones he'd already finished. This had been the last image he'd received in his instructions.

Once again Hembleth's voice startled him. "Nothing about what you've ever done before will prepare you for this, Nigriv."

"What am I about to do?"

The older man pointed at the large stone filling the cavern. "You have to carve a stone out of it."

Nigriv couldn't believe what he was hearing. "No!"

"Yes, son, and it won't harm you for doing it."

As he said it images of what Nigriv had to do came into his mind, and a shiver ran down his spine.

"The Citadel knows it needs to do this but..."

"But, what?"

"It will suffer when you carve the piece from her body. And you'll not be shielded from that."

"Didn't she… it just give me those?" He pointed at the eleven stones on his bench.

"This is quite different, you're cutting this one out."

"And?"

"I have no idea, Nigriv, nothing like this has ever been done before."

If he'd hoped the old man would stay around for support he was mistaken. Slowly Nigriv walked up to the Citadel Stone and place his left hand on it.

He was surprised to feel a wave of immense love flow up his arm and through him. It was almost like forgiveness in advance and reassurance that no matter how he felt during this he wasn't being blamed. He was the only one that could do this.

Even with all of that Nigriv wanted to stop. He tried to pull his hand off the stone but it was stuck there out of his control.

His right arm lifted and held the tool out from the stone before pushing hard into the surface. The first teeth cut straight through like it was bread.

That wasn't a problem but the sensations from the Citadel rocked Nigriv. It was like his heart and mind were being burned, not on the outside but inside trying to get outward.

Strength flowed up his left arm, into his body making him feel twice as tall and invincible. He could feel a compulsion building within him and had to close his eyes, unable to watch what would come next.

It all surged into his shoulder and he pushed with everything he had onto the tool handle. The sense of heat within burst from tiny flames into a raging fire, searing out from his chest and through his torso, down his limbs and into his head.

Tears streamed down his cheeks at the depth of the pain he could sense.

Had his hand not been stuck to the side of the stone, and the power of it directing him, he doubted he could have remained standing.

Finally the tool could go no further and when it stopped moving

Nigriv's pain subsided, not completely, but enough that he was able to catch his breath.

They weren't done and even with this small respite Nigriv didn't know how he would be able to endure what would happen next. Another surge of strength entered his body and he was directed to twist his arm with all of the power he had.

He needed to sever the connection at the bottom of this cut piece, so it could be removed. With a major rush of energy his arm twisted violently, forcing the tool to do the same.

A shriek louder than anything he could imagine flooded the cavern causing him to wobble where he stood. His right hand now spun freely with the tool in it.

Scorching from the inside out, his ears aching from the loudness of the endless sound, and his head ready to burst, Nigriv felt as though he would melt from within.

So this was it... I get to remember my brother by going to be with him...

And then he was gone.

NIGRIV

here was distant sound.

* * *

"THAT WASN'T EXPECTED."

"You say that like we knew what we were doing."
"True. Did it work?"
"I haven't looked yet. I wanted to check if he was alright."

* * *

"NIGRIV! NIGRIV! CAN YOU HEAR ME?"

Nigriv could, but everything felt heavy, his head, his arms, even his eyelids. No part of him felt like it wanted to work normally.

He could recognise Hembleth's voice but it was thickly muted.

"Can you open your eyes?"

He did and saw he was still in the cavern, but lying on the floor. *I'm not dead, I must have passed out.*

"You can hear me?"

Nigriv nodded. He didn't know why but he had no desire to talk, or perhaps he couldn't.

"We had no idea that was going to happen. I think you passed out from the sound, it was so loud, so intense."

It wasn't the sound, at least not on its own, but her pain. Oh Thenis, how much pain she suffered.

"Let's get you up on your feet and somewhere to sit more comfortably."

Nigriv struggled to stand and Hembleth half lifted, half dragged him over to a bench in the alcove.

"Stay here."

Nigriv wasn't going to try and go anywhere. He felt empty of everything and could have closed his eyes and slept for years. Hembelth came back holding the metal tool and tipped a piece of the stone out of it.

As the older man held it up Nigriv could see it pulsing with light. He could even sense the smallest of vibrations from it, a mini version of the Citadel.

"It worked."

Not quite, that needs to be finished off and smoothed.

Nigriv knew what he had to do, but he needed the strength to do it. There was only one way for that to happen. As much as he wanted to curl up and sleep, he'd made a deal and he wanted his reward.

Slowly he stood up.

"Are you well enough? You can just rest there for a bit."

Nigriv shook his head and stumbled over to the large stone, placing both hands on it. There was no anger, only compassion toward him and the sense of loss that the stone felt.

It couldn't shield him from how it felt but it was able to ease the pain he carried from doing what it had asked. The longer Nigriv stayed there the better he began to feel.

He had one task left to do and feeling refreshed, Nigriv went back to the alcove, took the stone from Hembleth and set to flattening the bottom and shaping the rest of it.

As he worked he wondered what would happen next. He'd done

his part, trusting that they'd fulfil their bargain, but he had no real leverage now that the work was done.

The last stone stood taller and thicker than the others and when he stood it on the workbench an idea came to him. He encircled it with the eleven other stones.

It was hard not to be impressed looking at them. Light pulsed through them all, white with blue hues.

"Majestic." The old man was staring at them as well. "Are you alright, Nigriv, you've not said a word, not since…"

Nigriv nodded. He still wasn't sure why he had no wish to speak, or whether he could, but at the moment he had no desire to try. The deep pain and sadness were still living in the back of his mind, even with the boost the Citadel had given him.

"You've done it, Nigriv. It's amazing and we're very grateful. Although, I know you didn't do it for our gratitude."

Nigriv waited for what came next.

"Just so you know, no one else will ever know of what you've just done and even if you were able to remember it after you leave here you won't be able to speak of it anyway."

That didn't matter to Nigriv, he would be glad to forget how this felt.

"We promised we'd give you a way to not lose your memories of your brother. You already know about the generalities of what happened at the Great Fair, and what we did."

Just tell me.

"To hide what had happened, we used the Occultation, but it's a blunt sword, not something that is easy to control or manage."

Nigriv listened, but more interested in his brother than any of this.

"It's taken more than we'd have liked from people's minds. Much of the past has gone, and within a generation there will be little or nothing about the distant past left for anyone. While it's not ideal we need to contain the amulets and the aftermath of their destruction, and if that cost is the memories, it's a cost we'll bear."

Easy for you to say.

"We hope to work out a better way to control the amulets, but for now it is what it is. Now the bit which affects you. Think of the Occultation like a massive bubble, son, that covers all of Dharatan. It's egg-shaped, of a sort, and reaches out past the land, covering some of the surrounding sea."

Nigriv wasn't sure where this was going.

"Which means, if you leave the area that it covers your memories will slowly return. That's the only way you can remember Ligriv and your past."

Now he understood. He would have to leave this land for good.

Hembleth showed him a map of lands to the west, including many different islands, all of which fell well outside the touch of what they'd done.

"I realise it might not be what you expected but it's the best we can offer. You can't live your life here in the cavern, so if you want your memories back, that's the choice you have to make."

While Nigriv had never left Dharatan, he wasn't wedded to it. If that's all it took to remember Ligriv, it was an easy choice for him to make. He wasn't tied to this place or anywhere, only Gantcy.

He knew she wanted to get away from the camp but he had no idea if she'd be willing to leave Dharatan, to go to some foreign land.

"What about Gantcy?"

"What about her?"

"Can she come with me?"

"If she wishes to, yes. Anyone can go."

"And her memories will return?"

"As long as you stay away, yes. If you return, not long after you reach the mainland everything will disappear again."

He thought he understood and it didn't seem much of a price to pay after all, but it bothered him that he'd be making that decision for her, without her knowing why. He had to discuss it with her first.

"Will I remember this conversation when I'm gone?"

"No."

"So I won't be able to tell her why?"

"No, son, like I said, nothing about this can be shared, not with anyone."

It made Nigriv uncomfortable but he also knew there were no other options.

"You don't have much time to make up your mind. We can secure you passage out of Rocknigh but that leaves you only a few weeks to get there. Boats won't leave port after that for half a year. The storms that come in spring mean no one will go again until after summer. If you don't make it by then or get on that boat, there's a chance you'll never leave."

Hembleth handed him a note.

"This explains what you need to do, and why. Outside of this cavern your memories will disappear quickly. By the time you reach the gate you'll have no idea what just happened. Only this note will tell you where you need to be and when. It's also your pass onto the boat. Understood?"

Nigriv nodded again.

"Good luck, Nigriv… whatever you choose to do."

And then the old man turned, walked toward the stone and disappeared as though the light had swallowed him up. Maybe it should have concerned him but after what Nigriv had just been through, it seemed perfectly normal.

He approached the stone and cautiously placed his hands back on the side of it, wanting to get a final taste of that warm feeling he'd had recently from it.

As he stood connected to it an image came into his mind of two small pieces of jewellery, both made from the little stone he'd broken. The Citadel was asking him to mend it.

Nigriv was happy to try and went back into the work space and saw the two pieces on his workbench. Nigriv didn't know how long it took, nor did he care, he simply worked away at the vision he'd seen, forging the two items the Citadel has asked for; a brooch and a pendant.

Both were very intricate and by the time he'd finished with them he knew that he'd just made the finest pieces he would ever create. Even *Ligriv would have been impressed.*

He was reminded about how much he wanted to keep his brother's memory alive, why he'd done all of this.

I'm done.

There was a pouch on the bench, which Nigriv opened, and saw it was filled with coins. A small note sat under it, explaining it was for him to take on his journey.

He took it and left the cavern, resolutely heading down the tunnel with the parchment in his pocket, knowing that he'd never be back here again.

NIGRIV

$\mathcal{N}$igriv had been so consumed with what was happening in the cavern that he'd not thought about how long he'd been gone or what Gantcy would be thinking.

Tears flowed down her face and she banged her closed fists against his chest.

"I thought you'd left me." He could see the fear and sadness that had grabbed her when he hadn't come back. It had been nearly five days since he'd left.

"Never."

As she stopped and stared into his eyes the pain she'd been feeling was evident.

"The only way I knew was that you never came down from up there. There's no one else is there?"

Nigriv shook his head vigorously. "Of course not."

"Then what?"

"I had to do something, something that I can't really remember. I know that sounds stupid but it's the truth."

"Nothing about this place is normal, Nigriv. I want to leave here."

He reached into his pocket and pulled out a parchment, he could remember that, and the pouch of coins.

"What's that?"

He handed it to Gantcy. Her face looked confused when she'd finished reading it.

"West?"

"Yes, across the sea."

"Why?"

He shook his head. "I don't know, but I am sure it's important. Something happened while I was up there, and I know it's ludicrous, but it's important. I know it."

She closed her eyes for several minutes then with a large sigh she shrugged her shoulders and opened them again. "We should do it, I'm sick of this place. Nothing good will ever come from here for us. And what else is there!"

Nigriv felt happy inside she'd agreed even if he didn't know why. He wrapped her in his arms, hugging her until she'd had enough. Maybe it was just that the decision had been made, maybe that was enough.

The next day they secured a ride to Watersend, and as they rode away Nigriv looked up at the spinning spire of sand with a deep conviction he'd never see it again, that this leaving was a permanent thing.

Within another day the mountain was barely visible and he and Gantcy simply stared out across the desert with their legs hung over the back of the wagon. *A sea of sand.*

He didn't know where that name came from, but it was there, something someone had said to him. He couldn't remember who or when.

It took the best part of a week before they reached Watersend and another day before they found a ride west. Spending a night in an inn, with a proper bed and a prepared meal, felt like a luxury but they had more than enough coin for it.

The next journey from Watersend was in a carriage, which seemed better to start with but was ultimately equally boring. Day after day of mindless travel following the river from Watersend to the western coast.

Crossing the ocean frightened Nigriv. He couldn't remember ever being on it before, or even in a boat. His concern wasn't made any better by the knowledge that he was doing this based on a note in his pocket.

By the time they arrived in Rocknigh Nigriv was agitated and anxious. He wasn't sure this was the right thing to do at all, and he wasn't just risking himself but Gantcy as well.

What else is there? He knew they didn't have any roots, or none they could remember. Gantcy didn't seem any happier than him, but he'd been so moody these last few days perhaps she was just feeding off him.

"You'll find boarding lodges down that way." The driver of their carriage pointed back the way they'd just come.

"Thanks." Nigriv handed over the rest of the cost of their passage and watched as the carriage drove away.

Standing at the edge of the port Nigriv breathed in the salty sea air. It seemed familiar in a way he couldn't explain, as though he'd been near it before, but like everything else it was something he just couldn't see in his mind.

"I reckon a decent meal and some ale would be the go right now. What do you think?"

Gantcy smiled. "I thought you'd never ask."

For the first time in weeks she seemed to have a lightness to her, more of the woman he'd become familiar with. She looped her arm through his and pulled him in the direction of the lodges.

Sitting in the first inn they'd come across, enjoying the hot meal and ale, lifted Nigriv's spirits immensely.

"What will it be like on the boat?" Gantcy asked him as she put down the remains of a leg of chicken and wiped her mouth on her sleeve.

Nigriv shrugged. "No idea, I've never been on one before."

It felt good to be in this city, in the inn, eating, drinking and enjoying the music from the lutist playing in the corner. *Maybe being in a city like this would be enough.*

"This feels familiar but I don't know why."

Nigriv nodded at her, he too could feel it. He thought back about what the note said. *If you want to remember, like you said you did, then follow these instructions to the letter.*

That meant they had to find the boat they were going to be travelling on. By Nigriv's calculations they had about three days left in the timeline he'd been given.

A bit later a tall stranger caught Nigriv's attention as he jostled several people out of his way heading directly toward their table. Nigriv suddenly went on alert and felt for the only weapon he had, his blade.

When the man got to their table, he stopped and looked down at them both. His face was stern, softened only by the bushy black moustache on his thin lips.

"Nigriv?"

With surprise he answered, "Yes, how...?"

"A friend told me what you look like. It's taken me half the night to find you."

"Who are you?"

"Your captain -- that is, if you're coming with me on my boat?"

Nigriv looked at Gantcy and saw she was as surprised as he was.

"No time for messing about, we leave by first light. If you're coming then you'll follow me now and get aboard. I should have been gone last week, I'm not waiting any longer."

Nigriv looked at Gantcy. Her face was a mixture of surprise and a smile. "You're sure?"

She nodded.

Together they stood and followed the captain back out of the inn and through the dark streets toward the port. Right in the middle of the jetties stood a tall ship with three masts.

The captain turned to them. "*The Maiden of the Sea.*"

All three of them walked up the boarding plank and onto the deck.

"I'm Hansan. As for your passage, it's been paid for and you're not needed to help. Stay out of the crew's way and hang on for your life when we hit the Sea of Storms, and you'll be fine."

"Understood." Nigriv wasn't sure what else he could say.

Hansan turned and hollered to one of the crew sat off to the side. "Fig, show 'em to their cabin."

The young man leapt up and hurried over before nodding at them and heading away.

Down in the level below deck he showed them to the back of the boat. He said nothing but pointed at the last door before turning and going back the way they'd come.

Nigriv turned the handle and forced the door open. They stepped into the room and took a look at their home for the next while. *I don't even know how long the journey will take.*

7 2

NIGRIV

*B*eing out on the sea felt strange to Nigriv and it took him several days to adjust to the constant movement. What made it easier was that memories began popping into his head randomly.

There was no reason or order to them but images and thoughts just appeared in his mind where before there'd been nothing.

"Ligriv!" he blurted.

"Your brother." Gantcy looked at him when he spoke.

"You remember too?"

"When you said his name I did, but there's some other things too."

Nigriv grabbed the note from his things and read through it again. As he did, the memory of speaking to Hembleth at the Citadel Stone crystallised.

"He told me this would happen."

"Who, Ligriv?"

Nigriv actually smiled at her comment, not mockingly but because for the first time in a while he felt good. "No, silly, Hembleth."

"You've never really told me who he is."

"There's not much to tell. All I can really say is that he's been around over the years more than once." As much as he wanted to tell her more he seemed unable to speak when he tried to explain anything else about the odd little man.

Nigriv knew there was a lot more to it but he couldn't grasp it all; he'd been with Hembleth, the man had given him a note and told him what to do, but everything else about it was foggy.

The longer they sailed from Dharatan the more of Ligriv's story came back to him. More of his past wasn't obscured like it had been, and the memory of the woman Tarna that had taken his brother returned. And again he relived his twin's death.

That brought back his anger. He was angry at her, angry at Hembleth and the voice in the Citadel stone. There was more about that stone, he was sure of it, but none of it returned.

Maybe in time.

The pair of them went up on deck and sat at the prow. Both had memories to relive that were back now, and the fresh air and beauty of the ocean was better than being locked in their cabin.

"I'm sorry to take you away from your home." Nigriv turned to her.

"Home? My home is with you, Nigriv, has been from the day I first met you, always will be."

Little by little Nigriv settled into the returned memories, feeling more complete than he had since the sand storm. Gantcy too seemed a lot happier remembering her mother and her life in Barrack.

Once they'd become reacquainted with their past, things became very dull. Without anything to do on the boat they either sat staring at endless ocean or lying around in their cabin.

Weeks passed and the ship stopped at a tiny island where the crew unloaded goods from Dharatan and topped up their own supplies for the next leg of the journey.

Back out at a sea, little by little the weather turned on them as they approached the Sea of Storms. At first it was just the ocean swell that grew, coupled with ever-increasing winds.

The sky grew darker, clouds hurtling by, rain harder than rocks pelting the crew and fogs thicker than blankets, leaving zero visibility for the captain.

Nigriv quickly learned this was only the beginning and he and

Gantcy had to retreat below deck once the bow of the ship coming up against waves higher than some ridges Nigriv had climbed.

Down below, Nigriv and Gantcy had to tie themselves to their bunk with sheets, to stop from being thrown about as the ship twisted and rolled, bucking against the sea.

As the sea battered the sides of the ship, the constant groaning of the hull's wooden planks caused Nigriv to fear for their lives. He wished he'd never set forth on this trip and even more that Gantcy was safe back on Dharatan.

One storm would pass giving them a few hours' reprieve before another would hit. In those moments he would occasionally leave the cabin only to see that outside the weather and seas were still at war with the ship.

The few times he did venture up on deck during lulls he was amazed at how stoic the crew seemed. All of them went about their tasks calmly but none did anything without having a line attached to them.

At some point the front mast had been damaged, snapped halfway up, but the ship was still moving quickly through the turbulent water. Nigriv cautiously made his way to the captain stood by the wheel.

"I warned you."

Nigriv nodded, there was nothing to say.

"A handful more days and we'll be clear of it. But we have to find our way through some rough passages first."

"Anything I can do?"

"What you're doing. Stay out of the way below deck, that's the safest place for you."

Nigriv walked the deck, holding onto rails, getting doused with spray from the ocean as he did. Soaked, he made his way back toward his cabin and changed before he settled in with Gantcy. "A few more days he says."

She nodded, her face pale and unhappy, but there was no choice but to ride it out.

The next storm felt far worse than any before it, raging constantly with no respite. At times Nigriv could hear items scraping across the deck, crashing into something as the ship rolled in one direction before sliding back and hitting another side.

All he could imagine was that previously tied down cargo had snapped its lines. Everything felt threatening, trapped as they were below in their small cabin without fresh air or light.

Water seeped under their door from waves crashing over the decks above and the two of them sat on the edge of the bed staring into the darkness. Nigriv had never felt so out of control in his life.

For an age the storm raged. It was impossible for them to tell night from day and mostly they just sat together holding hands. Nigriv had tried to nap, as had Gantcy, but it was futile.

The sound of timber snapping caught his attention and he clambered to his feet, untying his bind.

"Where are you going?"

"I don't like the sound of that."

"Then I'm coming with you, don't leave me down here."

Nigriv knew better than to argue and waited while she untied herself. Suddenly the boat came to a dead stop along with a massive crunching sound. Gantcy flew toward him and they both crashed into the door.

His back was sore from the impact but nothing felt damaged. He got to his feet, yanking her up with him. "That's not good."

The cabin door wouldn't open easily and it took him several goes banging his shoulder against it before he forced it open, falling forward into the passageway. Outside their room the water was already at shin depth. "Hurry, we need to get upstairs."

He dragged Gantcy by the hand as they sloshed through water and climbed the stairs to the deck. Rain pelted them, obscuring any view except what was directly in front of him.

He couldn't see anyone. The boat looked abandoned, until they reached the captain's wheel and his foot thudded into something solid.

Nigriv knelt down and found Captain Hansan dead, a piece of wood lodged in his neck. *That's not good.* As he stood Nigriv looked at Gantcy and shook his head.

The rain was easing a little, enough to help them see more of the boat and their surroundings. Waves still crashed over the deck drenching them, followed by icy cold winds.

He held Gantcy's hand firmly and led her toward the captain's cabin. It was mostly intact and they sheltered there until the last of the storm blew out.

When the rain was all but gone they searched the deck looking for others. They found more bodies, some prone on the deck, others flung overboard and hung by their lines off the edge.

Little by little the sky cleared until sunshine beat down on them. It was a respite that helped Nigriv maintain some form of optimism despite the situation.

"Over there!" Gantcy pointed to their left.

Nigriv could see it too, an island roughly half a mile away. He felt safe enough to lean over the edge of the ship and could see the rocky reef their vessel was lodged on.

For now they were stuck on the rocks but he had no idea how long the boat might stay intact. They needed to get off this wreck and over to that island.

"We need to find anything that's useful, Gantcy. You start at that end."

"Like what?"

"Food, supplies, tools, rope... anything. I'm going to check for a boat."

It didn't take him long to find the shore boat at the back of their ship and while Nigriv wasn't confident about how they'd get away from the rocks, it was better than trying to swim.

When he returned to Gantcy he had to smile, she'd already gathered a decent pile of gear on the deck. If she was worried she wasn't showing it.

"The boat's safe but we'll have to manhandle it ourselves."

Gantcy looked out at the choppy sea and turned back to him. "In this?"

"What choice do we have? No one is coming for us."

She looked like she wanted to burst into tears for a moment, then it changed. "Right."

Nigriv helped her sort through what she'd found earlier to load what they could into the small wooden boat. "We should look for weapons."

Gantcy looked at him with a tinge of fright.

"We don't know what animals or others are on that island."

She nodded and they headed toward the front of the ship, searching again.

Nigriv heard something moving and grunting coming from debris on the left-hand side.

"Gantcy, someone's here, come help me."

Someone was moaning amongst the debris. They started pulling at wooden planks and rubbish, tossing it across the deck.

Nigriv saw a hand, then an arm, and they frantically pulled at the wreckage clearing it out of the way. Eventually they saw it was Fig, alive and sporting a big graze on his head.

"It's okay, lad, we're here. Can you hear me?"

The young man nodded.

"Does anything hurt… hurt more than your head?"

Fig looked at him and thought about what he'd asked before shaking his head.

"Alright then, we're going to pull you out."

It wasn't easy and Nigriv was sure the lad was in more pain than he let on, but they managed to get him free of where he'd been trapped. When he stood up on his own it was a big relief.

"They're all gone, Fig. It's just us. Understand?"

The lad nodded, looking about the ship, taking in their predicament.

"We have to go to that island. The shore boat is okay and we've gathered supplies, but it's going to be hard work. I need your help. Understand?"

Again the young man nodded. They all went to the boat and Nigriv inspected the block and tackle holding it in place.

"It will be rough. As soon as we hit the water it's going to bash us against the side, but we'll just have to row like mad if we want to survive."

Gantcy and Fig looked over the edge and nodded. Neither looked happy about it, but all three knew they couldn't stay on the ship. The sea was as calm as it had been the entire day and there was only a few hours left before daylight would be gone.

"We'll all get in, then lower ourselves from there."

Gantcy was the first in, then Fig, before Nigriv clambered in. The small boat swung in the wind but they had little choice, it was this or nothing.

"Everyone ready?"

The first part went smoothly, both men pulling hard on their ropes to lower the boat downward. Whether it was luck or not the swell had eased enough that they banged against the ship a lot less than he'd expected.

"Now!"

Gantcy used a pole to push against the ship, creating some space while he and Fig set to rowing, trying to keep the closest oar from breaking on the ship.

A foot at a time they rode the small waves until they were free of the ship, both of them pulling with what strength they could muster. Foot by foot they pulled away, dragged back a little by the swell, then bursting forward again.

It was only when they were free of the rocks and ship that both men took a break to catch their breath. While he felt exhausted Nigriv knew they had to get a move on.

"Let's get ashore!" he yelled against the wind and sea.

The further from the shipwreck they rowed, the more his fear began to subside and an exhausted hope surfaced. There was an island and they had some supplies, although Nigriv could see everything was soaked in the pooled water of their little boat.

He didn't stop rowing until they reached the beach, not knowing whether to laugh or cry when he was able to jump out onto land. All three of them dragged the boat up the beach.

They finally stopped and took in where they were. He was soaked, as were the others, yet Nigriv couldn't help but feel better. He wrapped his arm around Gantcy and hugged her to him. *At least she's with me.*

Even Fig had a small smile on his face. Nigriv had no idea why he never spoke but it had to be tough for the guy having lost his entire crew. Off in the distance another storm appeared to be heading their way.

"Let's drag this up to that treeline. We need to start a fire and the boat will act as a shelter from that next storm."

It took longer than he'd expected as they were all spent, but no one complained. They propped the boat against some trees and tied it in place to help create a makeshift shelter before collapsing, wet and cold, under it. At least they were safely on land for now, everything else could be worked out later.

As night fell the storm made landfall. Nigriv sat sheltered from the rain with his companions, trying to make sense of the day and his future. In the end he used the memories of the past that were all fully back with him to make peace with things.

I guess this is our new home.

73

YANTARNAYA

Anger didn't accurately portray the way being trapped inside this stone made Yantarnaya feel. This wasn't the bargain she'd made with the Debrua, not that she had any control over what it did.

The stone ignored her pleas. She could sense its displeasure at what had unfolded but it wouldn't communicate with her any more than that. None of this was meant to happen.

It had started when Ligriv had smashed the small piece of the Debrua. From that moment on the stone had reacted rashly, wanting to punish him. Yantarnaya had needed to bargain with it, to calm it enough to allow another amulet to be made.

While the Debrua was vast and powerful it didn't have the finesse needed to work within the lands of men. Which is why she was its channel. It was her that served its needs, to control all of these lands, to destroy the other stone.

Yantarnaya had needed to ease its fury at what that silly man had done. At the time it had been a simple concept: let her step inside, as a trade almost, while he made the last amulet. Then to let her free so she could direct the next phase of the plan. She would travel with Schevenal to the Great Fair and make sure things went as they should.

Instead Uksod, ever the eager young idiot, had lost control and killed the only lapidarist they had. Thankfully the amulets were complete, but now there was no one to do any more work on the Debrua.

Not that that was likely, given the way the stone had reacted. It had agreed to take Ligriv inside while the amulets were out in the world, and hold him there for as long as needed.

But only alive, not dead.

She was angry at both men, so typical that they couldn't control themselves and had to be manipulated to do what was needed. That had left only Uksod to vent her anger against.

After she had screeched and yelled at him for some time he had left her alone, at the bottom of the cavern, isolated from the world.

When Uksod returned she explained what he had to do. He took the High Prince and a single amulet into the Amber Room up in the palace. It was a tribute to the Debrua, to her, to everything about the orange stone, and the closest place anyone could connect with the stone.

Inside there was a hidden room, where the very top of the Debrua was visible, encased in a glass box except for the very tip of it. Uksod had explained to Schenvenal he needed to touch the amulet to that tip of the Debrua, to link it to him.

When that connection happened things changed dramatically. Schevenal learned more than he could have ever imagined, but she too found out much about him, including his strength.

That was a surprise. As the bonding between him and the amulet began she sensed him making his own agreement with the Debrua. He agreed to do its bidding willingly with one small request.

His amulet was only to be bonded to his descendants and no one else. It was a clever ploy from a man who wished to see his family rule for a very long time. While he didn't know their plan with the amulets he had sensed their importance. To the Debrua such a request was of no consequence, and it granted that as a condition before Yantarnaya could object.

She didn't know any more than anyone else back then, although her instinct told her it was a bad decision.

As the ruler of Enderk readied for the trip to the Great Fair, Yantarnaya encouraged the Debrua to place conditions on the remaining amulets.

Uksod was made to bring each one to the side of the Debrua, letting the stones touch and name each of the rulers that would receive them. Then he packaged each one, ensuring they were labelled correctly.

Should anyone receive the wrong one the results would have been deadly. That was the cost of these stones out in the world, but without their power none of their plans could work.

Each amulet would link itself to the ruler, and influence their thinking, driving them to visit Enderk. When they came the Debrua would bond them fully to the stone, and to itself.

It was only then, when all were bound, that the Debrua would release Yantarnaya. Only when all had become servants of the Debrua, would she then be free.

And that was where she had lost her mind. There was too much at stake for her to be held inside the stone, too many things that could go wrong. She had pleaded and begged for it to relent and set her free, even promising Uksod or anyone to take her place.

Nothing worked. Desperately she waited for Uksod to come to her, then explained to him that he would need to go in her place. But first she needed to gift him something.

Like always, he was cautious, but when she explained it was the circlet that Ligriv had made, his ego took over. It was a weakness the priest had, he liked the trappings of being in power.

Excited to wear such a royal-looking piece of jewellery he placed it on his head without considering what might happen. On the inside of the circlet, a small point of the gem touched his skin, enough to make permanent contact.

That was all Yantarnaya needed to control him. Now she could direct him without speaking. He stepped up to the Debrua as she commanded him within his head.

Uksod leaned his head forward, touching the orange gem in his circlet to the outside of the Debrua aligned to where Yantarnaya's hands were placed.

Instantly the Debrua bonded his gem to him, power flooding through it, melding the circlet to his head. The results were unfortunate, at least initially.

All that power had flattened him and he lay unconscious for days, causing Yantarnaya even more concern. He was the only person who knew she was down here; if he died then she had no one to help.

Finally he woke, his mind disturbed but intact. He'd missed the High Prince leaving for Dharatan and it took him several weeks to recover from the effects of his binding.

Much later it was he who reported to her what had happened at the Great Fair. How angry she'd felt beforehand was no comparison to what she felt now. The whole thing had been a disaster.

All of the amulets were missing and her chance to be free gone with them. Uksod reported how the High Prince had tossed his amulet into the ocean when crossing the land bridge as they raced home.

That bridge had been destroyed by the huge storms that had followed him back from the Great Fair, severing their connection to Dharatan, and isolating Enderk.

Everything had gone wrong. Yantarnaya screamed and swore at the Debrua, shrieking that this was why she had needed to be free, to go to the Fair, but the stone cared little for her tantrums.

As far as the stone was concerned it would all work out in time, and that she simply needed to find the amulets. How she was meant to do that stuck here wasn't its concern.

Which left Uksod with the job of finding them and bringing them back. Which seemed simple enough except neither she nor the Debrua could detect the power of the amulets anywhere.

Somehow they had been hidden from the world, that was all the Debrua could tell them. It knew they weren't destroyed, which was the one thing Yantarnaya had to hold onto.

Which meant Uksod's primary goal was to find the amulets and who had hidden them. Had she known before this began how long that would take, perhaps she might have handled everything differently. But she didn't know that.

All she could do was wait in the stone while her minion started his search. Somewhere the amulets existed. As the years passed it became clear that the only way this could have happened was by the involvement of her siblings.

They and the Citadel Stone were the only ones capable of such a feat, and yet even she didn't understand how that could have happened. Nor could Uksod hunt them down.

And so she brooded and her anger grew. Waiting until the time when she and the amulets would be free.

EPILOGUE

embleth hadn't been to the island of The Eyes in what had to be an age. That was confirmed when he saw Valina standing on the path leading to the temple.

She was an old woman now, yet it felt little more than the blink of an eye since he'd handed the young girl the original tooth in Malamig. He wasn't sentimental but the reminder that these seers aged like ordinary people saddened him a little.

Their sacrifice was immense but none ever complained or pitied their lot in this world. *Such is the way of things.* There was much that spun around the stones and their power, much more than even he could grasp.

"Valina!"

"Hembleth, what an honour." Her face was filled with joy and a large smile.

"It is my honour, dear, I wish it hadn't been so long since we'd seen each other."

"I am sure you have been busy."

"Often with things that seem to be of no consequence and then I discover many years of man have passed."

"I look that old?"

He didn't answer as he had no wish to either agree or lie to her.

She nodded. "It is the way of things. What brings you to us this day?"

"You do."

"I did not call… there has been no prophecy."

He chuckled. "Did you forget?"

"Forget what?"

"What you asked my brother."

Her face lit up. "No!"

Hembleth walked up to her and grasped her hands. "Of course, it is the least I could do for you. Can you show me the room?"

Valina turned and led him to the room of the world.

Like his brother, Hembleth was impressed. For people who could not see, they saw much more than people with eyes. What they treasured was not shiny or obvious.

Things that others took for granted appeared to have much more value to the seers. He felt better for a moment, that perhaps there was still hope for the world.

If only all people could be this way.

He reached into the satchel slung over his shoulder and extracted the tooth he'd collected when he first met the twins. Again that seemed but a day or two ago, yet this old woman was now using a crutch to walk and so much else had occurred.

Nigriv was far from Dharatan, alive at least, unlike his brother. And Hembleth's sibling who was instrumental in all of this was hidden from them and up to Revas knows what.

"Here." He handed it to her.

Valina ran her fingers across the tooth, which was larger than either of their hands, feeling every part of it.

"So different and yet so much the same."

She walked to a shelf and placed it there.

"Is that where the other one lived?"

Valina nodded then took a few steps to her right and pointed to the ground. "And here was where it was broken."

"Do you still have it?"

"No, should I have kept it?"

He shook his head, then realised that wasn't enough. "No, it's fine. Can I look around?"

"Of course."

She waited while he walked the rows of shelves looking at everything as well as inspecting the room.

"And there's still no clue as to what happened?"

"None. My best guess was a wind, but…"

"None exists here."

They both stood in silence for a time then he said, "Can we talk?"

"Of course, let's go out to the centre."

When they were both sat Hembleth spoke first. "I do not know what happened here, Valina but I am not sure it's a good thing."

She stayed quiet.

"Much has changed since your last prophecy came and went. We think that it was wrapped up in that."

"The powers touched here?"

"I can think of nothing else, nothing I care to consider at least."

"I don't understand."

"If not that, then someone must have been here."

"That cannot happen, I would know."

"Unless, that too has changed."

She considered his words for many minutes. "Which would mean we are not safe?"

"I doubt there is any concern like that, but it might mean there are others that we have to consider."

Again she sat without speaking.

"Even that doesn't seem right to me, Valina, so I think it's the other. Perhaps now that this has all come to pass, then all will be well."

"It is not over."

"What do you mean?"

"The prophecy, it has not completed yet."

"Sorry?"

"We do not know what a prophecy means but we know if it is still in play. And this one, Hembleth, is still very much in play."

He was shocked which meant a lot. There was little in these worlds that shocked him, but that he might have misjudged this was most unsettling.

"You're sure?"

"Very much so."

"But the words, we've all agreed that they've been done and completed."

"Not everything has to be singular in meaning. I do not know all that has come to pass, but I know that what was told is still alive."

"That is most concerning." He sat there shaking his head wondering where they might have been wrong. But it all appeared to have played out, to have been completed.

What they'd done to protect Dharatan and hobble Yantarnya had taken so much. "You couldn't be mistaken?"

"No, Hembleth, in this I am sure."

"I am glad that I came then, although not for what I have learned."

"Such is the way of things."

He stood and waited for her to do the same. "I best speak to my siblings."

"I hope to see you again."

"And I, you, Valina."

As he walked away out of the temple, he doubted that would ever come true. A twitch of sadness crossed his mind as he slipped from the island into the void, but only for a moment, before his mind turned to the problem of the prophecy.

It can't be true.

But even saying that, he could feel a current of something that confirmed its truth. This was far from done.

FROM THE AUTHOR

First of all, I wanted to say a huge thank you for choosing to read *Cut In Half.*

This was my first standalone novel and I really enjoyed the process of bringing the story to life. Being able to tell some of the origins of the In All Jest series as a full story was a lot of fun.

If you haven't read Spire Of Fools yet, there's a direct tie in between that book and this one, which will continue as the series progresses.

There are more side stories I am planning to write in the near future. I'd love to hear which of your favourite characters you'd like to know more about.

If you enjoyed *Cut In Half*, I'd be grateful if you could write a review. It doesn't have to be long, just a few words, but it's the best way for me to help new readers discover my books.

If you'd like to stay up to date with my new releases join my Reader Group at my website: kingdarryl.com.

Best wishes,
Darryl King

A Fool's Errand, In All Jest Book 1

Fool Me Twice, In All Jest Book 2

Spire Of Fools, In All Jest Book 3

The World of Scurra